I0641480

Silence of the Sparrows

Silence of the Sparrows

J.P. McCollum

RESOURCE *Publications* · Eugene, Oregon

SILENCE OF THE SPARROWS

Copyright © 2026 J.P. McCollum. All rights reserved. Except for brief quotations in critical publications or reviews, no part of this book may be reproduced in any manner without prior written permission from the publisher. Write: Permissions, Wipf and Stock Publishers, 199 W. 8th Ave., Suite 3, Eugene, OR 97401.

Resource Publications
An Imprint of Wipf and Stock Publishers
199 W. 8th Ave., Suite 3
Eugene, OR 97401

www.wipfandstock.com

PAPERBACK ISBN: 979-8-3852-6733-0
HARDCOVER ISBN: 979-8-3852-6734-7
EBOOK ISBN: 979-8-3852-6735-4

VERSION NUMBER 05/20/26

For my brother Kris, whom I have crossed the country for many times over. I would cross the world if he needed me to.

"Even the sparrow has found a home, and the swallow a nest for herself, where she may have her young—a place near your altar, Lord Almighty, my King and my God."

Psalms 84:3 NIV

Contents

Thanks

I would like to thank my family, my friends, and all my former students who encouraged me to keep telling my stories. There is nothing more important than the story we are all a part of.

Abbreviations

ADAMS   American Data Analysis and Measurement Supercomputer.

AI   Artificial Intelligence. Specifically, the ability of neural-network computers to analyze, learn, and solve problems without direct human input.

CAMO   Consolidated Agriculture and Mining Operations; government agency

CEP   Concealment, Evasion, Portability; Sparrow survival strategy

CME   Compulsory Monitored Education

COATS   Critical Operations and Tactical Service; Special Ops.

LEAD   Law Enforcement Autonomous Droid; The new face of law enforcement on the streets.

NADF   New America Defense Force; The descendant of the US military, it is divided up into four branches: Ground (Army), Air (Air Force), Naval (Navy), and COATS (Special Operations).

RAC   Regional Agricultural Communities; successors to the SACs

RDF   Regional Defense Force; All 10 New America Regions have a Regional Defense Force. They are the descendants of the National Guard units in the United States.

SAC   Sustainable Agricultural Community

SEMIC Trains   Supersonic Electromagnetic Intra-Continental Trains.

Part One

Chapter 1: **Slate Creek**

"WINTER COMES LATER EVERY year," Rod said, peeling off his cap, wiping his brow, and staring at the clouds.

"Not late enough," Jude said. "These soybeans are still small."

"We're going to have to harvest them in the next week. It's the end of their growing season, so we just have to make do with what we get."

Jude looked at his dad's weathered face. It wasn't the sun that aged him; it was long winters and hungry mouths. His skin was thin, revealing delicate, spidery veins beneath the surface. His glassy brown eyes were tired but proud and satisfied.

"We didn't get a second corn crop this season either. We're going to be pushing our luck with food this year," Jude reminded his dad.

"The second crop has been too small anyway. Our first crop was a good one, and we'll have more time to put up the greenhouse. That'll help us grow a few more fresh things, and together with the livestock and whatever we hunt, we will be fine. Your sister might have to rethink her vegetarian diet, but we'll have what we need."

Jude chuckled. His father was unflappable, even as he grew older and frailer. Over the years, countless communities failed, sending the surviving residents back to the cities to face what they fled in the first place, but not Slate Creek. Rod Kane was the reason they were a *Sustainable* Agricultural Community, and there was no shortage of SAC leaders plying him for his wisdom.

"Let's take a look at the wind turbines."

"Mom, the computer's hanging up again. I can't get anything done!" Maisy complained.

"The satellite signal is getting interrupted," Marren said, looking at the bottom of the screen. "Callum, go check the receiver and make sure it is pointing in the right direction, please?"

"Sure, Mom. You know it is, but I'll double-check, just in case," he said.

"Thanks for humoring me."

"Ready to do some canning this weekend?" Marren asked her flustered daughter.

"I'll be ready to do anything if it just works right!"

"I know, sweetheart, but sometimes the signal gets blocked by debris, other satellites, or even the mountains if the signal doesn't come in just right. It's a pain, but it's what lets us keep you around, you know? I wouldn't want . . . "

"I know, Mom. Don't worry. They won't take me," she said, looking to make sure Callum was outside. "I'm way smarter than Callum!"

Marren smiled weakly with the joy of knowing her daughter was her most accomplished student, but she also nursed the memory of what happened to Callum. Three years without her son almost made her throw in the towel, but Callum was not anything if he wasn't tough.

"The grid screen has been showing low output from turbine number four," Jude said. "I want to check it out."

"It probably just needs a lube. The older turbines always need more TLC, and I think number four is our most senior member. It's been on that hill since the Transition."

"In that case, I might as well go back to the shed and grab the supplies," Jude said, sighing and running his hand through his dark, wavy, shoulder-length hair. He didn't quite hit his dad's height of six feet, and his hazel eyes were definitely from Mom. His knack for anything technical was from Dad, and he also shared his mom's fierce sense of justice. He was a consummate fixer.

Most of the big talkers with their rifles, pick-up trucks, and camping gear were the first ones to head for the hills during the Transition, but they were also among the first to return to the cities during that first telling year. Rod was a different case entirely. As an engineer and university instructor, he took his time and planned their move to the last detail. Before he got his pink slip, he emptied their retirement, savings, money market, stocks, and bank accounts and purchased 150 acres of remote real estate near some of his distant relatives who were part of the Salish Tribe and lived on First Nation land. He bought, salvaged, and built wind turbines for the fields, and he assembled and installed several acres of solar panels on the steep mountain terrain. He developed a detailed crop management system and livestock management system, and he designed simple structures that could be assembled in days and used for a variety of purposes. By the end of the first year, it was clear his family would not depend on the New America government for anything.

"Don't forget to clip in," Rod said.

"I know, Dad. I've done this a hundred times."

"Me too, but it only takes one time forgetting to fall fifty feet. Sorry, son. You think more about safety when you get old like me."

"You'll never be old," Jude chuckled.

He clambered up the handles and clipped his harness into the loop at the top of the pole. "Looks kind of dry in here," he said when he lifted the hatch. "And it sounds cranky. Let's see if some lube makes it happy."

Jude went to work unscrewing caps, pouring oil, and pumping grease into joints. While he was up on the turbine, he checked the wiring and ran resistance tests to make sure nothing was hampering the flow of electricity. "How's it look on the grid now?"

Rod slid his fingers across the tablet and brought up the grid read-out. "It looks good. We've got a lot more flow to the battery."

"Alright, then I'm coming back down. You're right, Dad. If you keep up on these things, they'll outlast their supposed thirty-year life span a few times over."

"Callum, how's the receiver look?" Marren asked as she stepped outside. Callum was standing, staring at the sky, shielding his eyes from the sun.

"It's good," he said, clearly distracted.

"What are you looking at?" his mother asked, always a little on edge when it came to Callum.

"I saw a drone," he said.

"All the way out here? That's unusual. Consolidated Agriculture and Mining Operations must be looking for mineral deposits in the mountains. You know what they say: 'You don't see much of CAMO because they work in the ground.' I doubt they're looking for farmland in this terrain."

"It was a military drone."

"Are you sure? Maybe Cascadia is updating its topographical maps."

"It wasn't a Regional Government drone, Mom. It had the New America flag on it, and it slowed down over our land. They're watching us, I know it."

"Why would they want to watch us?" Marren asked rhetorically.

"They watch everything, Mom. They want to know what we're doing, where our land is, where we get our energy, if we might have any untapped resources, and if we have any more kids that might need to be extracted."

It was hard to argue that. Callum had firsthand experience getting plucked out of the SAC and sent to a Compulsory Monitored Education boarding school. Three years at CME almost broke him and his mom, and that was the last thing she wanted to think about.

"They're not coming for anyone," she protested with a tinge of defiance. "You and Jude have graduated, and Maisy is in the top ten percent in Cascadia for her age. Besides, the Regions do the CME extractions. If they were looking for land or scanning for mineral deposits, it would be a CAMO drone. If it's a New America Defense Force drone, it's probably just doing a routine land survey. I know you have reason to be on edge, but let's not jump to conclusions."

"I don't like it. We're out here to get away from the government. We're not a burden to them, and they leave us alone. That's the deal."

"Maybe you should go talk to your dad and let him know. See what he says."

"Fine."

Callum stepped heavily across the grass to the work shed. Noticing the wind turbine tool kit missing, he figured Jude and his dad were out checking the power grid, but something else caught his eye. The rope handle for the door to the underground cellar was protruding from the thinning piles of straw tossed in careless wisps across the shed floor. He reached down, pulled the handle, and inhaled the scent of earth and steel that wafted from below. Stepping down the ladder, he made his way to the cabinet in the corner, opened the door, and gazed at the rack of polished wood and metal that was his father's prized — and highly illegal— rifle and shotgun. Rod had transitioned to bow hunting a few years ago, but he maintained that they should always keep the guns "just in case."

He heard his mother's words: "Let's not jump to conclusions."

He heard his father's voice: "Every choice has consequences."

He paused, but then he saw the drone in his mind, the bold colors of the New America flag emblazoned underneath, designed to be seen and designed to intimidate. His face flushed, and his vision narrowed. He did his time. He survived three years in CME in Vancouver, and now that he was home, they send a drone hundreds of kilometers north into the rugged mountains of what used to be British Columbia to spy on their SAC? Including all of his father's relatives, the consolidated community of Salish and other First Nation tribes, and a handful of refugees from Vancouver, there were around 170 people in their SAC. They were of no consequence, unless now they had become the target of monitoring.

He pulled out the shotgun and cracked it open across his knee. He rummaged through a box at the bottom of the closet and grabbed a handful of shells, stuffing them in his jacket pocket. He carefully pulled out two shells, slid them into the barrel, and snapped the gun straight. He climbed the ladder, not bothering to close the cellar door, and marched into the sunshine of the mid-September day. The drone was probably gone, but like his dad said, "just in case."

Callum made his way into the fields, which were long, narrow strips of fertile land that were squeezed between the steep slopes of the Rockies. As he traversed the patchy bushes of soybean plants with their slightly emaciated pods, he heard the unmistakable buzz of a drone approaching from the south. He instinctively crouched and watched as the four enclosed propellers twisted and maneuvered the rectangular fuselage like a nimble helicopter. Aside from the clear New America flag painted on the bottom, it had at least four cameras and several scanners attached to the bottom. He watched, waiting for it to make its pass and leave, but it kept circling, as if it was determined to find something.

After passing by the house and shed a few times, it made its way out over the fields, roughly following Callum's path through the crops. He shut his eyes tightly, physically trying to push out his memories of the extraction three years ago, but the growing sound of the buzzing and flashing memories of Cascadian troops pouring from a transport drone flooded his vision. His breath quickened and his eyes narrowed, focusing on the approaching intruder. Nearing his position it slowed, no doubt zooming in on an image that would certainly match one in their database, and examining the illegal weapon he was wielding.

Finally, something snapped. Audibly growling, "Not this time, assholes!" he raised the shotgun, pumped the handle with a satisfying ratchet sound, and pulled the trigger. The exploding shot pierced the skin of the drone like a thousand tiny sticks of dynamite, sending it flailing backwards for a few seconds until it recovered its stability. As if it were completely unaware of the threat, it surged forward towards him, cameras rolling, attempting to get closer footage of the source of the attack.

Callum pumped the handle again, gritted his teeth, and baited the drone, patiently waiting for it to slow and get as close as it dared. Still wobbling from a damaged propeller, it wasn't an easy target, but it was closer. He fired again, aiming at the dead center of the flag. The thundering boom of the shotgun was immediately followed by the shredding of the aluminum skin, obliterating the flag and shattering several of the cameras. Propeller pieces snapped and fluttered to the ground, and this time the drone could not recover its stability. Leaning heavily, the remaining propellers surged, trying to make up for the lost lift, but instead the drone sped off at a long slope, finally crashing over the ridge at the end of the field.

Rod stood at the base of the wind turbine, watching Jude splice some brittle wiring that had become exposed on turbine number seventeen. The crack of a shotgun blast echoed over the fields, causing both men to freeze and stare at each other. Jude whipped his head around, scanning the horizon from his perch where he was clipped in. The second blast went off, and Jude caught the last few seconds of the doomed drone's descent over the ridge.

"Dad, the north fields!" Jude called down, unclipping his harness and scampering down to the base. "I saw a drone go down."

"Callum," Rod breathed as he shook his head.

"Let's go see what happened," Jude said, as if trying to console his father more than direct him.

"Two shotgun blasts and a downed drone," Rod said as they made their way to the house. "It doesn't take much detective work."

The men burst through the door to find Callum still holding the shotgun and explaining his prized kill to his mother.

"It was buzzing around, not just flying by. It had at least four cameras. It kept circling the house and the shed, and then it came at me!"

"It came at you or towards you?" Jude interjected, clearly hot under the collar.

"It came at me, so I fired at it. It was hit, and it still came at me, so I didn't wait to see what else it was going to do. I fired again and hit it good. It went down over the north ridge."

"What kind of drone was it?" Rod calmly asked.

"A government drone. It had a New America flag on it, or at least it did until I shot it off," he said proudly.

"How big? Did you see any weapons on it?" Rod asked.

"It wasn't very big. Definitely not a transport. I saw cameras, but I don't know if it had guns or not."

"Do you know what you've done?" shouted Jude. Rod put his hand on Jude's arm and restrained his tirade.

"Why don't you get some supplies, grab a radio, and head over the ridge to check it out? Take extra water and a camera, and make sure you're back before dark. Let's see what we're talking about. Maybe we can contact the nearest surveillance office and work something out."

As soon as Callum was out the door, Maisy piped in from her strategic eavesdropping point in the school room. "Well, this isn't going to end well."

"Dad, I'm sure they got plenty of footage, and they definitely know Callum's ugly mug," Jude fumed. "Even if you want to 'work something out,' they got him on video. He just invited the New America Defense Forces right into our SAC."

"Callum hasn't been back long. He's angry, and quite frankly, Jude, he just doesn't have the restraint you and Maisy have. We're going to have to be patient with him," Rod explained.

"Sure, Dad, but the NADF isn't going to be patient."

"Your dad is right," Marren said. "When he heard that drone, it triggered a deep fear in him. Still, Rod, do you really think you can intervene?"

"Let him go find the wreckage, and then I'll know where it came from and who to contact," Rod sighed.

"They won't like that their drone was blown out of the sky by a CME kid with an illegal weapon," Maisy chimed in. "You've got a lot of explaining to do, Dad."

"Thanks for the input, Maisy," Rod said, rolling his eyes.

For the next few hours, the air in the house was thick with anticipation and consternation.

"It's been three hours. He should have been there by now," Jude said, pacing the kitchen floor. Rod and Marren sat at the table, carefully managing their anxiety and expectations.

"I will try him, but if he hasn't turned on his radio, it won't do any good," Rod said coolly. A last-minute thought during the chaos of the Transition, Rod brought several old 20th and 21st-century Citizen Band mounted and hand-held radios for communicating in the fields. Low-tech solutions are sometimes the most valuable.

"Callum, this is Dad. Do you read me?" Rod barked into the handset. The house radio was probably in an old diesel tractor-trailer a hundred years ago, but Jude was able to resurrect it and mount it on a wooden box and wire it through a power converter. On a clear day, it could have a good ten-mile range, but the signal bounced off the mountainsides like a ping pong ball. CB signals didn't have satellites.

"If he's over the ridge, he probably can't hear me," Rod said. "Let's sit tight for a bit."

"A bit" lasted about three more hours, and finally, the race to dusk had arrived. No one was willing to pierce the tension in the air as the realization slowly dawned that Callum should be back by now.

"Well, he's not going to make it back by dark now," Maisy finally declared, looking out the window at the dimming sky.

"She's right. We'd better head out and see what's going on," Jude said.

"No one is going anywhere," Rod said with arresting authority. "I told him to be back before dark for a reason. If he doesn't come in with a good explanation by morning, then you can go after him. Be ready to go at 0600."

Jude knew when his dad reverted back to military time, his old army instincts had kicked in. During the Transition, he was a drill sergeant, ordering everyone around with precision and purpose until the structures were in place, the crops in the ground, and the power grid connected. It had been several years since he had taken this tone, and Jude began to wonder if he would ever hear it again.

No one was able to sleep. By 5:30 am, Maisy was up and shaking Jude. "Wake up! You need to get ready to go. It's almost six."

"I never really went to sleep," Jude moaned. "Why are you up?"

"I'm going with."

"I don't think so."

"You think wrong. If Callum fell and has a six-inch gash in his leg, are you going to sew it up?"

"Good point."

Jude stuffed his pack with protein bars, extra water, and a blanket, and Maisy stuffed her pack with medical supplies.

"Where are you going, young lady?" Marren asked, emerging from the bedroom, wrapping her robe around her waist and tying it off.

"She's coming with me. If Callum is hurt, I'm going to need her help," Jude interjected. "I'll take care of her, I promise."

Rod came in from outside, rubbing something metal in his hands. Turning the handle towards Jude and extending it to him, he said, "Just in case."

"Your pistol? Isn't that what got us in this mess in the first place?"

"It's not drones you need to worry about," he said.

"Alright," he conceded, stuffing the pistol in his pack. "I've got a radio, and it is charged up. Give us a couple of hours to get over the ridge, a couple of hours to search, and a couple of hours to get back. I'll radio along the way as long as the signal is good. If we're not back by noon, then you can send out the search parties."

"Thanks, Jude. Be careful, watch out for your sister, and go easy on your brother. He's . . . "

"I know, Dad. Don't worry," Jude said, patting him reassuringly on the shoulder. "You ready?"

"I'm just waiting on you," Maisy said, adjusting the straps of her pack. "Let's go get him."

Jude and Maisy made good time. Despite their ten-year age gap, they had always been close. They seemed to have more in common, and they spent more time together than she and Callum did, especially during the three years Callum was at CME school. "Compulsory Monitored Education." For a government program meant to help students, it sounded a lot like a jail sentence. In many ways, it was similar: boarding halls, controlled movement, mandatory lessons, and limited contact with family. "You are set up for success," they would boast, and it was certainly true. You would succeed or you wouldn't leave until you did.

Callum was stubborn. It took him three years to finally pass his exams and earn his release. Of course, Callum was always stubborn and never liked school. He loved working with his hands, which didn't leave him with many career options in the city, but it suited him well for life in a SAC. He had the stamina of an Ox, and he loved nature. Since he'd been back, he was a big help to Rod and Marren. He was a major reason Rod could keep the crop schedule on track.

Maisy could thrive anywhere, which was why the university was the real loser when they rejected her application for a pre-med program. She was unfazed; she knew her father's departure during the Transition was probably the reason they rejected her. She was only sixteen, and she had already completed her high school curriculum, the EMT training program, and three nursing courses. She was the only Kane child born in Slate Creek, and to her, the Transition was distant history.

"What were the old states that made up Cascadia again?" she asked Jude, striking up a conversation to break up the long hike.

"The US States of Washington, Oregon, Idaho, and the Canadian Provinces of British Columbia and Alberta. Slate Creek is in the old British Columbia territory," he explained between breaths.

"Do you remember the Transition?" she asked.

"I was pretty little, but I remember three things: I remember Mom and Dad talking about when ADAMS went online, when Mexico finally consented to join New America after they added the green stripe to the flag, and when Dad found out New America would allow people to live outside the cities in what they called "Sustainable Agricultural Communities.""

"I've never been to a city," Maisy said.

"I don't remember much, and I'm sure a lot has changed since then. There's a reason Mom and Dad left."

"Dad says when ADAMS went online, the government lost its humanity," Maisy recalled.

"When a computer makes all the decisions, it's kind of hard to dispute that."

"American Data Analysis and Measurement Supercomputer. ADAMS," Maisy recited.

"Was that in a history class or government class?" Jude smirked.

"Both."

"You know, a hundred years ago, students actually *went* to school."

"So do I," protested Maisy.

"You go to a screen in a room. I mean, people actually went to a building where other people would stand in front of a class and teach lessons."

"You mean like at CME schools?" she asked.

"Even at CME schools, you sit at a screen. You get extra help whether you like it or not, but nobody stands in front of a class and talks."

"That would be weird. If all they did was talk, it would be boring, too. I like to see something, not just hear it."

"I guess you were born in the right century then. Lucky you," Jude said, winking at his sister.

"We're at the ridge. Let's see what went down, pun intended," Jude said, trying to ease the tension.

They hiked up to the crest of the ridge and peered down into the grassy area below. A large black circle about ten meters wide was staring back at them. The grass had been obliterated by something hot, and there was no sign of Callum, his pack, or any part of a drone.

"Callum!" screamed Maisy. "Callum!"

Jude put his hand on her arm. "He's not here. They've already cleaned up."

Chapter 2: **Missing**

"DAD, DO YOU COPY?" Jude said into his radio from on top of the ridge.

"I copy, Jude," came the reply.

"Callum is gone, Dad, and so is the drone. Whatever landed here didn't leave much grass. My money is on a transport drone."

There was a telling pause, and then a somber voice came back: "10-4. Come on home."

Jude could hear his mother crying in the background. She tried to hold it in, but Jude heard her gasp and moan quietly when his dad responded. She was probably sitting right next to him.

"Tell Mom it looks like a clean pickup. I don't see any sign of a struggle. He's probably not even injured. We just need to find out who has him." Marren needed something to hold on to.

A crackle came back over the radio, followed by Marren's voice. "Thank you, sweetheart. Bring Maisy back to me."

"10-4 Mom. Be there in a couple of hours."

The family meeting that afternoon had lost its somber tone by then and took on an air of purpose and determination.

"Didn't Callum say it was a New America drone?" Jude asked his mom.

"He said it was a smaller drone with the New America flag on the bottom. It had cameras and sensors, but not any weapons that he could see."

"It was probably a survey drone. That is odd. I would expect a CAMO drone scanning for mineral deposits or examining water sources, but not an NADF drone," Jude said.

"It might have been updating topographical maps," Rod guessed.

"That's what I told Callum," Marren said, "but I don't think he bought that explanation."

"His face is in the database, so it stands to reason that the cameras picked him up and fed the video to the NADF. Now all we need to do is find out if the NADF picked him up, or if they had the Cascadia Regional Defense Forces come get him," Jude thought out loud.

"Unless he was doing something across regional borders, the NADF wouldn't bother with him. He was probably picked up by the Cascadia RDF," Rod said. "He's most likely in Vancouver."

"I'll start trying to contact someone in the RDF. Maybe I can find out where he is and what we can do," Marren said, retrieving her screen and beginning her search.

"He's an adult now," Rod said. "The RDF is not required to update us like they were when he was in the CME school. They might not give up much," Rod cautioned her. She continued her search.

"Maybe we need to go to Vancouver."

At Maisy's words, everyone froze.

"You don't know what you're saying," Marren objected instinctively. "Leaving the SAC is not an option."

"We left the city decades ago, and we haven't looked back," Rod said. "I don't think you understand the dangers. I don't even understand all the dangers, but I know the people are not like us. They are dependent on the government for food and housing, and they have no purpose or passion. They are trapped and angry. You, me, any of us would be walking targets."

"I wonder how safe Callum is in jail?" Jude said. "I don't like it, but Maisy's right. The RDF won't give you any information. I'm going to have to go to Vancouver in person and see what I can do. At the very least, I can make sure he has a lawyer."

Marren put her head in her hands, and Rod sat back and sighed.

"Well, if that's the plan, then we'd better send you with access to some money. A public defender is like a wet blanket; it might cover you, but it doesn't really do its job."

Marren looked up at Rod with a look of shock.

"What are you saying?" she demanded.

"The kids are right. There's not much we can do from way out here. Jude and I will need to head into Vancouver," he said.

"Dad, this place will be in chaos in a few days without you. The soybeans need to be harvested now before the cold and rain ruin the pods. Ironically, the only way you could afford to leave would be if Callum were here for the harvest."

Rod sighed and let his fist down on the table.

"Let me go over all the tractors and harvesters to make sure they are ready, and then I'll go to Vancouver. It can't take that long to find the RDF offices and hire a lawyer," Jude said.

"I don't like it. It's so dangerous, and I can't bear the thought of losing another . . . " Marren protested.

"Shhh . . . ." Jude whispered, putting his hand on her shoulder and pulling her close. "You're not losing your other son. Not only am I coming back, I'm going to bring Callum back. Somehow, some way, I'll bring him home."

She leaned in and hugged him back. "Please be careful. Don't take any unnecessary chances if you don't have to."

"I won't Mom. I promise."

"So, it's decided, huh?" Maisy said, lurking in the doorway to Jude's room. "You're going to the big city."

"I'm going to Vancouver, yes. We talked about this, and don't even think about trying to ask to come with. It's way too dangerous, especially for a beautiful sixteen-year-old girl."

"I can handle myself, thank you," Maisy said defiantly. "In any case, I wasn't going to ask anything. You think I'm beautiful?"

"Of course. You look like me."

Maisy rolled her eyes and disappeared into the hallway. Jude knew this was no hike to the ridge. He needed more than food and water, and anything could go wrong. His passport was implanted when he was born, but it hadn't been scanned in over twenty years. Was it still there? Was it still working?

Travel wasn't exactly easy. The Slate Creek SAC wasn't as far out as some of the SACs in the Yukon, but there were few roads in the Rockies, and nothing more than trails that led in and out of Slate Creek. Even if they could afford a flight, there wasn't a pickup point for a transport drone anywhere near them. His old electric dirt bike was going to have to do the trick. With portable power only able to charge small devices, he was going to have to find plug-in points along the way and stop before he had to get off and push. On the plus side, the bike could handle the rough trails, and the charge time was much faster than cars.

Preparation for the trip was more involved than Jude had hoped. Some of the tractors' batteries were in rough shape, and with no one else to help at harvest, they had to be reliable. While he was at it, he decided to give his old bike a new battery. He had plenty of nickel and lithium from their mining trip in the mountains last summer, and luckily, he bothered to refine and process it into usable pieces, but fabricating the batteries in the shop took a few extra days. They would have to make another mining trip next year before he started recycling and refabricating the power packs on the grid.

"Study the maps of Cascadia and Vancouver," ordered Rod that night at dinner. "The last thing you want to do is get turned around and find yourself at the Yukon border."

"Okay, Dad."

"I put contact information in your tablet for the Cascadian government offices and the RDF offices. I also made lists of hotels, markets, and a few other places you might need to find."

"Thanks, Mom."

"I put a couple of band-aids in your pack."

"Gee, thanks, Maisy," he said, rolling his eyes.

"Actually, I made you a first aid kit," she admitted. "As far as fitting it into your packs, that's up to you."

"I'll figure it out. Thanks, Maisy."

"When are you planning on heading out?" Rod asked.

"I've got everything done on the tractors and harvesting attachments. I'll finish packing up and head out in the morning. I've already stayed a few more days than I planned," he explained.

"I'll make you a few more protein bars tonight," Marren said. Jude had plenty, but he knew his mother needed to do something for him, and you really can't have too much food on a trip like this.

"Thanks, Mom. Those will keep me going."

Sleep was an elusive bandit that night. Nothing in particular was worrying him, but everything at once was. There were so many unknowns, especially in the city. For the first time since Callum came home from CME, he really missed his brother. He was rash and stubborn and a bit of a bonehead, but he was a good man, a hard worker, and a big help to

Rod and the SAC. The ironic twist was that the only thing that could make him feel better about leaving Slate Creek would be if Callum were still there.

Maisy fought a hard battle for sleep that night, too. How was she supposed to go back to her screen and concentrate while her brother was on the trip of their lifetimes? If the city was so dangerous, why did most people live there? She knew her parents were protective, but the Transition had been over for years. New America was the only country she had ever known, and she knew almost nothing about it except what she was taught in history.

The next morning, a king's breakfast was cooking in the kitchen.

"Mom, have you been up all night?" Jude asked, coming in and smelling the bacon.

"I finished the protein bars late, and I figured while I was up, I might as well throw together some breakfast," Marren said.

"Couldn't sleep, huh?" he asked, knowing his mom.

"Not a wink."

He hugged her and then headed out the door to secure his side packs on the bike.

"Don't those side packs slow you down?" Maisy asked, peering into the doorway of the shed.

"A little, but I'm keeping them light and balanced. I don't want to wear a pack while I'm riding because after a few hours, it's going to get really uncomfortable."

"Smart thinking," she said. "Did my first aid kit make it?"

"Of course," he smiled. "No offense, but I hope I don't need it."

"None taken."

"Are you going to survive while I'm gone?" he asked, half serious and half kidding.

"I won't even know you're gone," she smirked. "By the way, did my bike get a new battery?"

"Your bike is newer, and it's not taking a five-hundred-kilometer trip, so no, it didn't get a new battery, but the one in there has plenty of life left in it."

"Okay."

There was an awkward pause, made so by Maisy's uncharacteristically quiet pose.

"So where are you going to stay on your way to Vancouver?" she finally asked.

"There's not much between here and there, so I suppose I will be camping out unless I run across another SAC and they are friendly."

"Are you taking Dad's pistol?"

"I am well prepared to defend myself and ready to hunt if I need to."

"Do you think you'll find him?"

"What's with the inquisition?" Jude asked, tightening a strap.

"Curious minds want to know."

"I think the government will not be eager to help, but I think I can dig up something about where he is, and I should be able to hire a lawyer. I doubt I will return with Callum, but I've got a good chance of getting the ball rolling towards his release."

"That's better than I thought. I'll be happy when I know he's okay. I don't think Mom will be happy until he's home again."

"If he wants to stay home," Jude said, looking down at the door to the cellar, "then you guys shouldn't tell him where the guns are."

After the last-minute checks, the tearful goodbyes, and the final admonitions to be safe and careful, Jude sped down the trail towards an old, overgrown highway he knew would be the best route south. Battery power was his main concern; without cities between Slate Creek and Vancouver, he would have to depend on friendly SACs who may or may not have charging stations.

The trail came to the old highway, long since abandoned by the former Transport Canada Ministry. As he leaned into his turn and accelerated on the pavement, he caught a flash in his small mirror. He turned his head, but he was going around a corner. When he straightened out, he looked again, and behind him was another bike! His adrenaline surged, knowing he was being followed, and his two bags of supplies could be worth his life.

He slowed for a better look, formulating a plan for confrontation. As the bike approached, he went over the plan in his head: stop, dump the bike, grab the Taser, and take control of the situation. He slowed more, letting the familiar-looking bike get closer, and then he executed his plan. He screeched to a halt, laid the bike down, and pulled out his taser. He pointed it at the rider, who surprisingly didn't even hesitate to approach.

"That's far enough!" he shouted.

The rider stopped casually, staring at him through the tinted visor of the helmet. Jude noticed a waft of blond hair, the end of a ponytail, blowing around behind her. The rider slid off her helmet and looked incredulously at Jude.

"If you shoot that taser at me, I will beat you senseless, as soon as I recover."

"Maisy Marren Kane, what in the world do you think you're doing?" shouted Jude. "Have you lost your ever-lovin' mind?"

"Are those questions or statements?" she quipped.

"We're almost 50 kilometers from the SAC!" Jude calculated.

"I know. Why do you think I waited to catch up to you? I didn't want it to be too easy for you to haul me back home," she said.

"You're impossible!" he shouted, throwing up his hands. "What about Mom and Dad? They're going to be terrified when they find out you're gone. Did you at least leave a note?" Jude asked in his best big brother scolding tone he could muster.

"Yes, and they left me one, too. At least Dad did. I found extra protein bars in my pack and a note that said, "I figured you couldn't bear to sit out such an adventure. Be safe and tell your brother to calm down."

"He did not write that," Jude said unconvincingly.

Maisy reached into her side pack, pulled it out, and handed it to him.

"He's even sneakier than you."

"Like father, like daughter."

"Well, we'd better keep an eye out for a good stopping place. Daylight will run out on us pretty quickly," Jude said, finally surrendering. "Remember: no matter what, stay close."

"You lead the way. You already know I can follow you."

They traveled down the road, occasionally slowing or stopping for a downed tree or other obstruction, but overall, Jude was happy with their progress. As dusk began to threaten, Jude spotted a thin column of smoke in the distance, and he pointed it out to Maisy.

They turned onto a trail that appeared to lead to the source of the smoke. Suddenly, a pine branch swung into Jude, knocking him off his bike. He tumbled a few times and then jumped back onto his feet. He took his helmet off to find a thin, wild-eyed, dark-haired woman standing behind Maisy with a knife to her throat.

Chapter 3: **Squamish River**

"Don't move, Maisy," Jude ordered.

"I wasn't planning on it," she said flatly.

"Who are you?" the woman said. Jude noticed she was young, about his age, and had a silky mocha complexion and deep brown eyes. Her look exuded an air of caution more than fear or anger. He sensed she was only trying to protect her own.

"I'm Jude Kane, and this is my sister, Maisy. We're from Slate Creek, a SAC a few hundred kilometers north of here. We're trying to find our brother. We think he was taken to Vancouver. We saw the smoke . . . "

"Is your brother that yahoo who shot down a drone?" she blurted out unexpectedly, slowly lowering the knife.

"Yes. His name is Callum. He got spooked. He doesn't have good memories after three years in CME. How did you know about that?"

The young woman dropped the knife and handed Maisy back her helmet.

"A good journalist never reveals her sources," she said. "I have been trying to connect the SACs with some kind of news-sharing network for a few years now. It's tough when no one talks to each other. I take it you need something, or you wouldn't have ridden towards the smoke."

"A safe place to sleep and some water would be great," Maisy jumped in.

"And a charging station. These bikes are going to need some juice if we're going to make it to Vancouver."

"Water, food, and beds are no problem. The charging station hasn't worked in years. Lots of things haven't worked in years. My Dad is the

SAC leader, but he's gone downhill since my mom died. You'll see what I mean. By the way, my name is Zara. Zara Malik. Welcome to the Squamish River SAC."

"Nice to meet you," Maisy said. "Thanks for not cutting my throat."

"We appreciate the help. Maybe I can take a look at that charger," Jude said.

"My brother is a kind of technical genius," Maisy said.

"I'm not a genius," he said. "I just like to fix things."

"You mine Lithium and Nickel and make batteries. Who does that? You're a freakin' wizard," Maisy argued back. She was naturally confrontational, even when she was complimenting you.

"You can make batteries?" Zara asked.

"Well, yes. My dad was an engineering professor, and he taught me a lot. I guess you can say I try to take his theory and make it work. Mostly, I repair anything electrical."

"Well, I hope your head doesn't explode. Most of the things that are supposed to give us electricity are dead or close to it. Like I said, things have gone downhill."

She was not exaggerating. As they approached the SAC, the dirt path wound through fields of degenerate crops of corn with shriveled ears and soybeans with small, withered pods. They passed through a tall wooden gate into the main living area that looked to be arranged in a circle of houses and barns, and everything was dark. As dusk began to enshroud them, there were no lamps, no flashlights, nor any sign of light inside the houses except the flickering of a few small wood stoves.

Jude noticed that many of the structures were empty.

"Where is everyone?" he asked.

"You can only last so long without enough power," Zara said as if she were fighting the same bleakness that plagued her father as well. "We have decent farmers, but with so little power, the tractors are worthless, and the water pumps can barely get water to our houses, much less irrigate the crops. Everything is done by hand, and as you can see, we lose some of the crops we do have before they can all be harvested. It's just as well. Even if we could grow more crops, there's not much land left. CAMO has taken over about half of our farmland here in the valley. They claim they need it for the cities, and they can farm more efficiently than we can. It's hard to argue that when you see our fields. Most people gave up and went back to the cities, and a few found new SACs. A couple of people went up to Slate Creek, which is how I found out about the drone."

"That must have been the Carsons. I had no idea they came from another SAC. No wonder they love Dad so much," Maisy deduced.

"Your wind turbines are still up. Is any power flowing into your grid?" Jude asked, surveying the landscape littered with still turbines and damaged solar panels.

"I don't know. I don't even know how you would check that. My dad had an engineer set this system up, but no one who is still here knows anything about it."

Jude sighed and looked at Maisy.

"We're supposed to be going to Vancouver to find our brother, remember?" she reminded him.

"We can't get there without charging up the bikes, and we can't do that until I find some power around here."

"You have a week," Maisy said, pointing at him with her helmet.

"Plenty of time."

Zara led them into the circle of dilapidated structures and empty workshops. Broken windows, moss-covered roofs, and sagging floors were standard features on buildings that looked hastily thrown together with wood and metal scraps.

"We need to go see my dad, and then, as far as where you want to lay your heads, take your pick. We have a lot of vacancies," Zara said.

"What's in that building there?" Maisy asked, pointing to one of the sturdier buildings, once painted white, with a faint red cross on the side.

"That was our clinic at one time. We had a doctor and a couple of nurses when I was little, but they left years ago."

"What do you do when someone gets hurt?"

"Hydrogen Peroxide and gauze."

"What if someone gets sick or has a bad infection?"

"Liquids and rest."

Maisy shot a look at Jude, and he smiled wide and smug.

"You have a week," he said.

Maisy surveyed the fields, houses, and the shuttered clinic.

"Plenty of time."

Amar Malik greeted Jude and Maisy feebly as he sat at the makeshift kitchen table made of a piece of scrap plywood and roughly hewn tree limbs for legs. He seemed consumed by his arduous task of whittling on a piece of wood.

"Nice to meet you," he said. "I take it Zara gave you a tour of the SAC?"

"Yes, sir," Jude said.

"We've got some challenges. Our enthusiasm for leaving urban life behind has waned as nature seems to be catching up with us."

"Yes, sir. I might be able to help. If you don't mind, I'd like to start by looking at your grid in the morning."

"I'm sure you can't do our power supply any harm. Isn't Rod Kane your father?" he said, searching his memory.

"Yes, sir."

"He was an engineering professor, wasn't he?"

"Yes, sir."

"He must have taught you a thing or two."

"Yes, sir. He knew he couldn't do everything by himself, and I have loved anything electrical since I was old enough to try and stick my finger into a power connection. It's like I've had a fifteen-year apprenticeship."

"You are welcome to see if there is anything worth salvaging out there. How about you, young lady?" he asked Maisy. "Are you the hired help?"

"Hardly," she said incredulously, trying not to roll her eyes. "I've taken emergency medicine courses, nursing courses, and even a pharmacy class. Now I'm looking for victims to practice on."

"By all means, the clinic is yours," he said, almost cracking a grin at the corner of his mouth. "Turn it into whatever kind of house of horrors you want."

Zara showed them to a vacant shack that sat fairly evenly between her own house, the clinic, and a supply shed. "Make yourselves at home," she said, pushing the front door open to a dusty room with rough, uneven floors, tattered curtains, and several cracked windows. "This place still has windows, but I wouldn't lean on the glass."

"Thanks, Zara," Jude said. "I'll see if I can get the lights back on in the morning.

"You already lit this place up when you showed up. You and Maisy have given us something we haven't had in a few years," she said, walking back out through the doorway.

"What's that?" Maisy asked before Zara closed the door.

"Hope."

Jude unfurled his bedroll, kicked off his boots, and folded a blanket into a makeshift pillow.

"I'm concerned about this place," he said to Maisy as he lay down and stared up at the cobwebs in the ceiling.

"What about this place specifically?" she asked as she prepped her own bed. "The fact that their corn and soybeans are pathetic?"

"No, although they are pretty bad."

"The fact that they have almost no power?"

"No, although that is a huge problem."

"The fact that they've lost most of their people?"

"No, although that is a sign of a dying SAC."

"Then what in the heck else is there to be concerned about?"

"CAMO has taken over about half of their arable land. Do you know what that means?" he asked.

"It means someone might actually grow something," Maisy said.

"That's not the problem. The problem is encroachment. The SACs have always been sacred in a way. According to ADAMS' analysis during the Transition, Sustainable Agricultural Communities were not considered a threat, and they provide a kind of 'safety valve' for populations that are not well suited for urban life."

"We all read the same thing in New American History class," Maisy said, "but they are terrible at farming here. CAMO will get a lot more food out of that land."

"Don't you see the contradiction?" he said. "If ADAMS gave SACs a protected status, how can CAMO just take over some of their land? What was that drone doing before Callum shot it down? Slate Creek is not that far away."

"So, you're worried that they might come for us."

"If they did, what could we ever do? Can you imagine if we lost half of our land in the valley? We'd starve," he said.

"Maybe that's the point," Maisy said.

"That's what I'm concerned about."

The next morning, Maisy began to scrounge for furniture and linens she could use to set up shop in the clinic. As she looked around at the dirt, the cracked windows, the unreliable water supply, and the unsanitary conditions, she became overwhelmed. "This place is a dump. I wouldn't stitch myself up in here," she said, exasperated.

"Hey doc," Jude said when he had gathered his tool kit, "why don't you make house calls?"

"It's kind of weird, don't you think? What would you do if a stranger showed up in Slate Creek and came to the door asking if you needed any medical help?"

"If she were accompanied by Zara, I'd say come on in."

"Good point. I didn't think of that."

While Maisy took her medical pack and went to get Zara, Jude made his first stop: the main powerpack for Squamish.

"How's it look?" a man said from behind, startling Jude.

"Whoa! You scared me a bit there."

"Sorry about that. Akal Malik, Zara's brother. You must be the guy from Slate Creek."

"Jude Kane," he said, extending his hand. "I just got here, but at first glance, it looks like these batteries have some decent life left in them, but there is very little voltage coming in or going out."

"That's not surprising," he said. "We've been getting less and less from the solar panels and wind turbines, but it really took a dive last year. I couldn't see anything obvious, but then again, I don't know what I'm looking for."

"A slow decline is probably due to maintenance: cleaning solar panels, correcting their angles, tightening bolts, and lubricating the wind turbines. A sudden decline means a problem, usually a damaged power line. I figure if I can find that first, then I can teach you the maintenance," Jude offered.

"I'll take you up on that," Akal said.

"Well then, let's get started," Jude said, pulling the strap of his toolkit over his shoulder. He only brought bare essentials, but luckily, there were some basic tools, oil, and leftover wiring in the supply shed.

"I think I've figured out the pattern here, and we should start from the powerpack and work out. A bad connection close to the pack would kill all the flow from the outer panels and turbines."

"I'm following you, boss," Akal said. "If you figure this out, you'll save this SAC. We're about to lose everything and everyone."

"No pressure," Jude chuckled. In reality, he was ecstatic. This mission was what he lived for, and to think that finding this kink in the electrical flow to the grid would mean so much to Squamish River was a big bonus.

They hiked into the fields first, with Jude showing Akal how to service and repair the wind turbines and solar panels. After a few stops, Akal was able to get to work right away while Jude started testing the wiring and the connections. After twelve hours, they were both exhausted, out of water, and ready for a better meal than the nuts and jerky they brought with them.

"Any luck?" Akal asked, tightening his last bolt on a panel in the furthest field.

"You've done a lot more than I have. I shored up a few potential problems, but I didn't find anything that would cause your drop in power. I've been looking for a line severed by a tree or shredded in the blades of a wind turbine, but so far, the wiring and connections are testing fine."

"We're just going to have to hike into the mountains," Akal said. "We'll likely have to take the eastern mountains tomorrow and the western slopes the day after. The wind is great up there, but the steep grades are going to slow us way down."

When Maisy and Zara made the rounds, some of the doors could barely withstand the knock. One cabin made from roughly hewn whole trees looked sturdy but drafty. The door was made of scrap boards, and drug across the floor as it opened.

"Good morning, Jon. I've got Maisy Kane here, all the way from Slate Creek. She's passing through, but she has medical training, and she's offered to take a look at folks while she's here. How's that leg you tried to chop off last week?" Zara didn't waste time.

"It hurts like hell," he grunted.

"Can I take a look?" Maisy asked.

"Why? What's a little girl like you going to do for me? I've already sewn it up."

"I've got pain medication, antibiotics, and a saw. Depending on the extent of the infection, I hope I don't need the third thing."

"Alright. Take a look. I tried to keep it clean, but I think something's trying to mess it up. It stinks pretty bad."

Jon opened the door, and the odor hit like a brick in the face. Zara jumped off the step and vomited until she felt twisted inside out, but Maisy held it together.

"Why don't you sit and get as comfortable as you can with your leg propped up on this stool?" she said, sliding it in front of a stained, padded chair that looks like he made himself. Jon hobbled over, sat down, and groaned as he lifted his swollen leg onto the stool. Maisy gently slid his pant leg up to his knee and examined the wound, intentionally holding in her shock and disgust. She was brutally honest, but she also instinctively knew that walking people through their trauma and injuries psychologically was as important as their physical treatment.

The gash was clearly from an ax, and he managed to sink it deep into the shin bone at about a thirty-degree angle. He did stitch himself up, but between his shock, shaky hands, and the growing infection, the Frankenstein monster was in far better shape than him.

"So, what do you think, doc?" he asked. Maisy resisted correcting him. Now was not the time or place.

"The good news is your shin bone is still straight, more or less, and it should heal fine. The bad news is the infection is pretty bad."

"Are you going to need the saw?" he asked. Zara had managed to make it into the living room, but she wasn't looking too good. At the mention of the saw, she slinked back out of the doorway.

"I don't think so, Jon. Your stitch job and attempt at keeping your wound clean actually did some good. It slowed down the infection just enough to keep your tissue alive. I will be able to give you some antibiotics and pain meds, but that alone won't clear this infection. I'm going to have to get old-fashioned and physically clean out the infection from the wound, and then the antibiotics will take over from there."

The blood drained from Jon's face, but the old lumberjack still maintained a bit of a sense of humor, if only for his own sake. "Will that hurt more than the saw?"

Maisy chuckled. "About the same, I would say. At least this way, you come out with a leg. Don't worry too much. I'm going to knock you out cold and then dope you up afterward. You'll be pretty sore, but you should heal up in a few weeks."

"You look pretty young to be digging out a fella's leg. Have you done this before?" Jon asked.

"Of course." She didn't mention that it was a virtual procedure exercise on her screen in her trauma course. Sometimes, trimming the truth a bit could alleviate potential problems later.

Jude sat on a fallen tree to catch his breath and pulled out his tablet to check the grid. "This is it, isn't it?" he asked Akal.

"We've hit every panel, and this is the last turbine," he shouted, clipping in and pulling a panel off.

"I'm missing something. I haven't found any broken lines or bad connections, but we still don't have the power we should."

"It's a lot better since we've got all these panels pointing in the right direction and the turbines moving again," Akal said, his voice echoing down the side of the mountain.

"Yes, but we're not seeing what we should flow into the powerpack. We're still only at about 35% of capacity for this setup."

"Maybe you should check the power packs again," Akal suggested as he checked wires, oiled the gearbox, and tightened bolts.

"You mean the power pack," Jude said. "I did, and it looked fine."

"I mean packs, plural. We have two power packs."

"What?" Jude shouted up to him. "Where's the second one?"

"It's under the first one. You get to it through a passageway from the supply shed. My dad said the engineer who set up the system wanted it to last, stay at a constant temperature, and be out of sight in case of any problems. The bottom one is the main power pack. The one you saw was probably the auxiliary."

"You didn't think to mention this before?" he shouted.

Akal unclipped and zipped down from the turbine. "I figured you saw both. Besides, we needed to hit these panels and turbines anyway. We didn't waste any effort."

Jude sighed. "Just the effort I put into making myself crazy looking for this broken connection. Take me to the shed."

Maisy was able to put Jon under general anesthesia without much difficulty, especially after he prepped himself with a few homemade liquors to calm his nerves. Zara kept an eye on the portable monitors to make sure his heart rate and breathing stayed steady, and Maisy got to work pulling out the thin twine he used as his sutures and peeling the swollen, purple flesh back from the wound. Zara kept her eyes on the monitors for a distraction as much as help for Maisy. Maisy grabbed a shiny stainless-steel instrument and began to cut and scrape away at the wound, grunting and commenting along the way. "There we go . . . ooh, that was a good chunk . . . nothing like getting all this pus out of the way . . . " Zara hung on by her nails.

"I think I got most of it, but I really need more light," she complained. I need a good spotlight right on the opening."

Suddenly, the dim lamps they had turned on in an attempt to get as much light as possible sprang to life, glowing brilliantly and lighting up the room. "He did it!" Maisy squealed. "Just in time. Zara, grab that lantern and shine it straight into the opening. Hold it steady and don't look."

"Don't worry. I'm not about to look."

"I can't believe it. We trekked over the entire SAC, and a rusted connection between the main and auxiliary power packs was killing the power supply that whole time. I should have looked closer at the connections coming out of the pack. I would have seen them going down . . . "

"Woulda coulda shoulda," Akal said, smiling. "You still fixed it, and we managed to get the power back flowing from the panels and turbines at full capacity. You've essentially saved this SAC. Thank you, Jude."

"You definitely saved Jon's leg and probably his life, Maisy," Zara said. "I can't believe how you dug in there and cleaned it out. I never saw our old doctor handle anything like that. You have a gift." For once, Maisy was quiet and just smiled sheepishly.

After a couple of days in which Maisy made a few more rounds and made sure Jon's wound was healing properly, they celebrated at the Malik house with a few flasks of homemade liquor and a wild turkey donated by a grateful remnant in the community.

That night, Jude hooked the bikes up to the charger, and they retreated to their still sparse house for a sound night's sleep that was all but ensured by the food and drink they had. The next morning, they gathered their things, refilled their packs and canteens, and loaded up the bikes. They thanked Amar and Akal, but they were very disappointed that no one knew where Zara had gone. She knew they were leaving, and it seemed strange she would miss the send-off, unless it would be too much for her.

"She enjoyed having you two here," Akal explained. "Maybe she just couldn't bring herself to say goodbye."

Knowing they were already delayed in their mission and that winter was coming fast, they decided to head out and get as far south as they could as quickly as possible. They weaved through the wooded path and found their way back onto the old, abandoned highway. They had just built up speed when they came around a corner and slammed on their brakes as a pine tree tipped and fell across the road.

Jude and Maisy came to a stop and pulled off their helmets. "Keep an eye out, Maisy. That was no accident."

"Of course not. I just needed to get your attention before you left me in the dust." Zara stepped through the tangle of dry branches and stood between them, holding a ragged knapsack. "Sorry about the tree. In my defense, it was dead and leaning anyway. We need to talk."

Chapter 4: **Wilderness**

Jude and Maisy exchanged deer-in-the-headlight looks while Zara set down her very modest trove of earthy possessions and took a deep breath.

"Why do I get the feeling that you need help with something else?" Jude sighed.

"Because I do," Zara said, looking at the ground and then stepping closer and looking into Jude's crisp hazel eyes. "But I don't need you to come back to Squamish. In fact, it's quite the opposite."

"So, you need us to leave? We're already doing that, or at least we're trying," Jude said, working out his logic.

"I want to go with you to Vancouver."

"Why do you want to come with us?" Maisy asked.

"Because I need to get out of here. I'm happy— very happy— that both of you helped us so much. Even though CAMO is squeezing us, we have a real chance now, but my future isn't here. I don't want to hide out in the woods. I want to be a journalist, and if I'm going to report on what's really happening, I'm going to need to get out in the world. A trip to Vancouver is a great place to start."

Maisy looked at Jude and sized up the bikes and packs. "We can make it work. It wasn't in the original plan, but then neither was I. It's your call, Jude."

"Do you have anything to keep the bugs out of your teeth, the wind out of your eyes, and the rocks out of your skull?" he asked.

"I've got an old bicycle helmet, a knit scarf, and a pair of safety glasses."

"That'll have to do. Let's put your pack and my pack on Maisy's bike, and you can ride with me. That will even out the weight a bit."

"Thank you, Jude. I won't be a burden. I promise."

"I'm not worried about you being a burden. I'm worried about keeping you safe. Like I told Maisy, stay close."

"You got it," she said, pulling down her knit hat, wrapping her scarf around her face, and throwing her leg over the back of the bike. She reached around his waist, and he shuddered slightly as she took his words to heart and held on.

The second leg of the trip continued without much incident, aside from the occasional downed tree, washout, and startled deer that were not used to seeing anything on that road for decades. Jude kept a wary eye on the daylight, the movement of the clouds, and the map on his phone. Even with the extra weight of Zara, they were well within the margins of his meticulous travel plans, but there was always one thing he couldn't plan on: weather.

Fall in northern Cascadia could give you a preview of winter within minutes. The overall climate trend had been warming for over a hundred years, but as devastating as that had been for many parts of the world, the volatility of the weather was arguably more destructive. The average annual temperature was two or three degrees higher than a few decades ago, but what people felt was the sudden torrential rains that came with a fast-moving air mass over warm waters, followed by an arctic blast that would paralyze thousands of square kilometers.

Jude didn't say anything, but Zara could see him checking his phone and switching between the topographical map and the weather radar. She could feel his body tightening as he checked the sky more and more frequently. He kept scanning the remote landscape, and Zara found herself doing the same thing. She knew he was looking for shelter.

When the first flakes began to fall, she sensed his adrenaline begin to course through his veins. Maisy glanced over to Jude, and he shook his head as if to say, "I know. I'm looking." Their timetable shrank from hours to minutes with the rapidly accumulating snow. Plunging temperatures not only made two-wheeled transportation treacherous, but it also killed battery power and hid deadly obstructions on the already rough pavement. It also had a way of freezing people to death who couldn't find shelter in time.

Through the thickening flakes that stubbornly clung to her safety glasses, Zara spotted an angular shape protruding from the encroaching whiteness of the forest. She tapped Jude's shoulder and pointed. He waved at Maisy and then came to a stop.

"What do you see?" he asked through the visor of his helmet. "I don't see anything."

"Look between the ridges. See the stream?"

"I do now."

"Follow the stream and look just past that S curve. It looks like some kind of structure."

"I see it!" he yelled, looking at Maisy.

"Me too," she said. "But I don't think the bikes will make it. The trees are way too thick, and the terrain is too rough."

"Let's hide the bikes here. We're going to have to hike it."

"Do you think it's safe?" Zara asked. "I don't know of any SACs out here."

"I don't know. I don't see smoke, and I don't see anything that looks like a power system, but from here it's hard to say. We'll have to approach carefully."

They rolled the bikes behind a clump of trees and covered them with branches as best they could. "I doubt anyone will be coming down this road anytime soon, but I still don't want to advertise them," Jude said.

"We'd better get moving," Maisy barked, already ten meters ahead of them, "or this snow is going to cover that little corner of the roof we can see."

They hoisted up their packs and headed down the steep, wooded hill. The terrain was even worse than they first thought, with the snow hiding boulders, fallen saplings, and depressions. Jude instinctively brought up the rear, staying close to Zara and reaching for her arm each time she stumbled.

"Will you guys hurry up?" Maisy ordered. "Jude, you are being so chivalrous, but you're tripping more than she is. Maybe you should focus on your own balance?"

"Working on it," he huffed.

They finally made it to the tree line and got a better look at the structure. It looked like an old hunting cabin, left over from the 20th century. There didn't seem to be any movement, power source, or indications of human presence.

"I think it's just us, but let's stick to the tree line until we get right up to it. I don't want to be an easy target for an uneasy shooter," Jude warned.

They had descended into a narrow valley, cut out between the mountain peaks over millions of years by the now inauspicious stream that snaked its way into oblivion somewhere beyond the thick forest. The gently sloped sides of the valley were now covered in at least three centimeters of fresh powder, and nestled just inside the tree line was the cabin. A hundred years earlier, it was probably well outside the cover of the trees, but even through the funneled wind of the valley, there will always be a few stubborn seedlings that stick and grow just beyond the shelter of their towering parents.

The cabin was a simple log structure, about ten meters square, and judging by the long-rotted stumps and impressive new growth around it, the cabin was likely made from trees in the immediate vicinity. This far out in what was then known as the Canadian Rockies, the owner probably had little choice in building materials. The pitched roof was pitted and about as watertight as a colander, but the frame and support beams looked to be still quite solid.

"Aaah!" shouted Zara, falling hard to the ground and grasping her ankle.

Jude's first instinct was to hush her, but he thought the better of it and rushed to her side.

"What happened?" he asked.

"I rolled my ankle on that bowling ball of a boulder," she hissed, pointing to an impressive rock that lay hidden in a pocket of snow.

"That is a nasty one," Jude said. "Thanks for finding it before me."

"Ha ha," she grimaced. "Now I really *am* a burden."

"Don't say that," Maisy said as she knelt and examined Zara's leg. "Where does it hurt?"

"My ankle."

"Can you move your foot?"

"Yes," she said, groaning. "But it feels like someone just used a hammer on it."

"Good. If you can move your foot and it's still pointing more or less in the right direction, it's probably not broken, but we need to get your boots off and take a look."

Zara agreed and then looked at Jude.

"We need to get in out of the weather," he announced, and then he looked at Maisy. "Get her boot off before it swells while I look inside. I'll come back and help her to the cabin."

Jude took his knife and ducked from tree to tree, working his way to the back of the cabin. It had windows, about half broken and half surprisingly intact. The logs were hewn, stacked, treated, and chinked, but only traces of the brittle chinking were left on the logs now. He carefully crept up to the back door, peered through the latticed glass, and scanned the ancient kitchen. The view was obscured by decades of mud and dirt, but he could see the bare cupboards and thick dust that spoke of years of solitude, except for the occasional four-legged critter.

The door opened angrily, but it stayed on its hinges. Suddenly, a chittering squeal shattered the winter silence, and Jude jumped back with a guttural scream of his own. Several grayish blurs flew past him, and he turned in time to see a family of raccoons scampering off into the woods. The cabin had apparently been occupied, at least until now.

Jude ran back to Maisy and Zara, where Maisy was ready with a knife and a sour look.

"What was that screaming about?" she said, her eyes wild. "Was somebody in there?"

"There was a whole family in there, but they've moved out now."

"What are you talking about? You didn't hurt anyone, did you?"

"You know me better than that," he said smugly. "The raccoons are gone now, and except for squirrels and maybe a few other critters, it's all ours. Let's get Zara inside."

"And after that," Zara slurred, "tell Mr. and Mrs. Raccoon I said thanks."

"A full dose of pain pills on an empty stomach may not have been the best idea," Maisy said. "At least she's more comfortable."

"She's so comfortable she's almost unconscious," Jude grunted as they tried to get Zara on her feet. "This isn't going to work. Help me get her on my shoulder." Jude hoisted Zara onto his shoulder in a classic fireman's carry and made straight for the cabin, crossing the fresh snow and even ground away from the trees. Maisy carried the packs, needing to drag a few of them the rest of the way, and the three of them circled to the back door and hurried in. Maisy shoved the door closed as the howling wind of the blizzard blasted against and through the generous cracks in the old log cabin.

"Well, we're in out of the storm— kind of," she said, surveying the cracks between the logs, the holes in the roof, and the decades of dirt, leaves, and debris on the floor.

"We've got a solid structure," Jude said. "I think the builder knew what he was facing out here. These logs were heavily treated, and I suspect the floor joists and trusses were too. Take care of Zara, and I'll plug as many holes as I can."

"With what?" Maisy asked.

"Whatever is lying around," he said.

"That would be dirt, leaves, and sticks."

"Don't forget branches and moss. Callum and I built forts in the woods with less. It's not a problem."

This was one time when Maisy was happy to have Jude on her side. When Jude said it wasn't a problem, he had already worked out a solution, found his materials, picked out his tools, and fixed it three times in his head. He definitely inherited Dad's analytical brain. She and Callum got an extra dose of Mom's emotional side, but Jude had a way of never letting feelings get in the way of solving a problem. That is not to say he wasn't emotional; he was compassionate almost to a fault, but he was always in such control of his feelings. They very rarely spilled out at the wrong time, except maybe when Callum shot down the drone. She knew Jude was upset with himself for how he spoke to Callum, even if he was dead right.

With the adrenaline surge over and her heart rate slowing, Maisy started to feel the cold, and she knew it would be worse for Zara. Immobile, semi-conscious, and under the influence of relaxing painkillers, Zara's core temperature could drop dangerously low. Maisy wrapped her in two blankets and propped her up against a corner. She quickly went to work finding a heat source, and from the looks of the cabin, they were going to need a fire. Burning wood in a house made of wood seemed absurd to Maisy, but she figured the place was more than a hundred years old, and back then, there was not much else to work with.

Resisting the urge to start cleaning, Maisy gathered dry leaves, twigs, and sticks to start a fire in the large stone fireplace.

"Hey Jude, do you have anything I can use to start a fire?" she shouted through the gaping hole in the roof he was attempting to patch with large leafy branches.

"Sure, but hold on a minute. Let me make sure the chimney is clear."

She heard him stepping tentatively on the roof beams and then heard a scratching sound as he jammed a sapling down the shaft, breaking loose decades of soot, dirt, and foliage. The deluge fell into the fireplace, spilled out onto the floor, and then filled the living room with a swirling cloud of black and brown dust.

"Thanks," she coughed. "I think it's clear now."

Zara moaned and shifted in the corner, and Maisy knew time was not on her side. The sun, wherever it was behind the blizzard, was setting, and the storm was still ramping up. All of them, especially Zara, were going to need a strong fire to keep hypothermia at bay in the drafty cabin. The more the snow piled up, the harder it would be to find fuel for the fire, and they might be stuck for several days.

"Where are you going?" Jude called as Maisy headed outside.

"We need firewood," she shouted back over the howling, biting wind.

"Don't go too far," he warned her. "And there's a fire starter in my pack."

She gave him a thumbs-up and scrambled into the brush. While Jude gathered fresh branches, she looked for the driest, most dead-looking limbs and sticks she could find. On the first trip back, she started the fire, and on each return run, she checked Zara's vital signs and made sure the fire was going strong. On one return trip outside, she pulled a protein bar from her pack and tossed it up to Jude on the roof.

"You need all the help you can get. Take a break and thaw out if you need to. Don't ignore your body," she yelled to him. Logic was his language. Of course, he'd push himself to the end to make sure the cabin was as buttoned up as possible, but making him think about physical limits activated another part of his brain and gave him another problem to solve: preserving himself. With the temperature dropping, the race was on to plug up the cabin before he was frozen stiff. They were going to need as much insulation as possible to preserve the heat and keep them from freezing to death overnight.

On her ninth trip back out to gather fuel, Jude grabbed her jacket and stopped her. "That's enough," he shouted over the wind. "We need to get inside."

Maisy shook off her tunnel vision and glanced around the cabin and up at the sky. It was almost dark, and the snow had piled up to about ten centimeters already. Jude was right; time was up. They had to work with what they had at this point. They pushed their way into the kitchen, and then together they shoved the door closed.

"I feel the fire from here," Jude sighed. "Good work."

"Thanks. Now go sit next to Zara and get the blood moving to your extremities," she ordered.

"How's her ankle?" he asked, dropping his coat and gloves and sitting on the ledge of the fireplace, rubbing his fingers together.

"It's not broken. She sprained it pretty bad, and I wouldn't rule out a small fracture, but I think she'll be ok if I wrap it up and she stays off of it for a few days."

"By the looks of this storm, that shouldn't be a problem."

The next morning, the waning coals of the fire proved to be no match for the drafty walls and roof.

"I think I figured out exactly what 'a cold day in hell' is really like," Maisy said as she emerged from her sleeping bag. "Keeping a decent fire going is a full-time job."

"Let me get it going again," Zara said, sitting up.

"Don't even think about it," Maisy ordered. "You've got to stay off that ankle and let it heal."

"It's feeling a lot better," she said, standing up and delicately trying to put some weight on it. "Aaah!" she hissed through her teeth, jerking her foot back up.

"Ready for some more meds?" Maisy asked.

"Yeah."

"Don't worry, Zara," Jude said. "None of us are going anywhere right now. You're not missing out on anything."

"What do you mean?" Maisy asked.

"There's a meter of snow outside, and the wind has calmed down, but the snow is still falling. We're stuck," Jude declared.

"But I need to get more firewood," Maisy protested.

"It's kind of hard to find right now, and what you might find is awfully wet," he said.

"We're running out of water, and we can't live on protein bars forever," she half-whispered to Jude. "What are we going to do?"

"Insulate."

"Huh?"

"How do you think the Inuit tribes survived? Snow is a fantastic insulator. We're going to pile and pack snow into every crack in these walls and the roof. The branches I jammed into the spaces last night will work to help hold the snow. A small fire will keep us warm, and maybe we can uncover some firewood as we shovel the snow. We'll kill two birds with one stone."

Despite Maisy's doubts, Jude's idea was a big success. As she kept the flames going and the coals glowing, Jude sealed up the walls and plugged the holes in the roof, and the cabin slowly began to warm. The wind chill kept the snow solidly in place, with only a slow seepage down the inside walls. They packed snow in bottles and set them near the fire, and Jude sacrificed a pair of clean socks to filter the water. By nightfall the next day, they had endured the worst of the storm, and Jude predicted they might be able to hike out to the highway in the morning.

"I hope you're right. We don't have enough wood to keep the fire going the rest of tonight, and we've already tapped into our reserves of protein bars," Maisy warned.

"We'll be fine," Jude reassured them both. "We just need to pass a little time now. Got any ideas?"

"Never have I ever . . . been to a city," Maisy said. Jude and Zara raised their hands.

"Never have I ever . . . had a passport implanted," Zara said, raising her hand alone. "Boom. Two points."

"No passport?" Jude said to Zara.

"Born and raised on the SAC. Nobody was around to implant it."

"Never have I ever . . . sprained an ankle," Jude said with a devious smile.

"No fair," Zara protested.

"You won that one," Maisy said.

"Maybe we'd better try and get some sleep. We're going to be busy tomorrow," Jude suggested.

"Good plan. I'm going to use the outhouse in the house," Maisy said, heading into an alcove off the kitchen area. With no indoor plumbing and what was left of the outhouse buried in snow, they had to make do. "I don't envy whoever gets chamber pot duty."

When Maisy left, Jude rustled through his bag and pulled out some beef jerky and a protein bar.

"Work on these," he said, handing them to Zara. "You'll sleep better with something on your stomach. I know you're hungry."

"You are too," she protested, "and you've done most of the heavy lifting. I've just been sitting here."

"You've been healing. You need the protein. I'll catch a squirrel if I have to," he said with a smile.

"I shouldn't have come. I'm such a burden."

"Don't say that," he said, putting his hand on her knee and looking her in the eye. "I'm glad you're here, and so is Maisy. I have a feeling we're all going to have to lean on each other, and a tripod is always more stable than a pair of crutches."

In the morning, Jude turned over in his sleeping bag and rolled his face into a puddle of water. He jerked his head up and saw dim daylight peering through the walls, illuminating the small lake that had formed while they slept. The fire was out, and water was dripping down the chimney.

"I thought I wet the bed, but now we'll never know," Maisy said, sitting up and raising her arm, dripping with muddy water.

"What's going on?" Zara said, surveying the scene.

"Good news: a warm front has moved in, and we can get out of here," Jude said. "Bad news: we're soaking wet, it's still cold, and our wet bags and clothes will be five times as heavy. How's your foot?"

"It hurts, but I think I can start putting weight on it," Zara said.

"She really needs another day off it," Maisy said. "I don't know what we should do."

"We need to get out of here," Jude said firmly. "We need to move, get our blood pumping, and find a way to dry off, even if it is by wind on a motorcycle."

"How . . . " Maisy started and then stopped as she saw the wheels turning in Jude's head.

"I've got an idea."

Cutting two sturdy branches with what was left of the old rusty hand saw he used two nights earlier, he made poles and slid them through one of the tents they packed. He created a stretcher that could be drug behind him, and Zara climbed on as his reluctant passenger. Maisy was left to carry the rest of the gear, and they gave up on the soaked sleeping bags and left them behind.

Following the notches he made during the blizzard, Jude heaved the stretcher up the hill, over the rocks, logs, and foliage, and finally found the trees where they sheltered the bikes. Jude collapsed in exhaustion and caught his breath while Maisy helped Zara off the stretcher and got her on her feet, or at least her good one.

Jude looked at the branches and tilted his head, looking puzzled. He listened and thought he heard a noise coming from the highway, but he couldn't be sure. Pulling the three largest branches away, he confirmed his suspicions. The bikes were gone. Despite trying to replace the cover of the branches, the thieves didn't cover their fresh tracks, leading straight to the highway. They had taken the bikes only minutes before.

Chapter 5: **Vancouver**

STANDING BETWEEN THE TREAD marks, dripping and shivering in the thawing air, Jude sighed and shook his head. Maisy held her tongue, and Zara hobbled to a tree and leaned against it. They were exhausted, soaked, down one tent and three sleeping bags, much of their food, and most of their energy. Now they were stranded in the jagged mountains and vast wilderness of northern Cascadia.

"It's a long walk," Maisy finally said, breaking the silence but not the tension.

Zara looked up. "Walk to where?"

"Anywhere," Maisy said.

Zara slumped down and sat on the wet earth, extending her leg.

Jude sighed, put his hands on his hips, and stared into the sky.

"We're not walking anywhere. We don't have enough supplies, and we're barely mobile. Our best bet is to go back to the cabin where we have some kind of shelter . . . "

"And do what? Go swimming?" Maisy snapped. "Sorry. That doesn't help . . . "

"Shhh!" Jude hissed.

"Look, I said sorry—," Maisy protested.

"Quiet!" he repeated. "Do you hear that?"

"I hear it," Zara said. "It's coming from the road."

Jude followed the sound, stepping out into the road and then to the other side. He rustled through the overgrown brush that lined what used to be the shoulder of the highway, and he emerged with a four-centimeter square box that was emitting a high-pitched beeping noise and a flashing red LED light.

"Is that a tracker?" Maisy asked.

"It sure is," Jude said with a smile. "Do you know what that means?"

"It means someone lost a tracker," Maisy said with her signature raised eyebrow.

"Yes, and you are that someone," Jude said.

"What?"

"See the little 'RK' etched on the bottom?"

"Yeah."

"Rod Kane. Dad was worried about you. He put more than protein bars in your pack. My guess is our bike thieves spotted it and tossed it away."

"What's the beeping noise?" Zara asked.

"It sets off an alarm when it is detached from its host and doesn't receive a remote shutdown signal within ten seconds," Jude explained. "Dad wanted a plan B. Now he knows where we are, and I expect we'll have a survey drone overhead in a couple of hours."

"Dad did that?" Maisy asked. "I'm kind of offended he spied on me, but I'm kind of relieved he did."

Jude's estimate was not far off. After about an hour and a half, a drone with a mounted camera descended gently into Jude's hands.

"Are you kids alright?" Rod's voice crackled from the camera.

"We're okay, but someone made off with our bikes while we waited out a storm. We're stranded," he explained.

"Do you want to come home?" he asked, knowing the answer.

"Not a chance. Callum needs us, and we're closer to Vancouver than home."

"I figured you'd say that. I've got an old colleague that I can call for a favor. He's got a small fleet of transport drones."

"Better make it a four-person transport, Dad. We picked up a new passenger from the Squamish River SAC," he said, turning the camera toward Zara.

"Zara Mailk," she said, waiving. "Nice to meet you."

"Nice to meet you," Rod said.

Jude turned the camera back towards him, and Rod spoke in a lower tone. "Be careful, Jude. My friend is pretty good at keeping out of sight and flying under the radar, literally in some cases, but it is still risky. The government has been known to just shoot . . . "

"I know, Dad," Jude interrupted, eyeing Maisy and Zara. "We'll be careful, and we'll try and find better transportation back home."

"Alright. Make sure there is enough of a clearing for the pick-up, and keep the tracker with you. "I'll shut it down but keep it handy just in case you need to manually activate it."

"Got it. Thanks, Dad."

"Thanks, Daddy!" Maisy echoed.

"Thanks!" Zara added as Jude lifted the drone and released it into the air. "I can't believe your dad has drones. I've never heard of a SAC having that kind of technology."

"He built several of them for checking on the crops remotely," Jude explained.

"And checking on his kids remotely," Zara smirked.

The transport drone was an older model, but it flew smoothly and felt solid. The four enclosed rotors continued to spin as it touched down on the outskirts of Vancouver and opened the door for its passengers to disembark.

"It wasn't easy to find a blind spot this close to a city," the remote pilot said through the speakers in the cockpit. It cost a lot of money. It cost your dad a lot of money," he said. "I wouldn't plan on a return the trip home the same way."

"Got it. Thank you, sir," Jude replied. The pilot never revealed his name, and neither did his dad. Anonymity is paramount when you fly illegally.

"Thanks for the walking stick, Jude," Zara said, hobbling out of the hatch and leaning on Jude's shoulder with her free hand. "It really helps."

"It's a little less conspicuous than a stretcher," he smiled, "even if it is still made from a tree branch."

"As long as you keep your weight off that ankle, I'm happy," Maisy interjected.

"Yes, doctor," Zara huffed.

They gathered their packs and surveyed the vacant lot as the drone ascended and disappeared into the faint glow of the city lights against the cloudy night sky. Gravel, broken concrete, and tufts of grass and weeds eventually gave way to a residential street, and beyond that, seemingly endless rows of dull, gray, angular structures. Some were independent, others seemed to be connected, and two blocks away, there looked to be a multi-level building made of several dozen interconnected components.

"Are those houses?" Zara asked.

"Cubes," Jude said. "Dad told me about them, but I didn't realize there were so many."

"Do you mean these are the 'family comfort units' we learned about in history class? They don't look anything like the pictures we saw. They are so small and dirty."

"Everything looks dirty to you," Jude joked, nudging Maisy's shoulder. "The government had to do something. That's part of what sparked the Transition. ADAMS figured if eighty percent of people are unemployed, you'd better find a place for them to live and feed them, or they could tear themselves and everyone else to pieces. That's hard to argue. Hungry, homeless people are very dangerous."

"Or you could go live in the mountains," Maisy said.

"That works if your leader is an engineering genius like Rod Kane," Zara quipped. "I'm not so sure it was the best idea for some of the other SACs."

"Dad said the Cubes weren't pretty, but they were functional. They made use of the massive plastic waste and recycled it into these 10 x 10 x 10-meter cubes with solar panels, plastic windows, and standard plumbing and wiring that could be easily connected to other Cubes or regular power and water sources. All of them are gray, and all are the same size; that's one way to avoid neighborhood jealousy," Jude explained.

Maisy looked at him with a questioning look.

"What? Dad and I have lots of time to talk out in the fields. You don't learn everything in school."

"What's the plan?" Maisy asked.

"Let's find a hotel. We're tired, our clothes are still damp, and I could just about eat my own arm," Jude said.

"Good idea. I could just about eat your arm, too," Maisy said, charging forward playfully.

Most Cubes emitted only dim light through thick curtains and hung blankets over windows, but the large building down the street seemed to have more life. Two of the bottom-level connected Cubes had open windows and bright light shining out onto the street, and in front was a neat but unassuming sign that read, "Surrey Comfort Unit Hotel."

Jude looked at the girls and said, "It sounds better than 'Stack of Cubes Hotel.'" They entered clumsily through the narrow doorway, knocking their packs against the door jambs and stumbling up to the front desk.

"You look like you need a room or two," the portly, balding middle-aged man said as he assessed the wrung-out trio.

"We've had a rough few days. A room would be great. Preferably with a bed and running water," Jude said.

"You're not too picky, are you?" he laughed. "Five hundred a night or twenty-five hundred for the week."

Jude looked at Maisy's tangled hair, Zara's wrapped ankle, and felt his stomach growling. "Let's do a week."

Jude paid the man and then received the door key code on his phone. "Is that it?" Jude asked.

"Yes, sir," the man said. "Room 316. There are ladders inside down the hall and an elevator with ramps outside. Just so you know . . . ." he began, but then looked at Maisy and Zara and stopped. "You look pretty tired. Why don't you get some rest and then come see me in the morning?"

Jude instantly had a hundred questions, but his own weight was dragging him to the floor. "Thank you."

As they entered room 316, the scene inspired different reactions.

"I need a bucket and a scrub brush. Are the linens even safe to lie on?" Maisy said.

"A bed. A dry, soft bed. I'm in heaven," sighed Zara.

"It's smaller than the cabin, but it's waterproof. That's all I need," Jude said.

Maisy helped Zara lie back and immediately began peeling off layers of damp clothing and then unwrapping her ankle for inspection. Jude set down the packs, unwrapped several of the remaining protein bars, and devoured them as he took off his clothes and laid them over any protruding surface to dry them out. He wrapped himself in a blanket, and without another word, he slinked down onto the floor near the window, wadded another blanket under his head, and fell asleep.

"I guess we don't have to worry about privacy," Maisy said with a chuckle as she lifted off Zara's t-shirt and hung it from a lamp fixture.

"I'm not worried," Zara said. "Your brother is a good man."

"He'll always be my dumb brother," Maisy chuckled, "but now I suppose I have to admit he is a pretty decent guy."

Zara hissed as Maisy gently moved and turned her ankle.

"How does it feel?"

"It still hurts, but it's getting better. I'd say about fifty percent. It's much better than yesterday," Zara said.

"The swelling is going down, too. That's good. I don't think you have any fractures."

"It must be all the goat's milk my parents made me drink. I've got strong bones."

"I've got tired bones. Want a protein bar before we go to sleep?" Maisy asked.

"Did Jude leave us any?"

"Two. He's logical even when he's starving," Maisy said.

In the morning, Jude made a point to pull on some dry clothes and have a conversation with the hotel manager before the girls woke up.

"Feeling better?" he asked as Jude descended the ladder and emerged from the narrow hallway.

"Night and day," Jude said.

"My name's Jay," the man said. "I take it you made the trip from a SAC, and this is your first time in the city."

"Is it that obvious?" Jude asked.

"It's my business. Most of my guests are folks who have given up on SAC life and have returned to the city. I've been busy, and I keep hearing the same thing: CAMO is encroaching on their farmland. Is that true for you, too?"

"No, at least not yet. Our SAC is doing well, mostly because my father is a great farmer, engineer, and planner. I've seen the encroachment, though, on other SACs. It's like CAMO is watching for crop failures, sweeps in under the guise of needing to make the land productive, and then the SAC gets squeezed. So much for protected status."

"I'm glad to hear someone is making it work out there. What brings you to Vancouver?" Jay asked.

"My brother. We had some kind of government observation drone flying over. He got the brilliant idea to shoot it down, and when he went after it, he disappeared. We didn't see who or what picked him up, but it had to be some kind of transport drone. We are pretty far out there."

"What government?" Jay asked.

"What do you mean?"

"The observation drone your brother saw— was it an RDF drone or a NADF drone?"

"I'm not sure," Jude said.

"The RDF is the Regional Defense Force, and if they picked him up, they'd have most likely brought him here to Vancouver. I spent a few years in the Cascadian RDF, and when we picked up people, we took them to Vancouver. If it was the NADF, the National Defense Force, then he might be anywhere from Seattle to Washington, D.C. As long as it wasn't COATS, you can probably track him down."

"COATS?" Jude asked.

"Critical Operations and Advanced Tactical Services," Jay rattled off. I guess they are what used to be 'Special Forces' before the Transition. These guys get involved in pretty sensitive, high-level operations, so I highly doubt they'd fly all the way out to a SAC to pick up a single bad-tempered citizen."

"Thanks, Jay. That helps. Now, where can I get some food in this town?" Jude asked.

"There's a market down the street. I'd go today if you can. Tomorrow is UBI payday for this district, and the stores will be swamped."

"Universal Basic Income. Another way to try and keep out-of-work people from killing each other," Jude said, shaking his head. "I'm starting to see why my dad was so motivated to establish our SAC."

"One more thing, Jude," Jay said. "I know you don't get a UBI, and you spent a chunk of money here. If you need some more cash, you can always power the discs."

"What does that mean? Is that like gambling?" Jude asked.

"No. The power utility has set up facilities in several different neighborhoods where people can go and pedal stationary bicycles that turn electromagnetic discs and create electricity. It's not much, but when you have hundreds of thousands of people with nothing better to do, all that extra voltage adds up. They don't pay a lot, but they also don't ask a lot of questions. They do a quick security scan, but they don't ask for your passport ID."

"Good to know. Thanks, Jay."

Rod made sure everyone had a passport implanted after they were born. Jude never understood why, especially when they were so far north and nestled among some of the most rugged mountains in the world. Why would they ever need a passport ID out there? Now they were in the city, and his dad's foresight was saving them again. If they were going to get into any building, take any transport, or ask for any information, the first thing they would need to do is pass under a scanner. They would have to be careful with Zara.

"So, what have you been up to?" Maisy asked when Jude returned to the room.

"I've been figuring out where to find things, like food, money, and our brother."

"Any luck?" Maisy asked as she propped open the window.

"Yes. Jay was very helpful. Apparently, Squamish River isn't the only SAC getting squeezed by CAMO, and the floods of refugees are his main customers. He is used to giving guests pointers for surviving the city."

"What about your brother?" Zara asked, standing up on her good foot and buttoning her shirt.

"He said if he was picked up by the Cascadian RDF, he'd be here in Vancouver. If it was the NADF, he could be anywhere. We can start here. If he's not in Vancouver, we might be able to find out who took him and where to go from here," Jude explained.

"What's first on the agenda?" Maisy asked.

"Shopping. The market is down the street, and according to Jay, tomorrow is not the day to go. After that, we can plan our trip downtown."

"I can make a list," Zara offered. "I've read about how people can just find whatever food they want at the market. I've wanted to do this my whole life!"

"Do you hear that?" Jude asked, leaning his head out the window.

"What?" Maisy asked.

"Exactly. Nothing. It's too quiet."

"I hear transports and voices. What else would you expect?"

"I'm used to the chickens, the cows, the pigs, the horses, and all the other racket I never thought much about, at least until now."

"In case you haven't noticed, we're not on the farm," Maisy said.

"It's the birds," he said pensively. "I don't hear the birds. Where are all the sparrows?"

"I don't know," she said, stepping over and leaning against the window. There aren't any trees very close that I can see. Maybe that's why."

"I think you're right. The Cubes don't have window ledges. Where would they perch? I never considered that. I've never thought I'd miss the sound of birds in the morning."

Chapter 6: **City Life**

"How do they get all this food in one place?" marveled Zara.

The aisles of the market seemed as if they were overflowing with a thousand different foods they had never heard of and a few they recognized, especially in the meat and produce section.

"CAMO is busy," Jude remarked.

"I'm not eating anything out of a box," Maisy protested. "There's no way that can be good for you. It's probably not even food."

"There are a lot of things I can cook in the hotel, but we could also use a lot of this packaged food for our return trip," Zara said.

"Let's wait until we're heading home and we know how we're going to get there first, and then we can see how to poison ourselves," Maisy said.

Zara rolled her eyes. "I'm making a list in my head now. How much money do you have?"

"How much can we carry is a better question," Jude said, inspecting a box of breakfast cereal.

"There is so much food . . . " Zara uttered again.

"There are so many people," Jude said. "Our hotel has more guests than our entire SAC."

"What's for dinner, Zara?" Maisy asked as they approached the scanner to leave.

"Chicken tenderloins, rice pilaf, and peas, if I can ever thaw them out. I also want to try this dessert called 'cheesecake.' It sounds gross, but I tried a sample, and it is delicious! I don't have to mix anything to make it. Apparently, I just let it thaw."

"Cheese, cake, and thaw are three words that should not be in the same sentence," Maisy complained.

"Maybe I should stay back today," Zara said after they trudged back up to their motel room with the groceries. "I don't want to slow you guys down."

"I want you to come with us, but you do need to stay off that ankle," Maisy reminded her patient.

"I'm more concerned that someone might ask for a passport. We're heading into the city and inside government buildings. There's a pretty good chance someone will want to put you under a scanner," Jude said.

"What happens if they do?" Zara asked. This was the first time she even considered the consequences of living on a SAC, and now suddenly she felt more like an outsider than ever.

"I'm not sure. I've never been scanned," Jude said. "They could assume it's not working and tell you to go to a doctor to get it fixed, but they could also arrest you and send you to jail. I really don't know."

"So much for reporting from the big city," Zara complained. "Some journalist I'm making."

"We'll give you a full report," Maisy said, putting her hand on her shoulder and then gently taking her ankle and lifting it onto the bed.

"You've got a lot to write about here," Jude said. "This is a real city neighborhood. Imagine folks back in the SACs trying to get their minds around the Cubes. It might help them appreciate what they have."

"You're right," Zara said, smiling. "*Life in the Cubes*. It's pretty catchy for my first article, don't you think?"

"Perfect," Jude said. "We'll be back in a few hours. Wish us luck. If you need anything, just call."

"With what?" she asked.

"My phone," Maisy volunteered.

"You both grew up on a SAC. How do you have phones?" Zara asked.

"The same reason we have everything— our dad," she said.

"He made these just for us," Jude explained. "Of course, we're not near any kind of service, but he modified our phones to connect directly to each other, like the old radios in the twentieth century. They also still connect to networks and use the old internet protocols. I wasn't sure they still worked, but I was able to pay Jay and accept our room key."

"That's amazing," Zara said. "You're going to have to show me how to use it."

"Jay said the light rail stop for Surrey is only four blocks this way," Jude said, pointing down the street. "He said it can get us into downtown Vancouver in a few minutes, and the second stop after the tunnel is the closest to RDF headquarters. I figured we'd start there."

"Let's hope our passports still work, we find someone who can give us some answers, and we don't get mugged along the way," Maisy said, shaking her head.

Jude sighed and shook his head. "Can you at least break your negativity into smaller chunks, please? One obstacle at a time."

"Sorry."

At the light rail stop, people shuffled in lines between two posts about six feet tall that Jude assumed were scanners. Jude stepped through first, holding his breath. There was nothing. He looked around, and there were no officials anywhere. Maisy followed with the same result. It was then that he realized the scanners made no noise. It simply registered your signal as you passed through.

"What's the point of the scanners if there aren't any cops around to grab you?" Maisy wondered out loud.

"There," Jude pointed. "That's the cops."

At ten-meter intervals along the platform stood three android units. Roughly human in form, they stood two meters tall with black arms and legs, a black "head," and a white torso with the letters "POLICE" printed boldly across the chest. On each shoulder was a red and blue light, and on the helmet, back, and waist were larger lights that would flash in an emergency.

"What are all those bubble-looking things on the robots?" Maisy whispered.

"Probably cameras," Jude said.

"Why so many?"

"They want good footage from every angle, I suppose."

"How many angles do they need?"

Jude thought for a minute, examining the android closest to them.

"Every angle," he said, lowering his voice. "These are LEAD units: Law Enforcement Autonomous Droids. They don't have lethal weapons, but they record everything."

"You mean cops can literally let robots do their jobs?" Maisy asked.

"From what I read, they are used mainly for patrol. Detectives are still human, but they rely a lot on the recordings of the LEAD units and dedicated crime analysis computers. By the time they arrest most people, the artificial intelligence and video have already made the case for the prosecution."

The train's approach was so fast and quiet that when it arrived, both Jude and Maisy had to stifle a yelp. It stopped, perfectly aligning with the handrails, and then opened its doors. Jude and Maisy stepped in and took a seat.

"Where is everybody?" Jude whispered. "There weren't many people on the platform, but I thought there would be a lot more people than this on the train."

"How many people have jobs?" Maisy asked.

"Only about twenty percent."

"So, if you have a job, you're very fortunate and relatively wealthy compared to everyone else. Maybe they can work from home, or they can afford private transport. I bet not too many of them want to rub elbows with the lowly people from the Cubes."

"Good analysis! I bet you're right. I must be rubbing off on you," Jude said, nudging Maisy.

"The robot cops didn't come after us, so I presume our passports are still working?" Maisy asked.

"It looks that way."

"Then we shouldn't have any problem getting into government buildings. Obstacle number one down."

"Two more to go: finding someone who knows something and getting them to tell us something."

"I thought you said to break it up in chunks. One thing at a time," she teased, giving him a return nudge.

Jude smiled. His baby sister had grown up more than he had realized while he was busy with his dad. She wasn't as technical as he and Dad were, but she was smart, tenacious, and observant. She had Mom's mind for finding the human impact in a situation and Dad's heart for helping. It was a great combination.

"This is our stop," he said. "Let's go find our brother."

They climbed the stairs, passed through another set of scanners, and emerged onto the street. There was no hiding the fact that they were from out of town. Immediately, they both froze and craned their necks to stare in disbelief at the unimaginable height and size of the gleaming glass and steel buildings.

"Jay told me the RDF headquarters were near this stop, but . . . " Jude mumbled.

"Let's ask that guy," Maisy said, pointing to a food cart vendor.

"Good idea."

"Excuse me, but can you tell me which building the Regional Defense Forces headquarters is in?" Jude asked.

"Sure thing. What'll ya have?" the vendor asked.

"Um, I just need to know which building I'm looking for," Jude replied.

"And I just need to make a living, pal. Nothin' is free."

Maisy sensed Jude's blood pressure rising, so she stepped in.

"I'll take one of those sausage-looking things," she said.

"You mean a hot dog?"

"Yeah. A hot dog. and I'll take one of those pieces of bread that look like it's tied in a knot."

"You mean a pretzel?"

"Yeah, a pretzel."

"Coming right up."

"I thought you hated processed food?" Jude whispered to her.

"They're not in a box. I'm trying to help us out. Shut up."

"Here you go: one jumbo hot dog and one pretzel. Condiments are right here," he said, pointing to the neatly arranged containers of spicy mustard, regular mustard, relish, onions, and pickles.

"Yum, thanks," Maisy said, dressing up her hot dog while Jude paid.

"The Cascadian government offices are on Wendover Street, the next block over. The RDF is in there somewhere, but it's just admin people and maybe recruiting. There aren't a lot of uniforms there. The RDF base is over in Victoria."

"Thanks," Jude said.

"Thank you!" Maisy murmured with a mouthful of hot dog. "This is so good! You have to try it."

"Do you know what hot dogs are made of? Talk about processed foods!" Jude laughed.

"I don't want to know. It's good."

"I'll take a bite of that pretzel thing," Jude said, tearing off a piece. "Thick bread with rock salt on top. It should be disgusting, but it's not too bad."

They ate, gawked at the buildings, and made their way to the next block over. Callum weighed on their minds, but they couldn't escape the exhilaration of being away from home and on their first adventure outside of Slate Creek. If the Cubes offered them a vision of hopelessness, the city gave them a look at what could be. Unfortunately, they were reminded of how exclusive the city and any employment were with every person that passed them in new clothes or drove by in a sleek personal transport vehicle.

Wendover Street was the center of regional government activity, with a row of medium and taller buildings, all labeled with their respective departments. Jude searched for the RDF offices.

"Cascadia Department of Health and Medical Services."

"Cascadia Department of Human Services (UBI and Family Comfort Unit Administration)"

"Cascadia Department of Justice."

"Cascadia Court Complex."

"Cascadia Regional Defense Forces Administration."

"There we go, Maisy. Are you ready?" he announced.

"Just a second," she mumbled as she stuffed the last of the hot dog in, closed her lips, and wiped a spot of mustard from the corner of her mouth.

"You look like a chipmunk," Jude said.

Maisy wanted to give him a comeback, but there was no talking with that much food rolling around in her mouth. She finally finished chewing and said, "Okay, let's go."

They entered the turnstile bullet-proof door and approached a wide, semi-circle reception desk that had three kiosks for getting information. They were labeled "Recruiting," "Operations and Administration," and "Communication and Archives."

"I don't think they were recruiting Callum," Maisy said, "and I doubt he's featured in a press release."

"Operations and Admin it is," Jude said, stepping up to the screen.

He pushed the button for English and then waited.

"How can I help you?" a smooth female voice said.

"I'm trying to locate a relative, my brother, who I believe is in RDF custody. His name is Callum Kane."

"I have located a record for Callum Kane. He is no longer in RDF custody."

"Can you tell me when and where he was released?"

"Callum Kane was released to the Department of Compulsory Monitored Education in September last year."

"I know about going to CME. He was taken recently, about two weeks ago."

"Callum Kane is no longer in RDF custody."

"Was he not detained two weeks ago?"

"Callum Kane is no longer in RDF custody."

"Well, then where the hell is he?!" shouted Jude, slamming his hand on the counter.

"Callum Kane is no longer in RDF custody."

"Take it easy, Jude," Maisy reminded him, putting her hand on his shoulder. "Maybe we can find a person to help us out."

"It doesn't look like there are many people around," he huffed.

Maisy stepped up to the screen.

"Is there anyone here who can help us locate our brother? If he is not in RDF custody, where would he be?"

"Please wait . . . " the voice said. There was a short beep, and then another distinctly human voice came through the kiosk.

"Hello, this is Kyra. It looks like the system can't find any recent records of your brother."

"Yes, it was clear about that," Jude said flatly. "He was picked about a couple of weeks ago. If the RDF doesn't have him, who does? How can I find out?"

"Was he picked up in Vancouver?"

"No. He was picked up outside of Slate Creek, a SAC several hundred kilometers north of Vancouver in the Canadian Rockies. He thought it would be a good idea to shoot down a drone. I don't know what kind of drone it was because I wasn't there when it happened, but I do believe it was an observation or survey drone. I also know that CAMO has been surveying and even growing crops on lands outside of SACs in the north recently. Would they have taken him?"

"CAMO is a public corporation and does not have the power to detain people. They refer all law enforcement problems and investigations to us. If he shot down an observation drone, then he would have been picked up by a larger transport drone, especially that far out. Did you see that drone?"

"No, I didn't. By the time I reached the scene, all remnants of the survey drone were cleaned up, and my brother was gone. The drone must have been a big one because the grass and plants in the area were flattened and burned pretty good."

"Did you say burned?"

"Yes. The whole area was blackened."

"CAMO uses primarily survey drones, and the RDF transport drones are all standard four-way turbo propeller types. The only drones that have the kind of boosters that can blacken the ground are NADF drones."

"New America Defense Force drones? You mean he was picked up by the Feds?"

"Draw your own conclusions, Mr. Kane. I've told you what I know."

"Yes, thank you, Kyra. You've been very helpful," he said, still processing the information.

"You're welcome," she said, followed by a beep.

"Is there anything else I can do for you?" the kiosk followed in its silky voice.

"No. You're no help at all," Jude said.

"Wait," Maisy said. "Can you tell us where the nearest New America Defense Force administration office is?"

"The nearest New America Defense Force facility is located in Seattle, Cascadia."

"Thank you," Maisy said.

"I guess I have to take that back," Jude said.

They left through the turnstile and wandered onto the sidewalk.

"I wasn't dumb enough to think we'd be bringing Callum home, but I hoped we would at least find him," Maisy said with a sigh.

"We didn't find him, but we found where he *isn't*," Jude said.

"I can't stand the thought of heading back to Slate Creek and not being able to tell Mom and Dad anything except that Callum is *not* in Vancouver."

Jude smiled. "Who said anything about going back home?"

Chapter 7: **Seattle**

ZARA WAS WAITING WITH dinner ready in their motel Cube.

"How did it go?" she asked tentatively when Jude and Maisy walked in.

"The good news is Callum is not in RDF custody. The bad news is he is not in RDF custody," Maisy said with a sigh.

"But, we were able to find out that he was probably picked up by an NADF drone," Jude said.

"The feds have him?" Zara asked. "What are you going to do now?"

"How do you feel about extending your time in the field as a journalist?" Jude asked.

"I'm game," she said confidently. "What do I have to go back to?"

"Jude has it in his head we are going to Seattle," Maisy said, taking off her jacket and sitting Zara down to examine her ankle. "Have you been staying off it?"

"Mostly," Zara said. "It's starting to feel a lot better."

"I haven't got everything worked out, but we know the nearest NADF base is in Seattle. If we can get there and get onto the base, we should be able to find something out," Jude said.

"How do we get to Seattle?" Zara asked as Maisy re-wrapped her ankle.

"After we eat, I'm going to talk to Jay. I noticed he had a fondness for whiskey. After a few drinks, he'll be happy to give me advice," Jude said with a devious smile.

"None for you, though," Maisy warned. "It won't do us any good if you can't remember what he tells you."

"Don't worry," Jude said, laughing. "Remember when Dad made that still a few years ago? No thanks. I can't stand the stuff."

After dinner, Jude made a trip to the store, which had a bigger section of alcohol than bread, dairy, and meat combined. Alcohol and boredom tend to find each other. He returned with a brand of scotch he noticed Jay had behind the counter, and acted as if he was heading to his room for the night.

"Are you calling it a day?" Jay asked, noticing the small cloth bag.

"Yeah. I figured I'd have a glass or two to help me relax and then hit the bed," Jude said, pulling out the scotch conspicuously.

"Ooh, that's a good brand. I drink that all the time," Jay said, his large eyes betraying his fondness for it.

"Want a glass?" Jude asked. "The girls don't like it, and I'm sure not going to drink the whole thing myself."

"Well, I really shouldn't . . . " he stammered.

"Why not?" Jude said, setting the bottle on the desk behind the reception counter. "You've helped us out since we crawled out of the woods. It's just a little thank you."

"Sure, why not?" Jay conceded. He pulled out two glasses from a drawer and wiped them out. Jude filled both glasses about halfway. They made a quick toast, and Jay took a swig. Jude pretended to take a small sip, but never let the liquid past his lips.

"When you were in the Cascadia RDF, did you have interaction with the New America Defense Forces?" Jude casually asked.

"A little," Jay said. "I was regular United States Army before the Transition, so the RDF loaned me to the NADF to help out with training new recruits. I wasn't planning to retire to British Columbia, but by the time I got out, it wasn't over the border anymore. Everything from Oregon to the Yukon was now Cascadia."

"It must have been strange going from living in the United States to living in New America, especially after spending half your career in the U.S. Army."

"I grew up near the border in Washington State, so Canada never felt like a foreign country to me. Of course, it was strange, but it's not like we were defeated and taken over or anything. The Transition was rough for a lot of people, but it would have been worse if we hadn't done something. There were environmental disasters, AI processes were replacing most people's jobs, and of course, Congress was so gridlocked they couldn't do anything before the damn country went up in flames. You add Canada's fiscal crisis and Mexico's collapse, and we were staring at the edge of a real apocalypse. People moaned about computers taking over our lives when ADAMS went online, but that thing really saved us, if you ask me. Passing a law requiring politicians to get an analysis from ADAMS before making any policy put the knife in a lot of biased political BS and finally allowed us to start solving problems. That was the key move right there."

Jude poured Jay another glass, feigning that he was also adding more to his.

"Do you ever miss the good 'ol US of A?" Jude asked.

"Sometimes, but I try to remember the big picture. Besides, it made it easy for me to settle down in Vancouver, and the fishing is way better up here."

They laughed, and Jay polished off glass number two.

"One more?" Jude offered.

"I don't want to wipe out your new bottle," Jay weakly protested.

"One more won't hurt anything," Jude said, refilling the glass. "So, did you ever do any training at the NADF base in Seattle?"

"I did all of my training at the Seattle base. Those kids were pretty tech-savvy, but they needed a little old-fashioned discipline. They were always a little cocky until we got out in the field, and I started firing live rounds over their heads. They straightened up after that."

"It looks like the girls and I are headed down to Seattle. Got any advice on the best transport options?" Jude asked.

"Take a ferry," Jay said, starting to slur his speech. "It's faster and cheaper than land transport, and it's a beautiful ride."

"Is there any such thing as a cheap ferry?" Jude sighed.

"How adventurous are you?" Jay said with a devious smile.

"I'm up for a challenge."

"Take a cargo ship. There are dozens of containers going down to Seattle every day, and it's only a few hours. Sneak your way onto one of them."

"How do I do that? There must be hundreds of security cameras and guard droids."

"Not inside the containers."

Zara was as productive off her feet as she was when she was mobile. She used the motel screen terminal to set up a news site, and then called on all her contacts in the SACs to check in for news and update them on their adventure. The fresh stories, pictures, and colorful writing reeled in her audience, especially the younger ones who had never known life outside of a SAC. SACs were made up of people who fled into the wilderness to preserve their humanity, but isolation can be just as cruel as servitude to an AI-dominated society. People craved connection, and Zara hit that need square on with reporting from the perspective of someone who grew up on the land.

After a couple of days, Zara was back on her feet. With the packs refilled and evenly distributed, the trio was ready to move.

"So exactly how are we going to get to Seattle?" Maisy asked as she laced up her boots.

"Next-day shipping," Jude quipped.

The train zipped under the bay and stopped right at the shipyard, but Zara didn't have a passport, and Jude didn't want to find out what would happen when she passed the scanners. They hailed a cab, and like all personal transport vehicles, it was driverless. After a short trip over the bridge and down to the docks, they got out and walked to a small waterfront park that sat adjacent to the shipping yard. Jude wanted more time to study the layout, watch the loading and unloading, and mark all the security droids and cameras, but they were already there and didn't have unlimited supplies or time.

Jude was able to discern which ships were coming and which were leaving, how the containers were moved and loaded, and a good route to get to them without being detected. What was trickier was determining their destination. Sneaking into a container would be dangerous, and they could only survive about two days. If they ended up in a container that was headed to Singapore, they would arrive in a big steel coffin. They needed to get into a container going to Seattle, and they needed to get in just before it was loaded.

They snaked around the stacks of containers, camouflaging themselves from the security cameras by sticking close to dark-colored containers that most closely matched their clothes. Finding a row that was lined up and beginning to be hoisted onto the cargo ship by the enormous robotic cranes, Jude waited until a security droid passed and then whipped around to the doors. He retrieved his small, hand-held disc cutter and went to work on the lock. It took three tries, but the tool did its job, and the lock finally popped off with a snap and a clink on the pavement.

He checked his flank again and then twisted the handle, pulled open the door, and slipped in. He clicked on his flashlight and scanned the interior, looking for labels, bar codes, or anything that would confirm the destination of the cargo.

"What's in there?" Zara whispered, peering in the door.

"Pet food," Jude whispered.

"Can you tell where it's going?"

Jude scanned the stacks of products and finally found a label with a clue.

"It's going to a distribution center in Tacoma. I think we're in business."

Zara motioned to Maisy, and they slipped into the container.

"Jude?" Maisy said in the darkness.

"Yes?"

"How are we going to close the door?"

"Like this."

He pulled two large magnets out of his pack, stuck them to the door, and pulled it closed. Once closed, he moved the magnets until they were covering both doors, top and bottom, holding the unlatched door in place. "Now let's hope that crane keeps us nice and level, or we're going to go swimming."

It soon became apparent that it was not going to be their primary problem. Sitting in relative silence and waiting for the sound of the crane, they heard the zip and whir of the guard droid rolling back past their container. It stopped outside the doors, and they held their breath. They heard a rattling outside, and then a solid thunk and echo inside as the droid latched the handle from the outside. They were firmly trapped inside.

"Well, we don't have to worry about sliding out of the box with a few tons of pet food now," Maisy said, folding her arms.

"How long do you think it will be?" Zara said nervously, folding her arms and gauging their tight space between the pallets of dog food and the door.

"It only takes a few hours to get to Seattle," Jude said. "With loading and unloading, it will be about a day or a day and a half."

"Okay," she said, starting to shiver.

Through the darkness, Jude could tell she was fighting a case of claustrophobia.

"Let's get on top of the dog food, in case it slides when they lift the container," he said, taking her hand and helping her on top of the stack. He turned to help Maisy, but she had already pulled herself up. He climbed up on the stack and sat next to Zara, intentionally moving in close enough so that they were touching. He took out his cutting tool and shone the flashlight on it.

"See this?" he asked.

"Where did you get that?" she asked.

"When we were out working in the fields on tractors, solar panels, or wind turbines, my dad always taught me to never forget my tools. These containers are thick in the frame and walls to support the weight of being stacked, but the roof is fairly thin. As soon as we are settled on the ship, I will cut a nice hole in the roof, so as soon as we are set down in Seattle, we can slip out. Don't worry. There's always a solution."

Zara stopped shaking and leaned into Jude. "With you there is." Maisy rolled her eyes, but in the dark, no one could see. It was probably a good thing. Zara needed the reassurance.

Suddenly, there was a loud clang outside, and the container rattled. "Hold on, here we go!" Jude said with a hint of childish joy in his voice. It was as if he was enjoying the ride. Of course, this was the closest thing any of them had ever been to an amusement park. The container was lifted into the air, rocking and swinging as the crane hoisted it, swung it around, and then lowered it onto the deck of the ship. It set the container down with robotic precision and then released the clasps and moved on to the next container.

"See? We're all set for the ride," Jude said. Zara wrapped her arms around Jude's arm and leaned her head on his shoulder.

"I've got another great story to write."

Even with a completely automated process, the loading still took a few hours. When the rocking sway gave way to a bobbing and gentle thrust, they knew they were en route. A bulky cargo ship couldn't make the time the ferries did, but it was still only a six-hour trip. Unloading was much faster since the bulk of the freight was heading on to China, and they were more than happy to be one of the first containers to make it back to dry land.

Just as Jude was putting to bed his regrets about their choice of transportation, a loud clang shook the container.

"What was that?" Zara asked frantically.

"I think they stacked another container on top of us," Jude said.

"H-how are we going to get out?" Zara stammered.

"I'm not . . . I'll figure out a way," Jude said, putting a hand on her shoulder. "There is always a solution."

Jude took his cutter out of his pack and scanned the inside of the container with his flashlight. Starting with the sidewall, then the door, and then the hinges, he tested his cutter against the steel and quickly realized what he feared: it was far too thick, and the cutter was losing battery strength. As he put the cutters back and searched his pack for another tool that might help, he heard the whirr of a guard droid passing by. He stopped rustling through his pack and listened again. Clang. Another container was set on the dock. Whir. Another pass by the guard droid. Clang. Whir.

"Why didn't I figure this out before!" he said, smacking the side of his head. "They're not just security droids. They're handlers! They watch all container lifts, mark their placement, and track the rows and stacks for inventory and quick retrieval. They watch for theft, but they also watch for damage. That's why that one closed the door on us."

"Good to know. How does that help us?" Maisy asked. "We don't have a lot of water with us, and I wouldn't mind a real meal sometime in the next few days."

"Water. That's it!" Jude said. "We need to attract some attention. We want a droid to think there is something wrong in here. Let's pour out our water at the bottom of the door and make it look like there is a leak."

"Have you lost your mind?" Maisy said. "We will not survive more than a few days if we don't have water. We need that water."

"You're right," Jude conceded, "and dog food won't exactly leak through the doors. If only we had some liquid . . . "

"We do," Zara said, jumping down from the stack. "All three of us do, and right now we all would be happy to let some go."

"That is disgusting, but it might just work. Here," Maisy said, handing Zara a jug, "you and I can use this. Jude, you can aim. Make sure it runs out of here and not all over our feet."

"Hang on," he said, pulling out a file. "Let me widen the gap here at the bottom of the door."

"Okay, but hurry up! All this talk has me needing to go *bad*."

After working the file and widening the hole while the girls filled their containers, Jude took his turn.

"Turn around," he said.

"Our eyes are closed," Maisy said.

"I'd feel better if you were turned around. I don't need the extra pressure," he said.

"Fine. If it helps your stage fright, we'll turn around," Maisy said sarcastically. They held their tongues for a few seconds and then burst out laughing. Despite the distraction, Jude made sure there was enough "leaking" of their container to garner the attention of a guard droid.

"Shhh!" he said. "I hear one coming."

There was the whir of the wheels, which stopped right at the door, the zip sound of moving arms, followed by the clanking of the handles being turned. Jude burst out of the doors, knocking the droid back, followed on his heels by the girls.

"Oh, thank God," he said dramatically, addressing the droid. "We were chasing our dog at the park. He smelled the dog food, ran in there, and then we got locked in! If it wasn't for you, we might have died in there! Thank you so much. We need to go find our dog."

"Stop!" it ordered. They waited, and Jude tried to speak in a way and language the droid would understand. He knew it would run their story through a series of security algorithms to determine risk, and the more victimized they seemed, the less likely they were a threat. How could three people who just peed all over the place inside a locked container be trying to steal 18,000 kilos of dog food with backpacks? "We're sorry about the mess. It's so embarrassing, but we were stuck for several hours, and we had strong biological urges."

The droid scanned them, the container, and the area. It summoned a clean-up crew and then made its calculated decision.

"No product damage. No apparent theft. Unusual circumstances. No threat detected. I will escort you off of port premises."

As they made their way through the main gate, they peered down at the shore of the Puget Sound, and all three of them stopped and gaped. The towering, gleaming, sleek buildings downtown dwarfed Vancouver and their imaginations.

"Get some pictures, Z. This article will need them," Jude said, scanning the skyline.

"Yeah," she said absent-mindedly, taking Maisy's phone and snapping photos.

A jogger came towards them, and Zara quickly shoved the phone into her pocket. There's nothing worse than being an obvious tourist, especially if you don't have a passport.

The jogger noticed their dated, worn clothes and tired expressions, and probably figured them for SAC immigrants, but he didn't mention it.

"Good morning!" he greeted them, stopping for a sip of water and to whet his curiosity.

"Good morning!" Jude responded.

"You look a little lost," he said. "Can I point you in a specific direction?"

"As a matter of fact, yes. We're trying to surprise our brother who is at the NADF base, but we have no idea where it is," Jude said. "Vancouver is not as busy as Seattle."

"Vancouver, huh? It's beautiful up there. I think of Vancouver like a big SAC," he laughed.

"Ha! I agree. Sometimes I feel like we were raised in a SAC," Jude said.

"The base is actually in Bremerton, not Seattle, but it's not far. Just head down the waterfront to the ferry terminals and jump on the next boat to Bremerton."

"Thanks!" Jude said. "By the way, do you know how much it costs?"

"It's complementary, courtesy of the City of Seattle. They just scan your passport."

"Great! My sister and I will have no problems, but our, uh, other sister sometimes has trouble with scanners not picking up the signal. Is that a big problem?"

"Nah," he said, taking another sip of water. "It happens all the time. If she's with you, they'll just chalk it up to a bad signal and probably give her an order to take to the doctor for a replacement."

"Thanks!" Jude said, echoed by the girls.

"No problem," he said, resuming his jog. "Tell your brother thank you for his service!" he shouted from down the street.

They all waved, and Maisy looked at Jude and started laughing.

"Don't forget, Jude. Thank Callum for his service."

They picked up their packs and headed north along the waterfront.

"What do you think, Zara? Do you want to take the ferry with us and see what happens? I'll completely understand if—

"I'm coming. I doubt I'll hang for a 'faulty transmitter.' A journalist has to take risks to get the story, right? The SACs are going to want to know what happens with Callum."

"Alright, but let's stick with the 'you're my sister' story. You can be the middle child that never gets noticed," Jude said, smiling.

They made it to the terminal, walked through the scanners, and held their breath. As Zara passed the yellow poles, a small red light appeared on a barely noticeable sign just past the gate. Next to the light, it read, "No signal detected. Seek medical advice for repair or replacement."

"That wasn't so bad. I guess I need to talk to a doctor," she said, looking at Maisy.

"Make an appointment."

They proceeded to the front of the boat with a noticeably larger crowd than they saw anywhere in Vancouver. The higher concentration of tech jobs and New America administrative offices gave Seattle a much higher proportion of employed people than most other cities. The effects of controlling a larger chunk of the economy were everywhere: architecture, personal transports, personal watercraft, larger, more advanced hospitals, and actual schools. As impressive as the city was, reality was still lurking on the outside.

As they approached the dock in Bremerton, the compacted neighborhoods of old 20th and 21st-century houses with thousands of Cubes jammed into every available space came into clear view. Near the shoreline were older, larger houses, and the further away from the shoreline, the smaller the houses became. Individual Cubes, houses attached to Cubes, and multi-cube homes stretched out for miles; the money didn't flow far from the city.

Beyond the Cubes, as they discovered in a dedicated NADF transport, the military base was carved out with expanses of land surrounded by razor-wire fence and filled with solid, angular, utilitarian buildings and hangars. The sprawling base was a hive of movement and mechanical organization with small, four-person transport carts that zipped visitors and personnel directly to their destinations.

Security was more thorough at the front gate, but after a clean body scan, the tired soldier waved Zara through with her "siblings." They made their way to the administration center and once again found a large reception area manned by kiosks. Jude and Maisy each took one and frantically began typing in requests for information on Callum. After almost a thousand kilometers, being frozen, soaked, stranded, injured, exhausted, trapped, and disappointed, they needed some news.

By the sighs and whispered cursing, Zara could tell they were hitting a brick wall. Casually, she stepped up to a third kiosk and began typing. After an angry burst from Jude and a few choice words from Maisy, Zara calmly said, "I found him."

"What?" the Kane siblings said in unison as they ran over to Zara.

"I figured the name search wasn't leading anywhere, so I tried another angle. I 'reported' a drone shot down. The system matched the date and description, and I just followed the link. Look, the 'suspect' was here a week ago, but he's been taken to a detention center to await his trial. According to this link . . . " she said as she scrolled down the screen, "all trials for offenses involving actions against NADF troops or equipment are considered Domestic Terrorism and are investigated by the NADF and the State Department. Domestic Terror tribunals are held in Washington, D.C."

Chapter 8: **Borders**

THE WAVES GENTLY LAPPED the rocky beach as the salty breeze came in lulls and gusts. Jude ran his finger over the silky-smooth, weather-worn surface of the beach wood log they shared, following the indents and crevices with the tip of his finger. Nothing was this smooth in the mountains unless you sanded it that way, but here the saltwater had softly worn the tired, dead tree into a sculpture of serenity.

The weight of the moment hung in the air, but no one said anything. The peace of the afternoon sunset on the beach was a respite they all needed and one they wanted to savor. Finally, Maisy broke the silence.

"I don't want to go back home without Callum. I know that wasn't the plan, but . . . "

"Me neither," Jude interrupted.

Maisy smiled as she took a stick and began drawing in the rocky sand. She turned and looked at Zara.

"Maybe I should go back."

"Are you crazy?" Maisy snapped. "You're not going anywhere without us."

"But I don't have a passport. It's not like I can just go get one. I was never registered. All of my education was done anonymously because my dad didn't want the government to even know I was alive. My mom planned my classes and used proxy servers to teach me. I even read old twentieth-century paper textbooks. If I get caught, I will get transported to a CME School before you could say, 'Oh look, there's a transport drone.' I could be there for years."

"You should be aged out of high school curriculum requirements by now," Jude said.

"Mom looked into it when Callum went away," Maisy said. "They don't have age limits. You have to get a high school equivalency with a technical endorsement or stay in CME until you do."

Jude smiled mischievously and shook his head.

"What's so funny?" Zara asked.

"Paper textbooks? Is that why you carry a pen and paper?"

"They never run out of battery."

"I think Maisy has the final word on this one. I wouldn't want to cross her. If she says you're stuck with us, then you're stuck with us."

"You realize we will have to cross borders to get to Washington, D.C., right? They won't just waive me through. We have to get through at least three regions, maybe four," Zara said.

"Dakota, Texico, Lakeland, and Appalachia," Jude said. "The thing about regional borders is that they are pretty open. We don't have to walk through a scanner. We just have to take the scenic route."

"And how will we do that?" Zara asked. "It's a long walk to the East Coast."

"I didn't say I had it all figured out. I just said we don't have to cross the border where they are checking passports. There is always a solution."

"Somehow that seems to be true, at least around you." She looked into his hazel eyes and smiled. "I'm in, but no more sneaking into shipping containers. Let's go get your brother," Zara said, slapping Jude on the knee.

"I'm with Zara; no shipping containers," Maisy said. "Speaking of shipping, how exactly are we going to travel across the continent with no money and no transport?"

"We've got legs, and that's a start," Jude said.

"What about money, food, and other provisions? What about finding shelter? And realistically, how are we going to cover 4000 kilometers if we don't get some kind of a ride?" Maisy was as good at recognizing problems as Jude was at solving them, but sometimes she could identify them much faster.

"SACs," Zara said. "I've got contacts in every SAC in Cascadia, and a few in other regions. I've gotten more since we left Squamish. Apparently, the SACs like my stories, and they've been sharing them."

Jude and Maisy looked at each other and smiled.

"I knew I did the right thing by not kicking your butt on that highway back in Squamish River," Maisy said.

"Which time?" Zara chuckled.

"Your stories are really making the rounds?" Jude asked.

"Oh yes. I keep my stories to the point and don't use a lot of video and just a few pictures. Bandwidth is precious in some places. Some people have told me they print my stories with old mechanical copy printers and take them to some of the outlying settlements that are completely cut off. It's the only connection they have to the outside world. I guess I'm an inside link between the SACs and the rest of society."

"That's no small thing, Zara," Jude said. "With what happened to Callum and the encroachment of CAMO we saw in Squamish River, the SACs are going to need to be on the same page. This is a great way to do that."

Zara smiled and twirled her trusty ink pen.

"What's our next move, fearless leader?" Maisy asked, taking out an apple and sinking her teeth into it.

"Were you talking to me?" Jude joked.

"Of course," she said with her mouth full. "You're the one who says there is always a solution."

"I think we should take the ferry back to Seattle, and from there we'll start heading east. We're going to have to get creative with transport."

"By creative, you mean steal?" Maisy asked with her classic raised eyebrow.

"Maybe borrow," Jude said. "Or hitch a ride. We'll see what's heading east out of town. I've always wanted to ride a SEMIC Train. Maybe we can take one to the eastern side of the Cascades and then find a SAC over there. It's mostly CAMO farms and orchards . . . "

"Big Springs!" Zara shouted, startling them. "The Big Springs SAC is just outside of Yellowstone and near the Dakota border. I've got a few readers from there. I'm sure they'd put us up and help us cross the border."

"See Maisy?" Jude said, standing up and putting on his pack. "There's always a solution."

Once back over the Puget Sound in Seattle, it was a quick walk to the SEMIC station. The Supersonic Electro-Magnetic Intra Continental train system was one of the first federal infrastructure projects completed by the New America government after the Transition. It was a big carrot for Canada and Mexico, and without it, the annexation may not have happened. It followed mostly along established railways and highways, but it also had long spurs into the Yukon Region as far as Anchorage and deep into Baja, all the way to the Panama Canal.

Rod Kane had worked with some of the SEMIC engineers, and he spent hours telling Jude all about the genius of the system.

"Three things made the whole project possible: the cheap, light, and almost indestructible polymers used for the train and the track, precision electro-magnetic controls within the polymers, and the simplest and most brilliant idea of all: the vacuum tube," he explained. "When you hit the sound barrier, you realize why it is called a barrier. It'll blow any train off the tracks, but if you are moving in a vacuum, no air means no sound, and no sound means no big boom. It also means no air resistance. Once the train enters the vacuum tube, the ends are sealed, the air is sucked out, and the train is only limited by G forces. On the San-Angeles Tube test run, they were able to clock 2471.3 kilometers an hour. Mach 2 on land! Talk about breaking a record! Even outside the tube sections, the trains still hit over 325 kilometers per hour. Not bad for moving people's butts a few feet off the ground."

The engineering prowess was lost on the girls, but getting off their feet was very appealing.

"So do we have money for tickets?" Maisy asked. She suspected Jude was working a different angle, but she had to know the plan at all times. There had to be a plan, even if it changed a dozen times.

"I haven't blown through Dad's life savings just yet," Jude said, staring in awe at the tracks and scanning the entire station. "I think we can get creative here."

"We're not stealing a train," Maisy said. Zara laughed, but Jude only cracked a small grin. He was engrossed. The train was its own titular fascination, but he was also formulating a plan to get them on board.

"There are relatively few people on the train, see?" he said, pointing to the first two sections. "The rest of the train is light freight. It's packed in long, slender containers."

"I thought we said no shipping containers," Maisy said, crossing her arms. Zara turned pale but held her tongue.

"Relax. They are too small and too tightly packed," Jude said, walking up to the railing and looking down onto the platform. "There are twenty-five or thirty sections on this train, and only the first two carry passengers. That means only the first two pull up to the platform and line up the doors with the scanners. If we can jump on a freight section, we should be able to work our way forward to the passenger sections."

"Talk about coach," Maisy said, rolling her eyes. "Still, it might work. It beats walking, and we would be able to get a free ride and avoid the passport scanners."

"And the LEAD units," Jude said, staring down at the platform.

"They sure like train stations," Zara said, peering over the railing and trying to pick them out.

"Robot cops," Maisy said dismissively. "I will never allow a machine to have authority over me."

"Law Enforcement Autonomous Droids," Jude reminded them. "Just like the ones in Vancouver. There are no eyes behind those cameras, just algorithms. I doubt they would let us go without a good passport scan. They aren't outfitted with deadly force weapons, so they're not too lethal, but they aren't known for making exceptions or missing details. I'd rather stay out of their line of sight."

"So really no guns, huh?" Zara said, making a mental note.

Maisy looked incredulous. "Not yet."

Zara loved the romantic old stories of Hobos back in the early 20th century, living in camps by rivers, running and jumping onto moving trains, and traveling the country looking for work, food, and shelter. Of course, the romantic sheen appeared much later, after the memories of hunger and desperation faded from the public consciousness. Still, traveling anywhere, especially outside Cascadia, was exhilarating, and doing it by sneaking onto a train was a pure rush of adrenaline. She couldn't help but think about characters from adventure stories, spy novels, and even westerns as they dodged the LEAD cops and ducked around dark corners.

Jude figured out the train they needed to catch was heading for Salt Lake City, and it made a stop in Twin Falls, which is where they would need to make their exit. From there, it would still be about 400 kilometers to the Big Springs area, but once there, they could rest and resupply before making their crossing into Dakota. They were almost into October, one of the most unpredictable months of the year. Since the rapid acceleration of climate change in the years before the Transition, October had become known for setting high and low records in temperature, flooding, freezing, and wind. The first fifty-degree swing, from 36°C to -20°C, happened in October. Jude was keenly aware that this was not the time to get stranded in the mountains.

"The train we need doesn't leave till midnight," Jude said, rummaging through his pack and pocketing a couple of gadgets. "We're pretty much out of sight, so stay here for a while. I need to go do some homework and take a look at those freight sections, so we know what we're getting into."

"Literally," Maisy commented.

"Be careful," Zara called after him.

He nodded and jogged the short distance to the tracks where the SEMIC trains ran from the port on the Puget Sound to the passenger station along the waterfront.

"I've got to confess," Zara said, "I'm nervous about jumping on this train."

"I get it," Maisy said empathetically. "You are taking the biggest risk without a passport. I would lie if I wasn't a little apprehensive myself, but I also know the only way to get to Callum is to trust Jude and take some risks. He's in his element when he's solving a problem. To him, this is just another challenge."

"You don't think Jude is worried at all? What if we get caught?"

"Jude is so focused, he doesn't have any brain capacity left to worry, although I thought I saw a bit of concern when we were in that shipping container. He wasn't worried about getting out, mind you, but I think he was worried about you."

Zara grinned and then tried to melt her smile into a quizzical look. "Me? Well, maybe that was because he was trying to help me avoid descending into panic. That wouldn't help anyone."

"Sure, but it was more than that. I can tell by the way he looks at you. He's pretty cautious about his feelings, but he can't help grinning like an idiot around you. Even right now, he's making sure we can pull this off without putting you in a position like last time. He knows you don't like to be enclosed in tight spaces, so he's going to try and avoid that situation."

"I hope I'm not making this trip any harder on him," Zara said. "You guys don't need to be tiptoeing around me."

Maisy laughed. "Don't worry, Z. I've never seen him like this around a girl. Granted, we were related to a lot of them back in Slate Creek, but even so, I think he enjoys 'tiptoeing' for you. Watch him when he gets back. If he found a safe way to jump on that train, he'll come back giddy and rambling, and he'll probably be talking to you most of the time."

"I don't mind that so much."

"Oh brother," Maisy said, rolling her eyes. "You mean you have a sweet spot for him, too?"

"Maybe," Zara smiled. "I'm a sucker for long, dark hair."

Maisy and Zara stayed vigilant in their small alcove as evening gave way to nightfall in the big city. There weren't many people out, but they were still women alone outside. They stiffened at the passing sound of footsteps and sighed collectively every time they passed. Suddenly, they heard the approaching scuff of footsteps that didn't seem to be passing them by. As they got closer and closer, Zara stepped back and crouched down, while Maisy flattened herself against a brick wall.

A man stepped around the corner, blurting rather presumptuously, "Ladies . . . ."

Smack!

Maisy swung a right hook and knocked his head back so hard he lost his balance and fell backward to the ground.

"Ouch!" Jude yelled. "Son of a—

"Sorry! Sorry, Jude!" Maisy called out to him, taking his hand to help him up. "I thought you were someone coming to, huh . . . "

"Coming to do what? Practice street fighting?" he moaned, holding his right eye.

"I'm really sorry."

"Yeah, yeah," he said, waving her off. "Now Zara has something else for her next story."

"Do you have a cold pack, Maisy?" Zara asked.

"It's in here somewhere," she said, digging into her medical pack. She took out the small bean-bag-shaped package and slammed it on the pavement a few times.

Zara took the pack from Maisy. "Let me help. Jude, I'll sit here cross-legged, and you can lean back against me while I hold the pack over your eye. That might be more comfortable." Maisy smiled and shook her head, but she held her tongue.

"Aaah," moaned Jude as Zara applied the pack. She put her hand on top of his, and instinctively, he took hold of her fingers, being careful not to squeeze as hard as it hurt.

"As I was saying," Jude said, "we're in luck. I figured out that SEMIC trains were designed with flexibility of purpose. It's pretty genius, really."

"What's that mean for us?" Maisy asked.

"Did you notice the sections are shaped symmetrically, aerodynamically, and they all have windows, even the freight sections? The sections are all identical and can travel in either direction. Passengers load from the side, and then when the passenger sections are full, the rest of the train is used for freight. The seats fold down onto the floor, and the roof opens. Cranes load special freight containers called 'sleeves' onto the section, and then the roof closes."

"Like shipping containers?" Zara asked.

"In a way, but much smaller and lighter," he said, squeezing her hand gently. "They are plastic polymer containers, about three meters high, three meters wide, and thirty meters long. A regular shipping container can hold about six sleeves if it is full length, but the SEMIC trains were made for speed. Each section holds three sleeves: two on the bottom and one on top. The curved roof closes over the top sleeve, which leaves a lovely space on either side of the sleeve for a few hitchhikers like us."

"So, we're riding with freight again?" Maisy asked. She tried not to be dour, but being trapped in the big steel shipping container on the boat left a bad taste in her mouth, too.

"We're sneaking on with the freight, but before the train starts moving, we can crawl along the freight sleeve up to the passenger section and get in through the emergency exits that are on both ends of each section."

"What about alarms?" Zara asked.

"We've got five seconds before the alarm sounds."

"What's the catch?" Maisy asked. "It can't be that easy."

Jude sighed, took the pack from his eye, and sat up, turning to face Zara and Maisy.

"The train is Supersonic, which means the sections are sealed and pressurized when the train starts moving. The passenger sections get oxygen, but the freight sections don't. I calculated we would have about thirty to sixty minutes of oxygen in the freight section."

"Oh, that's all," Maisy said sarcastically.

"Not exactly. When the train enters the vacuum tube, all of the emergency exits are locked. If we aren't in a seat before then . . . "

"Then we suffocate," Zara said. "No air in the freight section and no air outside in the vacuum tube."

"Basically," Jude said, trying to salvage his cautious optimism.

"Well then, we'd better get ourselves a seat before the train starts moving," Zara said. "I'm not walking to the Dakota border."

As midnight approached, Jude pulled out a set of gray coveralls.

"Put these on."

"Why?" Maisy instinctively asked. "Are we making a Jude Kane fashion statement?"

"I think they're making a comeback," he quipped. "The freight sleeves are gray, so these will help you blend in and avoid security scanners."

"With all the grease marks on yours, will you actually blend in?" Zara teased.

"I hope so. I earned these stripes on solar panels and wind turbines in Slate Creek. I'm rather attached to my coveralls."

"Where'd you get these small ones for us, anyway?" Maisy asked. "They're awfully clean. Did you steal them?"

"I borrowed them from a laundry service."

They slipped on their quasi-camouflage outfits, secured their packs, and stole out from their alcove into the chilly night. The sound of the water lapping against the piers was only interrupted by the buzz of the occasional personal transport or laughter from a group of late-night revelers.

"Watch for my signal," Jude said as they approached the tracks. "When the front of the train pulls into the station for the passengers, the tops open, the security droids scan the freight sleeves, the cranes take all three sleeves and load them, and then the tops close. It takes about ninety seconds. We need to jump on top of the freight sleeves between the scan and the crane."

They both nodded and stretched their limbs like a couple of sprinters at the starting line. When the SEMIC train glided in, Jude gave the signal, and they ran through the gate before it closed after the train and slipped in among the stacks of freight sleeves. Jude pointed to the area where the sleeves were staged for loading, two on the bottom and one on top, lined up along the tracks. He pointed out the security drones as they made their way down the aisles scanning the stacks, and as soon as it passed, he signaled, and they ran.

They reached the front stack of sleeves just as the crane was attaching to the sides. Maisy jumped up, then Zara, and finally Jude grabbed the side as the stack was lifted. The girls stifled a scream as Jude hung off the stack, swinging in the air. He clung to the side, using the momentum of the crane to swing his legs up onto the top of the sleeve and pull himself onto the top.

They flattened themselves against the containers, blending in and spreading out their arms and legs to keep balance as the stack was swung over the train section and lowered in. As soon as they touched down, the sound of metallic clamps and the hiss of compressed air were quickly followed by the closing of the rounded top of the train section. There was another hiss, the clunk of locking mechanisms, and then an eerie silence punctuated by the muted panting of Jude, Maisy, and Zara.

Jude set his timer for thirty minutes. "Let's not waste any time getting ourselves a seat," he said as they lay flat in the half meter of airspace between the corners of the freight sleeves and the rounded top of the train section. They scampered along the containers on their elbows and knees, reaching the end of the sleeve before the train lurched forward and began its journey to Salt Lake.

Jude turned on a small flashlight and reached over the edge of the freight sleeve to turn the handle on the emergency exit door.

"Shoot."

"Maisy knew how understated her brother was, so his exclamation was not comforting.

"What's wrong?" she asked.

"I can reach the handle, but we won't fit between the end of the sleeve and the front of the emergency exit," he explained. "It's only about eight centimeters. I thought we'd have a bit more room, but I couldn't get an accurate measurement inside the section. My estimate is off by six centimeters, and we need that six centimeters to squeeze through that door."

"What about the other end?" Maisy asked.

"I don't know," Jude said. "It's possible there's a bit more room down there."

"I'm on it," Zara called out, surprising Jude and Maisy. "When I see my brother next time, remind me to rub it in his face. This is for all the times Akal teased me and called me 'lanky.'" She wriggled and writhed her way backward for nine meters, finally reaching the other end of the sleeve. Her feet hit the end, but there was enough room for her to twist and slip down between the end of the sleeve and the emergency exit. "I can fit down here," she called back to them.

Jude and Maisy wriggled backward down the length of the sleeve and with some squeezing and stretching, managed to get themselves upright between the freight sleeves and the emergency exit. Suddenly, the train jerked backward and began to accelerate.

"Now we have another problem," Jude said. "If we open that exit at 300 kilometers an hour, we're going to set off more than a few alarms. The five-second grace period only works if we are still. Also, we are at the wrong end. That door just leads to another emergency exit on the next freight section."

"I guess we're stuck," Maisy said. "You doing ok?" she asked, putting a hand on Zara's shoulder.

"I'm good. I'm standing in front of a door with a little window. It's the difference between being squished and trapped, at least in my mind."

"How much air do we have?" Maisy asked.

"About twenty-two minutes, and seven minutes until the vacuum tube tunnel. Hopefully, we won't be in the tube too long," he said.

Suddenly, the train lurched forward, and a deep hum accompanied the rapid slowing of the train.

"What's going on?" Maisy asked.

"A stop before the vacuum tube," Jude said, his eyes wide. "We've got five seconds on each exit door and ninety seconds to get into that passenger section. Get ready!"

As soon as they felt the train come to a stop, Jude cranked the handle and opened the hatch door. They launched onto the small platform between sections, and Zara swung the hatch closed as fast as she could.

Jude counted under his breath, "One thousand one, one thousand two, one thousand three, one thousand four, one thousand . . . " They jumped down to the ground and sprinted the length of the section and leaped up to the platform behind the passenger section. Jude climbed up, and then, while balancing on the narrow platform, he helped to pull up Zara and Maisy. He twisted the handle on the emergency exit and pulled the door open. "Go!"

"One thousand one, one thousand two, one thousand three, one thousand four, one thousand five . . . "

There was a squealing beep, then a click as Jude shut and latched the door. The girls quickly pulled off their packs and ducked down into a couple of back seats. Jude noticed a communication panel with a red light blinking. A screen appeared with the words, "emergency hatch opened" and a menu of selections beneath: "emergency in progress," "door malfunction," and "opened in error." He touched the button "opened in error," and breathed a sigh of relief as the red light went out and the screen flashed the words, "thank you," and then went dark.

Jude turned and saw, among the departing and boarding passengers, that a few people had noticed the short alarm of the door and looked at him suspiciously.

Jude looked down at his grease-stained coveralls and then smiled broadly. "Safety check complete. We're all set."

Satisfied with that answer, they all settled in for the journey. He took a seat behind Maisy and Zara, and they all breathed deeply as the train moved forward. They watched through the pressurized cabin windows as the buildings gave way to old homes and communities of Cubes, and then to CAMO's manicured fields, and finally, the train slipped through the opening of the vacuum tube at the foot of the Cascade Mountains. The rush of air slowly ceased, and the gentle pressure of G forces pressed them back into their seats as they accelerated to twice the speed of sound, and the spectacle of the tube turned into a smooth blur outside their windows.

As Zara typed frantically on Maisy's phone, relaying the story of their adventure to her growing SAC readership, Jude turned his focus to the feat of traversing 400 kilometers from Twin Falls to the Big Spring SAC. There was not much he could do, but he used his phone and the superb connection on the train to look at the map, locate the best route from Twin Falls to the SAC, and explore transport options.

When they arrived in Twin Falls, the girls prepared to exit through the emergency door to avoid the scanners, but Jude had a different idea.

"Look at the platform. The scanners here are nothing like Seattle, and I'm not even sure if they scan departing passengers. Just link your arms together and move together. Follow the others."

The girls nodded and put on their sister act. They smiled, giggled, and skipped through the doors, past the scanners, and across the platform.

"Turn left and head towards the city," he instructed them.

"Actually, we need to turn right and look for the transport pads," Zara said. "Trust me."

Jude looked surprised, but nodded in agreement and followed the girls to the pads. A middle-aged man standing next to a medium-sized four-person transport drone waved to them, and Jude noticed his hand was closed in a fist, except for his thumb and pinky fingers. He waved his hand and also twisted his wrist in a bizarre but inviting greeting.

"A little bird told me you three needed a lift to Big Springs," he called over the sound of the rotors.

Jude froze with a questioning look.

"That would be much appreciated," Zara called to him as he took the girl's packs and helped them into their seats.

"Don Porter," he said, shaking Jude's hand. "I run Big Springs, or what's left of it. We have a smaller but hearty remnant there. CAMO has been squeezing us, as you will see when we fly over. I thought it was just us, but thanks to Zara Malik and her stories, we've figured out we're not alone."

"So, Zara's the little bird that told you we needed a lift," Jude said.

"She's the sparrow that sang in my ear," he said, laughing. "My family runs to the screens when they see another update from her. You guys have been on quite the adventure. We're all rooting for you."

Jude smiled at Zara, and she winked back.

"We'll get you fed and rested and give you whatever you need to help you on your way. You're welcome as long as you want at Big Springs. When you're ready, we can help you get across the border into Dakota. Avoiding border crossings isn't too hard, as long as you enjoy the countryside."

"I don't mind at all," Jude said, staring at the vast expanse of flat land, rugged pines, and rocky hills. Technically, they were still inside Cascadia, but it was a world away from the Rockies he was used to. While he preferred the blue mountains and lush green landscape, he also enjoyed a change of scenery and the thrill of traveling so far from home.

The greeting was warm and lavish, despite the apparent dwindling resources on the SAC. They spent a week with Don and his family, giving advice, shoring up crop storage structures, repairing the aging solar panels and wind turbines, and tending to medical needs.

Zara chronicled their stay and shared everything she could in her reporting about helping Big Springs. Jude wrote a special piece on tuning up wind turbines, and Maisy wrote a step-by-step First Aid guide. Jude was also able to resurrect a small fleet of four electric ATVs that Don desperately needed for checking their crops. Listening to them whir to life reminded Jude of their motorbikes and how much they needed them now.

The morning of their departure, Don's wife and family sent them off with their packs stuffed with food, blanket rolls, and freshly laundered clothes. Don took Jude and the girls in his off-road transport, and he had his sons follow in three ATVs. They reached the edge of a large, wooded area, and Don pointed into the trees.

"The border is about five kilometers east of here, but you won't see any signs. We're inside Yellowstone now," he explained. "You'll have to watch out for wildlife, but there aren't many people. Beyond that, you'll be crossing the rugged area that used to be Wyoming. CAMO gets a lot of its minerals from this area, but they are mostly automated operations. If you find a SAC, they'll likely be pretty rough characters, so be careful."

"When the rocky hills give way to flatlands and unending corn, soy, and wheat fields, you'll be in what used to be Nebraska. About 1500 kilometers east is Omaha, and 800 kilometers southwest is Denver. Either way, it's a long journey, so I want you to take these."

His sons got off the ATVs and presented them to Jude, Maisy, and Zara. All three of them were speechless.

"Make sure and lock them up this time," Don said as his sons joined him in the buggy. "Thank you for everything, and be safe, Sparrows," he said, driving off and waving with his distinctive thumb and pinky finger twist. Then it hit Jude: it was a sign for them; *they* were the Sparrows. They brought the music of hope.

Chapter 9: **Omaha**

THE BULL ELK LOOKED up from his grazing, stared for a few seconds, and then went back to his lunch. Three does and their four fawns raised their heads and stared for a few seconds before deciding to trot into the trees for better cover. Most creatures had a similar reaction: the people weren't particularly loud, and they kept moving, so they didn't seem to be an immediate threat. Maisy, Zara, and Jude were thrilled with their wildlife show in Yellowstone.

The ride was beautiful, but it wasn't easy. Maisy and Zara struggled to keep up with Jude, but no one complained because they knew they had to make headway to beat the impending winter. The memory of the cabin was still fresh.

"I think we're through Yellowstone," Jude said as they pulled up to a ledge overlooking a valley. "I've got about 20% battery left. We'd better set up camp."

Maisy and Zara exchanged looks. "I've got about 5% battery left in my bones," Maisy said. "We all need to recharge."

"We'll get the tent. Why don't you gather some wood and make a fire like a proper caveman?" Zara said.

"I'm on it."

It took some patience, pounding of tent pegs, and fumbling with rods and fabric, but the girls got the tent up and laid out the sleeping bags.

"Don's family was good to us," Zara noted as she flattened her sleeping bag. "They gave us some good gear."

"Is it just me, or do you have an irrational dread of waking up soaking wet and freezing?" Maisy asked.

"Trust me, it's not just you," Zara said.

As they dug through the packs for what would be dinner, they heard leaves and sticks crackling underfoot behind them.

"You don't have to try and be quiet, Jude. I'm not going to hit you in the face this time."

"Good."

That was not Jude's voice. Maisy spun around just in time to see a fist knock her head back, and then everything went black.

"Maisy!" screamed Zara. Before she could stand up, something pushed her to the ground, shoving her face into the dirt.

A menacing male voice said, "Well, what have we here? We don't get visitors very often."

Another male voice responded, "We never get visitors this pretty, either. I think we should give them a proper welcome to Wind River."

Zara screamed and kicked, trying to fight off her assailant, clawing and scratching at his face and getting tangled in his long, black hair. In the struggle, she got a quick glance at Maisy, who was still unconscious and having her clothes torn off by her attacker, who also had long, black hair.

Suddenly, Zara heard a thump followed by a pained cry. "Aah!" After another thump, Maisy's attacker slumped over on the ground. Before she could see what happened, her assailant took a similar blow to the side of his head, and he fell to the side unconscious before he could make any sound. She looked up, and Jude stood over her with a large tree branch and his hand held out to her.

"Are you okay?" he asked.

"I am now," she said, panting as she stood up and wiped the dirt off her mouth. "They came out of nowhere."

"Go check on Maisy. I'm going to give our guests a place to sit and relax."

Zara ran to Maisy, fixed her clothing, and gently put her arm under her head. As she slowly roused, Zara reassured her and helped her reorient herself.

"What happened?" she groggily asked.

"We were attacked," Zara explained. "This time you didn't swing."

"Figures."

"Don't worry; Jude saved the day. He's getting to know our visitors right now," Zara said, pointing to the tree where Jude was tying up the men.

"We haven't been properly introduced," Jude said in a mockingly courteous tone. "I'm Jude Kane. I'm generally a pretty nice guy, easygoing, a little bit of a technical nerd, and I like to solve problems. I'm also a brother and a pretty big family guy. That means that while I'm smiling, I wouldn't hesitate to gut anyone who tried to hurt a member of my family."

The men grunted and squirmed but didn't say anything.

"We're on a pretty long trip. We know we're in Dakota, but that's about it. I don't think there's a real city anywhere near here, so I'm guessing you two live in a SAC?"

"SAC?" the smaller one said. "Ha! We've been in a SAC for thousands of years."

The taller one chuckled sadly. "Welcome to Wind River."

"So, you're Shoshone or Apache?" he asked.

"You should have asked that fifty years ago. Now no one really knows," the taller one said.

Jude pulled up a stump and sat down on it. "We're Salish, or at least part Salish. We live in a SAC that is on what used to be called 'First Nation' land. Our brother got scooped up by the Feds, and we're trying to get him back."

"The New America Defense Forces took him?" the smaller one blurted. "Good luck."

"The New America isn't much different from the old one as far as we're concerned. We've been livin' and dyin' on this land for a long time," the tall one said. "The only difference is they sent us a bunch of those ugly square things to live in."

"The New America government gave you Cubes, but didn't require you to move to a city?" Jude asked.

"Nope," they both said. "They probably figured we'd die out in a few decades. We have bad numbers. More drugs, more murders, less education, and no jobs. We don't have a great reputation."

"So I've seen," Jude said, crossing his arms. "I'll make you a deal."

"We're listening," the taller one said.

"If you take us to someone who can help us get some food and charge up our ATVs without killing us, we can forget our little misunderstanding here."

"You'll cut us loose?" the short one asked.

"I'll hold all the guns and knives, and you two can lead the way. We'll give everything back once we're there and I feel safe."

"Okay," the older one said. "My name's Cory, and this is my little brother Curtis. My uncle is the chairman of the tribal council. I hope you keep your word to forget about, you know . . . what happened."

"I'm a man of my word," Jude assured them.

Maisy came up and stood next to Jude, her arms crossed. "Which one of you dumbasses hit me?" she asked.

Curtis looked up and then averted his eyes. As he turned his head, she saw he was bleeding from a nasty gash behind his ear.

"You're bleeding pretty good," she said, sauntering up to him and looking the wound over. "I'm going to have to sew you up. If you try anything, I'll stick the needle in your eyeball."

He shook his head.

"You're more forgiving than I am," Zara said, joining them in front of Cory and Curtis.

"It's not forgiveness," Maisy said, retrieving her medical pack. "It's my job."

The next morning, Cory and Curtis led the way to their settlement. It was a shell of a former town, strewn with old twentieth-century mobile homes, manufactured homes, run-down ramblers, and Cubes scattered haphazardly.

When they arrived, Cory introduced Jude to his uncle Charlie, and almost audibly breathed a sigh of relief when Jude kept his word.

"What happened to Curtis's head?" Charlie asked. "And who knows how to stitch up a wound like that?"

"My sister Maisy is pretty handy with a needle and thread."

"Lucky him. I'm sure whatever he did to get that gash, he deserved it."

Jude smiled. "This is the first time I've heard of the New America government giving out Cubes to people not in cities. I think Wind River might be pretty unique. Do you get a Universal Basic Income here, too?"

"We made an arrangement during the Transition: we give CAMO mining rights and all the land they want, and we get the city perks of Cubes and a UBI here on the reservation. It sounded like a great deal, except there is 95% unemployment and no schools outside of online learning. These kids won't sit at a terminal and read about history when they don't have a future. Between overdoses and murders, there won't be much left of Wind River soon," Charlie concluded with a tired sadness in his voice.

"Do you think it was an intentional strategy?" Jude asked.

"I think that ADAMS computer running everything knew full well the government didn't have to smoke us out. It just cut off all hope, and we started smoking ourselves out."

"I'm so sorry, Charlie." Jude's admiration for his dad seemed to grow daily. Slate Creek was a rare, shining exception to what now seemed to be the rule: SACs had a finite shelf life. With a little squeezing by CAMO, attrition would accelerate. You didn't need to exert force to control the population; you just needed to make them hungry enough, and in time, they would submit themselves.

It took about ten days to make it through Yellowstone, across Wind River, and through the Great Plains of Dakota. After stopping to recharge in Wind River, they found SACs near Cheyenne, North Platte, and Grand Island, where they were able to exchange some medical treatment and technical know-how for a power source and more food and supplies. Zara's chronicling of the journey sent their reputation out in front of them so well that they were received like celebrities in the SACs. Helping the SACs slowed them down, but it also gave them a chance to make good friends, build a sense of a much larger community, and get what they needed to keep them going.

When they reached Omaha, they decided it was time to head into the city once again. They found a small motel in a former industrial area where they were able to get a couple of beds and store the ATVs. After 1500 kilometers of some pretty rough terrain punctuated by frantic stops at the SACs trying to help as much as possible while the ATVs recharged, they were desperate for a break.

Sleeping in and waking up in a warm, dry bed was a luxury not lost on any of them. With their muscles crying and their bones aching, it was after noon before they stumbled from their beds and enjoyed a warm shower and used a commode that didn't give them splinters.

"Is anyone up for a walk?" Jude announced. "I was thinking about checking out some of the city."

"I'm up for traveling on steady ground for once," Zara said.

"You two go ahead," Maisy said as she slung a towel over her shoulder. "I'm going to soak in the hottest bath I can stand."

Jude and Zara headed out to the street and walked casually toward downtown. Stopping at a bluff overlooking the city, they sat down on a public transport bench.

"Omaha is not Vancouver, and it is definitely not Seattle," Zara said.

"Nope. Downtown looks like it only has a few blocks, and the rest of the city is just these sprawling automated manufacturing plants, warehouses, and the Cubes," Jude said, scanning the area. "It's poorer here."

"And more dangerous," Zara said, pointing out three enforcement transports.

"Those aren't the police," Jude said, focusing on the nearest transport. "Those are Dakota Regional Defense Force troops. They're patrolling the city. Why would the Dakota RDF be doing the police's job?"

"Maybe because of that," Zara said, pointing to a few pieces of blackened, twisted metal sticking out of a metal recycling container.

"That looks like a LEAD unit, or what's left of it," Jude said, walking over to the container and examining scraps. "LEAD units are the only presence the police have on the streets. If they're being destroyed . . . "

"Then the police had to call in the RDF," Zara said, scribbling in her notepad furiously. "Now we need to find out how many units were destroyed and why. That thing was blown to shreds. If poor people are cobbling together homemade bombs, there must be some reason."

"Spoken like a real journalist."

Jude and Zara went back to the bench and sat down again. Jude stretched his arms across the back of the bench, and Zara shifted up against him and lay her head on his shoulder.

"Do you miss your dad?" she asked.

"After seeing the conditions in these other SACs, I respect him more than ever, but I've been too preoccupied to really miss him. I guess I can get tunnel vision sometimes. All I see is Callum."

"I understand. Sometimes I worry about Akal and my dad, but I think we're doing something much bigger than just us."

"We are, but that is because of you," he said.

"It's because of *us*," she reemphasized. "I'm not fixing power grids or stitching people up. I'm just telling the stories."

"That might be the most important thing we're doing."

"So that's why you put up with me?" she teased.

"What's to put up with?" he asked, smiling.

"Oh, just little things like dragging my sorry butt out of the woods and smuggling me past passport scanners."

Jude chuckled. "I'm a sucker for a pretty girl."

"Oh, really?" she laughed. "You just say that because you haven't seen very many girls."

Jude turned and looked into her deep brown eyes. "We've been through two Regions, three cities, and a dozen or so SACs. Trust me; no one comes close to you."

"I don't know if that is true," she said, her smile melting into a sultry look, "but I don't mind hearing it."

Jude had never *really* kissed a girl, but he felt a magnetic pull drawing him to her. As he leaned down, she put her arm around his neck and pulled him in, sending an electric tingling down his spine as their lips touched.

Crack!

They snapped their heads back.

Crack crack!

"Those are gunshots," Jude said, scanning the area and trying to determine where they came from.

"That sounded like it was only a couple of blocks away," Zara said.

"I'd better get you home," he said instinctively.

"Not before we check this out!" she snapped back. "We need to find out what's going on. If that was RDF troops, we might be able to figure out what's been going on!"

"Again, spoken like a true journalist."

A volley of shouting followed the shots, and Jude and Zara followed the voices. It didn't take long to find the scene. An RDF transport with three troops outside and rifles pointed was shouting commands to a group of teenagers. It looked like five boys, and two were sprawled out on the ground.

"Stop! Don't shoot!" the boys shouted with their hands in the air.

"Step away from the device!" the troops shouted back.

"You shot them! They need help!" the boys called back.

"Step away now, or we'll fire again!"

They started walking backward, holding their hands up.

"Don't shoot! We're not doing anything wrong! Please get help!" they kept shouting.

In the mayhem, Jude took a visual picture of the scene. They were in a vacant lot between two abandoned brick buildings; there were no people, businesses, houses, or Cubes in the immediate area. The deadly "devices" had fins and cones and were lying on their sides with wires coming out of the bottom. The wires led to controls that were lying on the ground near the injured boys, where they dropped them when they were shot.

"Are you getting this?" Jude whispered as they hid behind a trash bin.

"Of course. Are those bombs?" she asked.

"Rockets," he said. "They're homemade rockets. My dad and I used to shoot those things off all the time."

"Did the RDF shoot those boys over a couple of toys?" she asked.

"Maybe I can help," he said and slipped away before she could talk him out of it.

"Wait!" he shouted, walking towards the boys with his hands up. "Those are not dangerous. They are just rockets."

"Stand down! Stand down!" they shouted. Jude froze.

"Those are not IEDs. I can prove it!" he said.

"Stand down!" they shouted again. "Move away from the devices immediately!" Jude backed up.

Two more vehicles raced to the scene. Another RDF ground transport appeared, spilling out backup troops, and an ambulance drone landed in the lot near the injured boys. The troops swarmed the boys, cuffing them and dragging them back to the transports while the EMTs approached the injured.

"Those are just rockets. They're toys," Jude shouted to the EMTs. "They're not dangerous."

The EMTs hesitated, and Jude took his chance.

"Look, I'll move them away so you can get to the injured."

One of the EMTs nodded, so Jude stepped in, scooped up the rockets, and carried them to the trash bin. He pulled up the wires and the controls and threw everything in.

"Let's go!" a voice came from behind the trash bin. It was not a familiar voice. Jude turned and saw a middle-aged man, standing next to Zara, motioning him to come.

"Now, while they're busy with the boys. Let's go!"

Zara looked at him and pleaded with her eyes, and he knew this was his time to exit.

"Follow me," the man said, galloping down an alley and around an old building. "Trust me, you don't want to get tangled up with the RDF."

They weaved around a few more corners and then slowed to a walk as they emerged on the street. "My place is down the block. Let's get inside, and then we can make introductions."

They arrived at a modest-looking double Cube, but when they went inside, they noticed the Cubes were a front, attached to an older twentieth-century brick rambler in the back.

"Those Cubes are ugly as hell, but they do their job. For me, it's some extra space that hides my main house. It keeps would-be thieves at bay."

"Thanks for getting us out of there," Zara said as they made their way into the main house.

"No problem. My name's Jaxson, by the way. Jaxson Mason."

"Jude Kane, and this is Zara Malik," Jude said. "You're probably wondering why we stumbled into an RDF stand-off."

"Ha!" he laughed. "I figured you were from out of town. Things have been pretty tense here in Omaha for the last few weeks. Most folks with any sense try to avoid going outside unless they have to."

"I guess I'm the one without any sense," Jude said, throwing up his hands.

"You were trying to help, and you didn't know the back story. That's not such a bad thing," Jaxson said, pouring three glasses of cold tea.

"What's the back story?" Zara asked, retrieving her pen and pad.

"Is that paper and pen?" he asked.

"It worked for journalists for hundreds of years, so it works for me," Zara said.

"You are a girl after my own heart," Jaxson said, handing her the glass of tea. "I'm a history professor, and when little pieces of the twentieth century pop up now and then, it makes my day."

"I'm glad I could oblige."

"The back story is fairly simple: Omaha is one of the poorer cities," Jaxson explained as they sat down at the polished cherry wood dining table. "The UBI is lower here than in other cities, and the government won't raise it, citing a 'lower cost of living.' The Dakota Region blames the New America government, and the New America Congress says ADAMS calculates the numbers, and they are fair. Most people have a hard time affording food or anything else, so crime has been on the rise. Omaha PD decided to deploy about a hundred new LEAD units to fight crime, but many people see the LEAD units as just another example of technology ruining their lives. A few young people started making homemade pipe bombs and other IEDs and taking out the LEAD units. Omaha PD called the RDF, and here we are. The troops have been rolling through the streets for a few weeks now."

"We grew up on a SAC in Cascadia," Jude explained, "so I'm not completely educated about city life. As I understand, most people rely on the UBI since only about twenty percent of people have jobs."

"In Omaha, it's closer to eight percent," Jaxson said.

"So, ninety-two percent of people are unemployed and rely on a Universal Basic Income calculated by a computer thousands of miles away. Where is Congress? Isn't there a human somewhere that can listen to people and make a decision?" Jude asked.

"Congress is legally required to consult ADAMS before creating any legislation. They don't have to follow its recommendations, but since the Transition, most representatives have all but capitulated to the word of ADAMS. It is supposed to be the non-partisan voice of reason."

"I take it you don't agree," Jude said, taking a drink of his tea. "My dad was an engineering professor before the Transition. He founded our SAC and never looked back. I sense the same reticence to embrace a government that is driven by Artificial Intelligence."

"ADAMS broke the partisan gridlock and implemented the drastic measures that were needed to prevent a total collapse of society. That is hard to argue with. Annexing Mexico and Canada was a rational move, making reforms more uniform and fully implemented. But in all these rational moves, what happened to the US Constitution? Where are our 'inalienable rights'? Where was the consideration of history and culture before plowing ahead with the formation of New America? Rationality without human consideration can put us in a more precarious position than we were ever in before the Transition."

"Exactly how precarious?" Jude asked as Zara continued to write furiously and fill her small yellow notebook pages.

"Do you know why the UBI is not enough?" Jaxson asked. "ADAMS fixed the UBI to individual adults. Children do not get a UBI, and their parents don't get any increase. Your income is the same whether you have no kids or ten."

"We saw CAMO encroaching on SAC land all over Cascadia and Dakota, subtly starving and squeezing people out. In the cities, the UBI is doing the same thing as if forcing people to starve if they have children," Jude said, his mind racing.

"Eighty percent of people are a drain on the economy, so what's the rational thing to do?" Jaxson asked.

Zara stopped scribbling and put down her pen. She looked at Jaxson and then at Jude with wide eyes. "Reduce the population."

Chapter 10: **Art History**

"WE'RE CHECKING OUT OF the hotel," Jude announced to Maisy as soon as they stepped through the door. "We've got a better place, and it's free."

"Good to know," she said with a hint of irritation in her voice. "It's also good to know you two are alive."

"Sorry about that," Zara said, coming to Jude's rescue. "We had a little adventure."

Jude recounted the story to Maisy while Zara wrote her story and posted it.

"Professor Mason is an encyclopedia of knowledge about the Transition and New America," Jude explained to Maisy. "We won't stay long, but I need to probe his brain. He was in the thick of things when ADAMS came online. He watches the government, and maybe he can tell us something that will help us get to Callum."

"I haven't entertained much since my wife passed away a couple of years ago," Jaxson said. "She was certainly a better cook."

"We've eaten enough squirrels and protein bars to keep us from complaining for the rest of our lives," Jude said. "Your roast turkey is a delicacy."

"Yeah, we're not hard to please," Maisy said.

While Maisy and Jude were occupied with dinner and their host, Zara began to wander. Beyond the front Cubes, the old brick rambler was a virtual homage to the 20th century. The kitchen had standard integrated appliances, but the cupboards were made of smooth, dark varnished wood, and the countertops were made from slabs of genuine speckled and polished granite. Granite surfaces were outlawed over fifty years ago.

The living room was inviting with thick, fine, light beige carpet, leather sofas and recliners, and wood tables and bookshelves. She couldn't tell immediately, but she suspected the leather was actual animal hide, and the wooden furniture could be as old as the early 20th century. Framed pictures filled the smooth white walls, and many of them were vintage photographs of famous places. Zara noticed a beautiful black and white photo from what appeared to be the top of the Space Needle. There was a young couple posing for a shot on the outer deck, and behind them was the breathtaking panoramic view of downtown Seattle to the south.

"That's me and Lizzie," Jaxson said, startling her. "We were in between college terms, and we decided to take an impromptu trip into the city. That was many years ago."

"You both look very happy," she said, smiling as she stared at the photo.

"We were. We both had our share of 'suitors,' but we knew almost immediately after we met that we didn't want to waste time on anyone else. It was the best decision we ever made."

"You have so many paper books," she remarked, looking around the living room.

"I have many more downstairs in the basement. When libraries began purging their physical collections, I scooped them up. There's just something sacred about a real book. Of course, I didn't have all the room in the world, so I limited my collection to mostly fiction. As an old, grizzled history professor, I can say our story is more faithfully told in our literature."

"I agree."

"Are you hungry?" he asked.

"If your food is as good as your art, I'm famished."

They all sat down at the large oval wooden table, and after the clinking of serving spoons and muted groans of "yum" and "this looks so delicious," the conversation began in earnest.

"This may be because I was raised outside most of my life, but it seems to me the cities, not just Omaha, are relatively . . . *lifeless*," Jude said. "I don't see many people outside, and even in Vancouver and Seattle, where there are more people with jobs, there aren't many folks on the streets. There isn't a lot of machine noise, but there isn't much noise of any kind. I don't hear music or see murals. I don't even hear birds singing in the morning."

"Seeing is believing," Jaxson sighed. "Artistic expression has become heavily censored, especially music and literature. Anything that the government deems to be 'inciting unrest' is silenced. After a few years, many artists just stopped creating things they figured would never be experienced. The chaos of the Transition is the never-ending justification for the silencing of the people. Of course, no government can silence everyone," he said with a wink.

"I take it you don't hold your opinions in," Zara said as she sipped from a glass of cider.

"I hold them in at the University. I'm a rare old dinosaur to be still employed, and it wouldn't take much to send me off into the sunset. To be honest, I have always been supportive of the goals of the Transition and the New America government: halting the destruction of the planet, addressing the catastrophic unemployment that is the ugly underbelly of our AI-dominated economy, and maintaining law and order, especially after a traumatic period of unrest like the Transition. What I oppose, however, is the trampling of constitutional and in some cases, basic human rights, institutionally entrenched income inequality, and the dehumanizing effect of censorship. I write passionately about these things, but I just use a different name and a different forum."

"What forum is that?" Zara asked.

"There is an entire online world of dissenting voices. We have to keep moving, anonymously posting on randomly named and renamed blog sites that are routed through a dozen or so proxy servers, mostly in Africa and Asia. ADAMS keeps an eye on us, but the nonviolent groups I am part of are not a high priority. We know ADAMS is watching because the more radical and revolutionary bloggers tend to disappear after a few weeks. ADAMS doesn't just watch where we go; it learns from what we say and determines threat levels."

"I think we need to talk," Zara said. "I've been posting stories about our travels, and SACs have come to follow my stories closely. Since I am from a SAC and I'm learning as I go, they trust my perspective on what I report. So far, I haven't been too critical of the government because I don't know enough yet, but I had a few thoughts about the shooting of those boys yesterday. Maybe we can talk about the best way to be more of a journalist and less of a target."

"I'm afraid that relationship is very much the inverse. What's your goal?" Jaxson asked with the tone of a wise sage.

"To tell the truth," Zara said without hesitation.

"What if it hurts? What if it puts you in danger? What if it costs you?"

"Then it must be worth doing."

Jaxson smiled and nodded his head. "Then it sounds like you're already a journalist."

"I just post blogs. I've never been to college or anything."

"If people read what you report, you're a journalist. You need to turn your blog into a real newspaper. Most people don't trust the news because they know the official press is censored by ADAMS and the New American government. You have a unique opportunity to capture the attention of the SACs and the silent majority in the cities that don't feel like anyone hears or represents them."

"How do I create an entire newspaper?" Zara asked.

"Give it a name. I'll show you the technical end and how to stay ahead of ADAMS by posting from different servers and in different formats, but you need a solid name and a brand people can recognize."

Jude smiled as he took a bit of turkey. He chewed, swallowed, and then started whistling. Maisy looked at him, cocking her head and raising her eyebrows questioningly, and then grinned when the light bulb went on. Jude whistled a little louder, and Maisy began flapping her thumb and pinky playfully.

Zara stared blankly for a few seconds and then looked at Jaxson and smiled wide.

"Sparrow Press."

"How long do you think Zara and Jaxson will be down in the basement starting a journalistic revolution?" Jude asked Maisy.

"If they don't emerge in a couple of days, we'd better go down after them," she smirked.

"I feel like I'd better work off some of this dinner. Want to go for a walk?"

"Isn't that what you and Zara did when you almost got picked up by the RDF?"

"Good point."

"Couldn't we use a bit more money?"

"Always."

"Why don't we find the nearest power station and hit the discs? We can get a workout, get a little money, and stay off the streets."

"And if we do run into any police LEAD units or have to pass through scanners anywhere, we don't have to worry about Zara," Jude said. "Good idea."

"Aren't you glad you brought me along, even though I didn't give you much choice?" Maisy asked with a chuckle.

"I don't know . . . " Jude teased. "It depends on how much money you can make pedaling the discs. I'm not sure if you can earn enough to pay your way."

"I'll out-pedal you," she shot back.

"Wanna bet?" he wagered.

"Yeah."

"I'll bet you two chocolate bars. We'll pick them up on the way to the station. Winner takes both."

"Deal."

They made their way to a store, picked up the chocolate and a few other staples, and then caught a transport to the power plant. They were fortunate that Omaha, in a small concession to alleviate the widespread poverty, offered free transport to the power stations. People were desperate, and the stationary bikes were often full, but Jude and Maisy managed to find a couple of bikes side by side.

"Do we have to stare at these screens?" Jude said as they began their workout.

"You're used to always being outside. These city people are used to being inside. No one has a job. What else are they going to do?" Maisy surmised.

"At least they could show something worth watching," he complained as he swiped the screen with his finger, moving from one program to the next. "Sports, soap operas, anime, terrible canned dramas . . . pornography?"

"They do have documentaries," Maisy said as a leopard raced across her screen to the narration of a whimsical British voice.

"Look at the people, Maisy," Jude said in a low tone. "They are miserable. Do you see anyone smiling?" he asked.

"Not really. Then again, we are working out."

"I didn't realize how bad it was, even when Jaxson told me. It's not just painting and music. Everyone is afraid to express themselves. When you muzzle people like that, they suffocate."

"I appreciate Dad more every day," Maisy said. "He saw all of this coming."

Jude thought about Slate Creek, and a pang of homesickness ran through his body. "We need to find Callum and bring him home."

Later that evening, after a luxurious hot shower at Jaxson's house, Maisy could see that Zara was not herself. The girls sat on a sofa while Jude and Jaxson talked about history and politics over a game of pool.

"Are you okay?" Maisy asked.

"I'm good," Zara said unconvincingly.

"I don't believe you. What's wrong?"

"I got word from Akal this afternoon. My dad died last night."

"Oh, Zara, I'm so sorry," Maisy said, trying to absorb the shock and still comfort her friend. She gently reached over and squeezed her hand.

"It's not like it was completely unexpected. He really started dying after we lost my mom. I guess they can finally be together now."

"How is your brother doing?"

"He's doing alright."

"Is he going to step in and try to help keep Squamish River going?"

"No. He got word he was accepted into the NADF. He leaves in two weeks."

"Hasn't he wanted to do that for years?" Maisy asked.

"Yes. He hesitated when Dad died, but I reminded him that there wasn't much left in Squamish River for him. I convinced him he could do more good in the military."

"Good. I'm happy for him. How is the rest of the SAC doing?"

"CAMO has taken over most of the rest of the land, and between the dwindling population and the pathetic crop yields, there wasn't really anyone or anything there to stop them," Zara explained. Akal said he would try and make a deal with CAMO to sell the land and see if he could distribute the money to the original landowners and their remaining families. The rest of the people in Squamish River are heading south to Vancouver or north to Slate Creek. Your dad said he would take anyone who showed up."

Maisy smiled as she pictured her dad welcoming the straggling remnant of the Squamish River SAC. "I hope you realize when my dad said he would welcome them to Slate Creek, he meant he would find them a place to live, and then he would put them to work in the fields. Everyone has a job in Slate Creek."

"I'm pretty sure the people motivated enough to trek up to Slate Creek will be happy with hard work in a successful SAC. The others will get food and shelter in Vancouver, but not much else. It's strange to think that in a few weeks the Squamish River SAC won't exist anymore."

"It will exist in your memories. Don't worry; you're basically family now, so you always have a home with us."

Zara looked up at Maisy with a small tear in her eye. "I know. Thanks, Maisy. It means a lot, especially now."

An alarm went off, and Jaxson grabbed his phone from his pocket.

"Hang on," he told Jude, putting his stick on the table. He read the screen, and the blood drained from his face. "We have a problem. You need to get out of here, *now*."

"What's going on?" Jude asked.

"The NADF, maybe even a COATS team, is en route now. Some LEAD units got footage of me leading you away from the scene with the boys this morning. My guess is they took the footage they got and ran it through their ADAMS terminal. Facial recognition led to an ID, which led to an address, and then ADAMS was probably able to link me to some of my writings that it kept in the low-risk pile. ADAMS did the math, and now I'm a high-priority threat. You don't want to be here when they come to the door."

As they scrambled to grab their packs, Jaxson called to Zara.

"Take this screen and my phone," he said, handing them to her. "Give me your pen."

She dug it out, and he scribbled out a series of letters, numbers, and symbols. "This is my master security code. Don't lose it. If for some reason you are caught, destroy the computer."

"Okay, I will," she said nervously.

As they headed up the stairs to leave, Jaxson rerouted them.

"Go through the back door in the kitchen," he shouted to them. "Go out the gate in the backyard and weave your way through the Cubes. Make yourselves disappear. When you get to your transports, head east to the Missouri River in the Council Bluffs district. You can follow it south to the northern border of Texico. Find Max. His information is in my phone. Follow the instructions; he's not an easy man to make contact with. Go!"

"What about you?" Jude turned and asked as he was going out the door. "What are you going to do?"

"I'm too old to run, too stubborn to hide, and too smart to think they'll ever let me go after this. I'm going to give 'em hell."

"I'll never forget you, Jaxson. Thank you."

"Thank you. You three have given me more hope than I've had in years. You're the Sparrows, right? Now fly!"

Jude hurried behind the girls, with Maisy charging ahead and weaving between Cubes and around corners. They got to an alley and dove down behind a recycling container. "Let's wait here for a bit," Jude said. "The streets are going to be hot now, and if we're running down the road with packs on, we'll stand out like flies in milk. Let's lay low for a few minutes."

As they sat down with their backs against a brick wall, trying to catch their breath, no one said a word, but they each knew what they all were listening for. Every sound made them tense up and hold their breath. There were almost no people on the street, and dusk had descended over an hour ago. If ever they needed to be invisible, it was now.

Suddenly, the muffled sound of men shouting drifted through the heavy air. There was the hollow bang of a polymer Cube door being kicked in, a volley of command calls, and then an eerie silence. After a few minutes, the peace was shattered by the crack of three rifle shots. Jude, Zara, and Maisy looked at each other, none of them speaking a word, and then they reached out, taking hold of each other by the hand, and hung their heads.

Part Two

Chapter 11: **Caves**

"Dr. Jaxson Mason?" shouted the commander.

"You could have knocked, and I would have answered."

"We don't knock first," he snarled.

Jaxson noticed the black clothing, tactical gear, and the lack of obvious insignia. This was not the Regional Defense Forces. This was a Critical Operations And Tactical Services team.

"Of course. Because individual rights have been thrown out the window in New America," Jaxson said, getting his jab in.

"You're under arrest for supporting and participating in terroristic activities."

"No, I'm under arrest for exercising free speech, a right that somehow didn't make the cut in the rush to create a new government during the Transition."

"Oh, we have a politician here," the commander said. "It's not a good idea to speak out against the state when you are employed by the state, Dr. Mason. Now your job is the least of your worries. We're not going back to the riots and chaos of the Transition. That is not only my job, but it's my personal mission."

"Those who would give up essential Liberty, to purchase a little temporary Safety, deserve neither Liberty nor Safety."

"Is that your wisdom, professor? You think we should all live in chaos so that you can spout your nonsense to whoever will listen?"

"That's not my wisdom. That's Ben Franklin. But I think he was right. Am I such a threat that it warrants sending in COATS?"

The commander smiled, then noticed a glass and dark mahogany display case with several rifles in the living room, nestled against the wall near the fireplace.

"Such a nice house you have hiding here behind the Cubes. Nice guns, too. You did know it is against the law to own firearms, don't you, professor?"

"I inherited those from my father's father. They are unloaded and secured, and they are legal under the classic, collector, and historical weapon exemption. They are quite literally 'grandfathered in.' I can show you my permit if you like." Jaxson struggled to hide the smug grin creeping up on his face.

"Well, now we have something in common, professor. I love old rifles. Do they still shoot?" the commander asked, changing his tune and catching Jaxson and the troops off guard.

"I suppose so. I haven't used them since I was a boy."

"Do you have any rounds in the case that we can load and try them out? I'd love to hold those pieces of history."

"I'm not sure. I kept a few rounds for each rifle, but it's been years. I can look in the drawers under the display case."

"Go ahead," the commander said, nodding to his team, who immediately lowered their weapons.

Jaxson rummaged through the drawers and pulled out a box that rattled with the sound of a few loose shells. He took a key, unlocked the cabinet, and pulled out a lever-action rifle. He handed the rifle and the box to the commander and said, "What do you think?"

"Beautiful," the commander said, turning the gun in his hands and examining every detail. "An original Model 71. Made from 1935 to 1958, it is a modification of the old 1886. And these are the .348 Winchester cartridges." He took three bullets out and loaded them in the chamber, and then cocked the lever.

Jaxson got nervous and muttered, "I've got a decent backyard, but there are a lot of Cubes surrounding me. I don't know if . . . "

Crack! The commander fired the first deafening round, hitting Jaxson in the stomach and blowing him up against the wall. He fell to the floor and doubled over, holding his wound. He lifted one hand, ripping in blood, and looked at the commander with rage.

"Well, what do you know? These were always very reliable," the commander said, smiling as he rotated the rifle in his hands. He cocked the lever again, fired, cocked a third time, and fired the last two rounds, both hitting Jaxson in the chest. His heart shattered, he slumped onto the floor, and he wheezed out his last breath.

"It's quiet. Let's get over to the storage place and get our wheels. Walk slowly and act casual. We don't need any attention," Jude said.

"Where are we going?" Maisy asked.

"Jaxson said to follow the Missouri River south. We need to get over the border into Texico and find a guy named Max."

"Texico's a big region," Maisy said. "How are we supposed to find him?"

"He's in Jaxson's phone," Zara said.

"And where is Jaxson's phone? Jude asked.

"Right here," Zara said, patting her pack where a conspicuous square bulge was sticking out, "along with his computer and pass codes."

"I hate to be the voice of questioning, but exactly how are we going to follow the Missouri River south?" Maisy asked. "The riverfront isn't exactly a paved road, and it is certainly not inconspicuous."

"Let's see what we have to work with when we get to Council Bluffs," Jude said.

"Let me guess: there is always a solution," Maisy said, rolling her eyes.

"Of course."

They managed to flag down a personal transport vehicle, and the owner offered to give them a lift for half the fare of public transport. It was a tight squeeze, but they managed. The owner spoke to them through a video screen.

"Where are you headed?" the owner asked.

"The storage units on 'I' street," Jude said.

"No problem," the owner said. "Hang on."

The owner sent the address to the vehicle, and it lurched forward. Zipping around potholes and sharp corners, they made good time, even if their stomachs still had to catch up. Jude paid the fare, and they went into the storage office to pick up their ATVs.

"Jude Kane," he said. "I need to get my ATVs."

The clerk stared at Jude blankly. "What ATVs?"

"They're in K-74."

"Um, I don't show we have anything in K-74. That unit is empty," he said, feigning an intent stare at his screen. Jude spied the reflection of the screen in the picture behind the clerk. He was in the middle of a multiplayer shooting game.

"Is that right?" Jude said, sniffing out the scam. "That's interesting because I dropped them off three days ago and prepaid a week's storage."

"I don't know what to tell you," the sniveling clerk said, going back to his game. Looking at his stringy black hair, thin moustache, and patchy scruff, Maisy's face began darkening to a shade of red that Zara didn't think was possible, but before she burst out, Jude shot a quick look at her and held up his hand.

"What dumb luck!" Jude said. "Do you think they were stolen?"

"Probably," he said, not even bothering to look up from the screen. "It happens all the time. I suggest you fill out a report with the Omaha PD."

"Okay, I'll do that. Do you mind if we walk around a bit just to make sure they weren't moved or misplaced by mistake?" he asked.

The clerk shrugged, glanced at Jude for two seconds, and then said, "Knock yourself out."

When they got outside, Maisy glared at Jude, while Zara hung back to watch the interaction. She resigned herself to the strategy of just waiting for Maisy to state the obvious and Jude to explain himself in some surprising way before she asked any of her own questions. Jude always had a plan, and Maisy always had to know what it was immediately. All she had to do was observe.

"Um, care to explain?" Maisy blurted out.

"Sure," Jude said in a suspiciously calm tone. "First, that rat-moustache little boy doesn't serve any purpose except to steal things he thinks he can get away with, especially if the customers are from out of town. This entire facility is self-contained with integrated cameras, locks, and payment scanners. He probably inherited it from his family, who probably owned it before the Transition. He only sits there to watch what kinds of things are being brought in and out.

"Second, we can probably find the ATVs if we follow the tracks. Our ATVs had a special hollow diamond tire tread pattern, and as you can see," he said, pointing to the tracks winding around the side of the K building, "they left us a trail to follow."

"Are we going to tell rat-moustache the gig is up or what?" Maisy asked.

"We don't want to interrupt his busy schedule," Jude joked. "My guess is that the ATVs are in that unmarked building in the back, along with a lot of other things that disappeared from people's storage units. I say we get our wheels and disappear."

"That will work, but it still doesn't satisfy my need to give that kid what he deserves," Maisy said.

"Why don't we leave that to the cops?" Jude said.

"Or the RDF," Zara chimed in. "I would love to see the look on his face when a couple of transports show up and troops bust into his office. He'll have a lot of explaining to do about his 'stockpile.' He might have to pause his game and talk to them."

"Now *that* will make me feel better," Maisy said. "Let's get our rides and get out of here."

Jude spotted the cameras near the unmarked building in the back of the lot and gently turned them out of the line of sight and onto the doors of nearby units. With the monitors in the office all reflecting a dull image of other storage unit doors, Jude and the girls followed the tracks to the back building.

The tracks disappeared beneath a large garage door that had a sliding latch and a fingerprint lock on it.

"Can you hack it?" Maisy asked.

"No, but I can cut it," Jude said, retrieving his ever-handier cutting tool. He cut through the latch, slid it out, and rolled open the door. The ATVs were haphazardly rolled in, sitting in front of a stash of television screens, transport parts, and electronics.

They quickly loaded up their packs, checked the batteries, and backed out, closing the door. Jude stopped to stealthily return the cameras to their original positions, and then the trio rode out of the front gate, waving to the cameras as they left.

Once they reached the river, Zara called in an anonymous tip to the Omaha PD, letting them know there was stolen property in a storage unit and insinuating that it may be materials used in making pipe bombs. Within two minutes, they saw an RDF transport drone descend on the "I" street storage facility.

"Alright, Zara," Maisy said as they rolled up to a riverside dock. "Where is this Max?"

"Give me a minute to get into Jaxson's computer, and I'll let you know."

"And Jude, how are we going to follow the river?" Maisy asked.

Jude sighed, looked at the river, and then looked at the map on his phone. "I have an idea."

Zara flipped open the screen and synced up Jaxon's phone. She mechanically tapped in the passcodes and, within a couple of minutes, found the information.

"Kansas City," she said. "We need to get to Kansas City, and he will give us instructions from there."

"Why can't we just call him?" Maisy asked.

"Jaxson's notes here say he will only respond to this email address, which is his most secure contact. It says Max is 'underground.' I guess that means he lives off the grid; he doesn't want the government to know where he is or what he does. That works well for us," Zara said, unconsciously rubbing the meaty part of her neck and shoulder where a passport would be implanted.

"Jude, you're up . . . " Maisy started to say, but he wasn't there. "Now, where did he wander off to?"

"Over there," Zara said, pointing to a group of people down by the river dock. "He's talking to those people with the boat."

"Oh boy," Maisy said with her now perfected eye roll. "Why do I get the sense we're not going to travel by land?"

Jude walked back up the bank with a telling smile.

"I made a deal," he said, "Our ATVs for their river raft. If we need to head downriver, we might as well use the river! This way, we can slip into Texico without worrying about scanners."

"I'd say that was a bad trade, but since my butt just recovered from our last ride, I'm not sad to see them go," Maisy said.

"Actually, that works out perfectly," Zara said, packing up the computer. "Because we need to go to Kansas City, and the river will take us right into town."

The river raft was a large, durable urethane boat with a small electric motor and enough room for six people, or three people and their gear. After loading up the raft, Jude revved the motor and launched them into the enormous lazy river, moving toward the middle and then gliding effortlessly downstream. Going with the flow of the current meant the motor wouldn't be used much, saving power and time as they slipped quietly into the Texico region and Kansas City.

"I got a message from Max," Zara said a few hours into their journey. She opened the message on Jaxson's phone. "He said he has to verify our identity with Jaxson." As they all looked at each other questioningly, the phone rang.

"Hello?" Zara said.

"Where Jaxson?" came a gravelly voice.

"Is this Max?" Zara asked.

"Who is this?"

"I'm Zara Malik. I have Jaxson's phone and his computer, which is how I got your secure email. I'm afraid Jaxson isn't with us anymore."

"What did you do?" the voice said angrily.

"He gave them to me just before the raid. He said he thought AD-AMS had tracked all his writings and finally connected them to him. He gave me his passcodes, his computer, and his phone just before the RDF showed up. He said to find you."

"How do I know who you are?" he asked.

"I'm the girl from the SAC that's been reporting on our trip across the country. I'm one of the Sparrows."

"Where are you now?"

"We're following the Missouri River south."

"Can you get over the border into Texico?"

"I think so. We're literally on the river in a raft. We can take it all the way into Kansas City if we need to."

"Good plan. Go through the city, past all the Riverboat Casinos, and east into the Independence District. You'll see signs for Liberty Bend, and there will be a park with a small dock. Meet me there tomorrow night. I'll be wearing a vintage Kansas City Royals baseball cap."

"We'll be there. Thanks."

"So now we've got a plan?" Maisy asked.

"It looks that way. I think our reputation is growing. As soon as I said I was a 'Sparrow,' it clicked for him."

"I just set out to find our brother," Jude said, paddling just enough to keep them straight. "I didn't set out to start something."

"Too late," Zara said. "People are poor and repressed. You two don't just bring compassion and talent with you; you bring hope."

"Yeah, well, you spread it," Jude said with a grin. "Now we're in this together."

After taking shifts keeping the raft heading more or less forward throughout the night, they made headway across the border into Texico in the morning, and by late evening, they floated past the large, anchored riverboat-style casinos in Kansas City. The music echoed off the water, and the pockets of laughter were punctuated by yells of drunken conversation and possibly arguing. At one point, a woman hung her head over a rail and let loose the contents of her stomach after clearly having had too much of everything.

Finally, they whirred their way out of the city, heading east. After spotting signs for Independence, they came to a large curve in the river and saw a sign that read "Liberty Bend."

"This is it," Zara said.

"I think I see the park and the dock over there," Jude said, pointing to a small floating dock anchored to a grassy area littered with trees, benches, and an aging playground. "Let's get over to the shore and wait under those weeping willows. If any LEAD units come by the park, I don't want them to have a good view."

It only took a couple of hours before dusk faded quickly into the night. The park patrons dispersed slowly, and the sun set below the horizon, igniting the lazy river into a fury of golden flickering fire. Crickets, frogs, and cicadas began their evening chorus.

"It is supposed to be October. Why is it still hot, and what is making all that noise?" Zara complained. "I can't hear myself think!"

"We're not in Cascadia anymore," Jude said. "I think the loud bugs are cicadas."

"Those are bugs?!" exclaimed Zara, jumping up from her spot on the grass. "How big are they?"

"Big enough to scare you, but small enough not to be dangerous. They're just noisy."

"Eeew!" she shivered.

Darkness brought increased caution, but it also brought relief for the thick-blooded Cascadians. Back home, they would be getting ready for the first snowfall, but here they were fighting off the temptation to take a swim. When a bouncing light came walking toward them, they tensed only momentarily until they made out the blue Royals hat in the darkness.

"Max?" Zara asked as he approached.

"Sparrows?" he responded.

"Yes, sir," Jude answered.

"You're going to have to leave the raft," he instructed. "Get your things and follow me."

Maisy started to object, but Jude had already thought it out. He knew this was the end of their river travels, and the raft wouldn't do them any good any longer. They took up their packs and jogged after their new friend.

"My name's Max, Max Simon," he said over his shoulder as they dodged brush and tree branches. It was hard to see clearly, but they could tell he was of medium height and thickly built, but not overweight. He had longer steel gray hair, but not down to his shoulders like Jude. He wore a charcoal button-down shirt, black pants, and, to Jude's surprise, black loafers.

"Thanks for meeting us," Jude said. "Jaxson was pretty insistent we find you."

"Here," Max said, pointing to a rugged, sand-colored transport with large wheels and a very wide, boxy frame.

"Is this a military transport?" Jude asked.

"It was. I got a good deal on it. Hop in."

They loaded up, and Max didn't waste any time tearing out of the brush near the park and finding an old, narrow highway long since neglected.

"Where are we headed?" Maisy asked. Jude and Zara shot her a look as if to say, "Don't ask that!"

"Like my transport, you'll see I like to recycle. Some old things can have very practical new uses with a little imagination."

It took about an hour and a half of driving on and off road, but they soon came to a large depression in the landscape, as if a meteor had decimated the area and left this solitary landmark. They came to the edge of the crater, and then Max hit the accelerator and dove over the edge. Zara let out a shriek, and Maisy froze, anchoring her white knuckles onto the door handles.

It turns out there was an actual dirt road that descended steeply into the abyss and led up to a curious set of iron doors set in a frame of concrete that looked like some kind of bunker. They looked to either side, and several sets of iron doors lined the crater in a semi-circular pattern.

Maxed pushed a button on his dashboard, and the doors began to swing open. "We're here, kids. Welcome to the Caves."

As they drove through the doors and their eyes adjusted to the interior lighting, Jude gaped at the web of passageways and pillars all around them.

"What is this place?" he asked.

"In the twentieth century, it was a limestone mine. The mining company had to foresight to mine only 75% of the minerals and leave the rest in regular pillars like you see here. When they had all they could get from this site, they sold the vacant mine to a developer who built concrete structures for warehouse space and offices. It's very convenient; the temperature remains 16°C and dry year-round. The only thing we have to monitor is ventilation. Distribution centers operated out of here for decades, but slowly abandoned the place when freight drones started replacing road freight."

Jude realized his mouth was hanging open and tried to salvage some of his dignity. He looked at Zara with wide eyes.

"Oh yeah. I'm getting this," she said, scribbling notes on her pad.

Max drove them to the front of an unassuming concrete and glass front, where they grabbed their packs and proceeded through the swinging doors into a sparse but comfortable lounge area with sofas and tables. I've got a restroom here, and a few spare rooms down the hall," Max said, pointing down the lit corridor. "And when I say spare, I mean it in every sense, but there are beds in each room, and they are better than sleeping on the ground."

"Or in a raft," Maisy said.

"Or in a shipping container or in melting snow . . . " Zara said.

"I'm glad you are so easy to please," Max said with a chuckle, the first sign of his caution melting. "Tomorrow we can swap stories over breakfast. I'm curious to know what you Sparrows have been up to."

Jude woke to the rousing smell of bacon, eggs, and coffee. Apparently, the ventilation system in the caves was working well because the smell of breakfast was marching forcefully throughout the subterranean complex. He pulled on his clothes, enjoyed using a real bathroom, splashed some water on his face, and joined Max in the lounge area that served as a dining and gathering room.

"You've got a great place down here," Jude said. "How in the world did you end up here? Does Texico have settlements outside of cities and SACs?"

"Not exactly," Max said, pouring two cups of coffee and sliding one to Jude. He nodded to the cream and sugar sitting in the middle of the table. "I was an attorney in Kansas City many years ago, working in the area of contracts, real estate, and business law. I also invested in property and developments, and I was doing well for myself, unlike the other 80% of society. Knowing what I did and who I did in Missouri, I got the early word that the developer was looking to sell these warehouses in a hurry. This place is not conducive to drone freight, so the tenants started leaving, and he knew he had to do something fast. The Transition hadn't started yet, but everyone knew something big was coming. Society was melting down faster than the ice caps, and I saw an opportunity: people would be desperate for secure shelter.

"I waited the developer out until he was on the verge of going bankrupt, and then I bought this complex from him for next to nothing. I was preparing to convert these warehouses into underground condominiums, but then the Transition happened, and everything changed. There was nothing but uncertainty: what would happen to the dollar? What would happen to rights, contracts, and legal agreements? What would happen to the courts and law enforcement?

"As soon as ADAMS recommended allowing SACs, I found a group that had the most realistic chance of succeeding. They were farmers and ranchers with land, soldiers and engineers with technical and survival skills, and a handful of professionals: teachers, lawyers, and a few doctors. I didn't plan to move out of the city, but I wanted to be part of this 'return to the basics.' I drew up a proposal, we voted, and then we formed the Ozark Sustainable Agricultural Community. We pooled our land and money, and this cave became our base of operations. Some folks still live in their houses, and I still have a place in Kansas City, but most of the rest of us live down here."

Jude was so laser-focused on the conversation, he almost jumped when he turned and saw Zara sitting behind him, scribbling notes.

"Good morning!" he said.

"Good morning," Zara said, never looking up.

"So now you know my story. What brings you kids all the way down here from Cascadia?" Max asked.

"Our dumb brother," Maisy said, wooed from her bedroom by the smell of fresh coffee. She poured her cup as one of the SAC members came in from the kitchen to announce breakfast was ready. They filled up their plates at the impressive buffet and returned to the table just before the regular group of families came filing through the kitchen in what appeared to be a regular daily routine before heading out to the fields, shops, and classrooms.

"Maybe we should start with introductions," Jude chuckled. "You know Zara Malik, our journalist in residence, and this is my sister, Maisy Kane. She is skilled in the field of medicine, and as far as I'm concerned, I'd rather see her than some academic stooge from one of the Universities that didn't know who they were shutting their doors on."

"Thanks," she said, "but don't count on me for any lab work or brain surgery. I'm basically a self-taught paramedic."

"I am Jude Kane, and we are on a long pilgrimage to Washington, D.C., to see if we can't help our brother Callum. He is a bit rash and impulsive, and after three years of CME, he is no fan of New America or any government authority. He spotted a drone flying over our SAC, Slate Creek, and decided to shoot it down. By the time I was able to get to the crash site, he was gone. We were able to figure out by the scorched earth in the area and piecing together clues from Cascadian RDF headquarters in Vancouver that he was taken by the NADF. Zara was able to get a little more information from the NADF base outside Seattle; he was taken to DC for trial. We don't know exactly where or what charges were filed, but we're figuring this out as we go."

"And on your way across the country, you're stopping in SACs and helping them with technical and medical issues. From what I've read," Max said, smiling, "you're making quite an impression."

"It turns out Slate Creek and Ozark are the exceptions to the rule," Jude explained. "Most SACs don't function as well as we do and lack much of the agricultural and technical skill it takes to keep things growing and working. I have to say, Max, I think CAMO knows it, too. I've seen evidence of their encroachment on most of the SACs we visited. If crops don't do well, they like to sweep in and claim 'the land must be cultivated to its fullest potential to provide enough food,' but then nothing is ever given back to the SACs, and they have no recourse. Have you seen this here?"

"They've tried. We had a couple of fields with weak corn crops because it was so dry, and CAMO sent a couple of drones out. As soon as we spotted them, the ranchers drove a couple of hundred head of cattle onto the fields. I did a survey and staked out our land borders along with some firmly worded trespass warnings. So far, we haven't seen them back."

"SACs used to be protected. Why do you think the government is allowing CAMO to squeeze us?" Zara asked.

"I think the government is *using* CAMO to squeeze us," Max said. "Now that the Transition has been over for ten years, the next thing they fear is people rising up and demanding the rights and ways of life they had before. The most likely place this would come from is the SACs. I think we've gone from being a 'relief valve on social services' to a threat."

"Jaxson had a theory," Jude said. "He thought it was more than that. Now that the Transition is over and things are stable, ADAMS has figured out that it is dangerous to have 80% of people out of work and not contributing to an economy that just doesn't need that many people when

AI does most of the work. He thought that ADAMS and New America might be trying to reduce the population."

"And now he's dead. I don't know if he wrote that anywhere, but if he did, I'm sure ADAMS would have connected the dots once he was identified. It would have put him on top of the threat pile," Max said. "Your help to the SACs and your platform with the Sparrow Press have put you three in an important position. The SACs need to know what is going on."

"I never wanted this," Jude said with a sigh. We set out to find our brother, not start some kind of movement."

"Maybe not, Jude," Max said, putting his hand on Jude's shoulder, "but how many more brothers will disappear if we don't come together and stand up for our lives?"

Chapter 12: **Sparrows**

AFTER SOME MUCH-NEEDED REST and a good restocking of supplies, it was time to keep moving. Max promised to work his magic with his old political connections, some of whom worked for the New America government, and see what he could find out about Callum. He also asked Jude if "The Sparrows" could pass through a struggling SAC in the southeast corner of the Lakeland Region, near the border of the Appalachia Region. In exchange, Max would give them an older personal transport vehicle to use for the trip.

"You know I'd help folks no matter what," Jude said. "I'm not asking for compensation."

"Of course," Max said. "But how else will you get there? Think of it as a loaner vehicle. Once you have your brother, just swing back through the Ozark SAC and return it. We'll figure out better transport all the way up to the nether regions of Cascadia at that time."

"I can't think of a reason to turn that offer down," Jude conceded.

"The transport is another older former military transport, but this one is smaller than the one we rode in the other day. It's one of the first electric Jeep models that were used for moving people and things around military bases. It's a bit cramped, but it has four seats and some storage, including a hidden compartment behind the back seat where you could store something, or someone, you don't want the border scanners to see."

"Perfect," Jude said, anxious to see the new wheels. "Where is it?"

"It's in the storage warehouse," Max said. "No one can figure out why it can't hold a charge. I figured if anyone could fix it, you could."

"I'll take a look," Jude said, a bit deflated.

"Tell me what you need. Whatever it is, I can get it. I have friends in Kansas City."

They dug out the old EJ150, which was originally marketed as an Electric Jeep with a 150-mile range. Of course, since the Transition, the old United States part of New America was dragged kicking and screaming into the Metric System, and 400 km, or about 250 miles, was the new standard vehicle range. Jude was hoping he could modify the vehicle and turn it into something closer to an EJ500, with the 500 being kilometers.

"The battery is shot," Jude declared in less than an hour. "I've grown up on a SAC, so I don't know what the parts availability of these things is, but it wouldn't take much to rebuild the battery. Can we get to a junkyard? The more old parts I have, the fewer things I have to fabricate by hand."

"Your wish is my command," Max said with a smile, realizing his plan to rope Jude into bringing the Jeep back to life was working perfectly. They headed off across the dirt and old, dilapidated highways to a salvage facility outside Kansas City, deep into a Cube neighborhood.

The girls didn't let the grass grow under their feet while Jude was busy. Maisy was introduced to Dr. Julian Robinson, who put her to work in the Ozark clinic. He was impressed by her tenacity and skill, having never been trained in a hands-on environment. Of course, he didn't tell her that straight out.

"Are you an RM?" he asked as she was sewing up a deep gash just above the knee of a young man who thought he could use his knee to break loose a stuck mower blade.

"No," she said, not looking up. "Evidently, I'm not University material."

"How do you know how...where did you learn to stitch like that?" he asked.

"I just do it like I learned on the screens," she said.

"You've had no hands-on training?"

"Do farm animals and a couple of emergency situations count as training?" she asked.

"It depends. Did your patients survive?"

Maisy laughed, still focused on the stitching. "Yes, I believe so."

"You know that the AMA has changed the classification of 'Physician Assistant' to 'Registered Medic,' right? Which classification were you hoping to study for?"

"Nurse first, then Medic," she said. "A Medic without real patient experience isn't worth their salt if you ask me."

"If you were a Registered Nurse, I'd say you were a little out of your league, and if you were a Registered Medic, I'd say you need to fine-tune your suturing skills."

"What do you think so far?" she asked, stepping aside.

"Hmm," he mused. "I would have used a smaller gauge suture to reduce the size of the scar, but the placement is not bad."

"I used the higher gauge because this kid is a farmer, and that gash is right in the middle of a high-movement area. This wound is going to endure some pulling and stretching while it heals. I'd hate for a small thread to pull out."

"I'm sure it will be fine," he said, trying not to concede her point but realizing she made the right call. "If we get any more wounds that need stitches, please let me take a look before you tie them off."

"Sure thing," she said.

Zara took her chance to put Jaxson's advice to use. If they were going to start spreading the word to the SACs about standing up to government oppression, the big guns would swing around and stare them in the face very quickly. Zara thought about Callum, and then she thought about her father. The crushing burden of the SAC on top of her mother's death drove him quite literally into the ground.

If SACs were so hard to survive in, then why did people live in them? What motivated them to give up housing, food, and medical care to live in the woods and fields and eke out a living as if they went back in time several hundred years? The answer: being human.

Zara knew it was time for the Sparrows to give voice to their purpose, and she wrote a simple manifesto that was featured in the first official edition of the Sparrow Press:

People need to know their lives have value, whether or not they have some sought-after skill, money, or talent. They need to be treated equally, regardless of any status or condition. They need to be treated with dignity just because they are human beings.

With AI replacing most jobs and the majority of people relegated to subsisting on government housing, food, and medical care, we can easily survive, but we aren't truly living. When people are thought to have less value than other people, then equality is a slippery, elusive dream. When equality gives way to a new social hierarchy that lowers the status of the unemployed, then the dignity that comes with a life of work and purpose vanishes just as quickly.

Without value, there is no equality, and without equality, there is no dignity. We must work to ensure all people are treated with value, equality, and dignity. These must be our values as New Americans. These must be our values as human beings.

The foundation was laid. From now on, CAMO encroachment, unfounded arrests, punishment without due process, and suppression of speech would earn a relentless barrage of criticism and a call for the restoration of the rights everyone lost when the Constitution was suspended at the beginning of the Transition. The Sparrow Press was no national force, but it gave voice to a national discontent brewing for the past ten years, and it was growing stronger with the new generation. Now, if only Zara could help Jude unlock the lion within. He was a true leader, but he was hesitant. She couldn't blame him; they were about to put all three of their heads on the chopping block.

Jude and Max returned with a cache of junk that made Jude as giddy as a kid with his first science set. It took him only a few hours to use the parts and supplies to create a battery that dwarfed the power of the original EJ150, and he affectionately renamed it "The Sparrow Wagon." He couldn't be sure until they hit the road in the real world, but he was confident they could get 500 km out of it with a full charge. The bigger battery was heavier, but over the next couple of days, he was also able to replace the All-Wheel Drive with a simple, lighter rear-drive axle, add a solar panel to the hood, and add later-model regenerative brakes to slow down the rate of discharge.

"Thanks for your help, Jude," Max said somberly as they loaded up the Wagon.

"I didn't do anything," he said. "We're the ones going to enjoy this thing, at least for a few weeks."

"I don't mean the Jeep," Max said. "The Chillicothe SAC could really use your help. I hope they don't hold you up too long, but without a major improvement in crops and infrastructure, they could collapse. If CAMO is circling them like we've seen, it will be sooner rather than later."

"We'll do everything we can," he promised.

"Me too," Max said. "When and if I find anything out about Callum, I'll let Zara know."

They shook hands firmly, but the girls dropped the pretense and gave him affectionate hugs as if they were saying goodbye to a favorite old uncle. With the Sparrow Wagon loaded and charged, they headed east for the Lakeland Region border. Zara wasn't happy about squishing herself into the hidden box, but Jude promised not to lock or latch it, and after only about half an hour, they were safely past the scanners, and she was able to re-emerge and reclaim her seat. As a consolation, Jude and Maisy gave her the entire back seat to stretch out in for the rest of the trip.

Unlike Cascadia, Dakota, and especially Yukon, the cities were much closer together in Lakeland. They drove through several Amish and Mennonite SACs along the southern border of Lakeland in what used to be the state of Indiana, and then past Cincinnati, along the Ohio River, and then north to the Chillicothe SAC, nestled in old farmland between the Ohio River and Columbus.

They enjoyed smoother roads in the country, and as they were driving the last few hours to the SAC, Zara tried to poke the lion.

"I didn't call out the government, at least not yet, but I felt like we needed to put our actions into words," she said.

"It's not like I disagree, Zara. I love what you wrote, and people need to hear that, especially in the struggling SACs. It's just that . . . " he trailed off.

"It's just what?" Zara asked.

"I'm no revolutionary leader. I'm just trying to get my brother back and help a few people along the way. I'm no messiah."

"You give people hope, Jude."

"I fix wind turbines and solar panels and show people how to grow better crops. I'm not a savior."

"You're a savior to every person you help. It's not about picking up a gun, Jude. That's not what we're about at all. It's about helping people and standing up for what is right. You serve people because you are a genuine, good man. It also helps you have a borderline addiction to solving problems and fixing things."

Jude chuckled and smiled at Zara. "So, what are we even doing here? What are the Sparrows?"

Maisy felt compelled to jump in. "We're some kids trying to get our brother back, helping people along the way, and giving people a voice they thought was silenced in the Transition."

"We're showing people their lives are still important," Zara added. "You're not just fixing things; you're giving them hope. It's your humility, your sense of justice, and your intelligence that make you the leader you haven't realized you are yet. And by the way, those are also some of the qualities that have caused me to fall in love with you."

Jude looked back at Zara, his eyes wide, trying to keep his eyes on the road and fumble a response, and utterly failing. Maisy crossed her arms and sat back, smiling, watching Jude turn three shades of red.

"I'm sorry," Zara said. "I kind of blind-sided you with that one. I meant what I said, but feel free to wait until you've had a chance to get your head together to come up with your brilliant response."

"It's just that...I . . . well . . . " he stumbled.

"Cat got your tongue?" teased Maisy. "Good grief, Jude. Just say it! You love her too. It's so obvious it's embarrassing."

"I do!" he interjected. "I can't even imagine my life without you in it," he said to Zara, staring at her in the rearview mirror. "I just don't know how to say it properly."

"You just did," Zara said with a wide, satisfied grin.

The Sparrow Wagon left the road, and following the GPS coordinates Max gave him, Jude drove down a narrow dirt path between two fields strewn with the remnants of a corn crop. The hills were dotted with rusty, still wind turbines, and they spotted two groups of solar panels overgrown with vines and weeds.

"Dear God," Jude sighed. "Max wasn't kidding."

"This place is worse than Squamish River," Zara said.

Jude looked at Maisy, and Maisy looked at Zara.

"We're going to need to give them at least a week or two. They won't make it through winter without our help."

"I don't think Callum is going anywhere," Maisy said.

"After posting my manifesto on Sparrow Press, it wouldn't hurt to lay low for a bit," Zara said.

Jude stopped at a sign posted at the corner of a field:

"Notice: unused, underused, and misused land may be subject to mandatory development by Consolidated Agriculture and Mining, Inc. (CAMO) under the Necessary Land Use Act." Jude clenched his fists around the steering wheel and looked back at Zara.

"That wasn't your manifesto. It was ours."

Chapter 13: **Eviction**

JUDE SOON REALIZED THEY were driving into the center of a circle. As the dirt road rose over a rolling hill, the houses and barns came into view. Given the sickly scraps of corn and the condition of the power grid, they were shocked to find large, well-built farmhouses and large, sturdy barns. The structures looked very well-maintained, and the landscaping was immaculate with lush, green grass, weed-free flower beds, and perfectly manicured vegetable gardens.

They were greeted by a stout, dark-haired man with a full, neat beard, black jeans, and white t-shirt, dirt-caked work boots, and a broad smile.

"I'm Jacob Miller," he said, extending his hand as Jude stopped the vehicle under a large oak tree. Jude got out and shook his hand.

"I'm Jude Kane, this is my sister Maisy, and this is Zara Malik," he said, introducing the girls as they emerged.

"Are you the Sparrows?" he asked with wide eyes.

"That's what they call us," Zara said, taking her place confidently next to Jude.

"Max said you would come, but I wouldn't believe it until I saw you myself. Thank you! Please, come inside."

They all went inside, followed by a trail of a few older women and a litany of young children. They sat at a large oak dining table, and the women began bringing tea, water, and biscuits.

"This is my wife, Marla," he said, pointing to a sturdy but demure, blond woman wearing a headscarf, a jean skirt, and a striped t-shirt who was taking the last batch of cookies out of the oven.

"Give these ten minutes to cool down and they'll be fair game," she said with a warm smile. She took a seat at the table while the rest of the brood scattered, but not necessarily out of listening range.

"Did Max tell you we're on our way to Washington, D.C.?" Jude asked.

"He said your brother was arrested, and you are going to try and plead his case," Jacob said.

"There is a lot we don't know, but one thing we do know is that it is unacceptable, especially now in peacetime, for the government to arrest someone and take him away without letting him contact someone. What is his charge? Will there be a trial? Where is his attorney? We're going to find these things out."

"These are basic rights," Jacob agreed.

"It's a long journey from northern Cascadia to Washington, DC, so we have had a chance to meet quite a few people. It turns out a lot of SACs have fallen into hard times with shrinking crop yields, failing infrastructure, and shrinking resources. We've been doing what we can to help with these things as we go," Jude said modestly.

"We appreciate your help," Jacob said. "As you probably noticed, we didn't have as big a crop this year because the tractors were dead, and the tractors are dead because we have no power."

"No power? How did you grow anything?" Jude asked.

"The same way our families have done it for centuries," Jacob said with a smile. "Horses and back muscles. Most of us living here in Chillicothe were Amish, Mennonite, or married in at some point, but we left the community. After the Transition, our families decided to come together and use a combination of Amish traditions and modern technology to create our SAC. It was perfect, except that after paying for solar panels and wind turbines, we didn't know how to keep them up. We're farmers and carpenters, not engineers. When the power finally went out last winter, we had to completely revert to the old ways of farming and living. Fortunately, some of us have relatives who haven't shunned us completely, and we got some help with the fields, barns, and a few animals to start breeding."

"That would explain the beautiful homes and apocalyptic-looking fields," Jude said. "Luckily, we can help. I am an engineer."

"We can't thank you enough," Jacob said. "We were raised with horses and hand plows, but that limits how much land we can work, and as you might have seen, CAMO is threatening to take over some of our land. We need power for the tractors, and it would be nice not to have to pedal a generator for the kids to go to school on the screens."

"It's not just you," Jude explained. "CAMO is knocking on everyone's door. We think they are trying to intimidate the SACs into giving up land, and we fear that is part of a bigger plan by the New American Government to squeeze us out."

"Squeeze us out of the SACs?" Jacob asked. "Why? We're not a burden. That's why ADAMS recommended we be given legal status."

"It might be that CAMO just wants more land, especially here between Cincinnati and Columbus. I also think it has to do with ADAMS realizing there are too many people who can't contribute to the economy. It could be they are trying to speed up the natural attrition of the population. SACs are harder to control, so if you can push them into the cities, then you have everyone in one place. People who are poor, crowded, and miserable and have easy access to birth control are less likely to have children."

"Dear God," Jacob sighed, reaching over and taking Marla's hand.

"Don't give up just yet," Jude encouraged him. "Let's get some power flowing again and work every square meter of land so they don't have an excuse to try and take it over. Once the tractors have juice, I'd go ahead and turn over all the fields before winter, just so the CAMO drones can see you have no intention of letting them near your land."

The next morning, Jude and Jacob were up early. Jude was getting ready to train a small army of homegrown technicians, and Jacob was assembling the volunteers.

"I can get every wind turbine and every solar panel up and the entire power grid humming like a kitten," Jude announced to the twenty young men and women who gathered on hay bales in the central barn. "But I am not going to touch a thing. I'm going to show you how easy it is, and you all are going to do it."

Smiles and murmurs fluttered through the group.

"Jacob has a group heading out in front of us to clear the brush so we can get to the turbines and panels. While they are working, I'll show you how to clean terminals, splice wires of different gauges, and use a tester to see how much current is flowing. If you can do these three things well, you know 80% of what it takes to keep the power flowing," Jude said as he gathered some wire, connectors, and tools on a rickety wooden table in front of him. "The first thing we're going to do is strip wire. It's all downhill from there."

As he handed out wire and cutters, he felt a nudge at his side. "Don't mind me," Zara said. "I'm just observing."

"Why don't you get some wire and a pair of cutters and jump in?" he said.

"Why not?" she said, taking a pair of cutters and snipping off a length of wire.

"Work it gently," he said. "I'm assuming they won't have wire strippers, so I'm teaching them to strip the wire with cutters manually. Be careful or you'll . . . "

"Cut the wire off?" she said, holding up the ragged end with strands of copper wire dangling.

"Snip it clean and try again," he said. "A little more gently this time."

She worked the cutters around the plastic coating, gingerly pressing and turning, and finally pulling the coating off, revealing the shiny copper threads beneath. "I did it!" she exclaimed, and then looked around, realizing she was louder than she thought.

"Me too!" came a reply. A young man held up his stripped wire proudly.

Next came wire splicing, where Jude showed them how to slip connectors over spliced wires and melt them together with mini-torches or cigarette lighters if that's all they had.

"Electrical tape is handy, but if that's all that covers a connection, it's a weak spot. If that weak spot is in the back of a turbine fifty feet in the air, you're not going to want to climb up there in zero degree weather to fix it. If you do it right the first time, then you will save yourself a world of trouble later."

"You're a great teacher," Zara said, sliding a connector over her section of twisted copper wires.

"I sound just like my dad," he laughed. "I can hear him now: 'Do it right the first time! Don't be lazy or you'll work harder later!' It drove me crazy, but he was right."

"I was thinking," Zara began, looking at him sheepishly, "that maybe we could go get some coffee or something."

"Are you asking me out on a date?" he said, smiling.

"Maybe," she said.

"Then I accept," he said. "I warn you: I've never been on a date. I have no idea what I'm doing."

"I don't either. It's not like Squamish River was the center of the known universe. I don't even have a passport, so technically I'm not even a real person."

"You're the most real person I know," he said, kissing her gently on her head. "You just haven't volunteered to tell ADAMS where you are all the time. As far as I'm concerned, it's none of his business."

They both laughed, but it was soon interrupted by shouting outside the barn. They all ran outside to see a large, ten-person New America Defense Force drone descending into the center of the circle of houses. Jacob came running to the front of the crowd, which instinctively moved back, offering up Jude and Jacob to speak for the SAC. They looked at each other for a second and then focused on the commander approaching them with two soldiers behind him. No doubt there were at least four more still in the transport.

"Welcome to the Chillicothe SAC," Jacob said. "What can I do for you, commander?"

"It doesn't look like you had much of a crop this year," he said.

"Corn takes a lot out of the soil. We let several fields lie fallow," he replied.

"I see," the commander said, letting slip a flicker of irritation that his initial intimidation tactic didn't work. "I've come on behalf of the New America Defense Forces to serve you notice that the Chillicothe SAC has exceeded its maximum allowable population of two hundred and fifty people. You have thirty days to vacate this land. If you choose to relocate to a city in Lakeland, your files have already been marked by the Department of Human Services. You do not need to apply; your eligible services will be expedited."

"Vacate?" Jacob said, stunned. "This is our life! You can't just. . ."

"Excuse me, just a moment, commander," Jude said, interrupting and taking Jacob by the arm. They stepped back and spoke in a hushed tone.

"How many people are really here?" he asked Jacob.

"A little over three hundred."

"How many families could visit their relatives in the Amish and Mennonite SACs?"

"Most of us, I suppose. Many of us are shunned, though."

"What if a dozen or so families went east to visit their families in Lakeland, even if they were shunned and had to come back a couple of days later? Is that possible?"

"I suppose."

"Good."

They turned back to the commander, and Jude spoke up.

"Sorry about that, commander," Jude said. "They haven't counted heads in a while, so we had to do some calculations. There have been well over three hundred people who have come into the Chillicothe SAC, but they have also had quite a few folks rejoin their families in the Amish and Mennonite SACs. I believe the current population is at about 170 people."

"That's not what our information shows," the commander said firmly.

"Well, I'm sure we can clear up the discrepancy. Out here, when people move from one SAC to another, they don't pass by scanners, so the system often has outdated location information," Jude said with an even, confident tone. "If you return with scanners, we can make sure everyone is out of the fields so you can do a head count. It would give you an accurate, up-to-date census of the Chillicothe SAC."

The commander was deflated. He knew his orders, but Jude made too much sense to logically argue with him. How could this SAC kid know so much about passports, scanners, and tracking people?

"I'll give your proposal to my superiors. Expect us to return within the week, and when we do, be ready," he barked.

"Yes, sir. We can have everybody assembled within a couple of hours," Jacob said, trying to seal the deal with a unified front.

The commander returned to the drone and flew off, leaving the people stunned. "What's our next move?" Jacob asked Jude.

"Let's keep our technicians here to get the power back on. Anyone else who has family in Lakeland that they can go to should leave right away. No one should cross any borders or use any trains; the scanners would pick that up, and our story would be blown," Jude said, now addressing the group that had gathered in the circle. "Plan to stay a week or so. After the NADF comes back with their scanners and does their census, Jacob will send word, and you can return."

"We don't have time to waste," Jacob echoed. "Before you leave, give me your contact information so I can let you know when it's safe to come back. Let's go!"

The group scattered, frantically calling and emailing the family they could. The people with the closest families left first, many of them taking the horses they borrowed with them. Others used the ATVs that were used for managing the crops, others had family come get them in personal transport vehicles, and some left in traditional horses and buggies.

Three days later, as Jude was supervising the repair teams in the fields, the distinctive, shrill cry of the bullhorn siren echoed across the rolling hills, and everyone froze.

"That's Jacob," Jude said to his team. "They're here."

The teams scrambled down from wind turbines and out from underneath solar panels and made their way to the circle. Seconds after the alarm, the unmistakable roar of NADF transports grew louder until they touched down near enough to the houses that they shook on their foundations. The commander brought three teams with him this time.

"Good morning, commander," Jacob said as he approached.

"Is everyone assembled?" the commander asked.

"We have a few stranglers coming in from the fields, but they'll be here in a couple of minutes."

"Set up over there," the commander ordered, pointing to a gravel area near the big oak tree. "Line up your people. They'll march through the scanner one at a time. While they're being counted, my troops will spread out and make sure none of your 'stragglers' need help in making their way to the scanner."

The operation proceeded with military efficiency. A large, yellow box, open at either end, was erected and powered up. Screens were pulled out, covers opened, and keyboards appeared. Troops corralled the crowd behind the scanner, and when the light turned green, they marched each person through, directing them to a separate area on the other side. Another group of eight troops poured from one of the transports on electric motorcycles and fanned out across the fields.

Jude and two of his crew were walking across the corn fields when they were met by the first motorcycle.

"Where are the others?" the soldier demanded after lifting the visor on his helmet.

"We've got two crews over there at the solar panels," he said, pointing north, "and two more at wind turbines there and there," he said, pointing northeast and due east. "They're on their way."

The soldier nodded and then tore off towards the solar panels to verify the story and ensure everyone was counted. As Jude and his team neared the barn, he saw the scanner and his heart stopped.

"Zara!"

He took out his phone and sent a message to Jaxson's old phone. Zara hadn't had it long, and he was praying she kept it with her.

"Meet me in the barn," he typed just before breaking into a run.

He didn't hear a response on his phone, but he would check once he got to the barn. The SAC was crawling with troops, and they only had a small window of time to figure out how to hide her before the motorcycles returned. If they were being this thorough, they were probably going to sweep the houses, too.

He slid open a side door, but the cows were right there in the pen, and he didn't want them to start bellowing. He ran around the back, slipped through the large door, and pulled it closed behind him. He checked his phone, no response. He sighed and pounded his fist on a bale of hay. How could he be so careless? Why didn't he think of a plan for her the minute the NADF left last time?

He took out his phone and sent another text, this time to Maisy.

"Where's Zara? Get her to the barn if possible."

He waited, panting and peering out a window. The line was moving methodically, and the others from the field were joining the group. No response from Maisy. Jude waited a few more minutes until his absence would be conspicuous, and he decided to take his turn through the scanner and then find Zara.

He walked casually to the line, finding Maisy and standing next to her. "Did you get my message?" he whispered.

"No. We turned our phones off and hid them."

"Where's Zara?"

"Safe."

Puzzled, he decided to trust his sister and make his way through the scanner.

"Cascadia?" the RDF soldier said as Maisy passed through the scanner. "What are you doing in Lakeland?"

"I don't live here. I'm on vacation with my brother, and we were just passing through."

"Where's your brother?" the soldier asked.

"Right here," Jude said, stepping through the scanner.

"I thought you were the one talking to the commander about the population here," the soldier said suspiciously. "Why did you present yourself as a leader?"

Jude had to think on his feet. "I'm a SAC consultant. I travel the country and advise SACs on maximizing crop yields, repairing and maintaining power infrastructure, and construction. Maisy here tags along, but her vacation has turned into a lot of work. She helps with basic medical care and education. We're very busy."

"I imagine you are," the soldier said. "I see your movement in Vancouver and from Seattle to Twin Falls on the SEMIC train, and I see here you just crossed into Lakeland a few days ago. How'd you get all the way to Lakeland without passing through the border scanners in Dakota and Texico?"

"SACs are remote, especially in the west. We have to travel over rough terrain, and we don't often pass through official border crossings," he explained.

"I see," the soldier said, and then waved them on.

They joined the growing crowd of scanned people just as the motorcycles returned, escorting the remaining work crews. They joined the line as the soldiers stored their motorcycles in the transport, and within minutes, the NADF finished scanning everyone.

The motorcycle troops, now sporting military caps and hand scanners that resembled cattle prods, lined up for orders from the commander.

"Search the houses and any other structures," he said.

They snapped into action. Kicking in doors, slamming drawers, and knocking over lamps, they made it clear that their mission was as much about intimidation as it was a census.

Jacob and the SAC members let out muted shrieks, cries, and sobs as the soldiers ransacked their homes, tearing through every level and every room. Jude squeezed Maisy's arm, and she looked up at him, knowing exactly what he was thinking. "It's fine," she mouthed to him. "It will be fine."

After an excruciating thirty minutes, the troops returned to their commander and made their report: "No other persons, weapons, or contraband were found, sir."

"So that was the reason for the big scanner," thought Jude. They weren't just counting heads; they were looking for any reason they could to delegitimize the SAC. Finding guns would make it easy.

"What's the final headcount, sergeant?" the commander asked.

"One hundred seventy-seven, sir," she replied.

The commander sauntered up to Jacob and looked at him incredulously. "It appears you've had a bit of an exodus," he said. "I'll make my report. Pack it up!"

At his word, the NADF powered down the scanner, gathered their gear, and retreated to the transports. Within twenty minutes, the transports lifted off and were gone.

"I can't t-thank you enough," Jacob said to Jude, shaking his hand. He was still trembling, but his smile was genuine. "If it weren't for the Sparrows, we wouldn't be here."

"I'm just glad we were here," he said. "Speaking of being here, where's Zara?" he asked Maisy.

"Come with me. I need your muscle."

They ran to the back side of the barn, and Maisy led him into a small shed just beyond that. Together they ducked inside, lifted the cover off a well, and shone a light down into the shaft.

"Are you okay?" Jude called down.

"That was absolutely the worst game of hide and seek I've ever played," Zara called back among the sloshing and dripping of water. "And I have to pee like crazy."

Jude chuckled in relief. "Need me to pull you up?"

"I've got it," she said, gripping the rope and stepping up the smooth cement sides of the well. "This thing is only about ten meters deep. They have a shallow water table here."

Jude and Maisy pulled her over the edge and helped her to her feet.

"Thanks, Maisy," Jude said. "I can't believe I didn't think of a plan before they got here. I'm so sorry, Zara."

"You were a little busy trying to save an entire SAC. I'm fine," Zara said, laying her head on his chest. "Besides, Maisy's got my back, too."

"That's right. The girls have to look out for each other in this operation," she said.

"What happened? Are they gone for good?" Zara asked.

"It looks that way. The final head count was 177. They couldn't find any other reason to shut it down, so they hit the road. It looks like the SAC is safe for now."

"You did it!" Zara said.

"*We* did it," Jude reiterated, hugging Zara and patting Maisy on the back. "I believe there is a bit of a clean-up party going on right now, and it sounds like there is more party happening than clean-up," Jude said. "I guess the Sparrows better make an appearance."

Chapter 14: **Leaving Egypt**

"WITH NO MORE PEOPLE to scan, no more laws to invoke, and no more reason to stay, the New America Defense Force packed up their troops and their gear and flew off over the beautiful rolling hills of the Chillicothe Sustainable Agricultural Community."

Zara wrapped up her story, ran it through the grammar check, and proceeded to post it in the latest edition of the *Sparrow Press*. Jude said they had about two more days of work to go to get the power grid up and running again, and after that, Zara figured they would move on to Appalachia and make their way to Washington, D.C. She heard her phone buzz at the arrival of an email, and her heart leaped when she saw who it was from. She hadn't heard from Akal since he left Squamish River for the New America Defense Forces.

"Should I send out the word for the other families to come home?" Jacob asked Jude when he came into the main house. Zara was only paying partial attention from her place in the workroom as she read the email.

"I'm not sure. My gut says we need to tread lightly. We managed to rebuff the NADF. We were simply standing up for our legitimate rights, but they may not see that. The Transition is still fresh for some officials, and they could be watching the area now. If they detect a lot of movement . . ."

"Then they'll be back, and it will be game over," concluded Jacob.

"Maybe have one family move at a time," Jude suggested.

"Maybe not," Zara said, appearing suddenly in the doorway from the workroom.

"What?" Jacob asked.

"What?" echoed Jude with a look of dread.

"I got an email from Akal, my brother who is in the NADF," she explained to Jacob. "He said he has been following the Sparrow Press when he can get to a civilian computer. He's in a café off base now. He said the military never gives them official word, but unofficial word has come down the ranks: COATS is being deployed."

"Oh God help us," Jude said, collapsing onto a chair at the dining room table. "We poked the bear."

"I am lost," confessed Jacob. "And I hate to be a stooge, but despite our use of technology, we do try not to take the Lord's name in vain."

"It was not in vain, my friend," Jude said. "We need God's help on this one."

"I don't understand. What is COATS?"

"Critical Operations And Tactical Service," explained Jude. "They are the elite fighting force in the NADF, trained for sensitive missions in unfriendly foreign territories. They specialize in getting in, getting the job done, and getting out before anyone wakes up."

"Why would they come here?" Jacob asked. We're certainly no military threat."

"We defended ourselves peacefully and legally. That is a much bigger threat than violent resistance. Resistance can be vilified for being violent and put down quickly with no backlash from citizens or politicians. Peaceful, legal resistance can be infectious, and that is exactly what the New America government fears most," Jude said. "If COATS is being deployed, then they want to make their point quietly. One day, a SAC is making a successful defense, and a few days later, it no longer exists. The government gets the land it wants, puts down resistance quickly, and instills a fresh dose of fear in the hearts and minds of the next generation coming up. Control is maintained, the public knows nothing of the operation, and CAMO shows up next Spring with plows and planters."

"Akal says he can't confirm they are coming to Chillicothe, but he said the buzz has been pretty consistent that this is a domestic mission not far from Washington D.C.," Zara said.

His pulse quickening, his face flushed, and his heart racing, Jacob gripped the back of the kitchen chair to steady himself. Once again, he looked into Jude's eyes with pleading and uttered the words, "What do we do now?"

Jude shifted into problem-solving mode. Zara recognized the tunnel vision look he got in his eye, and she knew a plan was about to form.

She was happy to hold on for the ride, but Maisy would need to know the details.

"Have Marla gather the other SAC leaders. Zara, can you please help Marla and get my sister while you're at it?" Jude asked.

"I'm on it," Zara said, disappearing in a flash out the front door and across the yard to the barn where Maisy had set up a makeshift vaccination and pediatric check-up clinic.

"What's up, Zara?" Maisy said, looking up briefly while attempting to hide the needle from her next booster shot victim. "What's that cow's name?" she said to the terrified five-year-old girl in her dark blue dress and white bonnet, struggling to contain her wispy blond locks. Distracted by the question, Maisy slipped in the needle, depressed the plunger, and pulled it out before the girl could give her an answer.

"Betsy," she said, and then looked at Maisy in wonder. "All done?"

"All done. You did very well."

"Yay! Mommy, that didn't even hurt!" she said, scampering to her mother. The desire to vaccinate their children was one of the major factors luring many of the former Amish and Mennonite faithful to the SAC. Vaccination in traditional Amish communities was still resisted and feared.

"Maisy, can you take a break?" Zara asked.

"I'm a little busy," she said, looking for her next patient.

"We have a situation."

"What kind of a situation?" Maisy asked, finally giving Zara her attention.

"The kind of situation where your brother is coming up with a plan to save the lives of everyone in this SAC."

"I thought he just did that."

"He did, but now we've got big guns coming. Literally. COATS is on its way."

"Here? How could that happen?"

"Akal gave me a heads up. We need to move fast."

"Yeah, we do," she said, finally turning deadly serious. "Mothers, we've got a meeting in the house."

"Marla, you will want to bring some of the women," Zara said, addressing Jacob's wife.

"The men are the leaders. I don't know if they want us interfering," she said, nervously folding her arms over her stomach and straightening her skirt.

"The men are going to need you now more than ever," Zara said. "Let's go." They weren't accustomed to having a choice, and in this case, Zara didn't give them one.

The crowd of husbands, wives, and family leaders assembled in the living room of the main house, where Jacob and Jude stood in front of the stone hearth. The tension in the air was thick, and Jacob wasn't holding up well. Jude instinctively looked to Maisy, who ran and got him a chair and a glass of water. "Relax. Let Jude give them the bad news, and then you can fill in the blanks. We've got your back."

"Thanks," he said, wiping his ashen brow. Marla deftly sauntered up behind him and took a seat on the hearth behind him and put a hand on his shoulder. He took her hand in his and held it tightly.

"Folks, just a few days ago, we stood up to the NADF and their attempt to take away your land. It was brazen. We all know this is valuable, fertile land between Cincinnati and Columbus, and CAMO would want nothing more than to roll their combines over these hills. You were brave, steady, and should be proud."

There was a muted murmur of ascent, but they were always cautious not to cross over into the vanity of pride.

"Unfortunately, I have some bad news," he said. The room fell deathly silent. "We have received word from one of our sources inside the NADF, the New America Defense Forces, that they plan to deploy COATS. There is only one reason to deploy the world's most elite fighting force: secrecy. They want to accomplish their mission quickly and quietly, where the regular NADF failed publicly."

"What does that mean?" one of the men asked. He was a large, burly man with the traditional black pants and shoes, suspenders, and a buttoned long-sleeve shirt. His curly red beard extended down from under his brimmed straw hat, past his hairless upper lip, and down from his chin to his chest.

"It means they will take this land. They may resettle you, force you into the cities, or worse. I don't want to terrify you, but I have seen what the NADF can do. I can't imagine what COATS would do in the cover of secrecy."

"Do we know these troops are coming for sure?" the burly man asked.

"No. Honestly, I only have confirmation that they are deploying domestically, not far from Washington, D.C.. They may not be coming at all," Jude admitted. "If they are coming, however, they'll be here before you see them coming, and they'll execute their plan before you know they arrived. Do you want to wait for them to come to your door in the middle of the night? Do you want to hope on the lives of your wives and children that they will let you leave together? That they let you live at all?"

The murmurs grew tense, with husbands and wives exchanging glances, words, denials, and resignations. Jude could sense they were still trying to grasp the impending flood.

"I am not your leader, but I am your friend. I advise you all to pack what you can carry and find your way to any other community where you have family or some connection. When my brother disappeared, all that was left was a patch of blackened earth. I'm afraid that's all that may be left of Chillicothe in about three days."

A wave of resistance began to swell in the room, but Jacob stood and raised his hand, quieting the group.

"My brothers and sisters, it is no easy or pleasant thing to hear all you have and all you hold dear is about to be ripped from your tired arms. It is natural to resist this terrifying reality. Unfortunately, it can also be deadly. I'm afraid our grand experiment, our ten-year Rumspringa, has come to an end. We must now choose: do we join the English in the cities, or do we return to our extended families and traditions? We don't have the luxury of living between any longer, enjoying the life of tradition and the life of convenience. It is time to make a choice, but know this: remaining in the Chillicothe SAC is not one of those choices. We must leave, and we must leave now. The troops could be at our doors tonight!"

With that word, the burly man sighed deeply, tipped his hat, and took his wife's arm. "Come, Sarah. Let's gather the children and pack the wagon. It appears we are fleeing like the children of Israel fled Egypt." After his exit, each man followed suit in somber capitulation.

Most families chose to return to communities where they had some kind of parents or relatives, hoping to find them accepting. Some of the older children and young adults were less inclined to return to farming without tractors, cooking without refrigerators or electric ovens, or houses without screens. A few opted to emigrate to Cincinnati or Columbus, including some of Jude's repair crew who developed a taste for technical work. In the cities, they could get more training and a vocational certificate. If they were extremely lucky, they might even get a paying job.

With the migration well underway, Jude, Zara, and Maisy packed up the Sparrow Wagon.

"Hurry up!" Maisy called out to Jude. "I don't want to be the last ones out of here, and I definitely don't want a front seat to see COATS in action."

"Give me a minute," Jude said, adjusting the angle on a small 360° camera he was mounting on the well house where Zara hid during the first incursion.

"Is that a camera?" Zara asked. "What is it going to pick up behind the barn here?"

"COATS won't use the front door," Jude reasoned. "And when they do come, this little well house is the safest structure. They won't want to damage the water supply and the pump. Whatever happens, maybe we can see at least part of it."

"Good idea," Zara said. "Exclusive footage, proof of violation of a SAC, proof of no resistance . . . "

"Proof of the real story, which is exactly what the government doesn't want."

Jude pushed a button, pulled out his phone, and opened the screen. A dancing, clear image bounced up on his phone, and a small mirror on the world around them opened up. "Now this is what I call a newsfeed."

Finally packed up, they bounded down the dirt path, through the bare fields, and headed west.

"Where are we going?" Maisy asked. "I thought Washington, D.C., was east?"

"It is," Jude said, glancing at Maisy. "But I think now would be a great time for us to lie low and see what happens to Chillicothe first. It won't do us any good to show up in the capital, grasping at straws. We need to stay out of sight and make a plan, and the best place to do that is . . . "

"Back at Ozark with Max," Maisy said, finishing his thought.

"I know you're anxious to get to Callum, Maisy. I am too. It's just that . . . ," Jude tried to reason.

"I get it," she interrupted. "It won't do us any good to show up empty-handed. We've come this far; we need a plan. Max is a lawyer, so maybe he can help us."

"You wouldn't mind spending a little more time with Dr. Julian Robinson, either," Zara chimed in from the back.

"Maybe," Maisy said coyly.

After three days, Jude began to second-guess his decision to have Jacob evacuate the Chillicothe SAC. The only thing his inconspicuous camera picked up was the gentle breeze and tumbling scraps of dried corn shuck pieces. By the early morning of day four, however, his instincts proved lethally true.

As soon as sounds started streaming through his phone, he threw back his blanket, pulled back his hair, and ran out to the "operation center," which was Max's office in the underground warehouse that felt in every way much more like a bunker now. He flipped on several screens and synced his phone feed with them for a better view. He turned his phone around, scanning in all directions, but nothing was in sight yet.

"What do we have?" Max asked, stumbling in with disheveled hair, crooked glasses, a poorly tied bathrobe, and slippers.

"Sounds like transports to me," Jude said. "It's still pretty dark."

"At that volume, we should be able to see them," Max said.

Jude continued to turn his phone, scanning the area.

"What are they doing?" Jude said, shaking his head. "This isn't good."

"What is it?" Max asked.

"SAC residents. Four of them."

"Why are they there? I thought you evacuated the place!"

"We did, and we were the last ones out. They must have gone back for some of their things. I think I recognize them; they are some of the younger ones who worked with me on the wind turbines. It looks like they're trying to salvage some of the things they had to leave behind. They're worming through the houses around the circle, carrying small packs. I'm guessing they're sweeping for heirlooms and valuables that didn't make it in the evacuation."

"If we heard transports, COATS is already there," Max said.

"There, on the other side of the barn," Jude said, pointing to a corner of the screen. "Did you see that?"

"That's a small transport," Max said. "What are they doing?"

"I'm not sure," Jude said, squinting at the screen and wishing he hadn't put the camera right behind the barn. They watched as what looked like four COATS operatives, cloaked in black and moving silently, zipped from structure to structure, communicating with hand signals and disappearing into and out of houses, sheds, and finally the barn. It wasn't until they met up in the barn that Jude finally saw their objective: working from the outer fields in, leave nothing standing.

The four Chillicothe refugees tried to hide behind the barn, where Jude resisted the temptation to yell into the screens, "Run! Run!" It didn't matter; they were accosted within minutes. The dialog was difficult to hear clearly, but even in the dark, the scene was obvious. The COATS operatives lined them up against the barn, holding them at gunpoint. Jude could see the terror in their eyes as they pleaded for their lives under the spotlights, trying to explain they had evacuated and were only returning for trinkets. One of them covered his face and stood silent, trembling as a growing dark streak crawled down his khaki pant leg. The operatives didn't bother with conversation. They radioed to their commander, most likely asking for direction, and then received their orders. They didn't hesitate. Shots rang out, and the four Chillicothe residents instantly collapsed to the ground. The COATS operatives each took hold of the back of the shirts or jackets of a victim and dragged the bodies into the barn.

Using advanced incendiary devices, they set a hot chemical fire to every building, razing them all to the ground within minutes. Jude was able to tilt his phone and just catch the small transport drone lift off, lighting up its boosters and blasting into the sky with bone-crushing speed. He turned the phone, scanning the fields, now able to discern plumes of smoke from the former farmhouses, corrals, and storage sheds scattered throughout the SAC. He scanned the northeast corner of the SAC, where the majority of wind turbines and the solar panel field were, and they appeared to be intact. The well house, as he predicted, was also untouched as the camera continued to faithfully stream the fiery annihilation. They knew what to hit and what to save. Unfortunately, the intense heat of the barn finally took its toll, and the camera slowly melted down, blurring the video feed and finally cutting out to an eerie, silent black screen.

"I hope you recorded that," Zara said, standing behind them with an angry, fiery look and her arms crossed.

"I've got it all right here," Jude said solemnly, holding up his phone.

"Good," Max said. "Give them a few hours, and the official story will be all over about how a tragic, terrible fire destroyed the entire Chillicothe SAC, and how the people must have fled or died in the flames. By tomorrow, CAMO will be rolling its giant plows and staking out its crop boundaries."

"Let's work on the video feed," Zara said, putting a hand on Jude's shoulder and giving a big sigh. "I want people to see what they did. I want them to witness the executions. I want them to see those COATS operatives and their transport slinking off into the sky. I want them to know exactly why those buildings were burning."

"Are you ready?" Max asked, crossing his arms and raising his eyebrows in a friendly but firm warning. "If you publish a story that is critical of the New America government or the NADF, they will keep an eye on you. If you show video of the COATS in action, they will come after you."

"That's exactly what the world needs to see," Zara said, her eyes narrowed and her lips pursed. "They need to see COATS in action. They need to witness the murder and unceremonious cremation of those four people. They need to see what their government is capable of. Don't worry; Jaxson taught me how to stay ahead of ADAMS."

Chapter 15: **Schooled**

LIVING IN A SUBTERRANEAN world is safe and convenient, but it doesn't bode well for those rare morning people who enjoy the warm glow of the sunrise. Jude had to settle for a table lamp with an artificial yellowish hue. Sitting up, stretching, and pulling back his hair, he slipped into his house shoes and scuffed along the smooth concrete floor, down the hall, and to the door of Zara's room. She was, of course, still out cold.

He opened the door, slipped through, carefully peeled back her blanket, and slid into the bed next to her, enveloping her with his arms. She rolled her head along his arm, resting it on his shoulder, and moaned, "Why are you awake? It's morning. I don't do mornings."

Chuckling, Jude kissed her soft, tangled head and said, "I'm a farm boy. I get up with the chickens."

"Mmmm," she moaned, curling into his chest and letting out a long sigh.

"Where's Maisy?" he asked, noticing the empty bed across the room with the blankets tucked neatly and pillows square at the head.

"She left with Dr. Robinson. Something about learning how to do basic blood tests. I guess they had to go get some lab kits in Kansas City."

"I wish she had let me know," Jude complained.

"She probably wanted to let you sleep," Zara said accusingly.

"Oh yeah. That was considerate."

After a few minutes of snoozing in Jude's arms, Zara roused and finally opened her eyes. "I guess the evacuation put the damper on our date. Maybe if we're not traveling or fleeing for a few days, we can squeeze in dinner?" she asked, looking up at his soft, brown eyes.

"I've heard Kansas City has good barbecue. What do you say we head up to the city and see what's along the riverfront?" he asked.

"As long as we take the Jeep and not a boat."

"Deal."

As it turns out, being on the run doesn't do your wardrobe much good. Zara and Jude realized their trip to the city would have to begin with a little shopping. Max generously provided them with some e-cash for the trip, allowing them to avoid pesky passport ID scans, and he gave them some good pointers on where to find just the right clothes that would look good, feel comfortable, and still be durable for day-to-day.

Zara helped find Jude some sturdy, dark jeans and a charcoal button-down shirt with deep purple accents. Jude lent his opinion on a series of outfits, and Zara finally settled on a flowing, knee-length, sleeveless, black cotton dress that accentuated her form, but still left plenty to the imagination. Being active and still somewhat modest even though her father had relaxed his Islamic-influenced rules years ago, she opted to get a pair of shorts to wear underneath. She topped off (or bottomed, as the case was) the outfit with a pair of simple but sturdy black slides.

Confident they no longer looked like they had just returned from a day in the cornfields, they headed down to the riverfront to take in the sights and have a romantic dinner. Nestled in among the casinos was a place with tables outside overlooking the river and a menu that appealed to Jude's carnivorous side. Zara agreed after seeing the setting and the respectable vegetarian menu.

"How did I not know you didn't eat meat?" Jude asked as they sat down.

"It never really came up, I guess," she said.

"I'm sorry I suggested barbecue."

"Stop apologizing. Roasted corn, baked beans, whole grain bread rolls," she read from the menu. "Trust me, I'm already salivating."

Jude smiled at Zara, her eyes sparkling behind strands of hair that insisted on falling down over the side of her face. Her smooth mocha complexion, black glowing hair, and firm, slender arms stood out in her sleeveless dress in a way Jude never noticed before. She was stunning.

"What are you looking at?" she asked sheepishly, pulling a strand of hair and tucking it behind her ear.

"This is nice," Jude said, smiling.

"The food looks pretty good," Zara said.

"I'm not talking about the food," Jude said, never breaking his gaze.

"I thought you said you didn't know anything about dating," she said sheepishly. "That was a pretty good line."

"I've seen and learned a lot since leaving Slate Creek, but the best thing to happen to me was running out of charge in Squamish River. I can't imagine going anywhere without you now, even if I have to drag you behind me in a stretcher," he said with a chuckle.

She smiled and sighed, resting her chin on her hands and looking into Jude's eyes. "It appears I'm stuck with you then, Jude Kane. Even if I had a home to go back to, I've already found my new home. You don't have to drag me, though. I'll keep up with you."

When it came time to order, Jude suddenly thought about her name, her father, and her family. Malik. He didn't want to chew on ribs in front of a vegetarian, and certainly didn't want to eat pork in front of a Muslim.

"I'll have the barbecue chicken plate with fries, corn, and a side salad. Thanks," he said, turning the menu screen back to Zara. He looked at Zara, and curiosity got the best of him. "Before the Transition, where was your family from?"

"My great-grandfather immigrated to British Columbia from Pakistan. He was a very devout Muslim, and he was a big part of the Pakistani community. My grandfather was raised in British Columbia, and he was part of the Muslim community, but he worked and went to the Mosque with Muslims from other countries, and he caused the shock of the family when he told everyone 'It doesn't matter if you are Shia or Sunni. We're all followers of Allah and Mohammed.' By the time my father was born, he followed traditions, but like many religious people in the West, he was much more secular and more concerned with the unraveling of society. I think his fear, more than his business skills, drove him to start Squamish River. That's probably why it didn't fare too well."

"Is that why he never had a passport implanted in you? Do you think he was afraid of the government?" Jude asked.

"I know it's why. His fear drove everything. It probably drove my poor mother to the grave."

"I'm sorry, Zara. I guess that might explain your drive to be a journalist. You want to get to the truth and expose it. The more you know, the less you fear."

"Exactly. What about you? You're here because you're trying to save your brother. Did you ever envision this scenario?" she asked, taking a sip of tea.

"Not in a hundred years," Jude laughed. "I was trying to get to the point where I could take over for my dad. He works so hard to keep Slate Creek running like a machine, and I wanted to relieve some of that stress. He's a tough guy, and my mom is pretty strong. They've got a few years left in them."

"Maybe you were needed on a bigger scale than just Slate Creek," Zara said. "Maybe you were needed to take your dad's skills to other SACs. Did you ever think that might be the real purpose of your cross-country journey?"

"You mean like God's purpose or fate or something?"

"I don't think fate is that worried about people."

"So, you do believe in God."

"I guess I do," Zara mused. "I'm not religious. My grandparents would think I'm an infidel if they could see me now, but I can't shake the feeling there is more to life than what we see."

"Interesting," Jude said, taking his own sip of tea.

"What?" she asked.

"You remind me of my dad. All my life, I wondered why he and Mom seemed so wedded to my Mom's Protestant Christian tradition when he was an engineer and should have known better than to believe in anything he couldn't prove. He would always say, 'There's a lot more that we don't know than there is that we do know. You can't prove everything.' I don't know if that was the Salish influence of his grandparents or just his convictions. I'm not too religious either, but my dad taught me to keep an open mind."

When the food came, they suddenly realized how hungry they were. A comfortable quiet ensued between them as they dug in, and then Zara stopped for a minute and looked at Jude and his plate.

"You changed your mind, didn't you?" she asked. "I saw you looking at the ribs on the menu screen earlier."

"I like chicken," he said, wiping a spot of sauce from his mouth.

"You didn't want to eat pork in front of me."

"I thought gnawing on a slab of pork ribs in front of a vegetarian who came from a Muslim tradition would be pretty rude."

Zara smiled and sighed while she took a bread roll, sliced it, and buttered the sides. She put it up to Jude's mouth and had him take a bite. "Your lack of dating experience is definitely not a problem. You didn't have to win me with charm; your character did the job. I tried to be careful with my feelings at first, but it's far too late for that now. I'm in way over my head with you, Mr. Kane."

Jude was at a disadvantage with a mouthful of bread, but he managed to get out a response as he swallowed and took her hand.

"I know exactly how you feel."

Jude and Zara strolled along the riverfront, enjoying each other and both trying to figure out how to admit when it was time to return to Ozark. The decision was soon made for them when Jude's phone rang.

"Jude, we've got a problem," Max said. "We've got three kids that failed their online exams and are scheduled for extraction for CME. All three of them said their exam was completely different this month. They said the format was different, a lot of the material was not in the curriculum, and the pass threshold was moved from 70% to 80%."

"Are they still allowed to retake an alternative exam?" Jude asked. "That's what Callum did. He failed all of them, but they still gave him that option."

"Yes. One boy took it and failed, and the other two haven't tried the alternative one yet."

"Don't let them take it yet! Wait till we get there. I want to see the exams. My mom knows these tests and the education system inside and out. She might be able to help us figure out what is happening."

"Okay. I'll tell the parents to hold off."

"We'll be back in a few hours."

On the road back, Zara was unusually intent on her phone.

"What's going on?" Jude asked.

"It's not just Ozark," she said. "I'm getting messages and posts from SACs all over the country. Parents are saying the exams have changed, and kids are failing and getting scheduled for extraction. This looks like a move by the New America DOE."

"How fast can you post something safely?" Jude asked.

"A couple of hours after I write it," Zara said.

"Can you write a post and advise parents to register for the alternative exam, but hold off on having their kids take it for 72 hours? Tell them the Sparrows are working on it."

Zara smiled. "I'm writing it now."

Once back at Max's underground warehouse at the Ozark SAC, now affectionately known as "the Bunker," Jude met with Max and the two girls who were set to take their progress exams.

"They kept asking weird questions," one of them complained. "It was like we were taking the wrong test."

"You were," Jude said. "And they did it on purpose."

"What are we supposed to do? Do we just have to go to CME school in Kansas City now?"

"Not yet. Let me sit with you and see these exams. I've got a great source for figuring these things out."

They took their place at two of Max's large screens and pulled up the exams.

"Hey, Mom, this is Jude. Have you had a chance to do a little research? Sorry about the short notice. These girls only have a few hours left to take the test."

"Of course," Marren Kane said confidently on the other end of the video call. "It's nice to finally see your face again, by the way. Your hair has gotten even longer."

"Thanks. I've missed you."

"Me too, sweetheart. Let's help these girls, and then we can talk. I need to meet Zara and see who my new daughter is."

Zara was off-screen, but her ears perked up, and a tear formed in the corner of her eyes. She hadn't heard the words "my daughter" for a few years.

The first girl pulled up her exam, and then Jude fed the content of her screen to Marren. She captured the images of each question, and she scrambled to locate the answer in her library of Department of Education curriculum that went all the way back to the first years after the Transition, when Jude was just starting school. As a timed test, she had to work quickly, and sometimes she had to help the girl from her own knowledge, but she saved each question.

It took a couple of agonizing hours, but they were just able to answer all the questions before time ran out. The score report: 89%. She was safe. Sighs and cheers erupted in the room, and the overwhelmed girl burst into tears. "Thank you! Thank you!" she cried.

"Thank you, Mom," Jude said. "You saved another kid from CME. You should be proud."

"They caught me off guard with Callum, but not this time," Marren said with a fierceness that took Jude by surprise. "If you can send me the screens of these exams, I can find the curriculum they are drawing from and make a study guide that will all but guarantee they will pass."

"I'm on it, Mom. I'll make sure the screens come through me so nothing can be traced to Slate Creek. Max has a good setup here with an amazing firewall and access to a maze of proxy servers. ADAMS won't see a thing."

"He's already tried," Max said after Jude got off the call. "As soon as we got the passing score, I had a dozen or so bots all trying to get inside our network. I'm sure the Department of Education is curious about the student who passed and the system she was on. Not on my watch. This is an ADAMS free zone."

"That's great, Max. We'll need your cover while we feed my mom the exam questions. Once she's created the study guide, Zara can post it on Sparrow Press, and the SACs will have access to it," Jude said with a feeling of satisfaction but also misgivings. "What I don't get is why the Department of Education did this. Obviously, they wanted students to fail, but what is the point of extracting all these SAC kids and swelling up the size of the CME schools? Isn't that a lot more expensive than leaving them in the SACs?"

"It's probably part of the same strategy," Max said. "The SACs aren't collapsing on their own as quickly as the New America government hoped they would, so they're putting the squeeze on them. Kids in CME schools can be tracked and more easily convinced to stay in the cities."

"But SACs aren't a threat to stability. ADAMS calculated that early on, so why the change in tone now?"

Max shook his head with the knowing smile of an attorney who had seen this side of humanity for decades. "Because ADAMS is not in charge; humans are. They always want more power than they should."

"That makes me almost like ADAMS. As long as the government is required to consult it, there is some kind of rational voice," Jude surmised.

"President Blake Conner defines himself as the leader who brought us through the Transition," Max explained. "He's the president who came to power in the chaos of the Transition, and he's been reelected twice on the premise that he restored order. He doesn't remember the U.S. Constitution, and he is desperate to maintain the stability and security of his New America."

"So, his life's mission is to protect the country by controlling it," Jude said. "And controlling everyone is a lot easier if they are in the cities."

"Neither of those ideas ever work, and they do make people pretty miserable," Max said. "Historically, miserable people are a lot harder to control than happy people. It's really a self-defeating philosophy."

"We'll just have to do our part to help his philosophy defeat itself," Jude said.

"The university system made a terrible calculation when they turned you down," Dr. Julian Robinson said as he and Maisy drove back from the clinic in Kansas City, where they stocked up on the blood testing lab kits. "You put those medical students to shame in the clinic today."

"I wasn't trying to make anyone look bad," Maisy said. "I just didn't want that kid going home with an infection that bad in his toe."

"You have an eye for people. You're the only one who picked up on his limp and bothered to check it out. You're observant and very thorough."

"Thanks," Maisy said.

"I know I can be a bit of a stickler sometimes, but I don't want to miss anything when I see so many different patients."

"I understand. It can be a matter of life and death in some cases. I drive my brother nuts because I always want to know every last detail, but details matter."

Dr. Robinson shook his head in agreement and looked out his window pensively as the transport glided out of the city. "You know, I could really use your help. It's a stretch working in the clinic and the SAC. Maybe if you helped me at the clinic, we could see patients faster and have more time to help out at Ozark."

"I'm open to that," Maisy said, thinking about Jude and Zara.

"Come to think about it, I'm pretty sure I could get the medical school to admit you and give you access to the courses. Your work with me could be part of your rotations. You would have to pass the courses and complete rotations in other areas, but you could become a Registered Medic."

"Are you being serious?" Maisy asked, stunned.

"Absolutely! I have some pull at my alma mater, and once they see you in action, they will beg you to come."

"I don't know what to say! I should talk to Jude. Of course I want to. It's my dream! But I have to think about Callum and my parents."

"It's a standing offer as far as I'm concerned," he said.

"Thanks, Dr. Robinson," Maisy said with a hard grin.

"Please call me Julian. I think we've at least gotten to that point, don't you?"

"Yeah. Thanks, Julian."

With three large screens working in concert, Max sat and watched the news coverage of CAMO rolling into the former Chillicothe SAC. Jude, Maisy, and Zara pulled up chairs. The driverless, natural gas-powered behemoths marked crop boundaries, plowed between the wind turbines, and made a border around the solar panels. The only signs of the thriving SAC that had been there a week before were the dark circles where the burned buildings had been cleared and the ground raked clean in preparation for the plows.

"They got their land," Jude said, shaking his head.

"Yeah, but look how many people you helped before they got there," Zara said, rubbing his shoulders. "How many more people would have been killed if you hadn't told them to evacuate?"

"We," Jude said. "We saved people. Akal stuck his neck out to notify us, and no one would have listened to us without the Sparrow Press. We couldn't stop them, but we saved some people and exposed the COATS operation. We did some good out there."

"You also figured out how to beat the new exams, got the study guide out to the SACs, and saved thousands of kids from extraction to CME schools," Max said. "The Sparrows have been busy."

"Speaking of being busy," Maisy said timidly. Maisy was never timid, so Jude's ears perked up.

"What is it?" he asked.

"Julian . . . um, Dr. Robinson, said he could use my help in the city at the clinic and here at Ozark," she said. "He said he could even get me into the medical school. If I pass the courses and do my rotations, I could get my Registered Medic license."

"Wow! That's incredible! What's holding you back?" Jude asked, detecting her hesitation.

"I came with you to get Callum back. Family comes first."

"Are you crazy?" Jude almost yelled. "This is your calling if ever there was such a thing. Do it! Zara and I will worry about Callum. It's going to take a good bit of legal help and time to get him back. Go to school. Maybe by the time we get him out, you can brag about your Registered Medic status."

"Yeah, and he'll take credit for bringing me here," she said. They both roared laughing, knowing that's exactly what Callum would do.

Later that evening, Jude took Max aside. "How much would it cost to get a lawyer for Callum?" Jude asked.

"More than you have," Max said. "Which is why you need me. I've been able to get in touch with a defense attorney who has three qualities we need: he knows the federal criminal justice system as well as anyone, he doesn't like the New America government, and he owes me a favor. He's agreed to take on the case because I helped him save his house right after the Transition. Give him some time to find Callum and what he's up against."

"How do I thank you, Max?" Jude said.

"You already did. You brought us all hope."

Chapter 16: **Take It On the Road**

MAX WAS UP EARLY, and in the conference room amid the smell of brewing coffee and the gentle wind of the ventilation system, he was making marks on a giant interactive wall map. Jude, roused by the wafting smell of the fresh brew, pulled on his jeans and T-shirt, pulled back his dark, wildly wavy hair, and sauntered out to see what Max was doing.

"What are you up to?" Jude asked, wiping the evidence of the sandman from the corners of his eyes. "Preparing a high school geography lesson?"

"Resistance 101," he said, remaining focused on his map. "New America is not going back on its promise to the SACs without a fight."

"Why do I get the feeling Zara and I just walked into your classroom?" Jude said with a sigh.

"You have good instincts," Max said, flashing a smile at Jude. "Why don't you rouse your reporter and grab some coffee and breakfast? Class starts in half an hour."

One nice thing about an underground cement bunker is that it is much quieter than a normal warehouse. With the insulation of limestone, steel, cement, and the white noise of the gently humming ventilation system, sleep is not a problem, especially without sunlight to remind your body what time it is. Jude stealthily cracked the door to the girl's room and tiptoed in.

"What do you want?" moaned Zara as Jude gently rubbed her shoulder.

"Max wants us in the conference room. There's coffee ready, and I can grab a muffin or something for you," he whispered. Maisy was still out cold.

"I want a bagel," she said with her face still half-buried in her pillow and her fine, black hair swirling around her head in a tempest. She raised up on her elbow, her hair still covering her face, and her eyes barely open. "Plain, warmed, not toasted, and slathered with cream cheese."

"I'm on it," Jude said, smiling as he kissed the top of her rebellious head of hair.

By the time Jude returned to the conference room with the bagel and coffee, Zara was already there. She had thrown on a pair of worn jeans and a white tank top and pulled her hair back in a tight, severe ponytail that didn't let a strand out of place. They sat down and began to study Max's map.

"Good morning, kids."

"Good morning," Zara said just before her first sip of coffee.

"Good morning," Jude said.

"I've been thinking about our situation," Max said. "Chillicothe is the latest casualty, and it's not hard to see why CAMO wanted the land since it is so well situated between major cities. But that doesn't explain Wind River, Twin Falls, Squamish River, or even the drone over Slate Creek. By the way, I don't necessarily condone your brother's actions, but I love the message they got."

Jude smiled and shook his head, remembering Callum's disdain for the government.

"Wind River isn't even a SAC; they are a tribal area that signed over mining rights years ago. There is nothing out there in the frozen wilderness that CAMO, the Dakota Region, or the New America government could possibly want, but they are circling a dying community like vultures. They are cutting their Universal Basic Income, watering down education, healthcare, and law enforcement, and essentially encouraging the whole community to implode on itself.

"The story is similar with the SACs, but it's CAMO doing the squeezing for the government. The Regions don't seem to have an agenda except for enforcing New America policies in order to keep their funding, so when you look at the big picture . . . "

"It's the Feds we're up against," Jude said. "New America is coming for the SACs."

"Why?" Zara asked, still chewing on her bagel. "What's in it for them?"

"Control," Max said. "It's been ten years since the Transition, but instead of restoring the protections of the old Constitution, they are still 'suspended.' The government is operating under a series of declarations and agreements, but there is no constitution to provide a backbone or protect basic rights. They fear losing control again, like they did during the Transition. The cities are firmly under their grasp, especially since people depend on the government for just about everything, but the SACs are too independent. They can be breeding grounds for rebels."

"The ironic thing is that until the SACs started coming under pressure, no one thought about anything but survival. Now we're talking about resistance," Zara said.

"A whole government is rarely paranoid, but I'm pretty sure this increasing insecurity is coming from President Blake Connor," Max said. "He was always a hard-liner, never compromising and never giving the other side an inch. During the Transition, this made him a hero and helped him ascend to the presidency. He had a lot to do with implementing ADAMS' recommendations and restoring order. Now the war's over, but he's still fighting."

"And that's where we come in," Jude said, eyeing the map.

"We're not raising an army or anything, but we're not giving away the farms either," Max explained. "We're going to make it worth his time to leave the SACs alone. If his 'squeezing' strategies fail, he'll lose support in Corporate Congress. Our biggest weapon will be our success. That's where the Sparrows come in."

"Max, what can we do?" Jude said with a deep sigh, shaking his head. "Look at Chillicothe. Four people were executed with barely a thought, and the SAC doesn't exist anymore."

"Imagine what would have happened if you were never there," Max said, folding his arms. "Besides, you have a secret weapon. Your footage of COATS made their move much more politically costly than they anticipated."

"So, then what's our strategy?" Zara asked, curious to know where the secret weapon would come in.

"You already created a strategy, or at least guiding principles," Max said to Zara. "Sanctity of Life, Equal Treatment, and Human Dignity. The first thing we do is never forget our ultimate goal.

"Next, we help the SACs succeed. Jude, you've seen what they need: repair and maintenance of the power grid, long-term crop and livestock management strategies, and education help so we can keep the kids out of CME schools.

"Finally, Zara tells the story. Just like you posted the study guides for the progress exams, you can post instructional videos, like basic power grid repairs and crop rotation. The posts can go where you can't."

"What about SACs that need more than an instructional video?" Jude asked. "Zara and I are going to need to travel."

"That's where this comes in," Max said, turning and pointing to the wall map they had almost forgotten about. He pointed to the indistinct blobs that were splattered across the North American continent, filling in the most desolate and remote spaces. "These are the registered SACs plus a few more I know about. Depending on distance and need, maybe you two can take your show on the road."

Zara looked at Jude and then back at Max. "We had a reputation after we left Twin Falls, but in the hours since Chillicothe went down, I've been getting a lot of calls to 'send in the Sparrows.' Now that people know there is help out there, they have hope."

"It sounds like we have a lot of work to do," Jude said. "There's no sense in sitting around when a lawyer is working on the case for Callum. We might as well do some good and see the country."

"I'll put out the word," Zara said. "We'll have to figure out who is most desperate and most accessible and then go from there."

Max smiled and slapped his hand on the giant interactive wall map. "Feel free to fill in the blanks."

Jude and Zara decided to take the Sparrow Wagon to Kansas City to pick up a few supplies in preparation for their trip. Jude was after tools; he knew the SACs would need basics, and he wanted to be able to leave what they needed with them when he left. Zara became a teacher, getting ready for the school year, gathering spare screens and preparing lessons on how to securely access Marren Kane's study guides and the Sparrow Press.

"Is Maisy coming with us to the SACs?" Zara asked.

"She will want to, but I'm not giving her the option. She has a rare opportunity with Doc Robinson to become a real Medic, and she'll do the most good if she stays put and gets her education," Jude said.

"Since when does Maisy do what you tell her?" Zara laughed. "Like when you told her to stay in Slate Creek."

"She'll want to come, but she knows she needs to stay. When I demand she stay, that is just giving her a justification to do what she knows is best. It's kind of a mind game, but that's how she works."

"In essence, your 'demand' is really giving her permission to do what she really wants to do in the first place, but now she won't feel guilty for staying behind. Sound about right?" Zara asked.

"Yep."

"That's a pretty sophisticated understanding of the female mind," Zara teased.

"And it only took me twenty years to figure out."

Arriving in the city, they were somewhat of a novelty. Many people hadn't seen a classic human-driven vehicle, and some were nervous, especially given its rugged military trappings. Jude didn't want the extra attention, but he didn't mind it entirely either. He took some pride in his project. Only very few of the wealthy people with jobs had the money and guts to have a classic human-driven vehicle and navigate the streets with it.

Jude had ordered his tools and other supplies back in Ozark, but not wanting to bring attention to the bunker, he sent his order to a market drop site in the city. The site was little more than a brightly colored kiosk with a yellow square painted on the cement next to it where the drones would land with their packages. Jude checked in to the site, and while waiting for the drone, they ordered a coffee from the café next door.

Jude was focused on the time: the delivery drone was ten minutes late. Zara was focused on the area: there seemed to be several lingering characters watching the drop site.

"The drone is late," Jude said.

"I think we aren't the only ones waiting," Zara commented.

"They're probably waiting for their packages too," Jude said just before rethinking his conclusion.

"Or they're waiting for our package," Zara said. "Maybe we should call the police and have them send a LEAD unit over here."

"The first thing it will do is scan everyone's passport. I don't want to take that chance with you," Jude said.

"I don't like our chances either way," she said nervously.

Finally, the drone came into sight, flying erratically and clearly struggling to stay aloft. Jude could see one of the rotors had been damaged, but the determined little drone pushed on to the drop site as if it were its last stop. With a hard drop and a bit of a slide, it landed in the yellow square.

"Please stay here," Jude said to Zara as he went to pick up the package. "Just in case." She nodded and, always a prepared journalist, took out her phone and got ready to record.

Jude scanned the package with his phone, confirming delivery. Usually, the drone would return to the warehouse, but with the damaged rotor, it stayed in place with a flashing red indicator light and a message on the input screen: "repair needed- retrieval unit en route." Jude had planned to scan the area better when he took hold of the box, but he got distracted by the damaged drone and his instinct to repair it.

"I think you have my package," came a menacing voice from behind Jude.

"Nope, this is mine. I've got confirmation," Jude said, feigning ignorance of their intentions.

"I'm afraid not."

Jude turned and faced the young man, who was flanked by a slightly shorter wingman. They were both dressed in nondescript dark pants and T-shirts, and navy blue windbreakers, and both had their hands in their jacket pockets. Jude made a quick assessment; it wasn't worth calling their bluff.

Glancing at Zara, he slightly shook his head 'no' and handed the package over. "Fine. I hope you get some use out of this stuff."

"We always do," he said. "We sell it." They turned to walk away, and Jude had an idea.

"Wait!"

"What?" the taller one asked suspiciously.

"If you're just going to sell it, sell it back to me. I need this stuff."

"Are you serious?" he asked, glancing around.

"Yes. What do you sell it for? Twenty-five or thirty percent of what it costs retail?" Jude asked.

"Usually."

"Sell it to me, then. Save me the hassle of having to order all these things over again. I'll give you $300 now, e-cash, no questions."

"No way. You're just stalling until a LEAD unit gets here," he said, glancing around again.

"No. Let's just say I have my own reasons to stay away from the cops."

"Make it $600."

"I paid $900 for it already! That's 60%! I'll go up to $400."

"You admitted what you paid and that you don't want the cops involved. The way I see it, I have the upper hand."

"I think you had the upper hand when you pointed whatever it is in your pockets at me. $500, take it or leave it."

"Deal."

"Give me your e-cash code."

As soon as they were out of sight, Zara rushed over to him.

"Are you okay?" she asked.

"I'm fine. I just got a really bad deal on a bunch of tools."

"But you're not hurt, and no one is trying to scan my passport."

Jude looked down at the sad sight of the crippled drone, and he noticed the flashing red light was gone. He bent down and read the input screen: "retrieval unit unavailable." A smile came across his face, and he picked up the drone, hoisting it onto his shoulder.

"Jude?" Zara asked.

"Yes?"

"Why are you stealing that delivery drone?"

"I'm just borrowing it. If I can get a new rotor and the right size bearings and casings, I can fix it."

"Isn't the company going to come looking for it?"

"Maybe not. It's often more expensive to find and retrieve a drone than just buy a new one. If they wipe the memory, then it's up for grabs. I just might have something to show for that $500 I paid after all."

Zara rolled her eyes as she took his phone, unlocked the back of the Sparrow Wagon, and opened the hatch. "It's a compulsion with you, isn't it? You can't help but resurrect a poor, helpless machine."

"I can't leave it all alone on the street. That's just cruel."

"Did you get what you needed, kids?" Max asked when they returned to the bunker.

"And then some," Zara said as Jude wrestled the drone from the back of the wagon.

"You know you're supposed to take the package and leave the drone, right?" Max teased.

"It crash-landed. It was crying out to me for help," Jude grunted as he carried it to a table inside that served as his makeshift workbench.

"Are you sure they're not going to come looking for it?" Max asked.

"They wiped the memory. She works for the Sparrows now."

"That's good because the Sparrows are needed," Zara said, staring at her phone. "There's a SAC in the Gulf States that's lost three kids to CME schools. They've got a week before the next round of retests are due, and they stand to lose another dozen. The parents are in a panic."

"The GSA Region is next door. We can get there in a couple of days," Jude said, looking at the wall map.

"Good. It sounds like they need help accessing your mom's study guides, and they could probably use some tutoring. They sound pretty desperate."

"I guess I'll have to resurrect her later," Jude said, looking at his drone. With his hand on his hips, he smiled at Max and Zara and sighed deeply.

"Tell them the Sparrows are on their way."

Chapter 17: **Give and Take**

As THE ROLLING HILLS of the slowly melting Ozarks gave way to the flat grasslands and cattle ranches of the former State of Oklahoma, Jude and Zara got a sudden case of déjà vu. The First Nation lands, or Native American tribal lands as they were called down here, bore the marks of the same arrangement with New America as Wind River had. During the Transition, the tribal councils had negotiated for the same relative independence that a SAC was given, but they also got the benefit of a UBI, housing, and medical care in exchange for exclusive rights to all mining and agricultural resources. After the collapse of all but the few largest casinos, this was a lifesaver. Whatever land CAMO wasn't grazing cattle on was littered with cubes, run-down schools, dilapidated hospitals, and temporary buildings used to house the overflowing jail population.

"Different strategy, same goal," Jude said angrily as they passed through the desolate landscape. "Instead of taking away land bit by bit, they cut the UBI, education funding, and emergency services. They chip away at hope, purpose, and dignity. The communities collapse in on themselves eventually."

"I can't imagine growing up here. You either get out and go to a city, or you stay here and slowly die," Zara concluded. "You don't have a lot of options."

It took about an hour for the sullen mood to lift, but the clear skies and balmy late summer temperatures rearing their heads well into late October lifted their spirits.

"I don't suppose this SAC is anywhere near the water, is it?" Jude asked as they navigated through the busy highways of Dallas. "Are we going to get to play in the white sand and turquoise water of the warm Gulf beaches?"

"Not exactly," Zara said, looking at the map on her phone.

"Not even close to the beach?" Jude asked.

"Nowhere near the beach," Zara said. "We're heading into the southern end of the Smoky Mountains. The Blue Ridge SAC is about 150 kilometers north of Atlanta."

"Nope. Nowhere near the beach," Jude sighed.

"How long to the Texico/ Gulf States border?" Zara asked.

"About an hour and a half."

"I suppose I'd better start moving things and clearing out the storage compartment so I can get in. I'm not looking forward to cramming myself in there in this heat."

"Maybe you won't need to."

"Say what?"

"We have to go south anyway to avoid crossing the Appalachia border. I've never been there, but I've heard the southern regions are known for back roads," Jude said. "Besides, every time I get scanned, I'm tracked. ADAMS is going to start putting the pieces together soon."

"I like that idea. The checkpoints are only on the major roads, but how do we know which of these back roads actually go all the way through over the border? They haven't been maintained for decades." Zara was recalling the sometimes treacherous route they took on the motorcycles in the mountains of Cascadia. Missing bridges and piles of trees across the road were not uncommon.

"We can stop in Texarkana and ask someone."

"I know there are SACs in Louisiana that get a pretty constant flow of relatives visiting from cities. They smuggle food and supplies to the SACs, and then go hunting and fishing illegally. I've shared a couple of 'Swamp SAC' stories on Sparrow Press. If we find some outdoors-looking folks in town, I'd bet they would know."

"I say we find a bar."

With a little bit of e-cash and a promise to smuggle a few cases of canned soup to a swamp SAC in Louisiana, Jude and Zara were able to get good information from a few patrons before they were completely drunk and map out a safe route.

Even though the routes were passable, it didn't mean they were smooth. Decades of crumbling asphalt and cracked concrete meant it was a rough go, and the road was little more than a trail in many areas. The rugged Sparrow Wagon mustered the strength of its old military days and made the trek through the woods and fields impressively, but it did drain the battery faster. They stopped for a recharge in Monroe, stopped again in Jackson, Birmingham, and Atlanta before turning north and heading into the North Georgia Mountains.

After a tour of the swampy, stifling heat and humidity of the lower Gulf States, driving up into the thick forests of the southern end of the Smoky Mountains was a welcome reprieve. Not quite the jagged, snow-covered peaks of the Cascades and Rockies, the Smoky Mountains had a soft, alluring quality with trees carpeting over the summits. There was an abundance of fast rivers, gentle streams, pristine lakes, and quiet wildlife that thrived in the mild climate.

"Follow the road along the creek until you see a shack," Zara said, navigating from the directions she was given. "Zack said he would meet us here."

Jude wound around the curves of the creek, following the trail of reddish-brown soil that packed hard to make a sturdy road, but would be a slick and messy obstacle course in a hard rain.

"There's the shack," Jude said, nosing the Sparrow Wagon up to the edge of the small, ramshackle building. "That thing looks like an over-grown outhouse. Where are the other buildings?"

"All I know is that he said he'd meet us here," Zara said with a sigh. "Why don't we get out and stretch our legs? It's not a bad spot for a picnic."

"Good plan. I'm hungry and tired of sitting."

They found a convenient log on the bank of the creek and sat to eat their sandwiches. The gentle lull of the flowing stream, the birds chattering in the trees, and the cool breeze seemed to carry away their stress with the current.

"Look over there," Jude whispered. "There's a whole family."

Zara peered through the kaleidoscope of green, orange, and brown foliage, catching some movement. She picked out a doe and then swallowed a squeal as her three fawns pranced along behind their mother. After several minutes, a hulking buck followed, cautiously smelling the trail and scanning the forest.

"That's a nice eight-pointer," Jude whispered. "He's a beautiful beast. If I had something to shoot with, we'd have dinner for weeks."

The buck froze and looked up, but he didn't see Jude and Zara. He seemed to be staring off at something over their shoulders, but it was completely silent. Suddenly, the buck jerked and jumped, tearing off through the woods, but stumbling and struggling to clear small logs and saplings.

"Did he get shot?" Zara asked.

"He acted like it, but I didn't see or hear a thing."

"Me neither."

"That's because I'm a wicked shot," a short, stocky man said, standing behind them on the bank holding a compound bow with two arrows attached to it. His toothy smile showed through his curly red hair and his thick red beard and illuminated his glass-blue eyes.

Jude and Zara jumped and scrambled to their feet.

"I didn't hear you come up behind us," Zara said.

"Neither did that buck," Jude said. He smiled and held out his hand. "Jude Kane, and this is Zara Malik. We've just flown into the area."

The man chuckled and shook Jude's hand and then Zara's hand. "The Sparrows have landed. I'm Zack Nolan. Welcome to the Blue Ridge SAC."

"Nice to meet you," Jude said.

"Nice to meet you in person. Where exactly is the SAC?" Zara asked.

"If you can help me drain and tie up that buck, I'll take you to our little paradise in the mountains."

The Blue Ridge SAC was an impressive operation. Jude and Zara were encouraged to finally see a SAC that was managed almost as well as Slate Creek. Nestled in the foothills, there were dozens of small plots with a wide variety of crops growing in the valleys and gentle slopes, while the homes of the two dozen families were further up in the hills. Most homes were simple, sturdy log homes set on stone or concrete foundations dug down into the soft topsoil, and a few families retreated into old mine shafts where they took advantage of the constant temperature and protection from the elements. It took some doing to make the shafts safe and comfortable, but during strong storms, they never worried about downed trees or broken glass.

"This SAC is one of the best I've seen," Jude confessed to Zack as they sat and had some freshly brewed coffee at his kitchen table. "And your log house is impressive. Lincoln would be proud."

"Thanks. It's only taken ten years of constant work," Zack said.

"What is that delicious smell?" Jude asked, his nose perking up.

"Your stove is hiding something amazing," Zara said as she emerged from the restroom and sat down at the table.

"Athalia is making something involving potatoes, pork loin, cheese, and whatever else she got her hands on," Zack said.

"It's called Cheddar Pork Potato Casserole, and it's my recipe," a woman said, gliding down the stairs. A very tall, sturdy black woman with her hair tied in a scarf came and stood behind Zack, absent-mindedly kneading his shoulders with her powerful hands. She was barefoot, wore khaki shorts, a double-layered brilliant white tank top, and had the toned arms and legs of an athlete. Her face was soft and her skin silky, and she shared the same radiant smile as Zack.

"I'm Athalia," she said, extending her hand to Jude and Zara, "and you must be the Sparrows we read so much about."

"This is Jude Kane and Zara Malik," Zack said, making the introductions. "This is my wife, Athalia. She's the master chef around here and the reason I have this," he said, patting his stomach.

"Now you know you're the one bringing home all the food. All I do is cook it up," she said with a chuckle, retreating to the kitchen to attend to business.

"She was a chef at a fancy place in Atlanta," Zack explained. "I met her at the market where I was trying to sell some pork I had raised. She liked what she saw," he said with a twinkle in his eye.

"You or the pig?" laughed Jude.

"Both."

Athalia sauntered to the doorway and added her part of the story while holding a wet wooden spoon and wearing a hand towel on her shoulder.

"Most suppliers only get their meat from CAMO suppliers, and they won't tell us if it is real or lab meat. They say if you can't tell, then why should they? But I can tell, and so can some of the rich folks who came into the restaurant. I bought that whole pig off of my man that day."

"Lucky for me, I got her number," Zack said.

"That man would not stop callin' me!" she said, returning to the kitchen. She yelled from the stove, "Of course, I kept answerin' the phone."

"The next time we met, I took her home with me."

"I only said yes because the damn restaurant owner tried to take the credit for my recipes, and I quit. I had nowhere else to go," Athalia yelled from the kitchen. "That was five years and two kids ago. I don't know what's wrong with me. I just can't say no to that man!"

They all laughed, and Jude shot a smile at Zara. She shook her head and rolled her eyes. She felt much the same way.

"It sounds like you've had a few kids fail the exams and get pulled out for CME," Zara said.

"Yes," Zack said, losing his smile. "Three kids failed both exams and were pulled out by the Gulf States Regional Defense Forces. We've got twelve more that failed the first exam, and the alternative has to be taken in a few days."

"That's why we're here," Zara said. "The New American Department of Education has decided to randomly select exams from before the current term, sometimes years before. It's like they designed the tests for the kids to fail. Luckily, we've got a great teacher who can identify the curriculum used from the first exam and make a spot-on study guide that all but guarantees they will pass. They just need to study quickly."

"Deal," Zack said. "When should I pull the students in to show you their exams?"

"Now," Zara said.

While she went to work gathering information, feeding it securely to Marren Kane in Slate Creek, and calming the frayed nerves of the students, Zack and Jude took a walk to the creek.

"You don't have a lot of solar panels or wind turbines here," he said. "You must have another source of power."

"We do more gardening than farming, so we don't need to power farm equipment. We rely more on hunting, fishing, and livestock than on crops, but we still need power. Let me show you something."

They walked down to the creek and then followed it to the shack where they met. Zack opened the door, and Jude recognized the large black box immediately.

"Your batteries."

"Yes, sir."

"Why are your batteries down here near the water?" Jude asked.

"Follow me."

They walked down to the creek, and Zack pointed to a rolling wheel, about ten centimeters in diameter, attached to a brown box nestled half-submerged at the edge of the creek.

"I call it MicroHydroPower. If wind can rotate a piece of metal and make electricity, so can water. We don't have the Buford Dam like Atlanta, but we also don't have millions of people," Zack said. Jude could see a familiar pride in his smile.

"How much power do they create?" Jude asked. "It can't be much."

"No, but when you connect about a hundred of them, you get some voltage. The advantage of these little guys is that they run constantly, not intermittently. They give us about half of our power."

"Impressive! I've got to see your design," Jude said. "This could really help some of the other SACs."

"I'll show you everything if you help me with that beast," Zack said, pointing to the shack. "We've lost some capacity over the past few years."

"No problem. Batteries are my thing."

As Jude and Zack worked on the batteries and pored over Zack's Micro-HydroPower box design, they talked about CAMO, the SACs, and the Sparrows.

"Some SACs have to be mobile," Jude explained. "When CAMO tries to take over land, they end up chasing their tail. This works best in the wide-open spaces in the Midwest. Here, not so much."

"We haven't had encroachment yet, but I've seen CAMO drones. I think they're waiting to pounce," Zack said. "Bastards."

"You're doing exactly what you need to: succeeding," Jude explained. "Keep your plots of land planted and labeled at all times. Grow cover crops so CAMO doesn't think it's unused land. Keep your wind turbines and solar panels working and conceal as much as possible. You may hate to think about it, but make plans for a worst-case scenario. Figure out what is portable, how you could leave, and how fast you could do it. You may not get a chance to come back for anything."

"I think we all learned that lesson when Chillicothe went down," Zack said solemnly. "It's terrible what happened to them, but the Sparrows saved lives, and since then, you guys are the only people SACs trust. That includes me."

"Thanks," Jude said modestly. "It's really a matter of all of us communicating and working together. That's something the SACs have never had to do until now."

Marren Kane didn't disappoint. Zara had the study guide ready to go, and for four days, the students huddled together in a makeshift classroom in the Nolans' living room and studied for their lives. By the evening before the alternative exams were due to be taken, they were ready.

As the students turned on their screens and logged in, Zara knew anxiety would be the worst enemy.

"Attention, parents. This is not my first study session, and I can assure you we will all be past this anxious moment in a couple of hours. In the meantime, it would help the students to have privacy. Anxious parents make very anxious kids."

They nodded and agreed, dispersing to their cabins.

Jude and Zack retreated to the kitchen table, where Athalia had made some appetizers for the kids before the test. With their nerves, they didn't eat much, but Zack and Jude had no such inhibitions.

"We should have come sooner," Jude said.

"We didn't know the government was up to anything until we lost those kids. It couldn't be helped," Athalia said.

"That is true. Still, with food this good, I wish I had come here sooner."

They all laughed and passed around the plates of chicken skewers, hush puppies, and homemade potato chips.

After nervously grazing and chatting for an hour and a half, there was an eruption of cheers from the living room. The first student passed the exam and was safe. She jumped up, hugged Zara, and immediately ran home, leaving her screen on the table.

Soon, the cheers were periodic, and the crowd of twelve dwindled down to one poor young student who reminded Jude of Callum.

"If I miss one more question, then I'm out of here," he grumbled, wiping his brow.

"It's okay, Sam," Zara said. "You've still got twenty minutes."

"And ten questions. I'm not that fast, especially in math."

Jude walked over to his screen and scanned the questions.

"Did you ever put a board on a log and tip it back and forth?" Jude asked him.

"Uh, yeah," Sam said, happy for the distraction.

"If you put ten kilos on one side, how much would you need to put on the other to balance the board exactly?" Jude asked.

"Ten kilos."

"Equations are like that board. Keep them equal on both sides. Add and subtract, multiply and divide, and you'll find how much that "X" really weighs."

The lights came on. "Oh! I think I get it!"

He began to scratch out the equations on his tablet, and each time he got the right answer, everyone cheered. Finally, he got down to the last question, and he began to panic. "I can't miss this, and I don't know about exponents. How do you get rid of something that is squared? Do you divide it?"

"No," Jude said. "You have to get to the 'root' of the problem."

"Square roots!" Sam exclaimed. "I think I got this!"

He clicked his choice, and everyone held their breath.

"Congratulations. You passed with 80%."

The small contingent left in the living room roared with a cheer that echoed throughout the woods of the SAC.

The next morning, Jude and Zara packed to leave. The men gave handshakes and pats on the back, and the women held back tears.

"I'm leaving with more than I brought," Jude said to Zack. "Thanks for sharing your design on the Micro . . . "

"You're welcome for the brown box," Zack said. "And you are not leaving with more than you brought. Your work on the battery pack is going to help us keep the lights on for years."

"Hopefully, that works both ways. Some of the SACs could use your design and put it to work."

"Before you go, I have something for you," Zack said. He walked into the house and came out with a sleek black compound bow and six carbon arrows attached to it. "This is small thanks. You might need it sometime. You cover a lot of country, and you might get hungry for something fresh."

Jude stared at the bow with wide eyes and stammered, "I . . . can't . . . how will you hunt?"

"I have several, don't worry."

"Thank you so much, Zack. *Now* I can say I'm leaving with more than I brought!"

Chapter 18: **Detention**

THE ROUTE BACK THROUGH the heat and humidity of the Gulf States, although beginning to wane, still took its toll.

"I'm almost willing to cross through Appalachia to avoid this swampy section of the country," Jude complained. "And we never even got to the beach."

"Why not?" Zara asked.

Jude looked at her and then smiled. "Yeah. Why not?"

They detoured south, heading for Pensacola, but after Zara looked at the map, she reminded Jude that there was an NADF Naval Station there.

"I don't think we need that kind of attention, especially if we're rolling along in a modified old J150. Lots of checkpoints, lots of questions, and lots of scans," Jude said. "Let's go to Biloxi."

The Sparrow Wagon rolled into the sandy parking lot of the sparsely populated public beach, and they let out a long sigh. The wind was blowing wisps of sand as if reminding people that hurricane season was not quite over. Jude and Zara sat and stared over the white, silky sand and the rolling green waves crowned with dancing whitecaps.

"This is amazing," Zara said. "I've never seen anything this beautiful before, not even in pictures."

"Whitecaps mean something entirely different in the mountains of Cascadia," Jude said. "Want to go get our feet wet?"

After unceremoniously discarding extra clothes and accessories, they tore off down the beach toward the surf. Neither of them having spent much time in the sand, they flailed their arms and stumbled through the soft ground until they dropped exhausted at the edge of the waves. Jude rolled up his pant legs, and with the wind attempting to up-end her loose t-shirt, Zara tied it off at her midriff. Jude watched her tame the shirt and pull it tight, staring for a few seconds at her wild, wavy black hair dancing and swirling around her face.

"What?" she asked. "I know my hair is out of control. I forgot to put it up."

"No. It's perfect," Jude said, taking her hand. "Let's see how cold this water is."

They pranced to the edge of the water and let a small stream swish past their feet.

"It's warm!" Zara said.

"It can't be this warm. We're just not far enough out," Jude reasoned.

"I'll make you a bet," Zara said. "If the water is warm, we stay here for the night. If it's cold like you think, we'll go where you want."

"Alright, let's go."

They stepped further in, and soon a bigger wave met them halfway and washed over their feet and ankles.

"Hmm," Zara hummed. "Feels good."

"Let's keep going."

They went up to their knees.

"I'm not convinced. It's still shallow."

Zara shot a look at him with her raised eyebrow and then pulled his hand, leading them up their waists and soaking their clothes.

"How about now?" she asked.

"I don't know . . . "

She laughed and threw her arms around his neck, staring into his mischievous eyes. She smiled, gave him a light kiss on the lips, and then said, "How about now?" and pulled his head down until they both tumbled over into the water.

They came up laughing, soaked, and the bet was settled.

"I don't think our bathtub ever had water this warm," Jude said. "I guess I'd better get the tent set up."

As they trudged back to the Sparrow Wagon, the zephyr that charmed them when they first arrived grew to an angry howl that helped to dry their clothes but also gave them the gift of sand in every crack and crevice of their skin.

They dove into the vehicle, slammed the doors against the wind, looked at each other for a brief second, and then burst out laughing.

Jude's hair had a distinct Einstein quality to it, while Zara's mop was standing impressively tall. They were damp, sandy, and for the moment, a happy mess.

"So much for the tent idea," Zara lamented.

"I don't know," Jude teased. "If we do it right, we could get an airlift back to Ozark. Max would be impressed."

"Very funny. What are we going to do now?" she asked.

"I lost a bet, and I intend to uphold my end. We will camp at the beach. We'll just have to use the old Sparrow Wagon for shelter. I'm pretty confident it won't fly away."

Zara looked back at all their supplies. "I suppose we could move some of your tools up here to the front. With the seats down and the cargo area, we'd have a little room."

"We can drape our wet clothes over the front seats, and I can turn the fan on to dry them out," Jude said. "If you hand me the tools, I'll put them up front and stay up here for a few minutes to give you some privacy while you change."

"What about you?" she asked.

"I'm not worried about my privacy."

"Neither am I."

Jude took a deep, nervous breath. "Ok. Let's make some room back there and get into some dry clothes."

After some shuffling, they sat cross-legged facing each other in the cargo area. Length and width weren't the problem; when you can't stand up, changing your clothes is a minor athletic event. Zara untied her T-shirt and peeled it off, handing it to Jude. He draped it over the driver's seat, where it flapped subtly in the breeze of the fan.

"Help me with these," Zara said, tugging at her khaki shorts. Unbuttoned and unzipped, they were clinging stubbornly to her thighs. Jude took hold of the legs, squeezing his fingers between her skin and the material. She shrieked and convulsed, almost kicking Jude.

"That tickles!"

"I'm just trying to get a grip!" Jude said.

"Here, peel them down from the top," she said, lying back and raising her rear end off the floor.

Jude took hold of the shorts, gingerly grazing her hips with his fingers, and gently but firmly pulled them down, freeing her from the shorts and turning them inside out in the process. He hung the shorts next to the t-shirt.

"Whew, thanks," she said as she sat up. "Hand me that towel and the nightshirt from my pack."

"Hey, this is *my* T-shirt," he said as he handed it to her.

"It is?" she said, feigning ignorance. "I hope you don't mind. It's very cozy."

"Of course not. It looks a lot better on you anyway." He turned his back to her, and while she attempted to dry off, he peeled off his shirt and managed to wrestle off his jeans. He laid them over the passenger seat and then felt two thin wet things land on his shoulders. One shoulder held a black bra, and the other a thin pair of ladies' underwear. Zara had gotten all her wet clothes off.

"You can turn around now," she said as Jude turned three shades of red. "It's okay. We're both adults here."

Jude slowly turned, and Zara was sitting in his white T-shirt, attempting to tame her wind-tangled curls. He turned back, leaned back slightly, and pulled off his wet underwear. Strategically wrapping himself in a towel and attempting to get rid of as much sand from his nether regions as possible, he dried off and then pulled on a fresh pair of underwear.

"Sorry if you got an unsolicited shot of my behind there," he said.

"As far as I'm concerned," she teased, "you really have nothing to be sorry for."

Jude blushed even more but composed himself as he took in the sight of Zara in his T-shirt, swimming over her, her silky legs and delicate feet covered in wisps of stray sand, and her stubborn waves of hair pulled forcefully behind her head in a rebellious ponytail.

"You got your hair back under control," he said. "Can you do the same for mine?"

"Sure. Scoot over here. Don't worry about your shirt. It'll just get in the way."

"Okay," he said, maneuvering himself back-first into the pocket of her crossed legs.

"Closer," she said, pulling his shoulders back gently. "That's it."

She began unknotting the tangled ends of his hair, which by now reached a few inches past his shoulders. From there, she worked up, brushing out longer and longer strands of his brown locks.

"You have great hair," she commented as she worked.

"You have great hands. Clearly, you're better at this than me."

"I can show you how to do it."

"I'd rather let you do it. I'm enjoying myself."

She pulled his hair into a ponytail, put a rubber band into it, and cinched it tight. He started to lean forward, but she caught his shoulders and pulled him back again. She began to rub and knead his shoulder muscles, working her way down his back with her thumbs and palms.

"Ohhhh . . . " he moaned. "That feels so good . . . aah!" he blurted.

"Sorry, too hard?" she asked.

"No! I like it. It hurts so good."

She rubbed out a few more knots and then snaked her arms around his neck and pulled him back further until he lay against her, and she rested her chin on his shoulder.

"This must be what heaven is like," he sighed.

"Do you believe in heaven?" she asked.

"Maybe."

"My grandfather told us heaven was where each man had seventy virgins. I didn't like that story."

"I don't blame you."

"Maybe I'll sleep with you, so I won't be eligible."

"Wouldn't your dad be disappointed?"

"I think he lost his faith when he lost his hope. He never taught us much about the Muslim religion. Most of what I know is just family tradition."

"Dad and Mom were raised in the Protestant Christian tradition. When they established Slate Creek, they both insisted we learn about Theology and the Bible in addition to the state curriculum. I hated it! All I wanted to do was learn about science and technology like my dad. He always told me, 'Before you know what you're doing, you need to know why you're doing it.' That's probably one of those lines I'll find myself telling my own kids one day."

"So do you believe in God?" Zara asked.

"Yeah, I do," Jude said. "Do you?"

"Maybe."

He leaned forward and turned around to face her.

"What do you think about marriage?" he asked.

"Does anyone get married anymore?"

"I know they do in the Amish SACs!" he said, laughing.

"Yes, they do," she giggled. "And they also still wear dresses and bonnets and use horses and buggies. Why do you ask?"

"I'm just curious."

"You're more than curious."

He looked into her eyes, folded his hands, and took a deep breath.

"I can't imagine the next sixty or seventy years without you. Of course, you may not want to be stuck with me . . . "

"I'd like that. I'd like that very much."

By morning, the winds finally died down, leaving the Sparrow Wagon covered in dust and supporting drifts of sand against its wheels on the windward side. The light filtered in through the dusty windows as the sun rose over the Gulf, blotting out the memory of the clouds and winds of the previous day.

A hard rap against the window startled Jude and Zara, who both let out a sharp yelp. Peering through the haze, Jude could see a LEAD unit and a human officer with him. He swallowed his heart.

Grabbing his mostly dry clothes from the passenger seat, he pulled them on and stumbled out of one of the back doors.

"Good morning!" the officer said.

His badge said "Recreation and Parking Enforcement, Biloxi PD."

"Good morning," Jude replied.

"It looks like you got caught in the storm last night."

"Yes, sir. By the time we got back into the vehicle, you couldn't see too well."

"It happens all the time. I'm just making sure you're alright. If you don't mind, my LEAD unit will give you both a quick scan, then you can carry on."

Jude gulped. What about Zara? He had no time to react. The story about her being his sister wouldn't play out too well in this situation.

"Jude Kane, member of the Slate Creek SAC, Cascadia Region," blurted out the LEAD unit. "Female subject, no reading."

Too late to hide and too late to lie, Zara crawled out of the wagon to stand with Jude and face the music.

"Are you sure?" the officer said to the LEAD unit.

"Confirmed. No reading from the female subject."

"I'm sorry, but I'm going to have to take her in," the officer said.

"No!" Jude blurted, stepping in front of her. She's not going anywhere."

The lights, clicks, and whirrs turned on in the LEAD unit instantly. They were now on a live video feed.

"Look, you're not in trouble," the patient officer explained. "Don't do anything that would put you in trouble."

"We're sorry, officer," Zara piped in. "He's very protective. We're on our honeymoon, and he wants to make it memorable."

"How did you two get all the way to the GSA Region without a passport?" the officer asked.

Jude looked at Zara and had to think fast.

"I'm from Cascadia. I met Zara in Texico when I got this old Jeep from her uncle Max. We got lost on some back roads near Texarkana, and before we knew it, we were looking at the beach."

"Talk about a whirlwind romance," the officer said, chuckling at his own joke. "Don't worry. Detention is only twenty-four hours. We take the information you give us, verify what we can, and put that into a temporary passport. You have ninety days to get to a doctor and have your permanent passport implanted. It's for your protection."

"It's okay, Jude," Zara said, stepping around him. "It will be okay. Just come pick me up tomorrow."

Jude tensed, but he knew she was right. This was the path of least resistance. This was not the New America government, and she was not Callum. He repeated this to himself.

"Zarah Kane," she said to the LEAD unit. "My name is Zarah Kane, Z-A-R-A-H, K-A-N-E."

"Smart girl," thought Jude. Zarah Kane would be a lot harder to connect to the Zara Malik of the Sparrow Press.

"It's not a hotel, but it's not exactly jail, either," the policeman said as he led Zara to the female detention bloc. "The LEAD unit relayed your information, and we should have a nurse and the passport here by morning. Once it's implanted, you're free to go."

"Thanks," Zara said.

"Don't thank me yet," the officer said with a sheepish grin. "You have to put this on. It's for security."

She sighed and shrugged as he handed her a bright orange jumpsuit and led her to the female intake room. Within minutes, she was changed, tagged with an ankle monitor, and taken to her cell. Her cinderblock and steel suite was not entirely bare; it came furnished with a stainless-steel toilet and sink, a steel-framed bunk bed, and a roommate.

"Buenos Días," said the woman. She was older than Zara, in her early thirties, with thick, straight dark hair, an olive complexion that was slightly darker than Zara's, and a somewhat shorter and thicker build. Judging from her hands, she did a lot of physical labor.

"Good morning," Zara said. "So much for my French lessons."

"It's okay," she said with a slight accent. "I speak English. My name's Sonja. Sonja Orozco. I thought you might be Latina."

"No. My grandparents were from Pakistan. I'm third generation, and I only speak English and a bit of bad French. My name's Zara," she replied, shaking her hand. "Are you here for a temporary passport too?"

"Yes. I came on a freight ship. I got on and hid, but when I got off, I ran into the *policia*. They said I didn't have a passport, so here I am. At least I have a bed and good food. I make better tortillas, but they gave us chicken and good rice. I haven't had meat in many weeks."

"I'm so sorry," Zara said. "I didn't realize it was that bad in Baja."

"Si. That is why I came. We have heard there was someone helping the SACs up north. We have screens, but unless we are near a church, we have to use them in government houses, and they control what we see. We started to read stories about *Los Gorriones*, but soon they were blocked. I came here to see if I could learn more about them. In English, they are called 'The Sparrows.'"

Zara fell onto her bed. She checked the room, spotted the camera in the middle of the ceiling, and then crossed the room to sit next to Sonja and speak quietly.

"Do you believe in God?" Zara asked.

"Si, I am Catholic."

"I know about the Sparrows," she said.

"You do?" Sonja said, her eyes growing wide. "Where can I find them?"

"Right here."

The sight of Jude standing in front of the Sparrow Wagon in his jeans, grey T-shirt, and hair blowing in the breeze was like coming home for Zara. Rubbing the injection site and rolling her shoulder, she descended the steps in yesterday's clothes and threw her arms around Jude's neck.

"I'm so glad to see you. I can breathe now," he said, hugging her firmly and kissing her cheek.

"I'm fine. I was treated well. Other than wearing an ugly orange jumpsuit, I got a few free meals, and I met a friend."

"Sonja Orozco," she said, extending her hand.

"Jude Kane," he said, shaking her strong hand firmly. "Do you need a ride?" he asked.

Zara and Sonja looked at each other and smiled.

"Sonja came up from Baja looking for the Sparrows. Do you think we can help her out?" Zara said.

"I'm sure we can. Let's go."

"Did you get a chance to charge up the Sparrow Wagon?" Zara asked as they hit the highway, and she peered over at the gauges.

"Yes, I did. I also got some good information about some back roads between Lake Charles in GSA and Beaumont in Texico. The border won't be a problem."

"We've got passports now, at least for three months," Sonja said. "If we do get scanned, we'll be okay."

"No matter what, we stick together," Jude said. "Bienvenidos a Los Garriones. You're a Sparrow now."

Chapter 19: **Coasting**

"ARE YOU SURE, MAX?" Jude asked on the phone.

"Yes. The lawyer has been to see Callum, whom I am told was quite happy to hear that his brother and sister had crossed the country trying to reach him. In any case, it will be weeks before anything moves. We're looking at after the New Year. Maybe you and Zara should take a little time for yourselves. I heard California is nice this time of year."

"Max, it's November in the Northern hemisphere."

"Exactly. Mild weather, no snow. Go to the beach and don't get detained this time."

"Do you have family in Baja?" Jude asked Sonja as they headed for the west coast. The momentary silence spoke for her.

"I did, yes," she said solemnly.

"I'm sorry," Jude said. "I didn't mean to pry."

"It's okay," she said. "It's part of me. It's part of who I am. It's why I got on a cargo ship and came north to find the Sparrows."

"What can we do?" Zara asked her.

"You are doing it now. You are fighting for people."

"Can I ask what happened?" Zara said.

"My children always did well in school. We went to the screens at the government house every day. I made them study hard, and they didn't want to be taken to the CME school, so they worked hard. All three of them did their best and always passed their tests. In June, when they sat down and began their tests, they were all in English. Their classes were always in Spanish, but all of a sudden, this year, they said all the tests would be in English. They took English classes at school, but they don't know enough to take their tests in English after studying in Spanish all year! We knew it was on purpose."

"So, then they came and took them," Jude surmised.

"Yes. My husband Paulo was so angry that he attacked the troops. He was beaten down by the soldiers, and then they wanted to make an example of him, so they shot him right there. They killed my husband in front of us. My poor children were terrified. I have not heard from them since."

"Oh, Sonja," Zara sympathized. "I'm so sorry. What are the names of your children?'

"Paulo, after his father, Humberto, Y Eva. Paulo is sixteen now, Humberto is fourteen, and my Eva is only twelve. She is strong, though."

"You must be so angry," Zara said. "We've seen the Department of Education change the tests, but not the language. That was such a brazen violation of policy, it makes me think they will try whatever they think they can get away with."

"Of course," Sonja said. "We are poor, and many of us cannot speak English. What can we do? I was angry for many days, but then I thought about Paulo. If he had not tried to hurt the soldiers, he would still be alive. He gave them a reason to kill him. That is when I knew how we had to fight back. I heard about *Los Garriones* and how they help the SACs without fighting, and that's when I knew I had to find you."

With temporary passports in place, they decided to hit the GSA and Texico border on the main highway and save time, battery power, and their spines from the winding and unpredictable back roads. They pulled up to the checkpoint and rolled down the windows.

"Nice vehicle," the border agent said suspiciously.

"I'm a bit of an old-school gearhead," Jude said. "I found this old beauty headed for the recycling plant. I increased the batteries, added some regenerative brakes and solar panels, and took out the all-wheel drive to lighten it up. What do you think?"

The guard was impressed. "Very nice. Where are you heading?"

"California. I've been working with some SACs on their power grids, but now I'm taking a break. I just couldn't keep the girls away."

"I see. Your scans seem to agree. The temporary passports look valid." He looked back at Sonja, then at Zara, and finally back at Jude. "You're a lucky bastard."

"What can I say?" Jude said, smiling. "Girls love the Jeep."

"Get out of here and have a good time."

"Thanks."

"Baja is very dry," Jude said. "How do the SACs survive?"

"CAMO is not good at farming in the desert," Sonja said. "Many SACs have survived because we can bring life out of almost nothing. Where there is more water, we grow corn, lettuce, and even tomatoes. Where there is less water, we grow grass and raise cows. We build houses on stone and raise crops on every patch of land that we can sprinkle with water. Now CAMO is taking even these lands away."

"Why?" Jude asked, his engineering brain racking itself to understand what value CAMO would find in the deserts of Baja.

"That's why," Sonja said, pointing out the front window.

Between the main highway and the coast southeast of Houston was a vast area of endless pipes, giant drums, angular buildings, and a network of small roads. At what looked like a decidedly secure and uninviting entrance, there was a large sign that read, "Beaumont Desalination Plant." Underneath in block letters it read: CAMO.

"I can't believe it!" exclaimed Jude. "CAMO is their own water source!"

"We see these pipes and tanks come into Baja," Sonja explained. "Wherever they go, the SACs disappear, and the land turns green."

"A hundred years ago, this was all oil refineries and pipelines. They have replaced and maybe even retrofitted much of the infrastructure to create usable water. With this kind of operation, they could transform all of Texico and Baja. They could grow whatever they want in the desert," Jude said, his mind racing.

"I think they started in Baja," Sonja said. "We are poorer and our land is drier. First comes the tanks, then the pipeline, and then the big machines that till and plant the soil. Next come the soldiers."

"That's why they're being more aggressive about moving kids to CME schools in Baja. Once the kids are in the city, the parents are more easily persuaded to move to be near their children. It's a very coordinated effort between the Department of Education and CAMO," Jude said. "New America is going back on its promise to the SACs."

"Thanks for my next headline," Zara said.

By the time they reached El Paso, the Sparrow Wagon was in need of a rest and recharge. The final few kilometers over the hills before town almost stopped them in their tracks, but on the downside, Jude got enough juice back to get them just outside of town.

"What is that line along the river?" Zara asked.

"That's the border," Sonja replied.

"What border?"

"The old US-Mexican border."

"Whoa. Why is it still there?"

"It was big. It's broken down in places, like over there near the bridge. That used to be a border crossing."

"That is so strange," Zara mused. "I get wanting to stop crime, but why did they put so much effort into stopping people from looking for work?"

"Don't take our jobs," Jude chimed in. "Scapegoating, protectionism, and nationalism were normal. Of course, when there are no more jobs for anyone, the border becomes almost arbitrary."

"Look at the shacks people live in," Zara remarked. "They are everywhere."

"They have always been there," Sonja said. "For many people, Cubes were a big improvement. I have friends who went to the city and told me people keep their shacks for extra space and consider their Cube their main home. If the Cube is plugged in and piped in, they have power and working kitchens and bathrooms. That is more than many people ever had before."

"Speaking of Cubes, let's see if we can find a hotel," Jude said. "I'm beat."

"I'm afraid I have no money," Sonja apologized. "But if it is okay with you, I can sleep in the Sparrow Wagon."

Jude and Zara looked at each other and laughed.

"No matter what, we stick together," Zara said.

"And you're stuck with us," Jude added.

It didn't take long after crossing the border from Texico to California before they began to see sprawling desert Cube communities. For the first time, they saw planned Cube communities, where residents attempted to arrange the Cubes as aesthetically as possible and surround the neighborhood with inviting landscaping. There were awnings, palm trees, small additions, and every manner of trying to cover up the ubiquitous angular architecture.

They also saw many more double Cubes and quad Cubes, where families and friends combined their assigned units to create larger, shared living spaces. There were also clearly former multiple Cube units where someone got fed up and took their Cube with them, leaving a conspicuous gap and hanging connections in their wake.

The closer to the coast they came, the denser the population was. Signs of wealth and former wealth grew, with large houses and communities of large houses becoming more abundant. There was also a phenomenon they encountered that seemed to be unique to California: Cube Towers. They were not the Cube hotels they had seen in Vancouver that were three or four levels high and stacked in a large square. These were single cubes stacked on top of each other straight up twenty-five high.

"We are in California, right?" Jude asked.

"That's what the sign said," Zara replied.

"How is stacking twenty-five Cubes a good idea in a place known for earthquakes?"

"And there are so many wires all over the place," Zara said.

"Those are cables," Jude said, scanning the scene. "The scaffolding around the stacks isn't just for the elevators. They have anchor cables attached to the Cubes. It must be for some kind of suspension support. It doesn't seem sturdy to me."

"But it is cheap. How else can you get twenty-five families on the same one hundred square meters of land?" Sonja said.

Jude and Zara looked at each other with surprise and then back at their friend.

"What? I have built many houses and buildings. These hands don't look like this from cooking all day long," Sonja said.

As they drove and took in the massive urban landscape, it slowly dawned on Jude that it might be difficult to find another hotel. Usually, they rolled into a SAC where they were welcomed with open arms, but in California, they went straight to the cities.

"Do you know of any SACs out here?" he asked.

"Not in Southern California. There are a few up near the Cascadia border, but that is a thousand kilometers away."

Jude checked his e-cash balance. He wasn't planning on paying for so many hotels, and in the cities, you couldn't exactly hunt and cook over a fire. The Sparrow Wagon was a tight fit with Zara, which was fun and romantic, but with Sonja, there just wasn't room for the gear and the bodies. They needed to pay for food and shelter.

"Well, look at that," Jude said, staring at his phone.

"What is it?" Zara asked.

"When Max said to head to California, he didn't leave us high and dry. Should we look for a hotel near the beach?"

After checking into a very old motel a reasonable distance from the beach and paying almost double to secure the Sparrow Wagon, they hailed a transport and made their way to Huntington Beach.

"There's probably a lot more going on here than in Biloxi," Jude said. "Years ago, this is where they held professional beach volleyball tournaments and shot a lot of segments for big shows." He was giddy with excitement, and for a rare moment, he revealed how young he really was.

"I'm excited to see the Pacific Ocean," Zara said.

Sonja was conspicuously and judiciously silent.

The transport brought them to the old Pacific Coast Highway and pulled into a drop lot. Jude paid the fare, and they scrambled to the top of the mound overlooking the beach. To the south, behind a stone and steel barrier that extended out half a kilometer into the water, was a beautiful resort with perfectly trimmed palm trees, pristinely clean and sifted sand, umbrellas and beach chairs, swimming pools, and the echoing sounds of kids and families on vacation. On this side of the barrier was the public beach. Jude and Zara looked at each other in disbelief. Sonja caught up with them, still quiet.

"This is definitely nothing like the Gulf," Zara said.

"I can't tell if that's sand or dirt," Jude said.

They surveyed the beach, taking in the shocking disparity. The sand was brown, clumpy, and so full of garbage it was hard to tell what was sand and what was dirt. Faded and chipped concrete structures that used to hold restrooms and showers were now crumbling shelters for the few homeless people who managed to fight for their spot. Tents littered the beach, with bags, towels, and cooking implements strewn everywhere. Some of the waders were relaxing in the water, and some were bathing.

"Did you know about this?" Jude asked Sonja.

"I suspected it would be like the beaches in Baja. For so many people, there is nowhere else to go."

Among the cacophony of the water, the wind, and the myriad of voices, a shrill crying sound made its way to Sonja's ears.

"What's that?" she asked.

"It sounds like squealing or crying," Zara said. "Maybe it's coming from the private beach.

Sonja didn't respond and immediately took off following the sound.

"I think it's coming from a tent over there," Jude pointed down the beach. He and Zara followed Sonja as she honed in on the sound.

They approached the tent, and the shrieking confirmed they found the right spot. It sounded like two or more young girls crying and screaming in terror. Sonja unzipped the door in one fluid motion and threw back the cloth to expose a stomach-turning scene. A rough-looking, unshaven, filthy man who looked to be another beach-dweller was rifling through the pockets of a thin, defenseless woman who lay flat on her back. Upon looking closer, not only was she not resisting, her stiff arms followed the jerking motions of her body as he turned her back and forth searching for valuables. She was not only dead, but she was in full rigor.

Zara stepped back, covering her mouth and managed to get a few meters away before losing her lunch. A flash of anger swept over Jude, and he took hold of the man's ragged pants, pulling him off the woman and out of the tent. Flipping him over and recoiling for a swift punch to the mouth, he stopped himself. The wild-eyed man was missing teeth, donned a torn, soiled Hawaiian shirt with no buttons, and had bare feet. He put up his arms in a flimsy defense, and Jude regained his composure. Taking the wallet and few trinkets from him, he stood him back up and ordered him to flee, which he gladly did.

Sonja immediately assessed the three terrified girls who looked to be between ten and fourteen years old and took them by the hand and ushered them out of the tent. While Jude went back in to assess the body, Sonja sat the girls on a low concrete sand barrier and flagged a nearby LEAD unit.

"Pobrecitas," she said sympathetically. The girls looked to be Hispanic, but then so did Zara. "Do you speak English?" she asked.

They all nodded, and the oldest spoke up. "Yes. We translated for our mama all the time."

"Was that your mother?" she asked.

The girls resumed a subdued sobbing, but the oldest steeled herself and explained. "Mama was very sick. We tried to take care of her, but this morning she didn't wake up. We didn't know what to do. We were crying and trying to decide where to go, then that man came in and . . . "

"It's okay," Sonja said softly. "It's going to be okay." She took all three of them and enveloped them in a warm motherly hug. As she embraced them, she noticed they were very thin and frail.

The LEAD unit approached, ran an automatic scan of everyone, and unceremoniously declared, "Elena Garcia, deceased." It called for police transport to the Medical Examiner's office. Thinking on her feet, Sonja wanted to assess the girls before the LEAD unit whisked them off to some horrific foster care system and separated them. She asked the girls, "Tienes familia?"

"Si, pero estan in Baja. Mama brought us up here to look for a job last year after Papa died. All our family is back in Baja."

"Do the minor children require emergency care?" the LEAD unit asked.

"No," Sonja snapped back. "I am a friend, and I will care for them and bring them back to their family."

"Affirmative."

Jude rejoined them, holding an ashen-looking Zara's hand and extending his hand to the oldest girl. "These are yours now." He dropped a delicate necklace, two rings, and a couple of bracelets that looked like potential heirlooms. They were modest, but they were all they had of their mother.

"Thank you," she said, wiping a tear away.

"My name is Sonja Orozco, and I am from Baja too. I came all the way from Oaxaca. This is Zara, and this is Jude. They are from all the way up in Cascadia. We're going to help you. You're safe with us."

"My name is Maya," the oldest one said. "This is my younger sister, Olga, and this is my baby sister, Juanita."

Zara managed to compose herself and tenderly asked them, "Are you hungry?"

They all nodded vigorously.

"Well then, let's get something to eat. What do you say?"

They instinctively looked to Sonja as if asking permission.

"Vamanos, mijas. We will eat, and then we will go to a real hotel and sleep. Have you ever been to a real hotel?"

They all shook their heads no with wide eyes.

"After that, we will find a way to get you back to your familia. Does that sound good?"

"Yes!" they said, the younger ones finally breaking their silence as their fear and uncertainty began to melt away.

Sonja felt a tug on her shirt, and she looked down to see Juanita smiling at her. "Are you angels?" she asked with wonder in her doughy brown eyes.

"No, mija," Sonja said. "We are Sparrows."

Sonja and Zara let their heart run away with their appetites. When they returned to the hotel room with food, it was clear they would have enough for themselves and probably a good part of the neighborhood. Zara and Sonja enlisted the help of the girls to prepare the smorgasbord, strategically feeding them pieces of tortillas, a bite of beans, and sips of water to test out their starved stomachs. Jude would jump in as soon as he got off the phone with Max.

"What are you going to do?" Max asked.

"I think we're done with this California vacation," he said after explaining the events at the beach. "And Sonja needs to head back to Baja. She wants to reunite the girls with their families, and after that, she is going to establish a 'Sparrow School' to train SAC leaders."

"You mean like your parents have started doing in Slate Creek for Yukon SAC leaders?" Max asked.

"They are?" he said, surprised.

"Yes. You've started a movement, Jude."

"You should see what is happening, Max. I feel like I'm leading a lost cause. Between CAMO, the Department of Education, and just the struggle of living outside a city, SACs are disappearing."

"You're not leading a battle for land, Jude. You're leading a fight for hearts, minds, and unity. On that front, the Sparrows are winning."

"Leave it to you to bring perspective."

"Why don't you go back to Slate Creek and see your parents? It will be good for both of you. Family is everything, you know."

Jude paused for a moment, and Max could almost hear the gears turning in his head. "I have an idea," Jude said.

"Why do I have the feeling this is going to cost me more money?" Max moaned.

"I want to give the Sparrow Wagon to Sonja. She's going to be a force down in Baja, and the least we can do is give her some wheels."

"What about all your tools and equipment?" Max asked.

"She's going to need them when she's training SAC leaders."

"I want to argue with you, especially about that Jeep, but it makes too much sense. Give Sonja my regards and get a couple of SEMIC train tickets to Vancouver. I'll see about chartering a transport to Slate Creek from there."

"You're the best, Max."

"I know."

"You didn't get to see their faces, but we saved the lives of three beautiful girls today. You were part of that."

"I know."

"We're doing good things, Max. We're giving people hope."

"I know."

Chapter 20: **Winter**

WITH A LETTER FROM Callum via his attorney and a video call from Maisy, Christmas in Slate Creek was one for the books. Zara's fears of feeling like an outsider among the Kane family melted away as soon as Marren got her arms around Zara and drafted her to help transform the old school room into an office for Sparrow operations. Rod told incessant dad jokes and embarrassing anecdotes about Jude, and within a few days, Zara took her place as the newest Kane daughter, whether she liked it or not.

Despite Jude and Zara's Christmas break, Sparrow training was in full swing. A "Sparrow Handbook" put together by Zara, as well as a few video lessons of Jude explaining basic electrical maintenance of the power grid, construction shortcuts, and crop management, were circulating and being multiplied among the SACs. Sonja had also already made a Spanish translation of the handbook and began making her own video lessons in Spanish and tailoring them to the unique needs of the dry Baja climate.

"We're everywhere," Zara said to Jude as he came in from the fields. "The Poconos SAC in New England used Marren's study guide and got all their kids past the latest round of testing. SACs all over New England and Appalachia are moving fast to prepare for winter. Sonja's marching south, and Yukon SAC leaders are already putting their lessons from your parents into practice. CAMO is going to have their work cut out for them this Spring if they think they can cut in on SAC land."

Jude came in and sat down with a big sigh.

"What's wrong?" asked Zara.

He looked pensively at her with a weak smile. "Do you ever stop and wonder if we might be doing more harm than good?"

"How is that even possible?" she asked.

"What if we are starting something we can't finish? What if Spring comes, and CAMO comes back with troops?"

"You're worried we poked the bear."

"That's a good way to put it."

"The thing is, the bear is stealing our food. It promised to leave us alone, but it keeps circling the camp. At least now we can warn other campsites, make it harder for the bear to take our food, and if we need to run, we have some warning."

"That's a great way to put it. I just worry that we've encouraged SACs to get into a fight they can't win, and I don't want to be responsible for people getting hurt."

"If people get hurt, it's the government doing it, not us," Zara insisted. "The people who have electricity, healthy crops, and their children still home with them wouldn't blame you if things go bad. In fact, they are much better prepared now if that happens."

"Still . . . " he began.

"We took a stand at Chillicothe, and we did the right thing. We may have caused some waves, but don't forget they were on their way before we ever got there. In every SAC we've visited, we've helped people. We've never encouraged anyone to take up arms or provoke the government. We're doing the right thing, Jude. Don't forget that."

"Yeah, you're right," he said. He tried to shake the feeling, but it wouldn't quite let go. Jude felt responsible for the SACs. In the recesses of his heart, he felt the dull foreboding that things were going to get worse before they got better— if they ever did.

The wind was gusting through the majestic Canadian Rockies, and the billows of snow were so turbulent you couldn't tell what was falling and what was being kicked up. Zara stood in the office staring out the window at the storm, cradling her warm cup of coffee.

"Beautiful, isn't it?"

Zara jumped, nearly spilling her coffee. "You scared me," she said, patting her chest.

"Sorry about that. When my boots come off, I'm a bit of a sleuth," Rod said. With thick woolen socks, hearty denim trousers, and a thick red and black plaid shirt, he was well insulated.

"You and Marren have an enviable collection of old paper books," she said. "There is something timeless and profound about a library."

"I agree," Rod said, sinking into an overstuffed love seat he upholstered himself for Marren a few years ago. He set his coffee down on the end table and let out a sigh. "I love this time of year. The crops are in, the wind turbines are spinning out lots of power, and somehow hot coffee tastes so much better when you are watching the storm from this side of the window."

"Winter was always a panic in Squamish River. Windows were rattling and drafty, there was never enough good firewood or power for heat, never enough food in the pantries, and even the coffee was bitter and tepid. I've never really enjoyed the beauty of where we live. This is truly a majestic land," she said, still staring out the window.

"It's hard to enjoy anything when you're cold and hungry," Rod said, taking a sip of his coffee. "To be fair, I am a relatively obsessive engineer. I'm sure your father did the best he could."

Zara glided to the loveseat and sank into the other side. "It was better when Mom was around. When we lost her, he slowly sank into himself. Akal and I tried to take up the slack, but we ended up spending our time taking care of him and each other. The SAC needed leadership. Thank you for welcoming the Squamish families here."

"Of course. We're up here to live, not just survive. More hands, more help, and more love can't hurt."

Zara smiled and stared around the room. Noticing a shelf with several versions of the same book, she got up to inspect them.

"You have quite a few versions of the Bible. Do they all say something different?" she asked.

"No," he said. "They just translate the Hebrew and Greek in slightly different ways. Scholarship improves our understanding of ancient languages, and English is a living, changing language itself. Translation is a continual process of updating and fine tuning. Of course, those paper Bibles are almost a hundred years old, but they still hold up pretty well."

"I take it the Bible is important to you. Jude said you and Marren had the kids study Bible and Theology in school."

"Yes, we did. We never expected them to become Philosopher-Kings, but we hoped they would have a faith foundation."

"Before you know what you're doing, you need to know why you're doing it," she recalled.

"Exactly. I guess some of it did sink in," Rod chuckled.

"I think I believe in God, but I'm not so sure. My grandfather was a devout Muslim, and my father taught me about the religion, but he wasn't a strict follower of Islam. By the time I came along, it was just traditions we brought from Pakistan several generations ago."

"Religion has all but faded into tradition and history," Rod said, taking another sip of coffee. "And I think that is not necessarily a bad thing. Religion is about people trying to reach God with traditions and institutions, which eventually always fail. If you can tease the faith out of the religion, you might find some real truth."

"How do you do that?" she asked.

Rod got up, ran his finger across the hard paper and leather spines of his Bible collection, and slipped one out. He handed it to her and said, "Read everything in red."

The first cabinet meeting of the year with President Blake Connor took place in late January after his reelection to a third term.

"A few days from now we will celebrate the tenth anniversary of New America, and what a celebration it will be!" he said as the room erupted in cheers and applause. "I grew up in the tumultuous decades leading up to the Transition, and as long as I can remember, I vowed to do everything I could to never let our country fall into that kind of despair again.

"I still remember when ADAMS first went online. I remember the resistance to the radical solutions we had to implement, and I recall very clearly the day the Constitution was suspended, and the troops rolled out. I remember the blood that was shed to save us from destroying ourselves.

"I also remember the day that a restructure of the tax code and a Universal Basic Income was announced, and the calm that quickly followed in the streets. I remember Canada agreeing to join us and form a completely new nation called 'New America.' And I remember the day, five long years after the beginning of the Transition, when we added a green stripe to the flag and Mexico joined us. Within days the remaining small, bankrupt countries in Central America followed suit, and New America, now encompassing the entire continent, was born. Boy was Australia jealous!"

Laughter and applause erupted again, and President Connor soaked it in for a few moments. His cabinet had coalesced around its charismatic leader.

"In the beginning, ADAMS determined the people fleeing to the mountains, forests, swamps, deserts, and other remote hiding places posed no real threat. We all remember when the term 'Sustainable Agricultural Communities,' came into our vocabulary. SACs have always been small, with fewer than 250 people, and nothing more than radical outsiders that never fit into society anyway. ADAMS, and people with common sense, figured that most of them would return to the cities after the first winter, and many of them have.

"Unfortunately, in the past few months, we have seen a dramatic reversal of that trend. People are not leaving their SACs, and in some cases, more people are actually joining them. We ran a few tests: we cultivated some land where SAC crops had failed, we increased the rigor of the grade-level exams, and we sent some drones to survey the registered SACs. We met with fierce resistance.

"After a nearly complete failure rate with the new grade level exams, students suddenly were able to pass the alternative exams. We had a survey drone shot down in a SAC in the Cascadian Rockies, and we've seen SACs begin to stake out their fields in an effort to repel CAMO agricultural machinery. Until now, I have chosen mercy over force, but it appears these emboldened SACs are intent on rebellion.

"I'm not criticizing past decisions or advice, mind you; the timing may have been premature, and I appreciate that we didn't start a conflict before there was a clear cause. One of the first things I did after returning from the holidays was to have ADAMS reassess the threat level of the SACs in light of recent events. ADAMS' analysis of the sudden reversal of the trend is due to something or someone in particular. SACs are no longer shrinking and failing because they are getting help with energy production, crop and livestock management, and education. The group is very elusive, but ADAMS' meta-analysis was able to identify the group responsible from chatter picked up from SAC members online. They call themselves 'The Sparrows.' They are not only elusive, but they are subversive, teaching SACs techniques to resist CAMO, the Department of Education, and in some cases even Regional Defense Forces.

"I am disappointed in the regional governments that they have not picked up on this activity and have allowed these 'Sparrows' to run freely, but I also recognize they don't have the resources that ADAMS does. I have ordered the New America Defense Forces to share this information with the RDFs, and going forward they will partner with us in rooting out this latest threat to our stability and our democracy."

"Max! It's good to hear your voice. How was Christmas in Kansas City?" Jude tried his best to mask his curiosity. He was dying to hear an update on Callum.

"It was warm and full of friends and family. And by warm, I mean unseasonably rainy and warm. It was a very brown Christmas. Maisy sends her greetings along with a threat that if you don't get down here to see her soon, she will disown you," he said.

"That's not true. She would probably just sock me one good time. She grew up with older brothers. She prefers physical violence."

Max laughed on the other end of the line. "I have missed you, Jude."

"The feeling is mutual."

"I suppose you want to know what is going on with Callum?"

"Yes, I would. Being home has made me miss that hot-headed buzzard more than I thought I ever would."

"The attorney has met with prosecutors, and they told him they are no longer looking at this as simply destruction of government property. They are now treating this as a case of domestic terrorism."

"Are you serious, Max?"

"When he questioned them, they were pretty tight-lipped, but he said he got the sense they were being pressured from higher up. The only thing that has changed between the time Callum was arrested and now is the resurgence of the SACs. He thinks President Connor has gotten wind of the SACs turning things around and standing their ground, and he wants to stamp out any hint of rebellion. As for me, I think Callum is a visible sign of SAC rebellion, but I don't think the President has tied the Sparrows to Callum, at least not yet. There is still no hearing date set, and they are likely not going to be in a hurry. I'm sorry, Jude. I wish I had better news."

"Is there anything else we can do, legally?" he asked.

"I'm afraid not. We're up against the Executive Branch of the New America Government. This is considered a national security threat now. There's no one higher to appeal to."

"Yes, there is," Jude growled. "The people."

"I've heard that tone before," Max said. "Should I be worried?"

"It's winter, Max. It's time for the Sparrows to fly south."

"Okay, boss. Give me a couple of days to arrange a transport from Slate Creek to Vancouver. Are you going to take the SEMIC train to Washington, D.C.?"

"We'll come to Kansas City first. We need to see Maisy, and then we can meet in the Bunker and go from there."

"That sounds good. You need to be careful, Jude. Things might get hot," Max warned.

"Of course they will," Jude said. "Maybe then we'll see some movement."

"I'm not talking about Callum. I've got sources in D.C., and they told me that one of the first things President Connor did when he returned from the holidays was to have ADAMS run a threat analysis of the SACs. He wanted to know why the steady collapse of SACs suddenly stopped. ADAMS didn't reclassify SACs as a threat, but it did find out the reason for the recent success of the SACs was because of the Sparrows. That was enough to classify us as a threat."

"How did ADAMS find out about the Sparrows?" Jude asked.

"It picked up on chatter between SACs. It doesn't look like Zara's posts have been seen directly, but if ADAMS has algorithms that can pick out chats coming from SACs, it's only a matter of time until someone slips up and mentions the Sparrow Press."

"If it can identify online chats that consistently come from known SAC IP addresses, it will monitor them and may be able to hack in and work backward. ADAMS may already know who we are, where we've been, and what we've done," Jude said.

"I don't think so, at least not yet," Max said, trying to be reassuring. "And even if that happens, you haven't technically done anything illegal. You're just helping people."

"We'll see when we come for a visit. Our passports will be scanned half a dozen times by the time we get there. If we make it, we're still in the clear."

"Now I really can't wait to see you," Max said.

It took a week before the weather cleared enough for a transport to make it to Slate Creek. As Jude and Zara said their goodbyes and lifted off, they stared at the snow-covered mountains and valleys below.

"I can't even make out the highway we took on the motorcycles," Jude mused.

"You couldn't make it out if you were on a motorcycle on the ground right now," she said. "And I highly doubt we'd find the cabin again."

"Are you feeling nostalgic for the cabin?" Jude teased.

Zara rubbed her ankle. "I don't think so."

The scans before boarding the SEMIC train didn't throw up any flags, and they both let out a sigh of relief. At least they were clear from Vancouver to Kansas City. When they arrived at the station, Max had a surprise waiting for them: Maisy.

With a squeal and a jump, Maisy threw herself at Zara, nearly knocking her over. Next, she turned to Jude and threw a punch straight into his upper arm.

"Ouch!" he yelped.

"Baby," she said before embracing him firmly and kissing him on the cheek. "Let's get back to Ozark."

The first order of business back at the Bunker was to decide how to handle the new "fame" of the Sparrows.

"I can put the word out and ask the SACs to not talk about the Sparrows on open servers," Zara tepidly offered.

"Would that really work?" Maisy asked.

"Probably not," Zara admitted. "We've been all over the country. People are excited, and excited people talk."

"Don't do it, Zara," Jude said decidedly. "Don't censor the SACs. We're not the government. We don't control what they say or do or think. If the New America government figures out who we are, let them find us. If they do, let them accuse us. I would welcome the chance to go on trial for helping people."

"What about starting something you can't finish?" Zara reminded him. "You were so worried about people getting hurt."

"If they blame me, maybe that will take the heat off of the SACs."

"What about us?" Zara asked. "What about Callum?"

"Let's not get ahead of ourselves," Max interjected, saving Jude. "All ADAMS knows is that the SACs were helped by something or someone that goes by the name 'Sparrows.' At this point, it doesn't know who the Sparrows are or what they've done. When and if it finds out, there will be no crime to accuse the Sparrows of. This is a case I could win, and my bet is ADAMS will figure that out before anything goes that far."

"Okay, I feel better," Maisy announced unceremoniously. "In the meantime, what are we going to do about Callum?"

"I think we need to go to Washington D.C. We need to apply some pressure," Jude said.

"Just a reminder," Maisy said waiving her finger, "You and Zara are on the verge of being identified as the leaders of a group that has officially been classified as a threat by ADAMS. I don't think you need to be making a spectacle of yourselves right now."

"I didn't say we would make a spectacle of ourselves. I just said we need to apply some pressure. We need to get close to the action and then come up with a plan."

"You're covered in meat and going into the Lion's Den," Maisy said.

"We'll keep an ultra-low profile. I don't plan to make myself or Zara known," Jude promised. "Think about it: where is the one place our passports have never been scanned, and the last place you'd expect to find someone who is wanted by the national government?"

"Probably Washington, D.C.," Maisy conceded.

"I'll get you the information for my contacts in D.C.," Max said. Watching the young, passionate activists work out their plans gave him the hope and the life he needed to persevere. Now all he needed to do was keep them out of jail.

Part Three

Chapter 21: **Too Easy**

RATHER THAN DRAWING A straight line from Kansas City to Washington, D.C., Jude and Zara decided to avoid as many scanners as possible, just in case they were being tracked. Max was not happy about needing to supply the Sparrows with another vehicle, but Jude promised they were only borrowing it, and it would be returned in good condition. Max laughed.

"I'll believe it when I see it."

This time around, the vehicle was a compact SUV type with driver and driverless modes, but it was nowhere near as rugged as the old Sparrow Wagon. They packed every crack and crevice, which was tight even without Jude's tools and supplies.

"All set? Max said as they were checking off their lists and racking their brains for anything they might have forgotten.

"I think so," Jude said.

"Got it!" Zara yelled, pulling a hair straightener from her bag and then neatly packing it back in. "With my stubborn hair, I need all the help I can get."

"Especially at the beach," jabbed Jude.

"Very funny, Einstein," she said.

"Call if you get stuck or lost or in trouble. Call if you don't. When you get there, give me a call," Max said.

"Got it. We'll keep you in the loop," Jude assured him.

After a bumpy ride out of the bunker and over some rough fields, they found the main east-west highway and headed out.

"Where to first?" Zara asked.

"We have to cross into Appalachia between Cairo and Memphis," Jude explained. "Otherwise, we end up needing to cross two borders."

"I had no idea we were going to Egypt," Zara quipped. It took Jude a minute, but then he laughed.

"Good one! I never thought of that."

"You never answered my question," Zara said.

"Where to first?"

"When did you turn into Maisy?"

"When we figured out we are targets."

"If all goes according to plan, we'll stop and recharge in Poplar Bluffs here in Texico and then cross into Appalachia and stop in Nashville, Asheville, Roanoke, and then D.C."

"I approve," she said, looking at the map on her phone. "Are we stopping at any SACs?"

"We need to get to D.C. and get underground as soon as possible. When and if we become officially wanted, we'll have a lot harder time getting around."

"Agreed. We take the D.C. express on this trip."

After a rest and recharge in Poplar Bluff, they headed for the Appalachia border.

"We have a small problem," Jude announced as he looked at the map on his phone.

"What's that?" Zara asked.

"There are lots of back roads, but not lots of bridges. We have to cross the Arkansas River, and that means crossing a bridge, which means . . ."

"Scans," Zara said.

"We can try to go around through another region," Jude weakly proposed.

"No," Zara said. "It would take forever. Besides, if ADAMS just picked up on the Sparrows, I don't think it's identified us yet."

"It's taking a chance, but then again, this way we'll know if we're on ADAMS's radar yet."

"Let's do it."

Despite their brave faces, their anxiety reared up when they approached the daunting suspension bridge. Regional borders were not as strict as national borders, but they were a great way to track the movement of citizens. It gave regional governments an excuse to scan registration and passports, alerting them to possible warrants, citations, or other nefarious reasons for getting out of town.

"Welcome to Appalachia, Home of the Great Smoky Mountains," Zara read as they passed under the sign.

"So far so good," Jude said, taking a deep breath.

"Just make it past the checkpoint," said Zara, nervously tapping her fingers and bouncing her knee.

"It looks like the RDF soldier is just waving everyone by. Smile and wave, just smile and wave," Jude said with a plastic grin fastened to his visage.

As they approached, the soldier motioned for Jude to roll down his window. They exchanged a split-second glance of panic and then swallowed their pounding hearts.

"Good morning. Can I get you to pull over here for a second?" he asked, pointing to a parking spot next to the checkpoint building.

"S-sure thing," Jude said, trying to steady his hand and tongue.

He went back to waving traffic by, and another soldier approached the car with a tablet screen in his hand and a small box of what looked like coffee mugs.

"Is there a problem, sir?" Jude asked.

"That depends. Do you have any warrants?" he asked with a scowl.

"No, sir," Jude said.

"How about her?" he asked, nodding to Zara.

Jude looked at the soldier's hard eyes and thought he had a small chance to crack the tension.

"She's all kinds of trouble, but I don't think she has any warrants out."

After a two-second pause, the soldier burst out laughing.

"Good one. I know what you mean. The troublemakers are the most fun, though."

Jude nodded and smiled. Zara redoubled her effort to paste her smile on.

"We do a few random detailed vehicle scans every hour, and you were the lucky ones. Sorry for the delay. Just so you won't get the wrong impression of us here, I'm going to give you a couple of coffee mugs," he said, handing Jude two sand-colored mugs with various mountain and river images on them. "Welcome to Appalachia."

"Thank you!" Jude said to the soldier. "And thank you, God," he muttered under his breath.

"Holy monkey knuckles!" Zara blurted out as soon as the window was up. "That scared the living crap out of me."

"Me too. That is not how I expected that to turn out."

"I like your mug," Zara said, holding up one of the cups next to Jude's face with a wry smile.

"You're very funny. Speaking of, did you actually utter the phrase 'monkey knuckles'? Where did that come from?"

"It's an expression I just made up."

"As opposed to the more traditional expression, 'scared the crap out of me?'"

"That wasn't an expression. I need to find a bathroom."

Traffic, crowds, and ever-present surveillance saturated the streets of Washington, D.C. There were no Cubes, no run-down neighborhoods, or any sign of poverty. If you didn't have a job, you didn't live in the District of Columbia. Under the guise of extreme caution, every aspect of life was closely controlled. Employers, the New American Government being the obvious juggernaut, were required to secure housing for their employees and arrange any travel or transportation. Without a preapproved security clearance and a purpose for being there, you earned at least a day in detention and then an express trip to a dump site outside the city border.

Unfortunately, Jude and Zara didn't know this. Usually, one of the thousands of advanced LEAD units would intercept anyone without a D.C. security clearance, but they managed to dodge them as Jude followed specific directions to the attorney's office and parked under his office building using the security code Max gave them.

When Jude pushed the security button, a large nose appeared on the screen, leaned back, and then leaned down to reveal two black eyes under an impressive pair of gray bushy eyebrows.

"Mr. Boris Spence? I'm Jude Kane, and this is Zara Malik. We're here to speak with you about my brother, Callum Kane."

"You're early," came a gruff, gravelly voice through the speaker. "My assistant isn't even here yet."

"May we come up? We've been driving for two thousand kilometers. We don't mind waiting a few minutes," Jude pleaded.

The screen went black, and the door clicked. Jude pulled it open, and they made their way to the third floor. The building was sewn into the Tetris-like maze of medium-sized apartment buildings, office buildings, and ground-level retail shops. It was the closest thing to the old suburbs that still remained.

They made their way up the stairs and followed the smell of freshly brewed coffee to the reception area. The pot was nearly full, but there were no cups to be seen.

"That smells so good," Jude whined.

"It's torture to make coffee and not have cups," Zara said. "Cruel and unusual."

"Actually, we do have cups, don't we?" Jude said.

Zara looked blankly for a second and then remembered. She dug into her bag and fished out two coffee mugs.

"Welcome to Appalachia!"

They took turns filling the cups, and before they could sit back down on the sofa, Boris called to them.

"Come on in, kids."

They took a seat opposite him at his desk, and he settled into his leather high-back chair. He looked like he sounded: he had a large frame, thick salt and pepper hair, dark eyes, and a tired, honest smile on his face.

"I'll get right down to it: we have an uphill battle. I'm generally not a pessimist, but I want to manage your expectations," he said.

"We've watched SACs get squeezed out and children extracted to CMEs after unfair testing. We know what we're dealing with," Zara said.

"Well, it's not all bad for Callum," Boris said. "If they wanted to make him disappear, they would have done that a long time ago. I think they want him to be an example. They want to spin his story. That's a double-edged sword: they likely won't harm him, but they're in no hurry to let him go."

"Maybe we can plead his case," Jude said. "If his family vouches for him, that should be worth something, shouldn't it?"

"President Blake Connor is a Transition hero with no tolerance for dissent. The gears in Callum's case have suddenly stopped moving. I'm doing all I can to get them moving again, but it's not easy. I don't think sympathy will get you very far."

"How about persistence?" Zara said.

"That's a better bet," he said. "By the way, nice matching coffee mugs."

"They were a little gift from the border patrol when we crossed into Appalachia," Jude explained. "We got pulled over for a scan, and we thought we were in serious trouble. Instead, we got a welcome gift."

"The border agents gave you those mugs?" he asked.

"Yes," Jude said.

"After a scan?"

"He said it was a random, detailed vehicle scan."

"There is no such thing. They only scan passports and license plates. Give me your cups," Boris said, taking them and going into the kitchenette area. He poured the coffee out and then dropped the cups on the floor, shattering them. He bent down, picked up the bottom pieces, and turned them over. Small wires were protruding from the sharp, broken edges.

"Son of a . . . " Jude trailed off, angry at himself for not seeing the ruse for what it was.

"What is that?" Zara asked.

"Trackers," Boris said. "They welcomed you to Appalachia with a pair of homing beacons. You two had better get out of here fast! The trackers are off now, so they know you're on to them. They'll be here any minute."

Without another word, Jude and Zara fled out the door, down the stairs, and into the garage. They jumped in, and Jude flipped the switch. He backed out and went around the row of vehicles in the garage, pausing at the street entrance to look both ways before pulling out.

He lurched forward and then immediately slammed on the brakes, throwing them against their seatbelts and causing the tires to chirp on the pavement. A large black transport cut them off, and instantly four troops poured out and surrounded Max's vehicle.

"COATS," Jude said in a hushed breath.

"I think ADAMS knows who we are now," Zara said.

"Put your hands up. Don't say anything except to ask for a lawyer, no matter what," Jude said. Zara looked at him and nodded.

The troops pulled open the doors, pulled Jude and Zara out, zip-tied their hands, and guided them quickly into the transport. One of the troops got into the driver's seat of Max's vehicle, and in one fluid motion, they sped down the street. As they neared an inconspicuous building complex, the driver of Max's vehicle veered off in a different direction while they moved on a few more blocks.

There was silence in the COATS transport. The troops didn't ask questions, and the Sparrows didn't resist. They drove down a ramp into a large underground structure where the transport parked near a large sliding door, and the troops escorted Jude and Zara in.

They were guided to a pair of hard chairs, seated, and told simply, "Captain Bowers will be with you shortly."

After a few minutes, a tall, lanky man in his olive-green dress uniform donning prominent black COATS insignia came in and stood in front of them. Jude shuddered as he recognized the man: he was the commander they rebuffed in Chillicothe just before COATS came and razed it to the ground.

"Surprised to see me?" he asked. "I suppose I have you to thank for my new position. After our little incident in Lakeland, I made it my mission to find out who you really were. It took some time and the resources of the Critical Operations And Tactical Service team, but I put the pieces together. It's nice to finally put some faces to this pesky little subversive group. Welcome to Washington, Sparrows."

Jude and Zara were escorted to separate interrogation rooms. They were searched, seated at a bare table, and their zip ties were cut off. In lieu of the primitive restraints, they each received a hard plastic ankle band with a black box on it.

"I don't think you'll try anything in here," the interrogator said as he came in and ordered the two escort soldiers out with a nod. "But in the spirit of full disclosure, I should let you know that tracker can also deliver 50,000 volts and can transmit and receive signals anywhere in the world."

"Good to know," Jude said flatly. "Am I under arrest?"

"You are being detained."

"Why am I being detained?"

"You are the leader of the Sparrows, correct?"

"You didn't answer my question."

"You are being detained on suspicion of subversive activity. Now answer my question: you are the leader of the Sparrows, correct?"

"If I am not under arrest, I would like to leave now."

"That is not going to happen," the interrogator said, letting slip his first hint of irritation.

"In that case, I would like my attorney present."

"You're not in a local jail, Mr. Kane. You are in the custody of the New American Defense Forces under suspicion of anti-government activities. This is a national security situation. You have no rights."

"I beg to differ, sir. Even under international law, I am entitled to representation and humane treatment. On a more practical level, be assured, sir, I will not tell you so much as the time of day until my attorney is present."

"I see," huffed the interrogator. "You are very confident. I'm afraid your confidence is misplaced. You don't have the protections here you seem to think you do. We can be very persuasive."

"So can we," Jude said with a vicious smile.

"Who are we?"

"Not without my attorney."

The interrogator with Zara took a slightly different approach.

"We just need to ask you a few questions," she said. Zara didn't buy it.

"I'd be happy to help . . . "

"Great!"

" . . . as soon as my attorney arrives."

"Oh. I'm afraid that won't be necessary. It's just a few simple questions."

"I'm afraid it is necessary."

"May I remind you where you are?" she said, her tone shifting darkly. "You are in the custody of the New America Defense Forces. This is a national security situation. You don't have the right to demand anything."

"It doesn't sound like a few quick questions to me."

"Tell me about the Sparrow Press."

"Tell me when my attorney will get here."

"You're not listening."

"You're not understanding. I don't answer a single question until my attorney arrives."

"You'll be here quite a while. Don't you want to see Jude? He's already cooperating, and he'll be done soon."

"Nice try," Zara said.

"He put up a good front until we told him what would happen to you. He didn't hesitate. Apparently, you are his Achilles heel. He can't stand to see you hurt."

Zara hesitated but then decided to call her bluff. "I have no such sensibilities."

"We'll see about that."

Chapter 22: **Throw the Book**

"GOOD MORNING, MR. KANE," the interrogator said cheerfully as he entered Jude's holding cell three days later. "I trust you got plenty of rest?"

"You mean with the lights on and the music blaring? Oh yeah. That's how I fall asleep every night," he said. "And thanks for the bread and water every morning. That one meal has me stuffed."

"Good. We're going to be busy today. We have lots of questions."

"I'll save you some time," Jude snarled. "My answer to everything is 'get my lawyer.' Now, can we shut off the lights and let me get some rest?"

"I'm afraid we're just getting warmed up," the interrogator said, shutting the steel door.

A cement room, painted white and furnished with only a small bed, a stainless steel toilet, and a small sink, was designed for security and hopelessness. You never begin your initial interrogations with a fresh candidate. Beatings can weaken the will, as will other physical and psychological torture, but nothing softens up a victim like sleep deprivation and hunger.

"Let's wake you up a bit before we begin," he said, setting his steel chair in the center of the cell and standing in front of Jude, sitting on his bed. He pulled out a large cattle prod and jammed it into Jude's shoulder.

"Aaah!" Jude screamed, convulsing on the bed.

"Are we awake now?" said the interrogator.

"Yes," gasped Jude. "Haven't you read the research on torture? It's not only inhumane and ineffective, but any information you get is unreliable."

"Is that so, professor?" he said, jabbing him again.

"Aaah!" he screamed, contorting his body until he rolled onto the cold floor.

"Yes, it is so . . . .and now I know why. You just pissed me off, and there's no way I'd say a thing to you even if I had something to say," he panted.

"We'll see about that. I'm very patient," he said with one final jab into Jude's stomach.

"Aaah!" he screamed, flailing on the floor. "Go to . . . hell."

Suddenly, there was a knock on the door, surprising both of them.

"Excuse me," the interrogator said, walking out. Jude heard some muffled voices outside, and then the door opened again. To his shock, Zara, a female interrogator, and his interrogator all came in.

"Jude!" Zara called, running to him and helping him get up on the bed. "What have they done to you?"

"I'm fine," he groaned. "I just haven't slept very well."

"We've discovered something, and I think it will save us all a lot of time and discomfort," the woman said.

"I didn't say anything," Zara reassured Jude.

"Separately, both of you are remarkably resilient, but when it comes to your affections for one another, you are substantially more flexible," she said.

The interrogators took Zara, sat her in the steel chair, and zip-tied her wrists behind her and her ankles to the chair.

"Now, Mr. Kane, we've seen how pain doesn't seem to motivate you, but let's see how stubborn you are when Zara is in pain."

"Don't touch her!" screamed Jude. He stood up from the bed, but a quick jab with the prod from the woman sent him flailing back onto the mattress.

"Aaah . . . ." he groaned, "don't touch her. I'll tell you what you want."

"Jude, no! I can take it!" Zara yelled.

"But I can't," he panted.

A loud banging on the steel door interrupted them.

"What is it now?" Jude's interrogator huffed, stomping to the door. He saw who was outside and called to his counterpart.

"You'd better get out here, too," he said to her.

"Don't go anywhere," she said to Zara, closing the door behind them.

"I can take it, Jude," she said. "If you can take it, so can I."

"No," he said, still catching his breath. "It's not worth it. We can tell them something, and then let Max fight it out in court."

As if on cue, the door swung open, and Max came barreling in.

"What did they do to you?" he said. "Cut these ties off!"

"Max?" Zara said, stunned. "How did you . . . "

"We'll talk later. Did you say anything?"

"No," Zara said. Jude just shook his head.

"Okay, Mr. Simon, you've seen they are fine," a COATS officer said. By his insignia, he was a rank or two above the interrogators.

"I want to accompany them in the transfer," Max demanded.

"You're not in a position to tell anyone what to do, Mr. Simon."

"Of course not, and you're not obligated to grant any requests. I know where I am. I'm simply asking, and if you honor my request, it is only because you want to do the right thing."

"You're a lawyer, that's for sure," the brass said. "Go ahead, but the National Detention Center won't let you hold their hands during processing."

"Understood."

Four COATS troops dressed in their gray and black digital camo uniforms swooped in, cut Zara's ties, patted Jude and Zara again, and escorted them to a transport. Zara tried to reach out and steady Jude as he stumbled, but the soldiers stepped in between and took Jude's arm. They took their seats, sandwiched between the soldiers, and left the COATS base.

"When we reach the detention center, you can go in through the main entrance, Mr. Simon. We'll take the suspects to processing. The staff will let you know when and where to meet your clients," the unit commander said.

"Thank you, Commander," Max said.

Max was a corporate, real estate, and intellectual property lawyer, so meeting clients in a detention center was not in his comfort zone. Of course, fishing them out of COATS custody took some calls and favors, but the front of confidence seemed to have worked so far. He convinced a judge that COATS was barking up the wrong tree if they were looking for terrorists and that Jude and Zara were simply two SAC kids who had the idea of sharing technical, agricultural, and survival knowledge as a way to help make people's lives better. He argued that the Sparrows were as harmless as their name suggested, and the court agreed to the custody transfer until the details could be hammered out in a negotiation or hearing.

It took a couple of hours, but after processing, Jude and Zara were escorted to a secure meeting room. They looked a little ragged from three days in COATS custody and not too happy about the beige jumpsuits, but otherwise, they were healthy.

"I can speak with them both at the same time, and the cuffs are not necessary," Max said to the guard. "I take responsibility for them and my own safety. Besides, you're right outside the door."

"Fine by me. Don't sue me if they cut your throat," he grumbled as he took off the cuffs and closed the door behind him.

"I hardly recognize you," Jude said, still tired and sore from his interrogation but not losing his cheeky wit. "You got a haircut, shaved, and put on an actual suit. You look like a real lawyer."

"I am a real lawyer, but Boris Spence is the real criminal defense guy. Unfortunately, your brother is the one favor he's doing for me. You'll have to settle for me, but Boris said he would advise me, so it's not a completely lost cause," Max said.

"You're brilliant, Max. We have complete confidence in you," Zara reassured him.

"You don't have much choice," he grumbled. "Let's get down to business. First of all, where's my vehicle?"

Jude looked down at the table, shaking his head.

"Still in good order, I presume," he said.

"You presume?" Max said. "Why do you 'presume' and not know?"

"COATS took it. It's somewhere on the base. I'm sure we can get it back," Jude said unconvincingly.

Max sighed. "I'm sure they'll hand the keys right over."

"Thanks for getting us out of COATS custody," Zara said, putting her hand on Max's and refocusing the conversation. "You came just in time."

"We're not out of the woods just yet," he said. "We're in a better place to fight in court, but you both have been identified as the leaders of the Sparrows. The gig is up. Now I need to sell the peaceful, harmless vision of the Sparrows to a prosecutor who thinks he's found a subversive rebel group. That won't be easy."

"What can we do?" Jude asked.

"From in here, you can't do much except to stay true to yourselves. Remember your mantra: sanctity of life, equality of opportunity, and dignity of all people. You have more support than you might think."

"What do you mean?" Zara asked.

"I posted an update after I heard from Boris that you two had been taken. The SACs sent a deluge of emails to their senators, and the Appalachian SACs threatened to protest in person. The pressure paid off, and you guys became political hot potatoes. How else do you think COATS let us walk off their base?"

"Really?" Jude said.

"You're surprised?" Zara said to him. "You've done a lot to help so many people, Jude. Folks don't forget that."

"*We* did," he insisted.

"I'm going to try and get us a hearing as soon as possible, and if all goes well, we win the argument, charges are dismissed, and we all go home. Of course, they could delay the hearing, the hearing may not go well, and we go to trial, or they may decide to stall indefinitely and let you sit in here," Max said. "It's as much of a political issue as it is a legal one."

"At least we're closer to Callum," Jude said. Suddenly, he realized what he said. "We're close to Callum! Isn't he in here too?"

"Yes, but he's on a different block. They're keeping him with the rebels, spies, and terrorists. He's classified as a threat to national security, so he's with a group that doesn't see much daylight. You probably won't see each other, but if you do, making a scene won't exactly do your case any good."

"Got it," Jude said.

"Before I go," Max said, standing up casually and checking the window on the door to make sure the guard was still distracted, "I have a little present for you, Zara."

"Won't you get in trouble for bringing something in here?" she said quietly.

"In this case, you would be in more trouble if I didn't bring it. Your passport is about to expire, and that would complicate things. Hold still."

He made one glance at the door, quickly wiped down an area of her skin with antiseptic, took out an injector, pressed it between her neck and shoulder, and squeezed the trigger.

"Aaah," she hissed, rubbing the injection site.

"You now have your permanent passport, and I made sure your information is up to date. It will override your temporary passport on the other side," Max said. "You can dig that one out if you feel like it."

"How did you get . . . .?" She began.

"Don't ask. Plausible deniability."

"Right," she said.

"I'll keep you posted. Stay strong and don't forget who you are," Max said as he got up to leave. He rapped on the door for the guard.

"Thanks, Max," Jude said.

"Thanks for everything," Zara echoed, struggling to resist the urge to rub her injection site.

Jumpsuits are not flattering, but they are practical. A regular mealtime is not anything to complain about, even if the food barely resembles anything you could grow or hunt. Even keeping company with felons was not unbearable, but the one thing that made detention a hellish experience for Jude was being trapped indoors for twenty-two hours a day.

He tried to take solace in the fact that it was winter, but when he got a glimpse of the snow during rec time, he ached to take a sleigh ride or jump on a snowmobile and whip through the wind turbines. It's hard to cage a wild horse.

"Miss being outside, huh?" another inmate said, jogging up beside Jude as they walked the yard.

"Yeah. I grew up outside. I haven't been stuck inside this much since I was in the womb," Jude lamented.

"Ha!" the man laughed. "I miss it too. I grew up on a SAC. I'm not used to being so socialized."

"Really?" Jude asked. "Which one?"

"I grew up with the Amish, and then a few years ago, I left with my cousin to start a new SAC with other Amish and former Amish families. We liked the farm work and the community, but we thought we could do with more convenience and less tradition. It was called . . . "

"Chillicothe," Jude said, finishing his sentence.

"Yes! You heard of it?"

"Oh yeah. Are you related to Jacob Miller?"

"Yes!" he said. "I'm Kurt Miller, his cousin. Do you know him?"

"Yes, I do. He's a good friend."

"Then you probably know what happened to the SAC."

"I know. I was there."

Kurt froze in his tracks. Not wanting to get the attention of the guards, he caught up to Jude again.

"You were there?" he said in a hushed tone. "Did you join the SAC recently?"

"No. I was there with my sister and friend to help get the power grid back up and running. We just got things moving again when the NADF showed up."

"Holy crap. Are you Jude Kane, the leader of the Sparrows?"

Jude looked at him, smiled, and said, "That's me. You say it like I'm famous."

"You *are* famous. You're a legend!"

"I wouldn't go *that* far," Jude said.

"Jacob told me all about what you did and how you basically saved everyone from getting torched. He told me how you and your friend Zara started the Sparrow Press for the SACs and how you guys have been saving kids from CME extractions. You have given a lot of people hope and made their lives better. You guys are heroes!"

"I spent a few weeks in Chillicothe," Jude said, strategically changing the subject. "I don't remember seeing you."

"I was here by then. I was a runner. I took things to Columbus to sell and bought things there to bring back. SACs aren't supposed to sell to the cities, but we did it all the time. People loved our fresh veggies, real wool socks and sweaters, and fresh baked goods. I got arrested last summer," he explained.

"Fresh baked goods sound pretty good right about now," Jude moaned.

"How did you end up in here?" Kurt asked.

"I almost walked in. I came to D.C. to see if there was anything I could do to get my brother out of here, and apparently, I walked into a trap. ADAMS figured out that SACs stopped declining suddenly. It picked up on this group called 'The Sparrows,' and it figured out who was behind it. I knew it was a risk coming here, but I didn't think ADAMS could identify me and Zara so quickly."

"Want to see something?" Kurt asked.

"Depends on where it is," Jude said, suspecting a delicately placed tattoo.

"Here," he said, rolling his forearm over, revealing a tattoo halfway between his wrist and elbow. It was the image of a Sparrow. "I got it after Jacob told me what happened to Chillicothe."

Modesty slowly melted into reality for Jude. The Sparrows had become far more than a couple of kids helping SACs with their power grids. The Sparrows had become a symbol of hope and humanity.

"Is that cool?" Kurt asked. "Is it alright that I got a Sparrow tattoo? I know I wasn't there when everything went down, but I knew when Jacob told me about you guys, I wanted to be on your side."

"I think it's very cool," Jude said. "There's only one problem."

"What's that?"

"Where's my tattoo?"

Zara took a seat at the end of the table. There were claimed territories in the cafeteria, but without knowing who sat where, she'd have to figure it out by the looks she got. As the new girl, she got looks from everyone.

"Look what we have here, ladies?" a husky middle-aged blonde woman said. "Fresh meat."

Zara smiled nervously. She could smile politely and ignore the remark, or she could let them know who she was. Either way was a risk, but at least they would know she wasn't weak.

"I thought all the fresh meat was on the other blocs with the men."

The women at the table snickered, and the husky blonde said, "This is a girls-only club. We stick to our own kind."

Zara didn't like the insinuation, so she pushed back.

"My boyfriend is on the other side with the men, and his brother is upstairs with the terrorists or whoever they have up there. I guess this whole place is a family affair for me."

The murmurs rumbled down the table, but there were no more comments. She might have to prove it later, but for now, she had some street credit and a little bit of space.

On their way to the library, a young woman with a light Filipino accent caught up with Zara.

"Hey, wait up!" she called.

"Hello," Zara said cautiously.

"My name's Chiela."

"I'm Zara," she said, shaking her hand.

"I like how you stood up for yourself today. You let them know you're strong without trying to get in a fight."

"Well, I'm not a guy with something to prove," Zara said.

"I hope your guy doesn't have to prove anything over on the other side."

"Me either. Jude is pretty smart, and he's no pushover, but he's not a fighter. I hope he doesn't have to learn."

"Did you say Jude?"

"Yes. His name is Jude."

"Jude Kane?"

"You know him?"

"I feel like I know both of you! You are the Sparrows!"

Zara had to catch her breath and her step.

"Um, yes . . . how do you know about us?"

"I've read every post in Sparrow Press. I know about the SACs getting pressure from CAMO. I saw the fire at Chillicothe, and I read about all the SACs you helped. I can't believe you're here!"

"I can't either."

"What happened?"

"The SACs were shrinking and disappearing according to plan, but then suddenly they stabilized. ADAMS noticed. Eventually, it found out about the Sparrows, and then it found out who was behind them. We didn't think ADAMS had identified us yet, but when we came here to see about trying to help Jude's brother, we walked right into the trap."

"That's why there hasn't been a Sparrow Press post in a few days," Chiela lamented.

"They didn't let me keep my phone or my screen."

"That's okay. When we get into the library, sit with me at the screens. I can show you a trick that will bypass security. You can connect to your proxy servers and post an article, and they will never know."

"If you are from a SAC, where did you learn how to hack your way around security?" Zara whispered as they sat down.

"I'm not from a SAC. I'm from Seattle. I used to be a Network Analyst for CAMO. I noticed the mapping protocols were changed, and the plowing and planting machines were cutting into SAC land. I knew that must have been a mistake, so I managed to get in and correct the protocols. I found out that the people who changed the protocols were not happy that I figured out what they did, and they were very unhappy that I was able to assume their admin profiles and recode the parameters. A few days later, I was here.

"I didn't have a lot to do, so I hacked my way out of this network, and that's when I found Sparrow Press. Very good work hiding your posts, by the way."

"Thanks. It must not have been good enough, because ADAMS identified me pretty quickly," Zara said.

"That was probably from the chatter between SACs. If they talked about you and Jude, ADAMS picked up on it. I doubt ADAMS was able to see your posts directly."

"So, if I post from in here, ADAMS won't know?"

"Not if I have anything to say about it."

Jude and Kurt met up in the yard again.

"Nice tattoo," he said.

Jude looked down at the underside of his forearm and smiled. "I like it too. Good idea."

As they strolled, they noticed a small crowd gathered outside the security fence. They weren't making much noise or moving around, but Jude noticed a few of them held up signs. There were no words on the signs that he could make out, but he could see a clear image, even from a distance. The signs all had a picture of a sparrow.

Chapter 23: **Hearing Voices**

If anything will attract a LEAD unit, it's a crowd. Throughout January, the daily crowds outside the detention center steadily drew more and more participants. It became almost routine; people would arrive, carry simple signs that featured the outline, drawing, or even picture of a sparrow, and then disappear. LEAD units would arrive like bees attracted to pollen, but no citations were given.

By February, the crowds grew larger and more vocal. Braving the driving rains, snow flurries, and sometimes treacherous icy pavement, people continued to gather with their sparrow signs, but now they also began to chant phrases like "Let Them Go," "Send Them Home," and "No Crime, No Case." They added poignant slogans to their sparrow signs that read, "It's Not a Crime to Help Your Fellow Man," "The Sparrows Are Innocent," and "Justice for the Sparrows and Justice for the SACs." Jude and Zara's case had become news.

In keeping with the New America media policy, the official news outlets ignored or downplayed any kind of demonstration or protest in order to promote social stability and safety, but the Sparrows had managed to transcend that barrier with a fervor and tenacity that got everyone's attention, including the authorities.

"Why are they still out there?" demanded the voice on the other end of the line. The D.C. Police Commissioner was in a very tough position.

"Mr. Mayor, we have the crowds saturated with LEAD units. We have thousands of hours of footage. We have a dozen human patrol officers on the ground. There have been no violent incidents, and in fact, the protesters regularly bring hot coffee and doughnuts for the officers. These people don't break any laws."

"Don't give me that load of bull, Commissioner. There is no way hundreds of people gather to protest outside a government building and no one even throws a rock."

"These people do. It's almost like they are following specific training or instructions from someone. I'm telling you, Mayor, I almost think a lawyer coached them or something. They don't resist, they don't conceal themselves from LEAD units, and they don't even use foul language. I've got no cause to arrest any of them."

"That's absurd. You've got to be able to round them up on an unauthorized assembly or no permit charge."

"They don't set foot outside public property. They maintain they are private citizens speaking out on behalf of the Sparrows. They obtain daily visitor passes and leave the city by curfew. They are perfectly legal. We can't touch them."

"Hmmm," the Mayor stewed. "I'm getting hell from up above. They don't like people picketing outside a National Detention Center. What do they want? Who are these Sparrows?"

"There are two people in detention— kids, really— named Jude Kane and Zara Malik. All I know is that they have something to do with the SACs. Is there anything else you can find out on your end? The New America national court system doesn't like to share a lot of information with the local cops."

"I'll look into it. In the meantime, if they so much as sneeze on an officer, arrest them and break this thing up."

"Yes, sir!"

"Chiela, listen to this!" Zara whispered. "Max says it's working. The protesters are following the instructions Max had me give them. They are definitely reading the posts! No one has been arrested yet, and Max said he got a call from the prosecution's office. He thinks the protests are putting pressure on them to move us along."

"Finally! They want to drag their heels because they don't have much of a case, but this might force them to make a decision. Too bad I can't get protesters to demand my release!" Chiela said in her chirpy, sarcastic voice, but with a distinct hint of sad reality.

"Chiela Cruz, you are a Sparrow. I have no intention of leaving this place and forgetting you. Our mission isn't over until you and Callum are free," Zara said.

"Zara, you are a true friend. Thank you, but in my case, they have me tied up with 'violation of policy' charges. The only people who could fight for me legally would be people in CAMO, and as a disgraced ex-employee with knowledge of potentially illegal actions, I'm pretty much radioactive. No one in their right mind would touch me."

"Just because you can't see the end of the tunnel, doesn't mean it isn't there," Zara reassured her. "There is always a solution."

"Why am I seeing a reporter interviewing a protester in front of the National Detention Center?" President Blake Connor demanded of his staff, who stood just outside the Lincoln bedroom door as he glanced at the news on the screen, threw his tie around his neck, and started tying it. "How long have they been there?"

"Since mid-January, sir," a staffer replied.

"Mid-January? And the news is giving them coverage? Why don't we invite them to the White House to air their grievances? What the hell is wrong with the police that they allowed this to go on so long? A protest is just the first step of a riot. This is not the old United States. You don't get to start trouble whenever you want, especially on my front doorstep. Get me the Defense Chief."

"Yes, sir."

Callum was less than a hundred meters away, but he might as well have been on the moon. Messages had always been passed between attorneys, but inside the detention center, communication with Max was limited.

Rec time was usually measured precisely to avoid any groups of prisoners crossing paths on their way to or from the yard. One day, a newer guard didn't have his timer set, and Jude and Kurt were late filing back to the cell block. On their way, they watched as another group from the "terrorist bloc" shuffled across the gangway for their turn in the yard, flanked by double the number of guards.

Jude's heart started pounding as it began to dawn on him where these men were from. He watched eagle-eyed as they passed, carefully scanning each face. Towards the end of the line, a thin, slightly hunched man with a skitched head and a week's growth of beard peered straight at Jude and locked eyes with him. Jude stared blankly for a few seconds, and when the man slowly smiled, Jude's throat seized, and his hand reached toward him involuntarily. He almost couldn't recognize his own brother.

Kurt nodded at Callum and then took Jude's arm and whisked him along before the guards took notice. When they returned to the bloc, Jude nodded in thanks to Kurt and then retreated to his room, where he collapsed on his bed, buried his head in his thin, hard pillow, and sobbed.

The tears soon gave way to anger, and the pillow became a sad punching bag for a few rounds before he threw it at the door and then kicked it a few times. He finally bent down, picked it up, dusted it off, and tossed it on the bed. How was he going to tackle this problem? He came to Washington, D.C., to get Callum out, and now he and Zara were stuck in the same place. Callum had had an attorney for months, and there was no sign of his case going to court. He and Zara had been in custody for several weeks, and despite Max's strong case for their innocence, there was still no word. Maybe they weren't doing everything they could.

The next meeting with Max was just after Valentine's Day. It was good to see Max, but it was great to see Zara.

"The pressure is mounting," Max explained. "The official news has interviewed protesters, and I'm getting word from my contacts that they are getting rattled."

"Who are they?" Jude asked.

"High-level officials. It might have even made it to the top. I'm surprised I haven't gotten a call yet."

Some things Max was better off not knowing. He was the legal representation of the Sparrows; he was the legitimate face of the kids who just wanted to help the SACs. If they needed a plan B, especially one involving Kurt, Chiela, or Callum, Max shouldn't know about it. In his words, it was important he had "plausible deniability."

As they spoke, Zara slipped a tightly rolled slip of paper in the shape of a cigarette from beneath the tongue of her shoe and passed it to Jude. He felt its shape and then tucked it into the heel of his shoe. There was so much he wanted to say to her, but there was no chance in front of Max and no time before the guards came in. He bit his tongue and bided his time; he sensed the scrap of paper would confirm his suspicion that Zara was already ahead of him.

When he finally made it back to his cell, he turned his back to the camera and unrolled the tiny scroll. It was cryptic, but not impossible to decipher: "Literacy Center, Screen Two. Follow the protocol." What followed was a series of steps that Jude realized was a way to get around the firewall of the Detention Center and access one of the many proxy servers Zara used for the Sparrow Press. From there, they could access their email and communicate freely.

"Zara," he muttered to himself, "what would I do without you?"

Screen two, it turns out, was the least visible from the security cameras. Pulling up a few dummy tabs about literature and New America History, Jude followed the protocol and logged into his email account.

"You are brilliant. I got in fine," he began writing. "I'm so glad we can finally talk! I can't wait to see you outside these walls.

"Max is doing his best, but I'm not sure how much patience we should have. I saw Callum, and he's lost so much weight I didn't recognize him at first. I think he's been intentionally undernourished and tortured. He looks terrible, and I'm worried he won't last long enough in here for a trial. I'm also worried that this might be their plan.

"I think we should give Max a few more weeks, and if there is no word on a hearing for us, we might need to move on to plan B. I can't just sit and watch my brother die.

"With all my love, Jude."

When Zara and Chiela came back to the Learning Center the next day, someone was on screen two.

"Shoot," Zara said. "It's taken."

"Leave it to me," Chiela said.

She went to the woman on screen two, whispered something into her ear, and the woman immediately gave Zara a terrified look and then jumped up and left.

"What did you say to her?"

"I just told her you like that screen."

"What else?"

"I may have mentioned that your boyfriend is on the terrorist bloc and that you have training in a certain area that would make it a bad idea to cross you. I didn't lie."

"Callum isn't my boyfriend, and I wouldn't hurt anyone."

"Okay, so it was a little white lie. Sue me. Let's see if Jude sent you a message."

They sat down, logged in, and ran through the protocols.

"Here it is!" Zara whispered. Chiela casually leaned over, taking turns glancing at the camera and glancing at the screen. Zara read and then sighed and sat quietly for a few minutes. She thought about Jude's state of mind and tried to imagine how she would react to seeing Akal beaten and emaciated. Anger rises quickly and can cloud your thinking and cause you to question the principles you swear by. Sometimes you need an outside voice to remind you of the voice inside that was drowned out by rage.

"Dear Jude," she began, "I can't imagine the pain and worry you have for your brother. Being trapped in here probably feels like slow torture. I want to remind you of the most valuable thing the Sparrows have in our arsenal: we are on the right side of humanity.

"Anything we do besides going to court with Max fighting for us would be giving up our defense, our legitimacy as advocates, and the moral authority that people have come to see in us. We would break their trust. We can't fight within the law or resist unjust laws if we act as if we are outside the law.

"We will win, Jude, and when we do, we will have our best chance of fighting for Callum. Remember who we are, and who you are. We are fighting for more than ourselves and Callum. We are fighting for Chiela, Kurt, and the SACs. We are fighting to give the forgotten a new voice and a hope. The funny thing is, they are fighting for us, too. If you ever doubt it, just look out beyond the fence the next time you are in the yard."

"With all of my love, Zara."

It took Jude a couple of days before his emotional state caught up with Zara's logic. He was always superbly rational, so he decided he agreed with Zara before he felt like he did. Seeing Callum reduced to half the beast he really was took a harder toll on Jude than he realized. He actually began planning a way to escape the National Detention Center. That's not an idea he would have entertained if he had not seen Callum. Despite his anger and worry about his brother, she was right.

Kurt and Jude met up in the yard later in the day, where Jude took a much-needed walk in the fresh air to clear his mind. Luckily, he had enough restraint not to mention "Plan B" to Kurt, so he didn't need to rehash the entire conversation.

"I think I'd die if I were ever put in the hole," Kurt said. "This little bit of fresh air is my piece of sanity."

"I couldn't agree more," Jude said. "The fresh air . . . "

He went silent and stared up into the sky. Kurt followed his gaze, and soon everyone else did too. A fleet of NADF transport drones was descending onto the grassy area outside the fence.

Jude and Kurt ran to the edge of the yard and joined other inmates straining to see every detail. The transports alighted on the grass and poured out troops who quickly encircled the crowd.

"The protesters," muttered Jude. "The LEADs couldn't break them up because they didn't break any laws. Max was right when he said they had the attention of high-ranking officials. Someone called in the Army."

"I'm not an expert on the government, but I'm pretty sure only the president can deploy troops. At the very least, he has to approve it."

"You're right," Jude said pensively. "I think the Sparrows might have made enough noise to reach President Blake Connor."

They watched as the troops took up formation around the crowd. The protesters naturally formed a circle, but then they did something unexpected: they made an outward-facing ring, holding up their signs facing the troops. They stopped calling out, and they stood still to wait for whatever instructions they might be given. The troops took two steps toward the protesters, but then suddenly stopped. They stepped back and held their position. The protesters continued to hold up their signs and stand firmly and quietly.

"What was that all about?" Kurt wondered out loud. "They looked like they were about to open up on the people, but then they just stepped back."

"Those were their orders," Jude said, hanging on his fingers as he leaned against the chain link fencing. "Somebody told them to stand down."

Chapter 24: **No Deal**

"The troops are in place, sir."

"So why is there still a crowd of protesters standing there holding signs? I told you to kill this thing quickly."

"Yes, sir. I made a last-minute call to pull them back until I could consult you," the nervous Chief of Defense said. "This is a politically sensitive situation, sir, and I thought you would want to consult ADAMS before taking any action against civilians."

"You're looking out for my career?" President Connor snarled.

"I want to be judicious about the use of military force in a domestic context, sir."

"The National Detention Center is our jurisdiction," the President posited. "But I suppose optics can be an issue here, too. Have an analyst run this through ADAMS and report to me within the hour."

"We took the initiative to give ADAMS the parameters for this situation earlier, sir. I'll have the analyst up here straight away," the Chief said.

Half an hour later, the Assistant to the President ushered in the Defense Chief, the analyst, and a guest.

"What the hell is this?" President Connor blurted.

"I apologize for the surprise, sir, but this seemed like a good time for you to meet ADAMS," the Defense Chief said. He stepped aside, and a droid stepped forward and extended its hand to the President.

"It's a pleasure to meet you, Mr. President," it said.

President Connor hesitantly shook its smooth, leathery mechanical hand. "Forgive my surprise. I was not told I would be speaking to an android." He shot a quick glare at the Defense Chief. "I thought

ADAMS was an extensive neural network housed in a very secure facility underground?"

The analyst stepped forward, nervously wringing his cold hands, except when pushing up his loose wire-rimmed glasses or plunging them into his pockets. He was short, thin, balding on his crown, and donned a short-sleeved white dress shirt with a thin, crooked tie, black pants, loafers, and conspicuous white socks.

"Yes, sir, it is. ADAMS is a very advanced AI, and he not only analyzes vast amounts of data, but he also learns as he does it. This means he can be interactive. He asks questions, receives input from other sources, and problem-solves in real-time. He can give the best advice in a conversation rather than just a report.

"As you can imagine, holding a conversation with a machine that takes up an entire subterranean room is not practical. Our engineers decided to solve this problem by creating a mobile interface that was as humanly familiar as possible. They took a decommissioned LEAD unit, stripped it down, and rebuilt it with the most advanced humanoid features available. As you can see, this unit has light, thin aluminum and polymer coverings from head to toe and humanlike hands, which are made from synthetic leather that is laid over very intricate mechanical and hydraulic digits. The form of the face was taken from a human model, and underneath are dozens of small hydraulic pockets that act as facial muscles, allowing the droid to express common human emotions."

"Thank you for the engineering lesson," President Connor said coldly, "but you didn't answer my question. Where is the real ADAMS?"

"Oh, yes, sir. I apologize. ADAMS is very much still housed 'in the basement' as we like to say. This droid is linked to the main ADAMS framework, but it can travel and interact in a more human manner. Essentially, it is the face of ADAMS, sir."

"I see," the president said awkwardly. "Well, let's get to it. If we're going to have a conversation, let's sit down."

The analyst, the Chief, and other staffers took seats on the sofas, while President Connor and the ADAMS droid sat in high-back chairs facing each other.

"I have a predicament," the president began. "My highest priority is to maintain the stability of New America. You know well how hard we fought through the Transition to come to a place of peace. Now we have a vocal group of protesters outside the National Detention Center holding up signs and chanting slogans in support of two anti-government rebels being held inside. NADF troops are standing by, quite literally encircling the protesters as we speak. I need to make this situation go away quickly before it escalates. How do you recommend we go about doing this without inciting further dissent?"

ADAMS smiled coyly and explained. "I have analyzed the ongoing footage of the protesters from the LEAD units on the scene. The protesters are consistent: they appear regularly, they are organized, they are peaceful, and they have posed no threat to the LEAD units or human officers. The pattern of their behavior is relatively unique and indicates they are following the instructions of a leader with extensive knowledge of the law."

"That sounds a lot like what the D.C. Police Commissioner told the Mayor. They know how to dance around the law. I want them gone before they start something that breaks the law."

"You, of course, have the legal authority to declare this gathering a threat and remove them immediately. Historically, this has had mixed results in preventing further protests. The use of the military with unarmed civilians has the potential to incur condemnation from the public and potentially move their sympathies to the people they see as unfairly oppressed."

"It looks bad. I get it. What other options do we have?" President Connor asked.

"You can meet their demands."

"I'm not inclined to entertain the demands of dissidents."

"They are calling for the release of two individuals, Jude Kane and Zara Malik. Together they have become known among the SACs as the 'Sparrows.' In analyzing the communications between the members of SACs, it appears the Sparrows have provided technical assistance with energy production, agriculture, and education. The decline in the SAC population since the Transition had been steady until last year, but it appears to have stabilized. I cannot determine a direct causal relationship without complete data, but based on the reports of assistance I found among the SACs and the simultaneous stabilization of the SAC population, it is reasonable to conclude the Sparrows were a major factor.

"The protesters are calling for their release, claiming the Sparrows are only guilty of providing assistance to the SACs. Based on all the information I have analyzed, that assertion is correct. I can find no evidence of anti-government speech or actions. As long as SACs remain a legal entity, providing assistance to them is not a crime. If they are tried in court, they would likely be released, and the New American government could be viewed as aggressive or anti-democratic. To avoid further protests and negative attention, I recommend the release of Jude Kane and Zara Malik."

President Conner sighed and sat back, crossing his legs and rubbing his chin pensively.

"I don't like letting them go. They have a name and some kind of movement. This could come back and bite us later."

"Jude Kane has a brother named Callum who is being held on charges of domestic terrorism for shooting down a NADF drone over his SAC in Cascadia. If the Sparrows do become a threat in the future, it is possible to tie the entire SAC to the downed drone."

"Why can't we do that now?" the President asked.

"There is no direct evidence to link the SAC or even the Kane family to the downed drone. If Jude becomes involved in subversive behavior in the future, however, that argument will be much easier to make in court."

"I see. I don't like it, but it makes the most sense right now," he said. Addressing his staff, he ordered, "Let's cut them loose, and let the media cover it. They can celebrate the rule of law and the fairness of New America. We might as well get some public favor points for this while we're at it."

"Yes, sir!" they responded, getting up and leaving to follow their directions. ADAMS began to follow the analyst, but President Connor stopped him.

"I'd like to have a few more words with ADAMS. I'm sure he can make his way back down to the basement," he said to the analyst.

"Yes, sir."

"Thank you for your analysis," the president said.

"You're welcome, Mr. President."

"You're aware of my feelings towards the SACs."

"Yes, Mr. President. Your clear opposition to the legal status of Sustainable Agricultural Communities during the Transition is on record."

"I agreed with your assessment at the time. They were necessary, and they did in fact go through attrition at the rate you predicted. It appears these 'Sparrows' have interrupted that attrition, and my hope of seeing SACs die naturally is fading. SACs are breeding grounds for dissidents and terrorists, and if these Sparrows are giving them new life, the risk of rebellion increases. If we don't cut the head off this snake now, it will come back and bite us."

ADAMS sat still, processing with an awkward delay.

"It's an expression . . . " President Connor offered.

"Yes, sir. I understand. You are concerned that the Sparrows may cause a resurgence of independence among the SACs and possibly lead a rebellion in the future. My recommendation to counter this is to recommend that the Corporate Congress and the Senate draft a bill that will allow Consolidated Agriculture and Mining Operations to assert eminent domain without a lengthy court procedure."

"That is the best idea I've heard all day!" President Connor exclaimed. "If CAMO needs land to produce food for the majority of our population in the cities, then they should not be held hostage by small, inefficient, rogue farmers and survivalists. We could pass this into law in a few weeks."

"Of course, CAMO does have the land it needs to meet our needs and produce a surplus to sell to foreign countries already," ADAMS reminded him.

"The definition of 'need' can be flexible."

"Those troops stood there forever!" Jude said as he and Kurt stood in line with their dinner trays. "Do you think we'd hear it in here if there was some kind of conflict?"

"We'd hear about it," Kurt said. "Maybe the official news feeds will have something online when we go to the LC tonight."

"I doubt it. The official news doesn't like covering anything that makes the government look bad."

"I saw a story yesterday. They interviewed a protester."

"Really?"

"Yeah. Maybe it was too big to ignore."

"If anything is too big to ignore, it is the deployment of troops. Let's look tonight."

On their way back to their cells, a guard stopped Jude.

"Kane! You have a visitor."

"A visitor?" he asked.

"Your attorney. Let's go."

"It's not visiting hours . . . "

"Do you want to see him or stand here asking questions? Hurry up!"

Jude came in to find Zara, Max, and another woman in a business suit.

"Have a seat, Jude," Max said. "This is Val Sorenson from the D.A.'s office."

"Nice to meet you," he said cautiously.

They all sat down at the spare metal table, Jude and Zara facing Max and Val. Val began.

"We've reviewed your case. While some are not comfortable with the idea of the 'Sparrows' having such a large influence in the SACs, at this point, we do not have any evidence of crimes being committed against the government. We will continue to monitor your activities and look for any sign that the Sparrows are working to undermine the New American or Regional governments, but at this point, we are willing to release you both."

Sighs and smiles were exchanged, and a feeling of elation swept through all three of them.

"Thank you, Ms. Sorenson. I assure you, Zara and I just wanted to help people in the SACs. We always respect the law."

"There are a few conditions," Val said, clearly not sharing the vibes with the other three. "First, you will let your supporters know to leave the area immediately."

"As soon as I get my phone back, I can spread the word," Zara said. "I don't know who led the demonstrations, but word will get to them quickly that we are free, I'm sure."

"Next, you must agree to make sure your passports are up to date and functioning correctly, and you do not avoid scanners at borders, train platforms, or near any government facilities."

"No problem," Jude said.

"Finally, you must agree to report any subversive activities in the SACs. If it is found that you knew of anything and failed to report it, it will be assumed you are party to the activity and you will face quick and severe consequences."

"We just want to help people. I have no desire to pick a fight with the New America government or the Regional governments, for that matter. As long as we live in a democracy, if change is needed, it can be done within the legal and political process," Jude said.

"So, we're agreed?"

"Yes, of course," Jude said.

"Yes," Zara said.

"Good. You will be processed and given your belongings right away. Make sure to call off those protesters.

"Yes, ma'am," Zara said as they stood.

"Wait."

Jude's words reverberated off the concrete walls.

"Yes?" Val asked as Max and Zara looked on with wide eyes.

"My brother Callum has been here for months, and he doesn't even have a hearing scheduled. When will that happen?"

"I don't know. That's a separate case, and he is facing serious terrorism charges," Val said coldly.

"I don't want to leave without knowing my brother will have a hearing."

"You are not in a position to bargain for your brother, Mr. Kane. Mr. Simon, maybe you can explain this to your client?" she said with clenched teeth.

"Jude . . . " Max began.

"I'm not leaving without a deal for my brother."

"There will be no negotiation for your brother. You take the deal for yourself, or you stay. I have no problem releasing Zara and leaving you in here."

"I'm not leaving without Jude," Zara said. "And until I'm out, there's no one to call off the protesters."

"You admitted there's not enough evidence, and clearly the people holding signs outside the National Detention Center got someone's attention, or you wouldn't have come. It seems to me that we are in a position to negotiate," Jude said.

At this point, they were all standing, and Max was visibly uncomfortable. He was terrified Jude might have blown the deal to get them out, but he also knew how desperate they were to help Callum.

"Is there anything you can do to move his case along?" Max asked. "I think if we knew he would have a hearing, or we had some indication his case was in motion, it would go a long way."

Val crossed her arms and glared at them.

"I'll make this clear: there is no negotiating for a terrorist. We have him on video using an illegal firearm to destroy an NADF drone. It would not be a difficult task to prove your father owned that firearm and implicate the entire Slate Creek SAC in a plot to attack a military target. Now, unless you want your family, your entire SAC, and all your supporters outside to be rounded up by the NADF and join you in here, I suggest you take our deal and forget you mentioned anything about your brother."

Max looked at Jude, and Jude looked at Zara.

"I'm prepared to stay," Zara said, looking at Jude.

"No," Jude said. "We'll take the deal. We'll call off the protesters and go back to Slate Creek."

"Are you sure?" Zara asked, taking his arm with both of her hands. "I'm with you all the way."

"Yes, I'm sure," Jude said. He looked into her eyes and put his hand on her shoulder. "This is a lot bigger than Callum. We're responsible for more than just ourselves."

"Okay. Then let's go home," she said, embracing him for the first time in weeks.

The SEMIC train ride from Washington, D.C. to Vancouver, B.C. was a smooth, peaceful three-hour ride. After weeks of separation and uncertainty, Jude and Zara drank in the uninterrupted alone time.

"I'm sorry, Jude," Zara said. "We went to Washington, and we can honestly say we did everything we could. I know you're worried about your brother."

"I am worried, but I don't think we failed. We managed to get scooped up by COATS and survive; we managed to live for almost two months in the National Detention Center and learn what they know and what they fear about the Sparrows; we got out of the NDC because of the power of the Sparrows. We didn't fail. We're just getting started."

Chapter 25: **A New Course**

ROD AND MARREN WERE relieved and ecstatic to have their children back. Jude and Zara were happy to not wear jumpsuits, eat real, fresh food, and be able to go outside whenever they wanted, even if there was half a meter of snow on the ground. Callum weighed heavily on Jude's mind, but nearly implicating his parents was sobering. For the time being, they needed to stay in Slate Creek.

"Where is Jude?" Zara asked Rod who was reading in his study.

"I think he is in the barn stacking hay bales," he said.

"Why is he doing that? Hasn't the hay been inside for a few months already?"

Rod sighed and smiled. "Yes, but Jude likes to restack it halfway through the winter to bring the bales closer to the feeding pens. To be honest, I think he needs the distraction during the lull of winter. There isn't much to do when the crops are in, and the power grid is working. There's nothing like throwing thirty-kilo bales of hay to clear your mind."

"Men are so strange," she said, shaking her head and going out to the barn.

Rod chuckled. "No argument there."

Zara threw on her sheepskin-lined coat and snow boots and followed the trodden snow trail to the barn. She slipped in the side door and followed the regular sounds of quiet grunting until she saw Jude in the hay loft. She hid behind a beam and watched as he picked up the square bales, walked them to the edge of the loft, and restacked them. He was wearing work boots, dark khaki trousers, and had a bandana hanging from his back pocket. He had tossed his plaid shirt over a rail, his t-shirt clung to his torso, and his face and neck were glistening with sweat despite the single-digit temperatures outside. Since getting home, he had a good start on a beard that he hadn't outlined yet, and his hair was in a ponytail to keep it out of his eyes.

"I would offer to help, but I get the feeling the work is the whole point," Zara said, stepping up into the loft.

"After being pinned up for a couple of months, I needed this," he said, wiping his brow with his bandana.

"If you don't mind me saying, I don't think you lost any muscle tone in the NDC."

"I still worked out, but I hate exercising just to exercise. Work has a purpose, even if it is just to move something from one place to another."

She sauntered up to him and threw her arms around his neck. "I'm not sure about this farmhand look," she said, scanning him up and down.

"I'm sorry. I can throw my plaid back on."

"I'd prefer if you took something off."

"That doesn't leave much," he chuckled.

"Exactly."

She leaned in and kissed him deeply, and he wrapped his arms around her waist to pull her closer. After two more lingering kisses, she took her arms down and pulled off her coat, throwing it onto the hay-strewn wood floor.

"I'm warm now," she whispered.

Jude put his arms around her waist again, but this time he took hold of the bottom of her long-sleeve T-shirt and slowly began pulling it over her head. She raised her arms and let him lift it off without breaking her gaze into his eyes. She placed her palms on his chest and then slid them down to his belt and then circled his waist and pulled him close, kissing his neck and then resting her head on his chest.

"I'm ready."

"Ready for what?" Jude asked, gently running his hand down her back and kissing the top of her head.

"For you. Right now."

Jude pulled back slightly and stared into Zara's eyes.

"Me too, but . . . "

"But what?" Zara asked.

"I never thought much about it before, but now that I'm standing here with you, wanting you more than ever, I realize what it means."

"What, having sex?"

"It's more than that. It's the ultimate expression of intimacy. I don't just want you physically. I want all of you. I want your heart, your mind, and your body. I want you forever, all to myself."

"I'm all yours, Jude. You know that," she said, smiling and trying to work his belt loose.

He put his hand on hers, stopping her. "I want to make it official."

"You mean you want to get married? You want to get a license, plan a wedding, have a reception—all of that?" she asked, trying not to sound disappointed.

"I know it sounds almost historical," he said.

"Almost Amish," she commented.

"I don't want a big wedding, and I don't even need a government license. I just want a ceremony where I promise in front of my family, and in front of God, I suppose, that we will belong to each other for life. I want to make that commitment first."

Zara sighed and put her arms back up around his neck. "You do sound ridiculously old-fashioned," she chuckled. "But I can't begrudge the man I love wanting to make a commitment. We'll become a family, and I suppose it's only right to involve everyone else."

"Thank you for understanding," Jude said, leaning in for a firm, lingering kiss.

"Let's not drag this out too long," she warned him. "If I catch you out here again looking like this, I can't make any guarantees."

As Rod sat reading one of his dusty old paper novels in his leather chair, he heard the back door open and close, the banging of snow-covered boots, and the soft padding of two pairs of wool socks. He peered over his glasses as Jude and Zara came into the study hand in hand.

"Dad, we want to talk to you," Jude said nervously. He suddenly felt fifteen again, like he was asking to shoot a gun or drive a tractor.

Rod noted the various lengths of hay sticking out of their hair and smiled, taking off his glasses and closing his book.

"I'm all ears," he said, folding his hands in his lap. "Feel free to sit down."

They stepped over to the love seat and sat down, still holding hands, their white knuckles interlocking.

"We want to get married."

"Are you asking my permission?" Rod asked. "It seems to me that decision is up to you, and by the looks of things, you've already made that decision."

They were so nervous and excited that the subtle insinuation flew over their heads.

"I know a lot of people don't bother these days, at least in the big cities and the SACs I know of," Jude explained.

"Except for the Amish," Zara interjected.

"Except for the Amish," Jude laughed. "But we want to. We want to make a real commitment in front of God and our family. I want you to do the ceremony."

"I'm not a licensed minister," Rod said.

"You're more knowledgeable about the Bible and Theology than most of the crack-pot ministers online, and you've been the spiritual leader to me and this entire SAC from the beginning. You're the only one whose word matters to me."

Rod smiled and bowed his head, pretending to think but trying to hide a tear of pride. "Miss Malik, how do you feel about a Christian ceremony?"

"I had some time in the NDC to read and think, and I took your advice. I read the words of Jesus. I read all the stories about him, too. My grandfather taught me that Jesus was a prophet and a good man, but I think he was a lot more than that. Based on what I read and how I see Jude living, I'm all in."

"Well then, when do you want to do this?" Rod asked.

"Give me a few days to get some rings. I wish Maisy, Callum, and Akal could be here, but I just feel in my gut we should do this now," Jude said, looking at Zara.

"I agree," she said.

Jude didn't waste any time. He went into the shop, opened the safe, and rummaged around for the nuggets they had panned from the creek over the last twenty years. It wasn't much, but he could make it work. He fired up the stove, melted the nuggets, and repeatedly skimmed the impurities off the top. He then poured the refined gold into two circular clay molds, let them cool, and removed and polished them.

Being in the middle of winter in the mountains of Cascadia called for some creative choices when it came to the ceremony. Marren used several pieces of dried ferns and flowers she was saving to make the bouquet. Accommodating the extended family and most of the rest of the

SAC required the use of the barn, which was only slightly warmer than freezing. Heating a dry wood barn full of dry hay without setting it ablaze took some father-son engineering, but they managed with a few portable heaters outside and several makeshift air ducts.

While Rod had a rental tuxedo at his wedding and most of his suits never made it through the Transition, Marren managed to save and preserve her wedding dress. With a few alterations, she was able to present it to an overwhelmed Zara.

"I . . . I can't take your wedding dress, Marren," she said. "You must have saved it for Maisy."

"I did, but . . . " Marren started before she was interrupted.

"I don't see why we can't both use it."

They spun around and stood in shock as Maisy crossed her arms and soaked in the moment she so carefully staged.

"Maisy!" Marren said, running to her daughter and nearly toppling her over. "I can't believe you're here!"

"I can't either!" Zara said, not daring to make any swift movements. "Did Max send you?"

"No, I did," Julian said, coming up behind Maisy and squeezing her shoulders. He extended his hand to Marren. "Nice to finally meet you, Mrs. Kane."

"Thank you, Dr. Robinson. This means the world to us," Marren said, misty-eyed.

"Family is everything, and I know Maisy has missed you. When she said Zara told her about the wedding, I knew she needed to be here. Luckily, I have a friend who helped us with air transport."

Jude managed to patch together a respectable charcoal gray suit from his and his father's thin wardrobe, while Rod opted to cover his casual jeans and flannel shirt with a closely buttoned overcoat. They did their best to strategically place the heating ducts, but the barn was still chilly. Zara refused to cover the wedding dress, and Jude stood freezing in solidarity with his bride.

Due to the cold and the fact that all the guests had to stand, Rod kept the ceremony poignant but short. Upon presenting the bride and groom, the barn instantly turned into a reception hall. In keeping with Coastal Salish tradition, several of Jude's relatives had a "give away," presenting him and Zara with gifts of herbal teas, jams, handmade cedar roses, traditional blankets, jewelry, and a few traditional cedar bark baskets to carry it all.

Had it been summer, the revelry would have lasted all night, but the short daylight and frigid temperatures urged everyone back home within a few hours. While Rod and Jude gathered up the heating ducts and stored the portable heaters, Maisy followed Zara upstairs to help her change out of the wedding gown.

"You're next," Zara said as Maisy undid the clasps and helped her gingerly slip out.

"What? You mean to have the dress or get married?" Maisy asked with her signature incredulously raised eyebrow.

"Yes."

"I'm still only nineteen," Maisy said. "Let's see what happens when I finish my Medic Program."

"You're so sure and focused. I admire you. Maybe I'm just weak; I fell hard for your brother."

"He's worth it," Maisy said, reaching for a small paper bag. "Now, I have a present for you. It is a little gift for your wedding night, and I won't say what it is, but let's just say I hope it's not too cold in your room tonight."

"Thanks, Maisy," Zara said.

"Don't mention it. Seriously, don't mention anything. This is my brother we're talking about, and I don't want any images in my mind I can't get out."

Zara laughed and hugged her new sister. "Let's get your mom and have her help us pack this dress up the way she had it. I want to make sure it looks this good for you."

"Who's that?" Jude asked, wandering into Marren's school room and peering over Zara's shoulder as she typed away on a screen.

"Chiela," she said. There was no masking the sorrow in her voice.

"What's wrong? Is she okay?" he asked.

"She's fine. She misses me. That's not it."

"What is it?"

"She was able to hack into the security cameras and send me some stills."

Jude leaned down and looked at a series of pictures. They showed an emaciated Callum in various poses— in a fetal position on his bed, sprawled on the floor, and hovering face-first over the commode— none of them flattering.

"I know you said you almost didn't recognize him, but I didn't imagine . . . " she trailed off.

Jude sighed and sat next to Zara. "Can you thank her for me?"

"Sure."

"Can you ask her something else?"

"Of course."

"What are her prospects for getting out?"

"She said about as good as Callum's."

"That bad?"

"She said yes, because she basically defected from the inside. They won't let her see the light of day."

"Tell her we're working on it."

"What exactly are we working on?" Zara asked as she typed.

"I don't know yet, but there's always a solution."

"Speaking of solutions, I know the gears of your mind are still spinning and thinking of how to get Callum out of the NDC," Zara said. "You made a strategic call to save us, but you haven't given up on your brother. I at least know you that well."

"Yes, you do," he said with a smile and a kiss on her head. "I hoped the political pressure that got us out would help him, but it wasn't nearly enough. Besides, I don't want to put people at risk. The sight of the NADF surrounding the protesters was something I don't ever want to see again. It could have gone very badly."

"What if we apply pressure in other ways?" she asked.

"I'm listening."

"Congressmen can go in a back door and avoid protesters, but what if they go into their offices, turn on their screens, and have a few hundred emails in support of Callum Kane?"

"That will get the issue in front of them. If they keep coming, it would be like a constant drip; eventually, somebody will want to put an end to it."

"Do you remember what Jaxson said about art back in Omaha?"

"Yeah. He said censorship was strict because of the fear of stoking anti-government sentiment. I imagine that fear is even worse in the Capital."

"Imagine each morning Washington D.C. wakes up to chalk art, paintings, music, poetry, and maybe even sculptures surrounding the government buildings with messages in support of Callum."

"That's the kind of legal, slippery resistance that will infuriate the authorities. What do LEAD units do with art? Sending human patrols or the NADF would look ridiculous. I love it!" Jude said.

"Want me to send out the word on Sparrow Press?" Zara asked.

"Not yet. If people are going to do this, they need some cover. Send Chiela a message and ask her if she knows the GPS communications frequency of the CAMO and NADF drones. I have an idea."

Operation "Freedom Exhibition" was executed at precisely 0400 on Friday morning. A small army of Sparrows came into Washington, D.C., the day before, bringing their art and supplies. Some stayed in hotels, and many others were able to connect with sympathizers who lived in the city. They stayed up much of the night preparing their paintings, poetry, and video and visual art displayed on tablets. One artist using bronze had created a compelling image of Callum wasting away in a symbolic cube of iron bars and managed to bring it with him in several pieces.

At 4:00 am, they streamed into the streets wearing dark jogging clothes and carrying their art. The sculptor enlisted five other people to help him carry the pieces, and two more lookouts to go ahead and behind. They snaked through the streets, staggering the group and putting on the air of a morning jog to get past any LEAD units without raising suspicion.

When they arrived at the courthouse, the first lookout gave the others an order: "Stay behind trees! There's a security drone coming around for another pass. I've got this." He spotted the faint blinking red light of the drone, and as it approached, he aimed the GPS jammer at it and pressed the button. There was no sound, but the drone suddenly veered off course. Flying completely blind, the drone went into emergency shutdown mode and slowly descended straight down onto the grass.

The first lookout signaled the other, and they ran to the downed drone, throwing a thick blanket over it. While they wrapped it up, they gave a signal to the others, who bolted for the steps to the courthouse. They pulled the pieces of the sculpture from bags, cases, and cloth wrappings and laid them out. The sculptor quickly began assembling the pieces, with others helping to lift the sections, apply adhesive, and tighten bolts.

With the sculpture in place, they gathered the remaining supplies and met up with the lookouts who managed to scoop up the drone, shut it down completely, and take it with them.

As they "jogged" back toward their safe house, the first lookout took the drone out of the blanket and carried it to a LEAD unit.

"I found this drone just sitting in the grass not far from the courthouse. It looks like a security drone. I think something malfunctioned. It needs to be turned in, but I don't know where to take it."

The LEAD unit took the drone, scanned it, and said, "Security drones are the property of the New America Defense Force. I will deliver it securely. Thank you."

By 6:00 am, the operation was complete, with early risers waking up to works of art scattered on and around government buildings all over the city. By 7:00 am, Corporate Congressmen, Senators, judges, and other officials had inboxes that were overrun with pleas to free Callum. By 8:00 am, the SAC Sparrows had left the city, and commuters were arriving to a barrage of paintings hanging from doors, poems and stories written in chalk, tablets playing music and videos on window ledges, and the most conspicuous of them all: the sculpture of Callum behind bars perched prominently at the top of the giant steps in front of the courthouse.

Admiration and confusion soon led to panic as the authorities pieced together the clear message of the guerrilla art: release Callum Kane. The NADF went on high alert, and buildings were locked down as LEAD units, bomb-sniffing dogs, and NADF troops fanned out throughout the city trying to determine the threat.

By noon, the panic had settled, buildings were opened, and the Defense Chief was ready to make his report to President Connor.

"What the hell is going on?" he demanded.

"There's no threat, sir. We found no bombs, weapons, or any kind of injuries. It appears to be a coordinated effort to send a message."

"What message?"

"The artists, or whoever they are, are demanding that Callum Kane be set free. The same message appears to have been sent to the entire Congress, judges, and many others."

"We had those damn 'Sparrows' right here in the NDC, and we let them go. ADAMS said we didn't have anything on them, but now look what's happened!" he yelled.

As if hearing a summons, the analyst accompanied the ADAMS droid into the situation room.

"From my analysis, it is likely that whoever led the protesters was behind this carefully executed statement," ADAMS explained.

"You call this a statement?" he screamed. "It's a disaster! We look like fools who can't even stop a bunch of artists from defacing government buildings! How are we supposed to maintain order if we can't even stop these 'Sparrows'?"

"We don't have conclusive evidence it was the Sparrows, sir. Jude Kane and Zara Malik, according to messages between members of their SAC and other SACs, were married in a ceremony in Slate Creek this past Sunday. Neither of their passports has been scanned anywhere since returning to their home. It is highly unlikely they had the time or resources to coordinate this kind of effort.

"While certainly more visible and direct, this message was planned with a high degree of efficiency and care. Technically, public displays of art are not illegal, no buildings were damaged, and no threats were made. As in the NDC protests, they were careful not to break any laws or local statutes."

"You've got to be kidding me," President Conner said, shaking his head. "I don't care about laws and local statutes. This is an attack on the New America government. I want these Sparrows, or whoever they are, captured immediately. If they are demanding the release of a terrorist, I classify them as supporters of terrorism. Get the security drone footage and find them."

"It appears, sir, that about a dozen security drones malfunctioned last night," the Defense Chief said. "LEAD units all over the city brought in downed drones that they said had shut down. Initial reports from technicians show the drones functioned properly when they were turned back on. They also analyzed footage from when the drones shut down, and they appear to have lost their satellite connection somehow and landed and shut down as a safety precaution. There was no footage of anyone near them at the time. When restarted, the drones all seemed to have reconnected to the satellites and resumed normal function."

"I want heads on stakes, and all you can tell me is that we don't have any heads or stakes?" the President raged.

As the analyst attempted to whisk ADAMS away, it stopped and turned to the President.

"We may have a head, sir, if I analyzed your expression correctly. I have received a message intended for me directly and to be shared with you, sir. The individual does not identify themself, but they say, 'We're not done.' I cannot identify this person at this time, and I cannot confirm who 'we' refers to. I will continue to monitor communications."

The President's face turned an impossible shade of red, and correctly sensing the meeting was over, the Defense Chief ushered everyone out of the room. As the door closed, the muffled roar of yelling and banging was followed by the sound of glass breaking and what sounded like a chair being destroyed against the wall.

"Call maintenance," the Assistant to the President said into her communicator. "But tell them to wait an hour before coming up."

Chapter 26: **Fire in the Skies**

SATURDAY NIGHTS IN THE National Detention Center are more subdued than any other evening. Even in prison, people can sense the end of a week. Maureen Donovan was in the last hour of a long twelve-hour shift when she followed behind the kitchen workers, making sure everything was clean, put away, and all the inmates had left. As she turned off the lights and began to pull the door closed, she heard the faint squeak of a heavy door and the sound of labored breathing. She turned and noticed the door to the walk-in cooler was open slightly, casting a sliver of light into the dark kitchen. In the light, she saw puffs of warm breath and a bloody hand wrap around the edge of the door.

"Help."

"Code three! Code three!" Maureen shouted into her com unit. "We've got someone down in the kitchen!"

Maureen ran over to the cooler door, weapon drawn. She inched toward the door, slowly reaching toward it, and then she quickly jerked it wide open. A young female inmate was on her hands and knees, and blood was smeared over her cheek and neck.

Four more guards came charging in, guns drawn and pointed down. Maureen kept waving a portable scanner over the woman, but nothing happened.

"Do any of you recognize her?" Maureen asked the others. They all said no. "I've scanned her three times, and I've got nothing."

"That's impossible. Every inmate has a passport," one of the guards recited.

"Unless it was cut out," Maureen said, pointing to her bloody neck.

"I'm . . . not . . . an inmate," the woman moaned. She was shivering uncontrollably.

"What happened?" Maureen asked, holstering her weapon and throwing her jacket over the woman.

"She . . . asked for help . . . with a stack of meat boxes. She closed the door . . . then she came up behind me . . . and started choking me. I blacked out, and then I woke up in here. I felt an itching pain in my lower neck. When I scratched at it, it bled all over. I think . . . she stole my passport."

"Who stole your passport?" asked Maureen.

"The one you should be looking for."

"I'm sure she took more than your passport," Maureen said. "Code seven, repeat, code seven; unknown female inmate, most likely escaped with a stolen meat delivery truck, approximately two hours ago. She may be using a stolen uniform and passport."

"Dammit!" stomped one of the guards. "This means we're going on lockdown. We're going to be here all night."

"Tell me about it," Maureen said, helping the woman to her feet. "This is my never-ending shift."

Zack and Athalia Nolan were ecstatic when they found out about the pregnancy. Sitting on their porch and watching the trees, Zack loved to put his ear to her stomach and listen to gurgles and sloshes. He smiled and then stood up and looked out at the forest.

"You tell me what you want, and I'll make it," said Zack. "Pine is soft and won't last as long, but it's everywhere and easy to work with. If I can find some oak, I'll use that for something we keep, like a rocker."

"You can do that?" Athalia asked.

"Of course," Zack said confidently. "Well, I'll need some help with the rocker," he finally admitted.

"Shh!" Zack said. "Do you hear that?"

"I don't hear anything. Wait . . . "

The distant buzz bled into a high-pitched, muffled roar, and before they could get outside to see what it was, an explosion shattered two saplings nearby and sent splinters of wood shooting into everything like small missiles, including their skin.

"Aah," moaned Athalia, suddenly realizing Zack was on top of her. "What was that?"

"I don't know," Zack said, lifting himself off of her and helping her up.

"How did you get on top of me so fast?" she asked.

"Instinct," he said, wincing.

"Sweet Jesus, Zack, you look like a porcupine!"

"You can work on me later," he said between his teeth. "We've got to take cover."

He took her hand in his and grabbed his shotgun with the other, running down the trail towards one of their SAC neighbors. Giving Athalia a few yards distance, he raised his gun and fired three shots into the air.

Their neighbor emerged up the stairs from his converted gold mine to greet them.

"What's going on?" the neighbor asked, taking Athalia by the hand and leading her down the stairs.

"An attack. NADF drones, I think. I heard the boosters. Spread the word; tell the SAC to go underground until they hear from me. I will send word to the Sparrows and see what I can find out."

"Damn, Zack. Are you okay? You look like a porcupine."

"So I've heard."

Zara had three monitors up in the old school room, and two were playing a video of an attack. One was the Blue Ridge SAC in the GSA, north of Atlanta, and the other was the Ozark SAC. Messages kept rolling in; Twin Falls was hit, a Swamp SAC in Louisiana lost a barn, and in the most egregious case, an Amish SAC was hit in Lakeland, west of Cincinnati, with two bombs.

"Jude," Zara said as he came running in, keeping her eyes pinned to the screens, "They're bombing the SACs . . . "

"Come on!" he commanded, taking her by the arm. When she hesitated, he used both hands and pulled her out of her seat. He grabbed their coats as they ran outside, Zara being nearly dragged by Jude, and headed for the garage where Rod and Marren were waiting. They took Zara and led her down the steps, and Jude followed.

"They're bombing the SACs!" Zara cried as Jude caught his breath.

"They're bombing the SACs . . . that we've been to," he said, still panting. "They got the message last week with the art displays, and now they're sending us a message."

"How do you know this?" Rod asked, interjecting.

"Max sent me a message. He's looked at the footage from several attacks. The bombs aren't incendiary; they're mostly paper. The NADF stuffed some light ordinances with scraps from the Freedom Exhibition: paper, canvas, pieces of plastic, and shards of brass from the sculpture. They're giving it back to us."

"Dear God," Zara said, finally putting together the fleeing from the house and their location in the basement of the garage. "Are they coming here?"

"I'd put money on it," Jude said. "Callum, the Sparrows, the art protests, the NDC protests, and the SACs are in one big category now: rebels. We're the rebels."

"They just let you go from jail with strict warnings," Rod said pensively. "My guess is if they show up here, they won't just drop paper bombs. They'll be looking for the rebels that slipped through their hands."

Jude looked at Zara and then back to his parents.

"Conceal, Evade, Portability," Zara said. "It's time to practice what we preach."

"Take the ATV. Disappear into the woods. We'll rendezvous in three days and figure it out from there," Rod said.

"That's the only set of wheels you have left for checking crops!" Jude protested.

"We'll get it back, but if you two get detained, we won't get you back. Now go!" Rod ordered.

Marren quickly gathered food from the pantry shelves, brought it up the stairs, and stuffed it into the storage box of the ATV. Rod took the set of ski goggles hanging on the wall and handed them to Jude and Zara.

"We don't have any more helmets, so don't flip this thing," he said. "Now go!"

Jude nodded, tapped Zara's hands around his waist to make sure she was holding on, and sped out of the garage and across the snow-covered fields towards the tree line.

"Hold still," Athalia said, working a deep splinter from Zack's side. "Some of these buggers are deep, and they like to break off."

"That's pine: nice and soft . . . ouch!" he yelped.

"Sorry," she said. "Sometimes I have to dig."

"Thanks for taking out my quills. That's what marriage is all about, right?" Zack said.

"Thanks for getting between me and the splinters. That's also what marriage is all about."

Zack reached and gently rubbed the newly emerging baby bump on Athalia. "This is what marriage is really about."

"The Sparrow Press just posted," the neighbor said, coming in with his tablet. "The bombs were only sent to SACs that the Sparrows helped, or at least the ones ADAMS knows about. They were filled with the shredded remains of artwork from a demonstration in D.C. in support of the Sparrows, and they were meant as a message, not an attack. It looks like we're safe for the time being."

"Thanks," Zack said, wincing as another splinter came out. "Can you please let everyone know they are all clear to come out?"

"Sure thing."

"One more thing: can you post a reply to Sparrow Press? I want to let Jude, Zara, and all the SACs know that Blue Ridge stands by the Sparrows."

"You got it."

The roar of the boosters and blast of the turbo propellers as the NADF drones descended down into Slate Creek had Rod and Marren bracing for a blast, but there was no explosion. Instead, the sound of boots and orders filled the air above the garage, so Rod decided to emerge and assess the situation.

"Can I help you, commander?" he asked the officer as he watched a team of soldiers already searching the house.

"Who are you?" he asked, touching his weapon but not pulling it out.

"I'm Rod Kane. I generally keep things running around here."

"We're looking for your son, Jude, and his friend, Zara Malik. They are wanted for questioning in connection with the destruction of national property."

"I'm sorry to disappoint you, Commander, but Jude and Zara had been here until recently, but you just missed them."

"Where did they go?" he demanded.

"Well, while your 'destruction of national property' was taking place, Jude and Zara were here preparing for their wedding ceremony that took place on Sunday. Zara is now Jude's wife, and they are on their honeymoon."

"When will they be back?"

"About a month, I believe. In the winter, as long as we still have power, there isn't much that needs to be done until planting in the Spring."

"Where did they go?"

"They are visiting extended family in tribal areas in Cascadia and Yukon."

The commander pulled out a com unit and contacted his superior.

"The father says they were here and had a wedding on Sunday. They are gone on their 'honeymoon' visiting family. They could be anywhere on First Nation lands in Cascadia or Yukon. Should we track them, sir?"

The voice on the other end of the com unit was loud enough for Rod to hear clearly.

"No. You'd be wasting your time. Their passports are flagged, so they'll get picked up as soon as they cross a border or try to use transport. Come back to base."

"10-4, sir."

Without a second acknowledgement, the commander turned away and rounded up the men. Rod stood shaking his head and muttered to himself, "Should I tell them you called?"

Rod and Marren gave the NADF a day to make sure they hadn't decided to hover nearby, and then early the next morning, Rod pulled his flare gun from the cabinet in the basement of the garage and fired it off into the still dark haze of the predawn hours. He figured they would be back by noon.

He was close: they rolled back up to the garage at 11:30, shivering and wet but otherwise fine.

"No bombs?" Jude asked as they entered the laundry room and started stripping off their boots and soaked coats.

"Nope. There was just a surly commander and a few troops that made a mess, but no explosives," Rod said. "It doesn't sound like they're coming back for you any time soon, but you have made the naughty list. They've got a flag on your passports."

"We're not important enough to hunt down in the wild, but we're enough of a nuisance that they'll put out a net," Zara said.

"I just want Callum to have a hearing. We had artists display their work. No guns, no marches, no shouting. Why such a response?" Jude asked no one in particular.

"You're a threat," Rod said. "You've united the SACs. What once was a loose, scattered group of survivalists that were sure to die off or reintegrate into the cities has become a vocal group outside of the government's direct control. President Blake Connor never liked the SACs. He was the most vocal opponent of allowing SACs during the Transition, and now that they are not dying out as planned, so my guess is that he's looking for an excuse to wipe them out."

"And we've given him that excuse," Jude said, shaking his head.

"No," Rod said. "Think about it: drones over Slate Creek, CAMO encroaching on SACs all over the country, and what happened to Chillicothe. He was coming for us from day one, but he didn't count on crossing paths with you two. The Sparrows are the only thing stopping him."

"I wish we had a little more firepower," Jude said with a sigh.

"Maybe we do," Zara said, smiling at her phone. "Chiela Cruz has managed to escape the NDC. She wants to know where to go to join the Sparrows."

"How . . . ." Jude stumbled, his mouth gaping open.

"I don't know. I'd like to ask her in person."

"Ask her if she can get to Kansas City. She would be safe with Max in the Bunker."

"She said she can be there in a couple of days. She wants to know where we are," Zara relayed.

"Unless we can find a way to fly over borders without getting scanned, we're stuck in Cascadia," Jude said.

"She says that shouldn't be a problem. She wants us to send her our GPS coordinates and be ready to go in two days. She says we'll get express delivery."

In two days, Jude and Zara found out exactly what that meant. Freight drones regularly carried the same long, narrow intermodal freight sleeves that were carried on the back end of SEMIC trains. The drones operated relatively autonomously, and security was surprisingly lacking. With the right codes, you could hitch a ride with a freight drone, and there were no guards, pilots, or scanners to worry about. She sent Jude and Zara a schedule and the codes they'd need to get a jump seat. After a few hours and several transfers, they landed in Kansas City.

"Welcome back to Sparrow HQ," Max said as he drove them down the dusty trail into the Bunker. "We've missed you."

"Ditto," Zara said. "The NDC bed-and-breakfast wasn't exactly five-star."

"How's married life?" he teased. "I see you're managing to keep your hands off of each other for more than two minutes at a time."

"Barely," Jude said, earning him a sock in the arm and a kiss on the cheek from Zara.

"This time, kids, you need to share a room," Max said. "We have an extra guest now. I'm sure you won't mind."

"Chiela!" Zara screeched as she stood up and nearly knocked over her friend. "I have only one question: how?"

"How what?" she asked.

"Everything."

"Getting here is a story. Getting you here is pretty simple; we used to ship a lot of things by air at CAMO, and the freight companies don't change their passwords all that often."

"I'm Jude. Nice to finally meet you in person," he said, shaking her hand.

"Nice to meet you," she said. "I used to say men and marriage are never worth it, but I can see why Zara made an exception for you."

Dinner that evening evolved smoothly into a strategy session.

"What's our next move, fearless leader?" Max asked Jude.

"From what we know of President Blake Connor, he has always had a sore spot for the SACs. When they didn't collapse as quickly as ADAMS predicted, he wanted to subtly help them disappear, but then something got in his way: the Sparrows. With the SACs fighting back, he's going to keep changing tactics, and we're going to have to try and stay a step ahead."

"He has the guns. Why doesn't President Connor just send in the NADF and wipe out the SACs by force?" Chiela asked.

"There are two things holding him back," Max explained. First, military campaigns against your own people are political bombshells. They are very hard to spin. Second, he just can't afford it. Wiping out the SACs means adding thousands of people to the social service programs in cities. Medical care, education, and UBI payments would bust the budget."

"So, we're playing a political game," Chiela said with a devious smile. "I like it."

"The protests and the Freedom Exhibition clearly struck a nerve, and I don't suggest any one of you three go anywhere right now, but this publicity has bought us some political capital with people who are sympathetic to the SACs. I have an idea on how to use that capital."

"We're listening," Zara said.

"Three SACs posted video of the paper bombing, and one video was very good. Someone was taking a video of their litter of puppies when the bomb hit. No one was hurt, but the explosion, the screaming, and the mess were terrifying. I think we should post it publicly and let it go viral. A blatant attack on the SACs won't look good for President Connor."

"It'll remind people of Chillicothe," Zara said. "It will help our case in the eyes of the public."

"Not just our case," Max said. "It will help Callum's case. Good old Boris Spence can use that video to argue self-defense. The video proves drones don't just take pictures."

"I recommend a quiet, speedy trial of Callum Kane," the ADAMS drone offered President Connor. "Initial data indicates the bombing of the SACs, despite being non-lethal, is viewed very unfavorably by 87.3% of citizens. Continuing to hold Callum Kane could garner sympathy for him and the Sparrows."

"Tell the DA to move him to the front of the line, but I don't want him walking free. If the jury doesn't make an example of him, I will."

Chapter 27: **Trial**

CALLUM THOUGHT HE WAS having a lucky day when a guard brought him some "leftover" bread pudding. It must have been from the break room, because they never ate anything that good! He suspected it might be more than luck, however, by day three, when the treats kept coming.

Boris Spence paid a visit, and this time, Callum suspected something was going on.

"I have good news," Boris announced as he set his briefcase down on the bare table and they took their seats.

"Let me guess, we have a hearing," Callum said.

"Even better, we are going straight to trial. I have no idea why the sudden rush, but I'm not complaining."

"Me neither. I've actually had enough food for once. Evidently, they want to fatten me up for trial. It doesn't look good if prisoners show up looking anorexic."

"I imagine not. There have been some recent developments that work in our favor. Basically, we can argue self-defense with a lot more credibility. Are you up for going over a few things and practicing some questions and answers for the stand?"

"Sure. I don't have any other pressing appointments."

"Well, kids, we have some good news," Max announced the next morning. "Posting those videos of the attacks moved the needle, I believe. Boris met with Callum yesterday, and they are preparing for the trial."

"Are you serious?" Jude asked, still trying to absorb the news.

"I wouldn't joke about your brother, Jude."

"I can't believe it."

"If you ask me, the drone attack was a knee-jerk reaction by a President trying to display his power and intolerance for dissent. I think ADAMS did some analysis after the video surfaced and told President Connor that he better move up the trial or there could be more problems."

"If all goes well, we could realistically be bringing Callum home in a few weeks," Jude said.

"Don't get your hopes up too high for an acquittal. President Connor is going to want blood, so to speak. Still, Boris isn't a fool. He's got a few tricks up his sleeve," Max said.

"At least we've gone from waiting for nothing to waiting for something."

Callum Kane couldn't have felt more out of place sitting in court in a suit and tie than if he were sitting in a restaurant in his underwear. After the bailiff announced the judge and opened the court session, Prosecutor Val Sorenson took her turn first, laying out opening arguments.

"This is a pretty simple case, ladies and gentlemen. The crime was recorded, and we will all have a chance to watch exactly what the suspect did. Using an illegal weapon, a shotgun, he willfully and intentionally identified an NADF survey drone, took aim, and fired. The first shot damaged the drone, and the second shot took it out. Both shots were caught by the drone cameras in high-quality footage. The drone is part of the NADF fleet; therefore, this is not only an act of sabotage; it is an act of domestic terrorism."

Boris stood up, buttoned his coat, and sighed deeply.

"Behold your terrorist," he said, waving his hand over Callum. "This red-haired, nineteen-year-old from a Sustainable Agricultural Community nestled in the remote Canadian Rocky Mountains of Northern Cascadia. Before we pass judgment on this young man, maybe we should know a few things about him first."

The jury seemed agreeable.

"Can he handle a deadly weapon? I sure hope so! It is not uncommon for a bear or a mountain lion to wander into the community, and when they do, you'll want more than a bow and arrow! We have strict gun laws here in the cities, but the Slate Creek SAC is hundreds of kilometers from the nearest city, and the weapon is a necessity up there. If it is not allowed under a grandfather clause, then I'd be happy to argue my next case about the legitimacy of gun laws in Registered Sustainable Agricultural Communities.

"But that is not why we are here. In fact, we're not even here to dispute the fact that Callum Kane shot down an NADF drone. As Ms. Sorenson said, we have the video. We're here to decide if Callum is a terrorist or if he is a reasonable young man trying to defend himself against a real or perceived threat.

"Callum was a victim of not one but three years in a Compulsory Monitored Education school. He was torn from his family and their peaceful farm life and taken to Vancouver, where he was housed with strangers, fed strange food, and expected to work in front of a screen all day after growing up working in the fields. If that doesn't make you jumpy at the sight of a drone approaching, I don't know what will.

"Finally, I will show you clearly and, for some of you, surprisingly, that our government has not been exactly faithful in its promise to the SACs; we have documented NADF attacks against registered SACs. Whether it was regarding a land dispute with CAMO, punishment of some kind, or intimidation, we don't know, but if I were living in a SAC and I saw an NADF drone approaching, I know I'd take cover. Thank you."

"What if Callum manages to get out of this mess and come home? What are we going to do then?" Zara asked. "Do you want to return to Slate Creek, put down roots, and live a nice, quiet SAC life?"

"Maybe," Jude said.

"That was the most evasive, non-answer you could give."

Jude smiled and lay back on their bed.

"Part of me misses that life, but another part of me loves helping the SACs. Callum was always the farmer. He loves the soil, he loves the work, and he loves the independence. I was always more of a technical guy. Travelling around the SACs and helping them with their power grids was the most fun I've ever had. Besides, I don't think the NADF is going to just forget the Sparrows. Eventually, they will come back for us."

"Yeah, we really have poked the bear," she mused.

"He needed to be poked," Jude defiantly huffed. "With President Connor, I have a feeling the SACs are going to need the Sparrow's help more than ever."

"I always wanted to be a journalist. I had no idea how important or dangerous it could be," Zara said, lying back next to Jude.

"It's not exactly conducive to having kids, at least not now. I do feel bad about that."

"We're young, and I'm not quite ready to settle down with a few rug rats just yet. I know the time will come, and I'm not worried about it. You know what one of the best parts about kids is?" she asked.

"What's that?"

"Making them. Let's practice."

After showing the footage of the attacks and guiding Callum through a set of questions in order to explain his actions, it was the prosecution's turn to cross-examine. Boris wasn't looking forward to this part, but if Callum played his cards right, it would mean a big pay-off for them in terms of jury sympathy.

"Mr. Kane, is it fair to say that you hate the government?" Val Sorenson asked.

"I love my family and my SAC. I hated being taken away from them, and I don't trust the government," Callum explained.

"When you saw the drone, did you know it was an NADF drone?"

"I saw the New America flag, and I figured it was from the national government. I know what the Cascadia Regional Defense Force drones look like."

"I'm sure you do. Knowing it was most likely an NADF drone, why would you shoot it down?"

"I thought it was spying or attacking. From a distance, it's hard to tell cameras from guns. There was no reason for an NADF drone to be all the way out as far as Slate Creek. I felt like I needed to defend my family."

"Why would an NADF drone be a threat to you if you weren't breaking the law?" she asked.

"Why does CAMO try to plant crops on SAC land? Why were SACs attacked recently? You defend yourself first, and then you ask questions."

It was time to pivot to the bigger issue.

"Were you encouraged to shoot down the drone as part of the Sparrow movement?" Val asked.

"Objection! Relevance?" Boris interjected.

"Your honor, being part of the Sparrow movement would speak to motivation."

"Overruled."

"What is the Sparrow movement?" Callum asked.

"I will remind you that lying under oath will earn you a charge of perjury. Answer the question."

"I don't know what you're talking about. What does the drone have to do with a bunch of birds?" he asked.

The judge hammered down the mutterings of laughter. "Order!"

"You're claiming to not know what the Sparrow movement is? How is that possible when it was begun by your brother Jude and his wife Zara?"

"Jude got married!?" Callum blurted out. "Are you serious?"

"Judge, may I have permission to treat Callum Kane as a hostile witness?" Val hissed.

"Objection, your honor!" Boris said, coming to Callum's rescue. "The Sparrow movement is a very recent phenomenon. Callum Kane has been in custody since before this movement, and he has nothing to do with it. He didn't even know his brother got married while he was in detention. He's not lying; he doesn't know what you're talking about."

"Sustained. Stick to the charges, counselor."

"Yes, your honor," Val sighed. "You seem to harbor a lot of hostility toward the government, Mr. Kane. Isn't it true that you really shot down the drone because you couldn't help but take a chance to strike back at the government you hate so much?"

Callum started to speak, but after catching Boris' eye, he took a deep breath and let out a long sigh.

"I'm a farmer, not a fighter. Do you know what I really worry about? I worry about a good crop and harvesting it in time. I worry about the health of the new calves and piglets and maintaining the size of our livestock. I worry about the weather, irrigation, and maintenance of our structures. Above all, I worry that we have enough food and energy to make it through winter without starving or freezing. The last thing I want to do is to pick a fight with the government, especially the national government. Why did I shoot down the drone? Because I don't want them to pick a fight with me."

Boris sat back, crossed his arms, and smiled widely. It's always a big risk to put a defendant on the stand, but this time the kid nailed it.

"No more questions, your honor."

"Sir, the report you requested from ADAMS is ready on your screen," the clerk announced as the Judge returned from lunch.

He let out a long sigh and fell into his leather chair. "Thanks."

He turned on his screen and pulled up the report:

"I ran an analysis of the case of Callum Kane using the full text of arguments made, exhibits presented, and a comprehensive comparison to legal precedent. In light of the legal but unusual surveillance over a registered SAC and the repeated extractions to Compulsory Monitored Education, the argument for self-defense is viable.

"A conviction for destruction of property may be appropriate, but in light of the defensive nature of this incident, a terrorism conviction is not legally sound and would likely be overturned on appeal."

"My sentiments exactly," the judge muttered to himself, opening his cabinet and pouring a couple of centimeters of scotch from the decanter. "The jury will probably say the same thing. If only it were that simple . . . "

"Your honor, you have a call. It's the President, sir," the clerk announced nervously.

"Thank you. I've got it," the judge said, accepting the call on his screen. "Mr. President! I had a feeling I might hear from you."

"Zack, I'm bleeding," Athalia said, cracking open the bathroom door. "I'm worried."

Zack turned even whiter behind his carpet-like red beard. Athalia was a rock, tall and imposing, always confident and sure of herself. Seeing her genuinely worried struck him deeply.

"Let's get you in bed, and I'll find a doctor," he said, taking her hand and helping her off the commode. The water was a sickening yellowish-pink as it swirled down, and they both dared not say what they really worried about. Athalia was only 34 weeks along.

"Where are you going to find a doctor?" she asked as Zack helped swing her legs into bed and pulled the blanket over her.

"I'll find one."

Even though it made no sense, Zack knew he needed to call on the Sparrows. He had no idea how they could help him find a doctor from a couple of thousand kilometers away, but something in him urged him to turn to Jude and Zara first.

"I know this is not your area of expertise, but I don't know where else to turn right now. Athalia is bleeding, and we don't have a doctor here in Blue Ridge," he typed into his screen. He wasn't sure if or when they might get it.

Within two minutes, he heard the ding of a new email, and his heart leapt with the hope it was a response and not another request for help fixing a hole in someone's roof in the SAC.

"Do you have a midwife in Blue Ridge?" Zara asked.

"Yes, we do," he typed. "But I'm worried it's something she might not be able to handle."

"Call the midwife right away. Have her examine Athalia, and message me back with what she sees."

"I'll do it right now. Give me a few minutes. Thank you," he typed.

Zack grabbed his handheld CB radio, recently resurrected and tuned courtesy of Jude during their visit, and put out a call on channel 24, Blue Ridge's designated emergency and information channel. Jude was right; sometimes 20th-century technology is still the best tool out there for a SAC.

"This is Zack, calling for Madeline. Madeline, do you read me?"

Six seconds of silence followed.

"Madeline, do you read me? If anyone is near Madeline, please have her contact me right away."

There was more silence, but Zack took a deep breath and tried to think logically. Most people didn't sleep with their CB under their pillow, so it might take a few minutes for the word to get to her, and for her to get to a radio. He took the radio with him and went into the bedroom.

"The Sparrows are going to help us. They want Madeline to look at you and report to them," he said gently, taking her hand and rubbing it soothingly. "Help is coming."

"Thank you, baby," she said with a sigh.

"This is Madeline," the radio crackled. "I'm on my way over."

The exam was quick and decisive. As the midwife put on her latex gloves and got Athalia into position, she rattled off her questions.

"Has your water broken?"

"No."

"Any contractions yet?"

"I don't think so."

"What was the bleeding like? Was it a heavy flow?"

"It was more like spotting, but still heavier than spotting."

In hospitals, you had instruments, headlamps, and medications that could counter early labor and infections. In a SAC, you had your hands, your eyes, and in Madeline's case, her husband's flashlight.

"You plug has come out, which is probably where the blood came from. Your water hasn't broken yet, but your body is getting ready for labor. You will start feeling contractions any time now. Let them know we don't have a lot of time."

"Thank you, Madeline!" Zack said, running to the screen in the other room and relaying the information to Zara.

Thirteen hundred kilometers away, the Sparrows mobilized.

"Can you work your transportation magic for us again?" Zara asked as Chiela was sitting in front of three screens, scanning and typing away.

"Where are you headed?" she asked without looking up.

"Not me. Jude's sister, Maisy, and maybe her friend Dr. Robinson are needed in the Blue Ridge SAC. It's about 150 kilometers north of Atlanta."

"Are they SAC residents or city residents?" Chiela asked.

"Technically, they are Kansas City residents. Maisy is in med school, and Dr. Robinson works out of the hospital."

"A charity medical mission? That's easy. I can get them to Atlanta in a few hours, and they don't even have to be stowaways. I'll get them the legit codes reserved for medical and EMT transport. Can they get from Atlanta to the SAC?"

"I'm sure they can."

"Tell me when they're ready, and I'll send them instructions."

"For the record, you're amazing," Zara said. "Thanks."

"For the record, I never realized I could be a hacker and still be working on the right side," Chiela chuckled. "Thank you."

"Has the jury reached a verdict?" the judge asked after everyone was seated.

"We have your honor," the foreman stood and said.

"What have you found?"

"On the charge of Domestic Terrorism, we, the jury, find the defendant Callum Kane not guilty."

Quiet gasps and murmurs echoed through the courtroom. Two quick snaps of the gavel quelled the noise.

"On the charge of Destruction of Government Property, we the jury find the defendant Callum Kane not guilty by reason of self-defense."

This time it took four slams of the gavel to restore peace in the courtroom.

"Thank you, ladies and gentlemen of the jury. Please do not leave at this time," the judge said. "First, the court does not need your statement of reasoning with your verdict; guilty or not guilty is all you must decide. Secondly, it appears you were sympathetic to the defendant, as is evident by your attempt to justify your verdict on the second charge. As an officer of this court, it is my duty to ensure we follow the law, and in this case, I do not believe that has been done. Regardless of the motivation, the evidence is clear that Callum Kane did, in fact, destroy this drone with the full knowledge that it was government property. I concur with the jury's decision of not guilty on the charge of Domestic Terrorism; however, I must override the decision on the second charge. I find the defendant Callum Kane guilty of the charge of Destruction of Government Property."

With the final pound of the gavel, the court erupted into the dull roar of people reacting to, discussing, and reporting on the verdict. Boris Spence leaned over to Callum and put his hand on his shoulder.

"It's not a complete victory, but it's still a big one. We beat the charge that could have cost your life. We'll use the jury's verdict to ask for leniency in the sentencing hearing."

"How long will that take?" Callum asked.

"It will probably be within the month. Don't worry; they'll keep fattening you up as long as you are on the way to court."

"Thank you, Mr. Spence."

"Don't thank me yet. When you are on your way back to Slate Creek, then you can thank me."

"The contractions have definitely started," Athalia grunted.

"It's a little too early for that," Maisy said, setting up an IV pole. "Did you tell your baby to quit being in such a hurry?"

"We're going to give you some medicine to hold off labor for a few days," Julian explained. "We're also going to give you some medicine that will help make sure the baby's heart and lungs are developed enough to handle life on the outside. Try to relax, Mrs. Nolan. I've delivered babies much earlier than this."

"Yes, but have you delivered early babies this far out in the woods?" Athalia asked.

"There is a first time for everything," Julian said, smiling. "Don't worry. We've got antibiotics and ways to stave off infection. To be honest, I think the environment up here is a lot healthier than in a hospital. The baby's heart rate is strong. I think this kid is a lot like his parents and can't wait to meet them."

"Ha," Athalia laughed. "This kid will get a lot of things from us, but patience is not one of them." She grunted again as the next contraction hit, and Madeline was there to coach her through the breathing.

"Are you ready to officially start your OB rotation?" Julian asked Maisy.

"Bring it on," she said, snapping her latex gloves on.

"Good morning, Val," Boris said as he prepared to enter court. "We got called back for sentencing pretty quickly, don't you think?"

"I think we all want this to be over with," she sighed.

"I imagine the optics don't make your bosses too happy," he said.

"You have no idea."

After the judge arrived and the bailiff announced the court to be in session, the judge didn't waste time.

"In the matter of Callum Kane, now convicted of Destruction of Government Property, it would seem appropriate for him to make restitution; however, it is not likely a SAC resident would ever be able to repay the cost of a military drone. In any case, this is a criminal matter and not a civil one, and we are here to decide an appropriate sentence for the crime he has been convicted of. Will the defendant please rise?"

Boris and Callum stood.

"For the crime of Destruction of Government Property, I hereby sentence you, Callum Kane, to one year in prison. Your sentence will be conferred with credit for time served in the National Detention Center. At the end of this time, you will be required to make regular contact with your assigned parole officer in the City of Vancouver, in the Cascadia Region."

"You aren't walking, but aren't rotting in prison forever, either," Boris said, trying to comfort Callum.

"It's alright, Mr. Spence. I have a light at the end of my tunnel. I think I'll be alright."

"Jude!" Maisy cried from the other end of the phone. "We have a new baby boy! Little Archer Nolan is wailing his healthy lungs out. Julian said if he went to term, he might have been over four kilos!"

"Thanks, Maisy. Tell Zack and Athalia I said congratulations."

"Jude!" Max said as he came in for dinner. "I just got a message from Boris. The judge gave Callum a year, and he gave him credit for the six months he's already sat in the NDC. He'll be out in September!"

Jude sighed and sank into his chair. "Max, I think I'll say the blessing over dinner tonight. I've got a lot to be thankful for."

Chapter 28: The Halls of Congress

"WHO'S THE FRESH MEAT?" an inmate said, looking at Callum at the end of the lunch table.

"I'm not fresh meat," he said coldly. "I've just been upgraded from the terrorism unit."

"Why'd they move you over here?" the inmate said with a mixture of curiosity and disdain.

"I finally had my trial. Apparently, I'm not a terrorist, just a pain in the ass."

The table laughed, including the curious inmate. Street credit from the terrorist wing and a little humor wedged a crack into the prison social structure for Callum.

"Were you really in the terrorism unit?" an inmate said, catching up to Callum on their way out to the rec yard.

"Yeah."

"Is your name Callum? Callum Kane?"

"Who's asking?"

"I'm Kurt Miller. I met your brother when he was in here."

"I can't imagine my brother in prison. Even when I passed him, I almost couldn't believe it. He solves problems and follows the rules, unlike me."

"He helped my cousin Jacob and basically saved the lives of the whole SAC. He's helped a lot of other SACs, too. The Sparrows are kind of a legend."

"The Sparrows?" Callum asked. "I heard that in court as if it were some dirty word. Who are the Sparrows?"

"The Sparrows is a whole movement, really. Jude and Zara started it when they travelled across New America and helped SACs that were in trouble. Jude helped restore power grids, and Zara helped with tutoring and reporting. Her Sparrow Press is the only thing SACs trust. They basically are the resistance."

"The resistance? What are they resisting?"

"I guess they resist the government, but it's not like he's starting a war or anything. He just helps the SACs become more successful and helps them fight back when the government tries to break the rules. Even though Jacob's SAC was destroyed and taken over, the Sparrows got everyone out. Other SACs had CAMO trying to steal land, and the Sparrows stopped them. The Department of Education tried to change the exams so students would fail and have to go to CME, but your mom and Zara helped the SACs beat the system and pass the exams. I'm telling you, your brother and his girl are so smart."

"That's another way I'm nothing like him," Callum mused. "So why did he start traipsing across New America in the first place?"

"You don't know? He was trying to get to you."

Jude and Zara kept busy throughout the spring and summer. Max's bunker in the Ozark SAC became a headquarters for supporting SACs all over New America. While Jude was busy giving advice and making short trips to help get power grids back online or solving other problems, Zara was reporting any and all things related to SAC living. Chiela became the unofficial chief IT guru for the Sparrows, fine-tuning the masking procedures Zara had learned from Jaxson. With Chiela in charge of online publication and the monitoring of communications, Zara was able to recruit in-field reporters throughout the SACs and even in some cities.

She established Sparrow Press guidelines and began spending more time editing and studying official news sites to glean some of the best practices and divining the worst ones. She developed policies advocating truth, clarity, and no tolerance for spin. When it came to core values, the Sparrows already had their foundation: sanctity of life, equality, and human dignity. If any of these were violated, the Sparrow Press immediately mobilized.

"Will the Sparrow Press provide exclusive coverage of the release of Callum Kane?" Jude said, sauntering up behind her and sliding his arms around her neck as she sat at her desk.

"I'd be surprised if any official news outlets covered it, but you can bet I'll be there," she said, leaning her cheek into his arm. "When's the day?"

"It should be in a couple of weeks. I need to see if Max has heard from Boris Spence."

"Boris has been trying to set up the time and details with the NDC for a month now," Max said, coming in from the garage and throwing his suit coat and briefcase on the kitchen table. "They've been ignoring him."

"They don't have a lot of time," Jude said. "It'd be nice to have details before we go get him."

"It'd be nice to have details, period," Max said. Jude picked up on his tone.

"Why do I get a heavy feeling in the pit of my stomach?" Jude asked. "What do you really think is going on, Max?" By now, Zara got up from her screen and stood next to Jude.

"I don't know anything for sure. I don't want to be a pessimist, but we should pay attention. Boris said the judge who sentenced Callum was under pressure from high up in the government, and he got that straight from the Prosecutor Val Sorenson. Even though he overturned the jury on the Destruction of Government Property charge, his sentence was probably viewed as too lenient for someone who was supposed to be an example. He was killed in a somewhat suspicious-looking car accident a few days ago."

"Suspicious?" Zara asked. "As in it was probably no accident?"

"There's no way to know for sure, but self-driving cars have a .0001% collision rate, and his car drove off a bridge," Max said.

"That would take a pretty high level of sophistication to tamper with or assume control of a car's control unit," Jude said. "It smells like a government job to me."

"We know someone was pressuring the judge, most likely from the White House. The judge gave a light sentence, and now he's dead. With the NDC stonewalling Boris . . . "

"They're not going to release him," Jude said.

"When you connect the dots, that is a possibility. Of course, it is still a couple of weeks away. Maybe they'll just send him out the front gate on the big day."

"Either way, we'll be there," Jude said.

"What if he doesn't walk out those gates that day, or the next?" Max asked.

"I'll be there on the last day of his sentence," Jude said. "And I'll be there the next day, and the day after that until he comes out."

"And what if that takes weeks or months or years?" Max asked.

"Then we'll be on the right side of the law, and the Sparrows will go to work for one of their own," Zara said with a determined scowl. "If President Blake Connor didn't like the Freedom Exhibition, then he's really not going to like us in October if Callum is not back in Slate Creek."

Jude looked down at Zara and smiled. "If we don't get Callum, President Connor won't get peace. The Sparrows can make a lot of noise when they flock together."

"Val, why is the NDC trying to stonewall me? Callum Kane should be standing next to me right now," Boris said into his phone, restraining his legal bulldog persona.

"It's out of my hands now, Mr. Spence. The judge . . . "

"The judge is dead," he said. "These two issues aren't related, are they?"

"For the third time, Mr. Spence, it's out of my hands. The case file might as well be tossed into the Potomac as far as I'm concerned. I can't help you. Now, if you don't mind, I'm going to get myself a cup of coffee before it's no longer breakfast."

Boris hesitated and then ended the call strategically. "Fine, but I'm not going to stop knocking on doors at the NDC until I can get satisfaction."

She was good, and he almost missed the message. Phones at the D.A.'s office are subject to continuous monitoring by ADAMS, so they needed a new venue. On the corner of Third and Potomac, there just happened to be an overpriced but convenient coffee shop. They stopped selling breakfast items at 10:30.

"Funny seeing you here," Boris said as Val sat down. "What are we not discussing?"

"This could get me in serious hot water," she said as she shucked off her coat and draped it over her chair. "Or worse yet, the same kind of water the judge landed in."

"So why talk to me?" he asked.

"Because Callum Kane is the brother of Jude Kane. If Callum is not released, the Sparrows might rear their stubborn heads, and if that happens, all hell could break loose this time around. Maybe you can convince them that anything they try will not end well."

"How far up does this go?"

"The top."

"The top of the D.A.'s office or higher?"

"As high as you can go."

"How do you know?"

"Besides being told to bury Callum on this flimsy case, I have friends in the White House, several of them, who say he hates the SACs. He opposed them all through the Transition, and he views them as a threat to social and political stability. He wanted to make an example of Callum Kane, but he only got a slap on the wrist. To add insult to injury, just after Jude and Zara walked out of the NDC, the Sparrows pulled off an embarrassing demonstration in Washington. He's got a big chip on his shoulder, and the only card he has left to play is Callum Kane."

"So how does he plan to justify holding Callum illegally after his sentence?"

"He's the President. If it's in the interest of national security to hold an inmate on suspicion of terrorist activities, no one will get in his way."

"I have a feeling the Sparrows will get in his way."

"If they do, there won't be any negotiations. There will be blood."

"So how are you planning to get to Washington D.C.?" Chiela asked when they wandered into the workroom that Chiela affectionately referred to as "her lair."

"Teleportation. And while you're at it, we need invisibility too," Jude quipped.

"I'm good, but I'm not that good. If I were, Callum and I would be sipping fruity drinks with umbrellas in them on a beach somewhere by now."

"Ha!" laughed Jude. "Clearly, you don't know my brother. He's all about trees, mountains, and beer. And even if you couldn't see him, he could never be quiet enough to pull off invisibility."

"You miss him, don't you?" Chiela asked.

"Yeah. We need to get him out of there."

"What are your parameters again?" Chiela asked.

"We agreed not to avoid transport and border scans, which technically we have done so far," Zara said. "It's not our fault freight drones don't scan hitchhikers."

"What else?"

"The NADF showed up in Slate Creek wanting to 'question us' about the Freedom Exhibition, so we're pretty sure we'll get snatched up the first chance they get," Zara explained.

"You guys are in almost as much trouble as I am!" Chiela laughed. "Freight drones are handy, but we're already pushing our luck with as many trips as you've made. Someone's going to notice eventually. Driving is slow and risky. I've got another idea."

Jude and Zara looked at each other and then back at Chiela. "We're listening."

"I've been working on this little ditty here for a while," she said, holding up a thin, one-centimeter-wide round disk. I developed the hardware at CAMO, and since I've been out of the NDC, I've been tweaking the programming."

"What is it?" Zara asked.

"I think it would be a great necklace, but if you want to make an earring out of it, that will work too."

"I meant what does it *do*," Zara said, rolling her eyes.

"Oh, yeah. Of course. It's a transmitter. It sends a signal to your passport, masking the information and telling the scanner whatever we want it to. We can use this to give you completely new identities, no surgery needed," Chiela said proudly.

"Impressive," Jude said. "And again, technically, we wouldn't be avoiding scanners. How well has it performed?"

"It's done well in near-range testing, but I don't have a high powered mass scanner like they have at the SEMIC train stations. I was thinking you two could try it out."

"Is there anyone not wanted by the NADF that could be guinea pigs?" Zara asked.

"No, it's perfect," Jude interjected. "If it works, it passes a real-world field test. If not, who better to figure out what went wrong and why?"

"I know this is right up your alley, Jude, but don't forget, as soon as our names pop up, the NADF will get a call," Zara reminded him. "What will we do then?"

"Improvise."

With the transmitters needing to be within one meter of their passports and their passports implanted between their shoulders and neck, they opted to make matching necklaces that hung down underneath their shirts.

"Who are we again?" Zara asked as they packed their bags.

"Mason and Gloria Maxwell," Jude said. "They are Ozark SAC residents, and Max promised we have their permission to temporarily impersonate them."

"I hope they don't plan on traveling while we're gone," Zara mused. ADAMS would definitely recognize one couple in two places at the same time."

"Yeah, that would blow our cover! Max said they never travel, and they don't plan on starting now."

"What's the plan when we get into the city?" she asked.

"I think we'll start with the Smithsonian, which can take a couple of days. Next, I want to see the Lincoln Memorial . . . "

"Very funny. Save that speech for the guards at the D.C. border, Mason Maxwell. I was talking about us. What happens if Callum doesn't walk out of the NDC?"

"I don't want to be fatalistic, but my gut says they won't let him go. My gut also says they're ready for a fight, unlike the last couple of Sparrows demonstrations. You heard Max; we're up against President Blake Connor. He may be willing to cross the line to send a message like he did with the paper bombs on the SACs, but ultimately, he is still responsible to the people of New America. It's a battle for the truth, and that is where the Sparrows have an edge," Jude said, and then he sighed and put his arms around Zara. Holding her tightly and leaning into her ear, he whispered, "I can't let you or anyone else get hurt. I want my brother back, but I don't want to sacrifice anyone else to do it."

"Somewhere between doing absolutely nothing and starting an armed insurrection is the path we need to take. We're going to find it together," Zara reassured him.

The Kansas City SEMIC train station was busier than usual, and Jude couldn't decide if that was in their favor or not. Chaos can be your friend if you don't want to be noticed, but then again, Jude wanted to make sure the transmitter was doing its job. Finding out in a SEMIC train station gave them a much better shot of escaping than the security station at the D.C. border.

Most people passed under the scanners without giving them much thought, and some didn't even notice. Jude and Zara, however, had their eyes glued to the small readout screens on the turnstiles. This was their only indication of what the scanners read unless they were stopped and questioned, and by then it was too late.

The crowd was in a hurry, and like an amoeba moving through a slimy liquid, Jude and Zara were pushed past the dingy, forgotten readout screens too quickly to get a good look. They made it through the turnstiles and met up again on the platform.

"Did you see the readout?" Zara asked, trying to quell a growing panic.

"No. They were too dirty and faint," Jude said.

"Great. How do we know if Chiela's transmitter worked? The NADF could be on their way, and we'd never know it."

"We'd know it if they showed up in Baltimore to greet us."

"We can't just walk into their trap. We may never see daylight again, and Callum will be trying to get *us* out."

"Maybe not. I have an idea."

Zara's heart started racing even faster. Whenever Jude said those words, he was about to get them into trouble or get them out of it. She prayed it was the latter.

"Excuse me," he said, walking right up to a LEAD unit. "I would like to ask for a voluntary scan. My wife and I don't travel much, and before we begin our trip, I want to make sure our passports are functioning correctly. I planned this trip for months, and I don't want to run into trouble. This is a special time for us."

Zara stepped up and took hold of Jude's arm. "I told him he is a worrier, but he said he wants our time to be special. It would make him feel better to know our passports are working properly."

"The passports appear to be working properly," the LEAD unit announced mechanically. It didn't offer any further information.

Jude felt Zara squeeze his arm even harder.

"I'm sorry to bother you, but could you tell me if the doctor coded my passport with my legal name? I often go by 'Mack,' and I hope he didn't confuse my nickname with my legal name."

"Mason and Gloria Maxwell, current residents of the Ozark Sustainable Agricultural Community. Your passports are functioning properly," the LEAD unit said.

"Thank you," Zara said, nearly dragging Jude away with their luggage in tow. "Nice work, Mack."

"Thanks, Gloria. What nickname should we give you?" Jude teased.

"How about Zara? I've always liked that name."

"Defending Callum Kane was not a passion. It was a favor for Max Simon," Boris said as they had coffee in a strategically out-of-the-way Washington D.C. coffee shop. "I was on the fence, but any chance I get to stick a finger in the eye of the New American government, I take. I'm an old crony still bitter about the suspension of the United States Constitution. We have yet to see our full rights and protections restored, and until we do, I'll keep spitting on their shoes."

"We might be doing more than spitting," Jude said. "If we don't see Callum walking out of the front gate soon, the Sparrows are going to push back."

"I don't want to get involved, but I won't get in your way," Boris said. "When do you want to draw a line in the sand? Callum's one year is up in a few days."

"I'll give them a couple of weeks. If we don't have him by October 1st, they will hear from us," Jude said.

"Are you ready?" Boris said as he waved his phone over the terminal and paid for the coffee. "He's a hardliner. He'll get his hands dirty if he has to."

"We're ready for him to get his hands bloody," Zara said. "In fact, we're counting on it."

Boris Spence was good on his word. Jude and Zara were introduced to Nigel and Clara Morris, a British expatriate couple who came to New America to work as consultants just before the Artificial Intelligence boom caused jobs to become almost as rare as winning the lottery. Clara's position teaching high school math disappeared as quickly as most other jobs, but Nigel was relatively secure in his job as a security expert working for an IT firm that had a contract with the New America government.

Nigel and Clara rented out the third floor of the three-story house to boarders who worked with Nigel and spent most of their time traveling for work. Jude and Zara were given the basement, and with the understanding that they needed as little attention as possible, all three of them settled on the seemingly inevitable generic code name for their living space: "the flat."

"Boris Spence was not very forthcoming about the reasons for and length of your stay in Washington," Nigel said after they made their introductions. "I presume your need for privacy may have something to do with previously running afoul of the government."

"My name is Mason Maxwell, and this is my wife, Gloria. We have lived on the Ozark SAC all our lives, and we are on an extended vacation to tour our nation's capital," Jude explained.

"We live by and fight for three guiding principles," Zara added, "The sanctity of life, equality, and human dignity. We interact with other people in SACs and a few in cities that feel as strongly as we do about these principles. This is the reason for the screens and other equipment, in case you were concerned."

"Boris is a good friend, and we were not concerned," Clara said. "Thank you for letting us know all the same. We will need to have our story straight if the authorities show up at our door." She winked and followed Nigel into the kitchen to let Jude and Zara settle in downstairs.

"I'll let Chiela know her transmitter worked and we've arrived," Zara said, setting up her screen. "Then we can get down to business."

"I like the sound of that," Jude smirked. She gave him the classic raised eyebrow.

"What? You have to admit that was a perfect setup."

"It's a good thing you're cute."

"I let the NDC know time is up and that I would be coming to pick up Callum Kane," Boris explained on the phone. "I stopped asking for details and started telling them what would happen. I figured this way, they would have to at least respond before I showed up, raising hell. I was right. They finally responded; they said, "his case is being reviewed by the NADF, and he cannot be released until they deem it is safe."

"Damn," Jude said. "I knew in my gut they would pull this, but it still pisses me off."

"I told them they can't hold a prisoner who's been adjudicated past his sentence, but they pulled the 'national security' card. I know this comes from the White House. The NADF couldn't care less about a kid from a SAC."

"Well, now we know what we need to do," Zara chimed in. "Keep an eye on the news on October first."

As the Senator roused from his early morning REM sleep, he noticed an alert on his phone. Prying open his eyes, he unlocked it and found a strange message that seemed to take up the entire screen like an emergency announcement. He fumbled with the touch screen, but nothing responded. Without much choice, he read the message: "Callum Kane is being illegally detained and tortured in violation of New America law, a New America National Court decision, and International Law. Until he is released, the Sparrows will no longer be silent."

The Capitol Building was a zoo of security, investigators, extra troops, and the constant buzz of staff scurrying from office to office. He went straight to his office, inserted his key card, and opened the door. The first thing his eye went to was the same message displayed and locked on his desk screen.

Right on cue, the Senate was summoned for an emergency security meeting downstairs. Senators poured from their offices, many of them still swiping and tapping away at unresponsive phone screens.

Just as the last of the staff were filing in and the Capitol Security Commander was about to speak, a loud beeping sound emanated from every screen and phone in the room. The locked screens changed and displayed a new message: "We have your attention. You know our demand. Release Callum Kane, and the Sparrows will fly away." After sixty seconds, the message disappeared, and everyone's screens went back to normal.

"Well, it looks like we are back up and running," the Security Commander said. "I will let you all know what we find out. In the meantime, consider all communications on government phones and screens not secure. Adjust your communications accordingly."

The Sparrows sounded familiar, and after a quick search back at his office, he was reminded of "Operation Freedom Exhibition" that happened all around D.C. several months ago. Before that, a small band of noticeably peaceful demonstrators had gathered daily in front of the NDC calling for the release of Jude Kane and Zara Malik, the founders of this Sparrow group.

The Senator realized two things in that moment: first, they were smart in their non-violent confrontation strategies, and second, they were right. In every case, their demands were for something that was legally owed to one of their members. Since the Transition, New America operated under regular legal precedent, allowing judges some leeway in accommodating the small variances in Canadian and Mexican law that had not yet been codified in their respective regions, but New America had not yet formally ratified a new Constitution. The Sparrows could one day force this issue to a head.

Chapter 29: **Ring of Fire**

"ARENʼT YOU SUPPOSED TO be out of here by now?" Kurt asked Callum at breakfast.

"Three days ago. Iʼve got no word, not even from my attorney. Theyʼve blocked all communication privileges. Something isnʼt right," he said.

"Can they keep holding you even after your sentence?" Kurt asked.

"What am I going to do? Just walk out?"

"Well, if you tried, youʼd find your answer very quickly."

Callum stopped in line, smiled, and put his tray back in the stack.

"What have I got to lose?" he said.

"Callum, wait . . . " Kurt started.

"Iʼm done sitting around," he said, walking out of the cafeteria and down the hallway towards the front office. There were, of course, multiple layers of wall, gates, and doors between the cell block and the office, but you had to start somewhere.

"Where do you think youʼre going?" a guard said, accosting him in the hall.

"Iʼm glad you asked," he said with a smile. "My sentence is up, and I could use your help in signing out at the front office."

"What the hell are you talking about?" he barked back.

"My sentence was complete three days ago. I havenʼt heard from my attorney, whom I hoped would give me a ride, but I suppose I canʼt wait in here forever. I wouldnʼt want to be sitting in a cell just because I didnʼt ask to go home."

"Have you lost your mind?" the guard said, gripping his pistol but leaving it still in the holster. "Get back to the cafeteria and quit playing games."

"I'm not playing a game," Callum said, holding his hands up. "My sentence is up. If I'm not allowed to leave, I want to hear it, and I want to know why. I have that right. I'll go to my cell and wait if you want to check with the office."

"That's the craziest thing I've ever heard," the guard said.

"Will you check?"

"What are you trying to pull?"

"Lock my cell and look at my records yourself. In fact, the judge's sentence was reported in the papers. Do you remember that protest about eight months ago? Search the word 'Sparrows' and you'll see."

"Go on back. I'll check it out if I get time."

The guard made sure his cell was locked, and after a few minutes, curiosity got the best of him. He knew records couldn't be accessed by guards, so on his break, he ducked into the break room and started looking up articles on his phone. He searched "Sparrows," and he found a report on the protests at the NDC, but nothing else.

On a whim, he clicked on the word "Sparrows," and it rerouted him to the Sparrow Press website. It was a hidden hyperlink. It wasn't necessarily secure, but you had to know what to look for to find it. On Sparrow Press, he got full reporting on the NDC protests, the Washington D.C. "Freedom Exhibition" protest that was not covered in the official press, as well as the details of Callum's trial.

According to the sentencing, Callum should be free. There was another article, a more recent one, that reported on the suspicious death of the judge who sentenced Callum. Of course, this entire site could be Callum's invention, except that he remembered well the artwork displayed everywhere that morning, and not a single official news outlet even mentioned the "Freedom Exhibition." Something wasn't right.

After his break, he went to the front office and tactfully requested information on Callum's file.

"You know we can't show you those records," the admin assistant said.

"Then can you tell me if he was supposed to be released?" he asked.

"If he was supposed to be released, he would have been released," she said.

"There seems to be a problem," he said. "According to the media reporting on his trial, his sentence is up, but he is still here. I'm not trying to stick my nose in the admin side over here, but he's claiming it's time to go home. From a security standpoint, that can lead to problems on the cell block."

"I'll check into it," she said blankly.

The guard went back to his rounds, and before he could reach Callum's cell, there were already four guards there pulling him out.

"What's going on?" the guard asked.

"He's being transferred back to the Terrorism Unit," one of the guards said coldly.

"Why?" the guard asked, bewildered.

"They don't tell me that," he snapped back. "All I know is the NADF wants him held in the Terrorism Unit, so that's where he's going."

"I see you checked for me," Callum said as they shackled him and dragged him away.

"Yeah," the guard said, and then under his breath he muttered, "Sorry."

"I think I finally got on their last nerve," Boris said as they sat in their coffee shop. "I threatened to set up my office in their lobby if I didn't get answers. The admin finally told me she was allowed to tell me that he was transferred back to the terrorism unit. They claim the NADF wants him held 'for reasons of national security.' Do you know what that means?"

"It means the court decision is worthless now," Zara said.

"The NADF doesn't care about a kid from Cascadia," Boris said. "But they do what their Commander in Chief says."

"President Connor," breathed Jude. "He has his bargaining chip."

"I think that bargaining chip is going to start getting very hot very quickly," Zara said.

"Whatever you two kids do, be careful and leave me out," Boris said. "I need to be able to deny any knowledge of your actions. Don't get me wrong, I'll be cheering you along, but plausible deniability is the only thing covering my rear, and that still might not be enough. Be careful; Blake Connor is a hardliner, and he's not above spilling blood."

Jude and Zara returned to "the flat" in the basement of Nigel and Clara Morris' house and quickly called a meeting. As soon as Max and Chiela joined them on the screen, Zara gave them the news.

"Washington got the message, loud and clear," Zara said. "And their response was to put Callum back into the Terrorism Unit. He won't see the light of day again unless we do something."

"I expect nothing less than a large and maybe violent response from Blake Connor. I don't want to put you at risk. I don't want to drag you into something. Before Zara and I make a move, we want to give you an out," Jude said.

"Thanks, but no thanks, kids," Max said. "I'm in."

"I finally have something to fight for," Chiela said. "And it's not like I'm not already on the naughty list."

"Great!" Zara said. "I have a few ideas."

Callum got up from his bed and waited at the door of his cell when he heard the call for dinner. He was starving; he missed breakfast and lunch because of the transfer. He heard the buzz of the door unlock and turned the handle, but he was blocked by a guard.

"Not you, Kane," he said.

"What are you talking about?" he asked. "I missed breakfast and lunch. I'm starving! I'll even eat prison food!"

His attempt at humor fell on deaf ears.

"We've got orders to move you to isolation. They'll feed you there. Probably."

The atmosphere wasn't the friendliest in the Terrorism Unit, but after a few days in isolation, Callum would have gladly joined Death Row just for the company. They did feed him; he got a piece of bread and a cup of water twice a day. After two weeks, he was starting to swim in his orange jumpsuit, and he had to hold his boxer shorts up as he stood. He gave up on asking for more food after three days. Had he known they planned to starve him to death slowly, he would have attempted to escape. At least then, dying by gunshots would be quick. At this point, he was too weak to even try.

On a cool, early October evening, the Potomac was meandering its way to the Atlantic, lapping up against both shores in the gentle Autumn breeze that would turn much colder in a few weeks. It was quiet as most people in Washington were winding down from their workday or tourist activities, and darkness surrounded the dull glow of the city lights.

In the early morning hours, it seemed to some that there were a few extra stars in the sky, but for the handful of awake and curious sky watchers who bothered with binoculars, they soon found the extra twinkling in the sky was that of tiny LED lights on ultra-compact weather sensor mini drones. Rising from various hidden launch points, each drone was adorned with the image of a sparrow, preprogrammed with a location, and upon arriving, played a message on a continuous loop: "Release Callum Kane, and the Sparrows will fly away."

As the drones descended and found their recipients, Corporate Congressmen, Senators, officials, and hundreds of members of the official media awoke to the sound of Zara's voice chanting, "Release Callum Kane, and the Sparrows will fly away." Those who couldn't stifle the repeated sound destroyed their drones, but almost everyone brought them to work. After all, the President needed to be made aware of this.

The President was well aware. Dodging no-fly zones with low altitude and weather sensor permission codes, the Sparrow drones flooded the airspace around the White House and littered the lawn. Each drone sent to the White House had the name of a staff member printed underneath the image of the Sparrow, so for nearly an hour, there was mass confusion as staff members, after determining the drones were not a threat, rushed around exchanging drones as if they were a gift or contained an individual message just for them.

Eventually, the NADF Chief of Defense rushed to the White House to deliver his report. Not knowing if the President would want to see it or not, he carried the drone with him bearing the name of President Blake Conner.

"Let me see it," President Connor said coolly.

"Yes, sir."

He took the drone, turned it over a few times, and ripped the tape off the small hole where the looping message was coming from. He paused for a few seconds and then walked over to his desk and violently slammed the drone onto his desk, shattering the plastic housing. He took hold of the largest pieces and continued to slam the drone onto his desk over and over until it finally lay quietly in hundreds of pieces on the floor.

"Sir, we think . . . "

"I know you think it's the Sparrows. That much is obvious. Let me guess: you have no idea where they were launched from?"

"Not yet, sir."

"How did they manage to get a hold of dozens of drones?"

"Actually, it was a few hundred, we believe. They were sent to both houses of Congress, many officials, and the media."

"Fantastic. I don't suppose you can trace the purchase of a few hundred drones from our own government, can you?"

"It's not likely, sir. They were surplus weather sensor drones. They are regularly sold in large numbers to universities and private vendors, and according to initial searches, there were no large-scale purchases. They were likely obtained in dozens of separate e-cash transactions from multiple vendors."

The Defense Chief could see that the President's restraint was barely holding. Sweat beaded on his forehead, and his clenched fists were shaking as he stood over the pieces of the drone. The Defense Chief had to give him something.

"We'll hunt them down, sir. We will find them."

"I know you will," President Connor seethed. "The Sparrows crossed a line; they violated a no-fly zone. I hereby determine this group of invisible cowards to be a domestic terrorist organization, and I must act on the presumption that they have infiltrated Washington, D.C. I want troops in the streets, drones in the skies, and every camera looking for any hint of the Sparrows. Martial law is officially now in effect."

"ADAMS has not picked up on any passport scans by Jude Kane or Zara Malik. Should we send troops to Cascadia to try and find them?" the Chief asked.

"No. They are here. I know they are. If we have to scan everyone in Washington one by one, we'll flush them out. Until we do, a curfew is in effect."

At the sound of the latch clanging open on his door, a surge of adrenaline gave Callum just enough strength to stand. Two guards came in with a tray and a small tray table. They sat Callum back down on his bed, put the table and tray in front of him, and encouraged him to eat.

"Take it easy," one of them said. "If you puke it back up, we'll make you lick the floor clean."

He couldn't believe his eyes. There was a small feast in front of him, including sliced turkey, mashed potatoes, corn, green beans, and even a piece of cake. It wouldn't be easy to hold back, but Callum was determined to keep this rare infusion of nutrition down. He ate small bites, chewed slowly, and swallowed carefully.

"To what do I owe this honor?" he said between mouthfuls.

"You're going to need the strength," one of the guards said, twisting his baton in its holder. "We're sending a message to your brother."

Suddenly, he lost his appetite.

After their vigil near the National Mall, donning their altered looks, "Mason and Gloria Maxwell" made their way back to the flat. Jude's "Mason" had darkened hair pulled into a ponytail and a trimmed beard. He wore blue jeans and a plain dark blue t-shirt. Zara's "Gloria" had powdered gray streaks in her hair, a khaki skirt, and a plain red T-shirt.

The sight of NADF troops was nothing unusual, but the sight of troops deploying into the streets set alarm bells screaming for Jude and Zara. Zara's phone buzzed, and she quickly grabbed it from her bag.

"He just declared martial law. They're scanning everyone. Get back to the flat," the message said.

"What's going on?" Jude asked.

"Chiela said President Connor has declared martial law. We'd better get back."

A smile slowly grew on Jude's face as they headed home.

"What's that look for?" Zara asked. "Do you know something I don't?"

"It worked perfectly. His temper and his insecurity got the better of him. He's overreacted, and now we're pulling his strings. All he can do is show force, but that's not going to stop us."

"Are you sure?" Zara asked. "The whole city is under martial law now. Nobody can do much of anything."

"Exactly. Everyone is under martial law, so everyone is feeling the pain. It shouldn't be too hard to show people a picture of Callum before the trial and explain how our request to set him free resulted in President Connor punishing everyone."

"We can do better than a picture of Callum before his trial," Zara said, holding up her phone and showing him a picture. "I'm so sorry, Jude."

Chiela found the picture, intentionally left in a Sparrow Press blog thread, with the caption, "Actions have consequences." In the image, Callum is again thinner, but this time he has been severely beaten, bandaged, and then propped up on his bed in his cell. President Blake Connor was sending a clear message to the Sparrows.

Jude sighed and kept walking. "He's already played his best card, but we still have ours."

"We do?" Zara asked.

"People don't like martial law. People don't like seeing other people kept in prison after their release date, and they really don't like seeing them being beaten while in custody. Do you know why?" Jude asked.

"Because it could easily be any one of them," Zara said.

"Exactly. Even if they don't care about Callum, they do care about Constitutional protections, which have yet to be reinstated ten years after the Transition. Now that people are seeing abuses, they will start calling for a new Constitution to be ratified and demanding a new Bill of Rights. Do you know why they'll demand it?"

"Because the Sparrows will give them the idea," Zara said with a satisfied smile.

"Yes, they will, and that's President Connor's worst nightmare. It's a lot harder to control a population with guaranteed rights and protections," Jude said. "Hang in there, Callum. We're coming for you."

Chapter 30: **Recalculation**

THE CHIEF OF DEFENSE and the analyst decided to meet in the basement and consult with ADAMS before approaching the president with their report.

"Is there any indication that Jude Kane and Zara Malik are in Washington, D.C.?" the Chief asked the ADAMS drone.

"No, sir. There have been no scans since they returned to Cascadia last year," ADAMS said.

"Is there any way to track down who bought and released the weather drones?"

"It is possible, but not feasible. No large transactions have been detected."

"Is there anything we can say to satisfy our incensed president?" the Chief asked, grasping at straws. "He has classified the Sparrows as a national security threat. Bringing them down is now priority number one."

"That is not rational. The Sparrows continue to use non-violent and creative means to communicate their wishes. They are not a physical threat. The most efficient way to silence them would be to release Callum Kane."

"Clearly, you have not yet grasped some of the nuances of leading a nation," the Chief said with a sigh. "The threat is political and optical at this point; a group that calls into question the authority of the President could easily influence people and lead to civil unrest. The President will not allow us to return to the days of the Transition."

"I can explain my surveillance strategy and the intelligence I have gathered from the Sparrow Press. I have learned more about their purpose and goals. Perhaps that will meet with his approval," ADAMS offered.

"It couldn't hurt," the Defense Chief said. "Let's go upstairs."

"We can post a transcript, but I want to appeal to people in a direct address. I want to talk straight to them. Chiela, can we do that in a way that will still get to those who don't have a lot of bandwidth?" Jude asked as they met around the screen.

"Keep it under fifteen minutes," she said.

"Sounds good. We'll practice," Zara said.

"I want you to view it first, Max," Jude said. "Check my facts. I don't want to look like an idiot."

"Will do, boss," Max said with a classic thumbs up.

"Alright then. Let's get to work."

By the next morning, New America woke up to the first publicly broadcast video from Sparrow Press. Since most people in the cities had only heard rumors of the Sparrow Press, finding a video directly from the source and not officially sanctioned by the government made it a hot commodity, and it went viral within minutes.

"People of New America," Jude began, "I am Jude Kane, and this is my wife Zara." Zara sat next to Jude on camera with her arm on the back of his chair and her attention trained on him. "Together we founded the Sparrows, and it was quite by accident. We set out across New America on a mission to find my brother, and along the way, we helped a few of our friends in SACs. We have a simple philosophy: we believe in the sanctity of life, the equality of all people, and basic human dignity. To us, these are ingrained values, but for many others, these have been forgotten ideas. A small amount of empathy and compassion unleashed a powerful wave of encouragement, determination, and strength among the SACs.

"We are not a terrorist group, a mob, or some kind of dangerous militia. We are just New America citizens who want to be heard. We strictly forbid any use of violence, we don't use weapons, and we work within the law.

"On our journey, we noticed the incremental infringement on the rights of the SACs. Land was being gradually taken over by CAMO; grade-level exams were altered without notice, prompting several Compulsory Monitored Education extractions; and in one case, an accusation of overpopulation led to the eviction and annexation of an entire SAC.

"We eventually did find my brother, Callum Kane. He was held without trial for several months, and then he was tried and sentenced to one year in prison for destroying an NADF drone over our SAC in Cascadia. He broke the law, he received his sentence, and he served his time. Unfortunately, when his time was complete, he was not released from prison. When we asked for him to be released, we received this photo."

At this point, Zara held up the picture of the beaten and gaunt Callum in his cell. She paused for a few seconds so people could study the photo and undoubtedly screenshot it for sharing.

"The Sparrows are not calling for a rebellion; we are calling for a restoration. It has been ten years since the Transition, and we have yet to see the reinstatement of the Constitution. In Congress, the narrative is that we are no longer the United States, and therefore, we need a new Constitution that will be agreed upon by all ten regions, including those in the former countries of Canada and Latin America. We call upon President Blake Connor to make this his first and most urgent priority. We call upon him to restore a true and real Democratic Republic in New America.

"Do I want to see my brother released? Of course I do, but we have a bigger problem than Callum Kane. Until our rights are secured again under a constitution, we are all Callum Kane. We are all SACs at the mercy of the New America Defense Forces. We are moved by fear, trapped by power, and defenseless in our civil lives.

"Many of you are living in this now as martial law has been declared in Washington, D.C. The NADF is hunting for anyone associated with the Sparrows, and Zara and I are the grand prize. Our offense? We asked for Callum to be released. We were creative in our messaging, but we used no weapons, hurt no people, and made no demands outside of the law.

"If the government wants to find the Sparrows, let's make it easy for them: we are all Sparrows. This Saturday, let's not just speak our message; let's show them. In Washington, D.C., beginning at 8:00 am, in accordance with the curfew, I encourage you to unleash your own message. Voice your opinion. Demand the ratification of a new Constitution. Demand the protection of our democratic values. The government works for the people, not the other way around.

"Will you be arrested? That is a possibility, but I make three firm promises: first, the government cannot arrest everyone; second, you should not be arrested for speaking your mind; and third, you will be heard.

"As for our Corporate Congressmen, Senators, and President Blake Connor, I have an assignment for you: start working immediately to amend, ratify, and reinstate our Constitution. If you don't know where to start, I will help you:

'Congress shall make no law respecting an establishment of religion or prohibiting the free exercise thereof; or abridging the freedom of speech, or of the press; or the right of the people peaceably to assemble, and to petition the Government for a redress of grievances.'

It's time to go to work."

It has been said that Washington, D.C. is twenty-six square kilometers surrounded by reality. That Friday, it began to be surrounded by a very present human reality.

Jude and Zara's appeal spread virally throughout the country. The rumors, stories, and speculations surrounding the Sparrows were essentially set straight, and for the first time in more than ten years, people got the truth from someone besides the official media. Cities began organizing online communities sympathetic to the Sparrows, and the tension building during that week was palpable.

People began to stream into the Washington, D.C. area, and by Friday, the traffic was building outside checkpoints. In anticipation of some kind of mass demonstration on Saturday, President Connor called in thousands of NADF troops, tightened the already strict travel restrictions going into and out of the city, and deployed every functioning LEAD unit.

One thing ADAMS was still learning was the unpredictability of human behavior. While checkpoints along the highways into Washington D.C. firmly held to their policy and turned back cars, there was no way to stop the streams of people walking through streets, parks, and even coming in small boats up the Potomac like an army of ants invading a summer picnic in the grass.

The "fillers" went in first, infiltrating the city on foot and then finding troops or a LEAD unit and surrendering. The Capital was a popular tourist destination; an outsider wouldn't necessarily be aware of the martial law status, and travelling by foot (and thereby avoiding checkpoints) was not illegal. LEAD units and NADF troops were soon stretched thin throughout the city, detaining "tourists."

Detention centers, jails, and other holding facilities were quickly overwhelmed with peaceful citizens who smiled and cooperated. Transports were arranged to shuttle people out of the city, but for every hundred people dropped off outside the city limits, two hundred more would arrive. By early Friday morning, every structure used for detaining the incoming horde was overcapacity, and that is when the second wave descended on Washington, infiltrating and surrounding the Mall, the Lincoln Memorial, the White House, the Capitol Building, and other landmarks.

At exactly 8:00 am, Washington D.C. residents who were sympathetic to the Sparrows began spilling from their apartments and joining the throngs on the streets, in the parks, and around the landmarks. Unable to ignore the historic gathering of people, official media outlets launched their reporters, drones, and cameras to capture the demonstration and the government response.

"Get the Chief of Defense and ADAMS to the situation room," President Connor barked at his secretary as he cinched his tie.

"They are already there, sir," she replied.

He stormed down the hall, followed by a small army of aides and analysts with their briefcases and clipboards.

"What the hell is going on out there?" he bellowed as he barreled through the door and looked at the screen on the wall.

"I estimate a crowd in the tens of thousands," the ADAMS droid answered. "Precise numbers are difficult. Troops and LEAD units are scanning everyone they can, but they are overwhelmed."

"Are they even trying to control the situation?" yelled the President. "This isn't martial law. This is chaos, and the NADF has completely capitulated."

"Sir, we have detained thousands," the Defense Chief explained. "We have transported them back out of the city and turned them away at the checkpoints, but they continue to stream in on foot. We just can't be everywhere, and at this point we have nowhere to put them."

"You have guns, and they don't."

There was a brief, uncomfortable pause as the room absorbed the President's statement. The Chief took a deep breath.

"Even so, they are not in one place, sir. These are peaceful citizens, and the world is watching."

The world was watching, and the Sparrows had center stage. At 8:00, the residents joined the travelers in the streets, and the authorities were paralyzed. One by one, the tens of thousands of people began shedding their coats. It was a crisp winter morning, but the sun was shining, the sky was clear, and the people were ready to send their message. With the image of Callum Kane in an orange prison jumpsuit sitting bruised and beaten on his bed in the NDC fresh in their minds, the people donned their own versions of solidarity. They wore orange T-shirts, sweaters, and even jumpsuits, and emblazoned on each of them in everything from permanent marker to professional graphics was the phrase:

"We are all Callum Kane. We are all Sparrows."

On every orange shirt, above or below the words, they displayed the prominent image of a Sparrow. Some of the more creative folks brought black paint and shared it with others, wiping it below their eyes like an old American football player to reflect the bruises on Callum. After displaying their clear message, the protesters sat down, some of them linking arms in solidarity, as if daring the New American government to take action.

"I have to say something," Jude said as they sat hunkered in the flat.

"They can't hear you from inside the National Detention Center," Zara reminded him.

"We called for this demonstration. How can we sit here and keep hiding?" he asked.

Zara sighed. "You're right. We can't be cowards, but we can be smart. I have an idea."

As Zara adjusted the glasses on Jude, Chiela gave orders from the screen.

"The cameras on these glasses send a strong signal to your phone, so you're going to have to take off your necklaces. When you're out there, your passports won't be masked. You'll be Jude and Zara again."

"If I'm streaming live, I'd better me," Jude said. "I've never worn glasses. These feel weird."

"Don't worry. They look great," Zara reassured him. "You are so sophisticated now."

"You don't have to go with me. I can't stand the thought of you back in the NDC," Jude said, putting his hands on Zara's shoulders and looking deep into her gleaming brown eyes.

"I can't stand the thought of being away from you, no matter where we are, but this is bigger than us," Zara said. "I'm not going to hide either."

"Alright then," Jude said. "Let's do this."

The crowds in front of the Capitol Building were more than Jude or Zara could have ever imagined. The image of Callum had struck a nerve. After winding through the streets and pushing their way to the steps, Jude paired his glasses with his phone and focused on Zara.

"Are we streaming?" she texted Chiela.

"You're live. Start talking," she replied.

"Good morning, Sparrows!" Zara said. Suddenly, the crowd surrounding them backed away in a semi-circle, realizing Jude and Zara were there in person, and the live stream was happening right in front of them.

"We don't have long," Zara continued. "The NADF will likely be here to arrest us within minutes. Your response is overwhelming, and there is no doubt Congress and the White House have heard you loud and clear!"

The cheer was deafening.

"If and when my brother Callum sees the sea of orange and the thousands of you standing in solidarity with him, he will be overwhelmed," Jude said. "Without violence, without force, and without guns, we have made our demands clearly and powerfully today. The time to ratify our new Constitution is now, and the rights of everyone to believe what they want, say what they want, and live without fear of recrimination from the government is right now!"

The crowds roared again, waving and clapping, while those further away were watching on their phones. As soon as Jude went live, it wasn't just the Sparrows watching. ADAMS homed in on the location and notified the Chief of Defense, who gave the orders down the chain of command, and troops began moving toward the Capitol steps immediately.

"The authorities will come," Jude warned the crowd. "Let them come. Don't resist them. Don't fight them. We don't want anyone to get hurt. After all, the sanctity and dignity of every person is the heartbeat of our movement, right?"

"Yes!" cheered the crowd, clapping and nodding in agreement.

"And now a message for Congress: it's time to get to work on our new Constitution. Form the committee, gather the amendments, and start writing. History is waiting for you, and so are we."

Another roaring cheer came up from the crowd, and then after a minute or so, it began to die down, and then quickly went quiet as the troops arrived at the Capitol steps. Every phone was trained on Jude and Zara, and Jude let the cameras on his glasses continue to roll. The world was watching every move.

"If we shoot them right there, that would send a pretty clear message, don't you think?" President Connor said, watching the screen in the situation room. He was standing in the corner with his arms crossed, brooding.

"That could be technically legal under your broad powers to use military force to protect the public, but I estimate you would lose the battle of public opinion. Also, as I understand irony, your powers are not exactly clear as we have not yet officially ratified a Constitution for New America that would spell out those powers specifically," ADAMS explained. "Essentially, you risk a powerful backlash at this moment, sir. I urge caution."

"Maybe a backlash is an opportunity to reassure the public that the government is in full control," the President said.

"Did I ever tell you the story about losing my home in a fire when I was a kid?" the Defense Chief said, stepping forward.

"What the hell are you talking about?" President Connor shot back. "Now is not the time."

"Now is the perfect time, sir. I have the troops standing by. Let me explain."

"Make it quick."

"The fire started in the kitchen, but we were asleep. The alarms went off, and we were able to get everyone out by crawling on the floor. We got outside just as the fire trucks pulled up and rolled out their hoses. At this point, the roof over the kitchen was engulfed in flames, and the fire chief ordered the water to be directed to the neighbor's roofs, the bushes, and the other side of the house. My father was furious! 'You're missing the biggest part of the fire!' he yelled. 'Turn the hoses on the kitchen!'

"The chief was calm and assured, and he placed his hand on my father's shoulder. 'The kitchen and that side of the house are lost,' he said. 'The water would be wasted. By dousing the rest of the house, the bushes, and your closest neighbors, we can still save them. A fire that big is never drowned; it has to burn itself out. All we really do is contain it and prevent it from spreading.'

"I'm going to be frank, Mr. President. The fire out there today is pretty big. There are tens of thousands of citizens, and every one of them is peaceful. They are calling for the release of a prisoner who has already served his time, which is a legitimate cause. They are also calling for the Constitution to be reinstated, a promise made during the Transition that has yet to be fulfilled. That may be the most legitimate demand that can be made. No one is carrying guns or clubs. No one is calling for investigations or resignations. They are calling for their elected representatives to do their job. If your response is to put out this fire by force, it will be costly, and it will spread. If, however, you release Callum Kane, promise to initiate the Constitutional drafting committee, and lift the martial law, this fire will burn itself out within twenty-four hours."

"You think I should just give in to the mob?" President Connor asked.

"You're the President," the Defense Chief said. "You still have time to be the hero. You make the call, and you'll be the President who listened to the people and restored order. In a way, these people, these 'Sparrows' as they call themselves, have made you look good."

"ADAMS?" the President said, turning to the droid.

"I'll try an analogy as well. What does more damage: a boiler with its release valve opened, or a boiler that explodes?" ADAMS asked.

"A boiler? Like the kinds used in ships and heating homes two hundred years ago? That analogy is antiquated, but I get the point."

"My troops are standing by, sir," the Defense Chief said.

"Have them escort the two Sparrow kids who started this mess to the NDC and give them the brother. Prepare a written statement for the media. I don't want them to think they have enough pull to get me on camera. Tell them we will send our recommendation to the Senate to form the Constitution Committee this week, and I will lift the martial law as soon as the non-residents have left Washington, D.C. In fact, call it 'Curfew.' That sounds better. Also, don't mention anything about the Kane kid. Let's just let them go back to Cascadia and hope we never hear from them again. If I so much as see a sparrow sitting on my window ledge, I will grab a pistol and shoot it."

As the soldiers approached Jude and Zara, they held out their hands for the cuffs.

"That won't be necessary," the Lieutenant said. "Please follow us."

Jude looked at Zara and shrugged his shoulders. She did the same and walked with Jude, flanked by two Corporals. They got into the back of a transport, and for a moment Jude tensed and held Zara's hand. He worried the unpleasantries would be waiting out of public view, but as the transport began moving, the Lieutenant addressed them respectfully.

"It's not a long ride. We're on our way to the NDC," he said.

"I expected as much," Jude said.

The Lieutenant smiled and sat back. The transport rolled into the backside of the NDC, and the soldiers led them inside the intake door.

"Aren't you going to search us?" Zara finally asked after her curiosity got the best of her.

"Visitors only need a cursory scan, not a full search," he said. "We're not here for you."

As Jude and Zara looked at each other and tried to grasp what was happening, a gaunt figure in plain clothes that hung from his body waddled up to them and threw his arms around Jude.

"Callum!" Jude bellowed, followed by a long embrace and a fairly futile attempt to hold back tears.

"You're here for him," the Lieutenant said. "Sign for his things, and you are free to go."

"Thank you," Zara said slowly, still stunned.

"Thank you, Lieutenant," Jude said, scribbling his signature on the release form.

"Nice to finally meet you, Callum," Zara said with a hug.

"It's so nice to meet you. I'm normally the better-looking one."

"I don't suppose you want to hang around and do some sightseeing, do you?" Jude asked.

"Very funny," Callum said. "By the way, since when did you get glasses?"

As they walked out to the street to hail a transport, Zara put her arm around Callum's shoulders and spun him around in front of Jude.

"One last thing," she said. "Thank you, everyone! Not only are Jude and I walking out of the NDC free, but we have this fella with us!" she said, leaning Callum in front of the cameras. "It would not have happened without you. Today the Sparrows sent a clear message, and it appears we were heard."

Cheers erupted throughout Washington, D.C. as the message spread from screen to screen. As the crowds slowly began to disperse and bleed out of the city, spontaneous celebrations, singing, and a few drinks were had on the way.

"What is all that noise, and why are there so many people wearing orange?" Callum asked.

"The Sparrows," Zara proudly explained. "Just a few thousand people who came out to ask for your release."

"Really?" he asked, dumbfounded. "Why do they care about me?"

"Because we do," Jude said, taking off his glasses.

"Thank you for everything," Callum said. "Can we go home now?"

"Not quite," Zara said, reading her phone. "Your sister insists we take you to Ozark, where she can take care of you. She says, 'He's skin and bones, and Cascadia is way too cold right now. I need to fatten him up first.' Ozark is a SAC near Kansas City. Ever been on a private air transport?"

"The only transport I could afford was the free ride you get to CME or the NDC."

"You'll like it," Zara said. "Max said Boris Spence paid for first class. He wants you to have a steak on him."

"Thanks again, guys. Thanks for not giving up on me, even though I brought this on myself," Callum said.

"You didn't bring all of it on yourself, and we did a lot more than write emails and twiddle our thumbs," Jude said. "We started something with the Sparrows. I think the country will be better off now. People will be treated better, and the SACs will be stronger. You helped start a little bit of a revolution."

"The streets are clearing, and I estimate the non-residents of Washington will be gone by 1800, sir," The Defense Chief reported.

"Based on the passport scans, his estimate is accurate," ADAMS said.

"Good. Thank you for your honest input, Chief. I need people who tell me the truth I don't want to hear," President Connor said.

"Yes, sir."

"Why don't you go home and have a beer. You deserve it."

"Yes, sir," he said as he left with a smile.

ADAMS, can you stay for a few minutes?" the President asked. "I just need to ask some basic data questions. You can leave, too," he ordered the analyst.

"Yes, sir."

"Now that the main blaze has burned out, so to speak, I'm anxious to prevent this from ever happening again," the President said to AD-AMS. "Tens of thousands of people demonstrating in the capital could have easily turned violent. It's a dangerous situation."

"There is always that potential, sir."

"The people are nostalgic for the old US Constitution. That is fine, as long as my power to intervene and keep the peace is not impeded. We'll need to keep an eye on the Senate and the Corporate Congress. I want the right lawmakers on the committees to make sure they're not giving too much away."

"Yes, sir."

"I don't ever want to be surprised by the Sparrows again. I want surveillance on all their activities maximized. If they ever try and pull another 'demonstration,' I want to crush it before it starts. Do you have any suggestions for containing the Sparrows?"

"Yes, sir. The Sparrows began as an effort by two young people to assist the Sustainable Agricultural Communities. As SAC residents themselves, they are independent, and they have helped other SACs become more independent. If you are going to contain any future blaze, you would need to apply the water hoses to everything surrounding the Sparrows, so to speak. The Sparrows fought for the SACs. While we have no legal basis for such action, the complete legal and physical elimination of the SACs would serve to weaken or even eliminate the Sparrows."

"Your analogy was much better this time, ADAMS," the President said with a smile. "I agree with your conclusion."

www.ingramcontent.com/pod-product-compliance
Lightning Source LLC
Chambersburg PA
CBHW051142030726
47504CB00004B/999